8 DAYS

BARRI L. BUMGARNER

Linda,
Thank you for reviewing my novel!
Enjoy –
Barri L. Bumgarner

Published by Tigress Press, LLC
Columbia, Missouri

THE CHEMICAL OF the ages, he prophesized. A wondrous weapon of mass destruction funded initially by Uncle Sam. It was part of his spiel when bringing the other three on board. CIA, FBI, or some other alphabet group – it didn't matter who thought it up. When Nathan discovered that Aralco had access to it, he frothed. A WMD with the ability to asphyxiate, cause hallucinations, and ultimately saturate the atmosphere? And his own corporation had a contract with the Armed Forces to fine-tune it for warfare?

Destiny, he called it. Ten months later, they had the perfect omnipotent chemical cocktail – anaphylaxis with a twist.

"God only needed seven to create it. We just need eight to rectify the mistakes He made."

ISBN 0-9740848-9-1

No persons or places in this book are real. All situations, characters and concepts are the sole invention of the author.

Published September 2004

Published in the United States of America
Tigress Press, LLC
2509 Morning Glory Drive
Columbia, MO 65202
www.tigresspress.com

Dedication

This book is dedicated to my father, who I love with all my heart. Daddy, I hope you can read it in Heaven.

Acknowledgements

Many people had a hand in the successful publication of *8 Days*. I could not have done it without their inspiration and expertise. Thank you to all of them.

My mom has been instrumental in my love of books and edited my early manuscripts. It all started with poetry and has blossomed from there. Marsha Tyson motivated me to resurrect this manuscript and has read and re-read drafts – constantly challenging me to improve it. Patricia Browning Griffith read a *rough* draft many years ago and still gave me the inspiration to revise and market it. Helen Cope and Jan Summers, as readers and editors, have been amazing. This final product is better because of them. Much thanks to my novels' group for helping me grow as a writer. A huge thank you to Tam Adams for her patience and amazing photography – all photographs were taken by Tam, including my photo at the end of the book. Misha Franks helped authenticate the voice of Jessie. Stacey Woelfel of KOMU-TV aided my research of the chemical effects on the atmosphere – how television and radio towers would respond in the event of a catastrophe of this sort. To the Joplin Chamber of Commerce for permission to use Memorial Hall and for their supporting materials. To my agent who tirelessly works on my behalf.

And especially to Janet Musick, whose support and editing have not only made this book better, she's made me a better writer.

Part One: Disintegration

"I have a rendezvous with death..."
– Alan Seeger

Chapter One

Nationwide
Day One

THE NEW YORK City brownstone stood sentinel to an abandoned street. The perpetually buzzing neighborhood, even at two a.m., was suffocated by an eerie silence. The city that never slept was taking its first nap.

"Mommy?" A small boy sat up in bed and peeked over his blanket. A sour stench floated into his bedroom, reminding him of soiled pants back when he was a two-year old baby and couldn't hold it. "Mommy? I'm thirsty."

Something broke downstairs with a loud shattering crash, then a door slammed. The boy yelped and threw the covers over his head. After a few seconds, he pulled the comforter down and listened. Nothing.

"Mommy? I'm thirsty," he tried again. He brushed the blond stray hair from his straining eyes. He saw shapes and figures in the blackness and prayed they weren't monsters. He didn't believe his mom when she said the bulb in his nightlight had burned out on its own; he knew the one-eyed green man under his bed had eaten it.

His three-year-old ears listened for familiar sounds like Mommy's footsteps, the radio that made him dance like a monkey around the living room, or his Big Bird See-n-Say. But only a scary silence engulfed his bedroom, confusing and frustrating him – no honking horns that he loved to count as he fell asleep, no screams from outside or thumping music, not a single roaring engine or squeal of laughter. Nothing. So he did what always brought him the quickest response.

"MOMMY, I NEED YOU!" he shrieked, and held the piercing pitch until his throat went raw. He knew if his mommy could hear him, she would break her neck to save him.

No one came. After twenty minutes of chest-heaving sobs, he drifted off to sleep. When light finally filtered through his curtains, he woke, wondering why Mommy hadn't gotten him up for pre-school.

"Where are you, Mommy?" he rasped from his sore throat. He wiggled into his sweatpants and tugged his smelly Yankees sweatshirt over his head. He tiptoed down the stairs, flipping on every light as he went until he got to the living room. He stopped at the door, confused.

"Mommy?" But she didn't move. He took a few steps toward her, avoiding the shards of glass sprinkled all over the floor. She lay on the couch with her hand in the air as if she wanted a teacher's permission to speak. He reached out to touch her pale arm but couldn't bring himself to do it. Her skin looked like plastic, her eyes were too dark, and flies crawled all over her. There was a dark brown stain on the couch under her bottom. He now knew what the awful stench was.

"Please get up, Mommy," he pleaded in a tiny voice. He wanted her to look at him, to turn her head and say *It's okay, baby, my eyes are open because I'm awake.* But she didn't move, didn't answer.

Staring at his dead mother, he wet himself.

* * *

"WHAT THE HELL is this shit?" shouted Tito Marrero to his seven-year-old son.

"Dunno, Daddy," responded the happy-go-lucky boy just home from school. "It wasn't like that when I caught the bus this mornin'."

The two sat on their porch staring at trash someone had just dumped all over their neatly manicured lawn. The active neighborhood watch program had let them down. Tito started to pick up fast food cups, candy wrappers, and miscellaneous junk. He smashed the stray garbage into the dented metal trashcan. The headache came back with a vengeance.

"Dang it, I don't know what the deal is," he moaned as he massaged his temples.

"I haven't had a headache like this in ten years. If you don't count your granny," he added with a chuckle, but even the soft laughter sent a dull throb into the base of his skull.

"Let me, Daddy, I can make it go away. Come here." The second grader led his father by the hand and climbed onto the back of their vintage Chevy Impala. He pulled his dad's shoulders back where his small hands could reach. He kneaded Tito's tight deltoids with savage aggression, knowing his dad liked it rough.

"Oh, yeah. Oh, there, yeah, I feel the knots. That feels so good, Marcus."

"Mom!" Marcus shouted at his mother arriving home before *PB&J Otter, Rugrats,* and even *SpongeBob, Square Pants.* Her shift at University Hospital shouldn't have ended until after his cartoons, dinner, and *Wheel of Fortune*.

"Debbie, what're you doin' here, girl? You get off early?" Tito took his young wife in his arms and held her close, but she only stared at him.

With a swift motion, Deborah Marrero pulled out her Lady Smith and Wesson, her protection of choice for the late night shifts at the hospital. She held it less than six inches from her son's head.

"Mom? Don't, you're scaring me." Marcus shrank back as his mom aimed the gun at him.

Her right hand trembled, but she braced it with her left. She cocked the pistol, tears streaming down her face.

"I love you, baby," she whispered, then squeezed the trigger gently. The report brought a yelp of surprise from Tito, who watched with his mouth hanging open. Marcus crumpled to the ground like a discarded ribbon. Blood mixed with brain matter splattered all over the side of the Impala.

Tito stared at Debbie, his eyes clouded with confusion. She knew the look – she'd seen it in the mirror, and it had ridden on the coattails of an excruciating migraine. Somewhere far away, a voice told her to hurry the fuck up and finish it.

"Make it easy, honey. Give me a better target. You know I have to." She tried not to look at her son's body. Tito didn't object, because it sounded so logical. He dropped to his knees and raised his head to the business end of the gun.

Put him out of his misery.

She obliged the voice by planting a bullet into her husband's right temple, killing him instantly. Staring at the two people she loved most laying motionless in their own blood, she did what she thought was the only logical thing to do.

Placing the gun carefully in front of her, she opened her mouth and stuck the barrel between her teeth. She rested the hot muzzle on her tongue, the metallic gunpowder burning her lips. She shivered. What the hell was she doing? She closed her eyes, wondering what the voices and visions in her head meant. They didn't make any sense, but then neither did the sight of her son and husband dead in the middle of the yard with what looked like ketchup on their foreheads.

Could this really be happening to the world, all these scenes flashing before her? One of the voices whispered that she could be a survivor if she chose to.

"Shut up!" She didn't want to hear any motivating thoughts that meant she had to work hard at a life that no longer included the two men she loved.

When the gunfire echoed for the third time in the neighborhood, a few still functioning friends came out onto their front porches. A startled but lucid Karen Smithton dialed 911, unaware that what Deborah Marrero had done might have been the smartest decision of all. Smithton carefully replaced the receiver when no one answered at emergency services and went to find her cat. An hour later she remember she'd never gotten one – she was allergic.

* * *

THE HORDE OF shopping maniacs lining the streets of Chicago stopped abruptly along Michigan Avenue, State Street, and Superior. Heads turned to the sky and eyebrows lifted in question. Did someone up there just say something? They didn't know the majority of them would be issued a one-way ticket out of Dodge by midnight. *Don't wanna ride that train*, many of them would whine.

But about eighty percent of those within the contaminated area didn't know what they wanted. Famous people would forget they were somebody, rich folks wouldn't remember that they could buy the world, and the poor had no clue they were inferior to anyone. They all had one thing in common that day. Those who woke to fight the mysterious battle against an invisible foe would wish for a ship, a train, a bus, even a cab to take them on a trip out of town. But no dice. They learned the hard way that some people are chosen and others eliminated. What they couldn't comprehend was who chose? And why?

No deposit, no return, one old coot shouted in downtown Philadelphia, the city of brotherly love. Ironically, a seventeen-year-old high school quarterback punched him so hard in the face the senior citizen passed out cold.

All across the country, strange moods, altered personalities, and confused Americans went to bed for their final rest.

A mother of three somewhere in the suburbs of L.A. forgot to feed her infant son who screamed for her life-giving milk. She thought she might be missing a step of her late night ritual but it eluded her. She even considered checking to see if her dog needed water. But then she remembered he might have died earlier that summer.

He had.

An elderly man forgot to take his insulin. When he retreated to his bedroom, he had the strangest inkling that he might just be the Pope.

He wasn't.

In the Hollywood Hills, a couple forgot about their combating affairs and the sticky separation that caused more trouble in the media than it was worth, and consummated their newly revived relationship. He even thought it might make a difference in their future.

It wouldn't.

A small jet carrying a professional baseball team had a pilot who just happened to think he was Evil Knievel. The dive that sent many of the players reeling would wake them only thirteen minutes before Stage I began in earnest. The ball players shouted, wondering why life was so cruel as to wake them just in time to die. Frantically, they faltered for seatbelts as if a flimsy strap of woven canvas could save them.

It couldn't.

In a nightclub in downtown San Antonio, a smattering of people stood hanging around after a local band left stage. One drunken fan screamed for Mick, while another tried to pay tribute by urinating on the stage. Various onlookers debated whether the two men standing on the pool table had actually ripped their shirts off, or if their eyes deceived them. One blinked to make sure his eyes hadn't gone funky on him.

They hadn't.

Stripped to the waist, a woman near the back screamed, but not a single person made a move to help her. Within moments, an inebriated bartender unbuttoned his jeans and tried to rape her. She screamed and clawed at his eyes, drawing blood. But he pried her hands back and held them above her head. He yanked her jeans down just as another woman came up behind him and slammed a Jack Daniel's bottle over his head. Unlike its depiction in Hollywood, a hard liquor bottle packs a fatal punch when delivered with enough force.

And it had been.

Similar scenes took place in the nation's fifty largest cities. By morning, America would be in the grip of a sinister master plan orchestrated by four geniuses without a conscience. Or a way to stop it.

Chapter Two

Dallas, Texas
Day One

"EIGHT DAYS – DAMMIT, Jamie, that's the plan. Eight days, and that's the way we're doing it." Nathan Kirkpatrick ran a hand through his sandy blond hair. It felt slick – he hadn't washed it since they had come into the lab on Monday. Was it Thursday? Friday? He had lost complete track of time.

"It's cruel, Nathan. I mean, if we're doing it, why draw it out? Huh? We're not monsters, are we? That *wasn't* the plan." Jamie didn't want them to see her as the emotional female, but the experiment had taken a twist she wasn't comfortable with.

She looked down at their original genetic targets and then at the second grid – the total genocide they had progressed to. If they meant to weed out the minorities – the weak links, as Nathan referred to them – they had lost their focus.

"Lighten up, Jamie. We adapt when we have to. This is the only feasible way we can take it worldwide. That's what we agreed to, right?" Nathan looked at Kyle, who nodded, then at Bobby who looked like a trapped rat.

His heart isn't in this anymore, Jamie thought. She wanted to pull him by the sleeve into the other room to see what triggered the reservations.

"Bobby!" Nathan barked. Jamie jumped.

"Yes." Bobby's dark eyes, dark hair, and dark expression made his pale skin look ghostly.

The fluorescent lights flickered, pulsed off and on, and each of them stared up at the cylindrical bulbs as if looking would will them to stay on. A second later, the room was swallowed by total darkness.

"Damn. Does anyone have a fucking flashlight?" Nathan slapped his hand down on the table, angry that there were things he couldn't control.

"Is...is this Stage I, Nathan?" Bobby's voice trembled. He reached his hands blindly in front of him to make sure none of them were too close. Bobby liked space, even dark space.

"How would we know, Bobby? Jesus, I'm not God. Not yet, anyway." Nathan let out a fake demented laugh that goose-pimpled Jamie's arms. "We're uploading a wicked virus that will debilitate electricity and computer systems in the middle of the night – just in case some hotshot thinks he can stop our little operation. Don't want some think tank to get a whiff, know what I mean?"

"Shut up, Nathan. I think there's a Mag light in the first drawer here." She brushed her hand along the smooth countertop, then fumbled for drawer handles. She counted the third to the left and pulled it open. Just as her hands made sense of what she was feeling, the back-up lights clicked on and bathed the room in an eerie bluish glow. Equipment beeped, automatic recovery systems reset programs, and a steady hum of weakened electricity added to the ambiance.

"That won't set anything back, will it?" Nathan raised his eyebrows at Kyle, the computer whiz.

Kyle tapped buttons, restarting the laptop. "Give me a sec. Oh, yeah. That's it. YES!" He pumped his fist. "I'm so good. Okay, kids, we're back in business. Let's get this done."

"So where were we?" Nathan narrowed his green eyes and looked from Kyle to Jamie and then settled on Bobby, the weak link.

"I think before God tried to intervene with our tidy little plan, you were saying yes to something, *Bobby*." Nathan smirked. "Was that a *yes, Nathan, I agree?* Or a *Yes, what the fuck do you want?"*

"You're an asshole, Nathan. It's a *yes, I agree.* I just want to do this, okay? Why do we have to talk so goddamned much? Jesus."

"We don't." Nathan plopped down into the chair next to Kyle. "Hop up, Kyle. It's time."

Kyle, Jamie, and Bobby gathered behind Nathan and watched him initiate the second part of Stage I's release and Stage II of Operation X-86.

The chemical of the ages, he prophesized. A wondrous weapon of mass destruction funded initially by Uncle Sam. It was part of his spiel when bringing the other three on board. CIA, FBI, or some other alphabet group – it didn't matter who thought it up. When Nathan discovered that Aralco had access to it, he frothed. A WMD with the ability to asphyxiate, cause hallucinations, and ultimately saturate the atmosphere? And his own corporation had a contract with the Armed Forces to fine-tune it for warfare?

Destiny, he called it. Ten months later, they had the perfect omnipotent chemical cocktail – anaphylaxis with a twist.

"God only needed seven to create it. We just need eight to rectify the mistakes He made."

Jamie made a humphing sound. She wondered if Nathan thought someone was writing down his prophecies like he was Nostradamus or something. She freed her shoulder-length hair from the ponytail holder and gathered it in a dexterous motion she had done a million times. She tried not to let it sink in – that the four of them were in their twenties, smart enough to rival the greatest minds in the nation, yet the future they saw had so little to offer that their only recourse was extermination.

Did I agree to this? She had and she knew why.

"Nathan, did you call your mom? Did you give her directions to the tombs?"

"No, Kyle, I didn't. That was for the three of you with a conscience. Save all your little loved ones – for what, I don't know. I can't believe you would want them to live in the world we're dooming them to. Besides, I'm Hitler's successor, remember? I saved those who would continue my work." Nathan looked up at Kyle, met his best friend's eyes and held them.

Kyle studied Nathan's icy expression, flat and chilling in the gloomy light. Had Nathan always looked like Jack Nicholson in *The Shining*? The women at Aralco Chemical Company whispered about how cute Nathan was, comparing him to a young Harrison Ford – rugged, with a crooked smile and a mysterious nature. But they had no idea about the *real* Nathan Kirkpatrick. They weren't privy to Operation X-86, didn't have the security clearance. No one did, not even them. But it hadn't stopped them from stealing the blueprints for a chemical warfare project sponsored by the government's armed forces.

"Hey, Nathan, you gotta finish the upload." Jamie snapped her fingers in front of his face. "Wake up. We've got work to do. No time for sniffing butts."

Nathan shook the fog away and pasted on his best smile. But Kyle started snipping at Bobby about something. The two took to bickering like teenage sisters. And then it turned serious.

* * *

WHEN THE ACRID smell of gunpowder dissipated, before an intruder would attempt to thwart their getaway, Nathan Kirkpatrick finalized the deployment of X-86.

"Let the cleansing begin," he said, thumping the Enter key. The remaining three sighed. The fourth – soon to enter the early stages of rigor mortis – lay sprawled less than ten feet away.

The computer whirred, sucking the little bit of energy it could muster from the back-up power supply.

The traitorous back door had been slammed shut, and Operation Meltdown was a runaway train on a one-way track. There was no stopping it now. Stage I hadn't felt as final because it had been minor – mind-altering but not deadly. But not Stage II, Stage III, Stage IV, or Final Deployment. These wouldn't cause headaches, hallucinations or dementia.

For billions around the world, these meant permanent sleep.

Chapter Three

Georgetown, South Carolina
Day One

HAD IT EVER been this chilly in August? Becky couldn't remember off-hand, but with only twenty-five summers to reflect on, she figured she wasn't exactly competition for the *Farmer's Almanac*. She wandered through the front yard, shuffling her feet through the prematurely fallen leaves. The light sweater didn't block out the bitter breeze prickling goose bumps on her arms. She hugged herself and shook shoulder-length auburn hair from her face, but the wind whipped it back. A miniature funnel cloud swirled leaves around her. She kicked at them playfully, but her heart wasn't in it.

She used to love playing in leaf piles her daddy raked. Mama would giggle, bag those Becky didn't smash to bits, and then throw a few at Daddy. The memories made her feel hollow, but brooding wouldn't bring Mama back. She hugged her arms tighter, trying to ward off the odd summer chill. The porch thermometer read forty-one degrees. Becky couldn't comprehend it. In South Carolina, it seldom dipped below sixty, except in the wee hours of the morning. But at seven forty-five in the evening, forty degrees was all wrong.

Her gray-blue eyes turned westward and skimmed the horizon for Mr. Farmington's horses but didn't see the bays that pastured there. Nature's dazzling display of flaming color was broken only by the Carolina pines silhouetted against the fiery sky. The beauty fueled her melancholy. She wondered if the few miles inland gave way to some relief from the biting chill and longed to be there, anywhere that would lift the burden from her heart. It was no secret she had never been a fan of winter.

The Atlantic crashed ruthlessly on the beach to the east, ten-foot waves normally swarming with surfers, but they, like the sandy shore, were completely empty. Breakers roared in, rushed back out, and repeated the pattern, gaining ground with every trip. At that rate, Becky feared the house would be underwater by sunset.

* * *

"BECK? YOU OUT here?" Her husband came bouncing onto the front porch and was caught off guard by the cold breeze that riffled his close-cropped auburn hair. "It's cold as hell out here, feels like freakin' November!" He rubbed his goose-pimpled arms, sore from the day's workout but buff enough to make him smile.

"I know. Kinda weird after all those one-hundred-degree days." Her voice trailed off. She picked absently at a snag in the cream sweater.

"Beck, you okay?" He couldn't tell from her glazed look if this was about her mother or something else. Three months hadn't eased the pain of sudden loss, the cruelty of a vicious car wreck that hadn't allowed any closure. Becky's anger had slowly dissolved, evolving into the hollow ache that accompanied her most days. When the manslaughter charge led to a conviction and the drunken slob took up permanent residence behind bars, she would feel some sense of justice.

"Becky?" He reached out to hold her, but she didn't seem to notice. She had lost her usual Sandra Bullock smile. He loved to tease her about how much she looked like the movie star. Her gray-blue eyes made him quiver with love every time he looked into them. But he could tell she was hurting, and it hurt him to see it.

"Huh? Oh, I'm sorry, Jacob, I was just lost in my own thoughts."

An uneasiness crawled into his groin. She didn't call him Jacob unless she was angry with him or playfully scolding him. "Honey, let me warm you up." He pulled Becky to him, snuggling her with his warmth. He brushed the sandy brown hair from her eyes, but she was still miles away.

"Jake, have you ever wondered what it would feel like to die?" She stopped, seemed to drift for a moment, a stoic expression on her face. "Or just to know that you were going to? Like people with cancer or AIDS." Her voice tapered.

He wasn't sure if she had finished speaking, so he waited, staring out toward the water, mesmerized by the beautiful setting sun and the ocean sounds behind them. He loved the location of the home his parents had given them as a wedding gift three years earlier. It was less than a mile off the beach but surrounded by weeping willows, pine trees, and crepe myrtles.

"Oh, I don't know. Yeah, I guess." He stroked her face, expecting tears but not surprised there weren't any. Becky hadn't cried much since her mother's death. "Baby, I know this has been hard. I promise it'll get better."

"I know." She lowered her head and let out a long, ragged sigh.

"Geez, this is maudlin after-dinner conversation. I hope I didn't bring this on with my singing. I promise I'll quit, or I'll turn the stereo up louder. Didn't know I was that bad."

He chuckled, then pulled her closer to him and giggled in her ear. He nuzzled against her back, wrapping his arms in front of her – a standing spoon, she called it. He could tell his banter wasn't helping. The apprehension now worked its way into the pit of his stomach, and he knew, much as a mother knows her child's moods, that something wasn't right. He drew his arms possessively around his young wife even tighter. "No, no, honey, your whistling was fine. Didn't bother me at all. I'm just a little distracted, I guess, kind of down." As she uttered each broken phrase, she slid out of his arms and drifted back into the house.

Jake stood there a moment, the wind stealing the words as they passed his lips. "Singin', not whistling. I was singing." His bright green eyes searched the horizon for some insight into his wife's depression.

He slipped back into the house behind her. He contemplated building a fire but decided that was just too bizarre for a Carolina August. He wandered into the kitchen and noticed there was nothing for dessert, uncharacteristic for Becky. He caught a faint hint of Eternity from the bathroom and heard the familiar roaring bath water coupled with the thud of each item Becky put on the edge of the tub. Barbasol shaving cream, Pert shampoo, one of her Bath & Body shower gels, all the wonderful chemicals that skewered his hormones. He hoped the relaxation would help snap her out of the strange mood.

He thought of joining her. Instead, he grabbed a Sprite from the refrigerator and pulled a piece of fried chicken from under the foil covering last night's leftovers. He stretched out on the couch and relished the comfort of his nightly ritual of channel surfing.

The brain-dead entertainment reached an all-time low when Dirty Harry made someone's day by blowing the punk to smithereeens. Becky's voice broke through the haze but didn't filter past the automatic gunfire on TV. When she hollered again, Jake jumped, partially from being startled but mostly because of her previous mood. He was in the bathroom doorway before the TV's images left him.

Staring at his bubble-covered wife, he could still see the after-images of a bad guy falling victim to Dirty Harry's .357 Magnum.

"What is it, baby?" He took in the whole scene in one frantic look: his wife surrounded by the frothy white, steamy mirror reminiscent of *Fatal Attraction*, clothes strewn about, and the toilet seat up – shit, he kept forgetting. Everything seemed chaotically normal.

"Gosh, I just needed a new bar of soap. You left me a sliver again. Parts of me must be pampered, you know. Glad I didn't need anything too alarming; you might've hurt yourself. You didn't, did you? I could always massage it for you." She flashed a wicked, please-mess-with-me smile, and his heart and nether regions went topsy-turvy.

"Yes, you must be Zestfully clean. Here, let me help. Always glad to oblige my ladies." He returned her seductive smile while doing all he could to get out of his shorts and T-shirt as quickly as possible. He considered hopping in fully clothed.

Their fingertips met as he handed her the bar of soap. He didn't have the patience to open it at this point, and little electric jolts pulsed through his entire body. He paused before sliding into the tub behind her and kissed her nose, looking deep into those slate blue eyes that had captivated him from the moment he'd met her. Their thoughts collided on that wavelength that made him instantly want her.

They made deep, sensual love between time in the bathtub and the awkward clamor to the bedroom. He lay peacefully with her in the niche of his shoulder for three blissful hours, savoring the closeness, the overwhelming passion, and the harmony of feeling her naked body next to his.

It would be gut-wrenching for Jake come morning – the reality that they would never make love, cuddle, or talk again. Her death would madden him, but it would be nothing compared to what he would witness by noon the next day.

Chapter Four

St. Louis, Missouri
Day One

"WHAT IN GOD'S name are you doing, Jessie?" Justin watched his eight-year-old daughter in utter disbelief. Her nimble fingers dexterously manipulated the screws that tightened the plate on his dad's antique Victrola. She brushed a stray brown hair from her hazel eyes with the back of a hand like a mechanic irritated by a bead of sweat. Her signature pigtails belied her maturity.

"Honey, there's no way that piece of junk is ever going to work," he insisted, but she wasn't listening. She whipped about, her pigtails flipping this way and that as she worked.

"Daddy, relax. Have a little faith. I know what I'm doing." Jessie rolled her eyes in her holier-than-thou manner and sighed. Small skillful hands took the handle and cranked it dramatically. As soon as she finished, she pulled out an old standby the two of them loved to dance to. The first time the song came on, her daddy said, "Girl, let's get jiggy with it!"

Jessie's fit of giggles had made him so happy, they played it three times. Chuck Berry's *Maybelline* slipped easily onto the tiny prong in the middle of the turntable. The record hitched as the needle caught each snag. Had it been a regular LP, Springsteen, her daddy's favorite, would have gotten the nod, but the dinosaur technology forced her to rediscover her grandmother's old 78s, and she had done so with glee.

She preferred 'N Sync, if only the Victrola could handle compact discs. She placed the needle farther into the record, past unforgiving scratches, then clapped with enthusiastic anticipation. A tinny, faraway Chuck Berry asked why Maybelline couldn't be true, and Jessica Bayker accompanied him off-key.

"Well, I'll be damned," Justin mumbled. His daughter had just fixed an eighty-year-old Victrola he'd considered junk for years. He had kept it for sentimental reasons.

"It's not nearly loud enough!" he shouted. He reached for the doors and opened them to let the steel speakers declare louder about the things Maybelline used to do. He twirled his daughter about the garage, not wanting to stop her celebration dance. She had spent so much time in her room since her mom bailed on summer plans two weeks earlier.

He had second-guessed himself continually about whether he had done the right thing by maintaining sole custody. He loved Jessie more than life itself, but not at the expense of her happiness. It was more than he could say for her mother.

* * *

THE BATTLE HAD been cutthroat, his victory a result of his substantial salary and stable lifestyle as a defense attorney. A kid just couldn't grow up with a mother jetting off to different cities three or four times a week. He had struggled with the overnight flights Rachel had volunteered and then used it against her in court. She reasoned that a female pilot had to do twice as much to get half as far.

She had exemplified that at a fanatical pace. He'd felt it in his gut when the flirting evolved into affairs. While Jessie was learning her numbers, the alphabet, and how to tie her shoes, her mommy jaunted cross-country with a certain co-pilot Rachel had stopped talking about. Justin hadn't known the pilot, but he knew what her silence meant. He defended liars for a living, recognized the eye movements of the guilty, and was sickened that he now compared the woman who once stirred his soul to common criminals.

Jessie's first day of kindergarten had been the beginning of the end. Rachel was on an overnight flight to Seattle but had promised she would be back so they both could escort Jessie to Country Day Elementary School. When Rachel called and said she wouldn't make it, claiming the flight had been delayed due to weather, Justin raced to his Gateway. The storm report on the Internet showed Seattle as partly cloudy with the usual thirty-percent chance of rain. No raging storms as Rachel claimed, no stifling fog or heavy winds – just excuses.

Justin festered that night and finally called to give Rachel an ultimatum, but she got in the last word by not being registered at the airline's usual hotel. She had specifically penciled the number on the side of the refrigerator – another lie in a slew of deceptions. He tried to reach her cell phone, but she had turned it off.

When he tucked Jessie in, he did it for the first time as a single father. The legalities might not be final, but his decision to follow through with it was.

The lawyer in him laid it out cut and dried. Cheating left Rachel no room for appeal, no silly motions for joint custody.

She had gotten home the afternoon of Jessie's first day of school and was greeted by Justin sitting on the couch with a letter in his hand.

"Know what, Rachel? Your daughter started kindergarten today. She was so excited. She wore this new jumper, the one with balloons on the strap and the bowtie buckle – oh, wait, I bought that for her last weekend and you haven't really been home, so you've probably never seen it. Hmm. You are her mother, aren't you?" He swallowed, keeping his anger in check. "Maybe I have you mistaken for someone else – someone I used to love and sleep with."

"Oh, don't start with me, Justin. I was working. This *is* the twenty-first century. And what do you mean, *used to love?*"

He didn't answer. Instead, he tossed dated photos on the coffee table. Seeing herself hand in hand with another pilot in an intimate cuddle, Rachel didn't bother denying it. She didn't speak at all.

"And you," he said, then paused. He took a deep breath and looked Rachel dead in the eye, no longer swayed by her Cindy Crawford-like beauty. "You will be apartment hunting on Jessie's second day of school. Unless, of course, you want to shack with Mr. Power Ranger. These..." he shook the envelope, "these are the terms of the divorce I will be filing." He dropped the letter on the end table with a muffled *thunk*.

"Jesus, Justin. Let's discuss this like rational adults. If..."

But he didn't listen. He stood, tapping his watch to signal that there were more important appointments pressing – school let out in less than ten minutes.

When he got home, Rachel was gone. Jessie didn't bat an eye when he explained that Mommy had an unavoidable emergency flight. She was used to it.

Rachel returned after midnight to pack her things and box a few keepsakes. She carried them to her BMW without a word. Justin was relieved to see emotion as Rachel stroked Jessie's cheek and whispered goodbye, tears dropping into her daughter's hair. For a frantic moment, it occurred to him that she might try to take their daughter. But he was sure Rachel knew better.

Justin filed for divorce four days later. Rachel didn't fight for money because her salary rivaled his, though with assets he nearly doubled her income. She felt compelled to battle for custody of their daughter, but it didn't last long.

Like everything else, it got in the way of Rachel living her life.

* * *

Dear Diary,

Daddy said Momma called today when I was swimming at Anna's. I think he just says that so I wont be hurt that she did not call. I got a postcard from her last Friday. A real pretty beach with palm trees somewhere in Florida. It said she wished I could be there but I dont think she means it.

Diary, I think maybe my momma doesnt like me anymore, or shes just kinda forgotten about me, with me not there and all. I dont like it that Daddy lies for her. That makes me sad. I miss my momma, but I know I hurt her feelings that day in the big chair. Even the judge guy cried when I said it.

Well, Diary, I'm going to go to sleep now. My head hurts from thinking about Momma. I miss her, but Im getting used to it. Sweet dreams to Momma and Daddy.

Love,
Jessie

* * *

JUSTIN WOKE FROM his nap, another headache pounding until he thought his skull would crack. The late afternoon sun filtered through the blinds, and he knew by the direction of it that Rachel had forgotten to call Jessie before her five o'clock flight.

Justin hated conjuring stories to account for his ex's shortcomings, but he'd continued the charade for his daughter's sake. He knew the excuses had worn thin and that Jessie saw through them, but how could an eight-year-old accept that her mother visited once or twice a year because flitting about the country was more important? Justin refused to be a party to it, so he continued the façade – for his sake as much as Jessie's.

"What the...?" Justin held onto his shirt before it got tugged off his arm. "Wha...well, don't pull my arm off, squirrel bait. What?" He couldn't disguise his grin. Just looking at Jessie's toothless smile made his heart swell.

"Let's make popcorn and watch an old movie. Please, Daddy, can we pleeeeease?" She looked at him with puppy dog eyes, one pigtail drooping across her cheek as she cocked her head. He marveled at her ever-short attention span and resigned himself to an evening of Buzz Lightyear, Shrek, or Simba – the stack of paperwork on his desk would have the night off.

The two pranced around the kitchen while Justin looked for pizza coupons, called in their usual, and Jess poured two ice cold Dr Peppers. He hadn't asked what movie he was in store for, but he had his suspicions. It had been three months since she'd watched one of the *Toy Story* movies, and that was darn near a record.

"Wait, Daddy. I have a better idea." Her wicked grin told him she wanted something bigger.

"Spit it out, little girl." He still couldn't get over how happy she was. He knew he was going to do whatever it took to please her, to keep the sparkle in those hazel eyes.

"Let's go to the game. Albert's only two away from the record, and I could see it. You said it would be in this series, remember? C'mon, Daddy." Her knowledge of baseball amazed him. She paid close attention and he liked that – usually.

He raised one eyebrow, prepared to object. His headache wasn't any better.

"C'mon, Daddy, you got to see the Cardinals win the pennant when I was a baby. Junior's gonna try to stay in the wildcard race and break that one guy's record you don't like. He could do it, and I could be there to see it! C'mon, Daddy, c'mon, let's go, can we please?"

Justin hemmed and hawed, toying with his daughter. She was right. Being in the park as a kid when Ozzie, Willie, and the other heavy hitters blasted their way through the play-offs only to clash with the Royals in the I-70 series had been a religious experience. He could take a few aspirin and be good to go.

"I don't know; the game's in two hours. It'll take us at least forty-five minutes to get there. You still have those free tickets for terrace seats?"

She nodded her head emphatically. Her school had given tickets to second-graders who completed ten books by the end of the school year. Jessie had done that with her eyes closed – by Christmas. One love Justin passed on to his daughter was books, and they had multiple sets of free tickets to show for it. He hoped they would have the same program her third grade year.

"Geez, I'll have to cancel the pizza because it'll take too long, but we'll have to eat first."

"Eat first? Daddy, are you goofy? We have to eat hot dogs and peanuts at the game! You can have a beer, and I'll have lemonade. C'mon, Daddy, don't be a poop." She pulled at his shirt, making him laugh.

"Or..." Her eyes gleamed with a new thought.

"Yes, your majesty?" Justin put his hands on his hips, playfully mocking her.

"We could go eat at Hard Rock afterwards?" The questioning plea tugged at his heart. She was spoiled to the nth degree and he knew she loved that.

Justin fulfilled all her wishes. They celebrated as their Redbirds won with a walk-off home run, in spite of Junior's gallant efforts with two of his own. The game measured up to her hopes, and her happiness satisfied Justin. She showed off for all who sat around them that Albert's magic number was a measly *one*.

At Hard Rock Café, they ate until they nearly popped. He bought her a new Hard Rock T-shirt, sparing nothing for the return of his happy little girl. After he glanced down at his watch and saw how late it was, he made Jessie's night by suggesting they stay at the Marriott. The game had run long due to extra innings, summer was nearly over, and Justin knew bedtimes would soon return with the school year schedule. It dawned on him that his baby was going into third grade in eighteen days.

Jessie nearly bounced out of her skin as she waited for her dad to pay for their room. He loved the bobbing pigtails and what it meant to see them. She had only been in two hotels in her life, and nothing as luxurious as the Marriott.

The desk clerk returned Justin's Chase card, had him sign the slip, and handed him the card key for their room. Justin had splurged, and they took the elevator to a top-floor suite – with the ballgame rush, suites were the only vacancies. And he had a wonderful surprise for his daughter as they stripped to their skivvies, put on their new jerseys, and flopped onto the massive bed, heads down at the end so they could watch TV.

Jessie squealed with glee as Woody filled the TV screen. Buzz Lightyear's "to infinity and beyond" delighted her.

"How did you get this movie, Daddy?"

"The hotel has oodles of movies, Jess. This is a classic." He ruffled her hair and pulled her to him. He covered them both with the comforter.

All was right with the world. His baby girl was happy and that was all that mattered.

As he dozed on and off throughout the movie, he couldn't help but chuckle each time Jessie shouted, "To infinity and beyond!" with Buzz and Woody.

A smile creased his face as he drifted to sleep. He would die a happy man that night.

Chapter Five

Brandisburg, Arizona
Day One

"HEY, STEVE, COME here – hurry!" Timmy Edwards stared at his computer terminal like it was the black plague. His Barney Fife image made him hard to take seriously, but Steve heard a frantic tone in his best friend's voice. Most nights in the silo were too boring to stay awake. This would not be one of them.

"Holy shit! Timmy, what the fuck did you do?" Steve punched a few buttons to clear the screen that appeared to be going berserk. Visions of Tony Andrews' wrath swam in his head. Boot camp had been a cakewalk in comparison.

"Hey, I didn't touch the sonuvabitch. It just started going nuts on me!" Timmy rubbed his forehead. He wondered why all the weird shit happened on his watch. Working in conjunction with Beta Tron Chemical Corporation – BetaCorp to those in the loop – and the Army had its ups and downs, but manning the silos as part of Tony Andrews' military-endorsed operation gave him a connection to the civilian world that he liked. It wasn't all about mess halls, barracks, and sergeants busting his hump. He got to have the best of both worlds – private apartments, forty-hour work weeks, and real food. Defending Andrews' Fortune 500 dynasty ranked high on enlisted personnel's wish list – BetaCorp manufactured most of the military's chemical warfare weapons and produced some of the most advanced technology to combat enemy advancements. The Iraq contract alone made BetaCorp millions.

"Let me have a look," Steve snipped, shooing Timmy out of the way. Both men stared at the computer terminals surrounding Timmy. Readouts that made no sense or meant chemical warfare was imminent scribed across the screen so fast they could neither read nor calculate them – streams of numbers, chemical symbols for poisons and toxins and extensive unknowns, a list of cities blended together with no separation between words. Warning lights flashed on the panels next to each technician's desk.

Steve dropped his manual with a dull thud onto a table. Both of them jumped. Nerves bounced off the confining walls like ping-pong balls vying for freedom.

Steve thumbed through the pages to the *Emergency Protocol* tab. Without hesitating, he started barking orders to Timmy and coordinating procedures they knew were both frightening and serious.

Neither had any idea that what they misunderstood as a chemical leak was already wreaking havoc on the atmosphere and affecting millions, even manipulating the weather.

"Okay, who makes the call?" Timmy's foot tapped as he prayed Steve would step up. "Wanna flip?"

"I will. Give me the list of questions. Print that readout, too, would you?"

Timmy did as he was told, grateful not to have to hear Andrews tear into him. The last time he had a conversation with the company CEO, it cost him a week's pay – just for being a few minutes late more than once.

"Mr. Andrews? Sorry to disturb you at home, sir, but this is Corporal Steve Singleton, along with Specialist Edwards. We, um, have a situation here at Site #906, and I just forwarded you some information. Can you log on?" Steve tapped a pencil on the table until Timmy grabbed it from him. An eternity seemed to pass while both men waited. Steve read and reread the printouts while Timmy paced.

"Hmmm," the old man finally said.

Steve could picture the CEO sitting there chomping at the bit – mob-personified with slicked-back black hair, olive skin, and narrow, beady eyes too dark to tell if they were black or brown.

"I don't understand. When did you receive this information? This can't be right."

"Uh, our readouts are off the charts, sir. There is definitely something in the atmosphere – we didn't receive information from anyone. Our systems picked this up. But look at this – the image I'm sending you right now shows someone is manipulating our satellites to coordinate some kind of chemical release over the course of the next eight days. And there's a list embedded. I'll send that, too."

Steve could hear Andrews type and then heard a printer kick into action.

"Shit. This is not good. Tell you what, Corporal, you got your manual handy?"

"Yessir." Steve's heart thudded in his chest, terrified of the impending decision.

"I want you to go into lock-down and wait for my go. We're going to have to get a fix on this satellite. But I have to make some calls. You boys follow protocol – it won't take long. I'll be back in touch in less than ten minutes."

The phone was dead before Steve could respond. He dropped the receiver into its cradle and replayed the conversation for Timmy.

"So let's do it, Timmy. He'll be callin' back in a few and I don't want him pissed."

"Me neither."

Both men held their badges with an oddly shaped key attached, lifted the Plexiglas cover, and plugged it in. It took a synchronized turn of each key to activate any military intervention.

"This locks us down for good and gets the ball rolling. You claustrophobic, Timmy?" Steve chuckled, but a twinge of fear gripped his privates. He wanted to call Beth, but he knew he would panic his wife and there was no point in doing that. "On my count. Five, four, three, two, one," Steve chanted, and both turned their keys. A five-minute countdown popped up on a main computer terminal.

"That's it," Timmy muttered.

"Yeah, that's it. But we still have loose ends to tie up. When the countdown is over, all systems become automated, except what we activate with the missiles. I hope it doesn't come to that, but we'll find out pretty quick. We have to get everything else switched over before we move to the air chamber. We can arm the silos from in there." They scrambled around for the necessary manuals. Timmy grabbed his coffee cup, and Steve plucked his wife's picture from his corkboard.

"Can we do it all from in there? I never thought we'd really ever have to do any of this." Apprehension coiled Timmy's stomach, adding nausea to his gamut of emotions.

"Yep, that's why I got this baby." Steve pointed to the laptop and tapped the enter button. He studied the updated information and felt his insides swim.

"How long will we be in there?" Timmy's voice trembled.

Steve didn't answer his partner. For nearly twenty seconds, Timmy's gut churned as he did everything possible not to look at the countdown.

4:31…4:30…4:29…4:28…

"Timmy, we got a problem. You see this?" Steve pointed to data on the computer's screen.

"Well, that's just not possible, I mean – oh, my God. Terrorists are usin' our satellites to attack all these cities. But...I don't get it."

Steve did. He stared at the lists – eight release dates and times and coordinates for some vehicle to deploy an unnamed chemical into Earth's atmosphere. Deep coded instructions for an unmanned plane called a microtron. *Probably a tiny robot designed to self-destruct with completion of its mission.*

"I'm givin' him two minutes to call us back – he said he'd call in ten and it's been seven. But time's wasting, and I'm not gonna go into that air chamber not knowing. I need to talk to Beth." He looked at the phone, but both men knew it would only call coded numbers. Cell phones didn't work deep in the silo. Before either could contemplate ways around it, the phone rang.

"Deploy your missiles, Corporal. Now." Tony sounded frantic, but Steve thought there was something else. *He's excited – I think he's smiling.*

"Sir? All of them?" Steve's hand trembled, and he snapped his fingers for Timmy to come front and center. "Which protocols – I mean, how many of them do you want us to fire?"

Timmy's heart lurched. *We're firing missiles. Oh, God.* He glanced at the countdown on the main terminal's screen.

3:33...3:32...3:31...

"All of 'em. And hurry. I'm sending you the coordinates. I just talked to Basinger at Aralco, and we're both going to try to take out the satellites." They could hear Tony typing as fast as he could.

Steve couldn't know it, but he was right. The old man was smiling like an alley cat in a mouse café.

"What about other silos, sir? Are they a go, too?" Steve watched his best friend collapse into a chair and wondered if Timmy was up to the task at hand.

"Yes. Now it's your turn, son. Do your duty – quickly. Seems a lot of people are already, um, out of commission, and we need to be quick."

"Yes, sir."

"You boys do your part, and I promise you'll be rewarded."

Steve heard the click and dial tone before he could argue.

"I gotta get outta here, Timmy. We're going to die. The old man doesn't get it. The orders have already been downloaded. Taking out the satellites won't stop it, nothing will. I gotta get to Beth, and if I..."

"HEY!" Timmy shouted, trying to stop his buddy's tirade.

Steve clamped his mouth shut, shocked at Timmy's interjection.

"We follow orders, Steve. You preach it three hundred and sixty-five days out of the year, but now you're freakin' out on me.

C'mon – show me what to do and let's get our jobs done. Lives may depend on it. You can guess all you want about the satellites, but I'm more afraid of Mr. Andrews, aren't you? I don't need a court martial either."

Steve nodded, then grabbed the manual and each of their emergency procedure cards. He tossed one to Timmy and both men popped them in half. They pulled the piece of paper from the middle of the broken plastic sheath. He thumped buttons on his terminal and papers started scrolling out of the printer almost immediately. He yanked them from the tray and slapped each page onto the desk in front of the two of them.

"I really want to call Beth first. Just in case. How can I do that?"

"Steve, you can't. We'll get fired and discharged. You know protocol. We deploy the missiles, get in the chamber, and wait. That's what we're trained to do."

They glanced at the terminal.

2:09…2:08…2:07….

"I'm leaving, Timmy. I don't care about my job because tomorrow, it's not gonna matter. Are you really gonna try to stop me?"

Timmy rested his hand on the butt of the Glock fastened to his belt. He unsnapped the tab and lifted the pistol to feel the weight of it. He'd never drawn on anyone before – other than during training.

Steve watched Timmy analyze the gun in his hand. "Ah, Timmy, c'mon, man. Look!" Steve's voice rose as he pointed to the computer screen.

Timmy looked, but it didn't really make sense to him. All he knew was that procedure was procedure, and he meant to follow it.

"Timmy, I'm not going to die a slow death down here. I gotta get to Beth. I know you're not married, but imagine how I feel. Don't you wanna help your parents, man?" Steve's face contorted, panic needling him. He glanced at the main terminal.

1:26…1:25…1:24….

"All I know is they count on us to do the right thing. We have a responsibility, Steve."

Timmy gripped the Glock but let the muzzle point to the floor. "I…I don't wanna do this, Steve, but you know the drill. We've been trained for this. We chose this role when we enlisted. You don't just pick and choose what orders to follow."

Steve studied his friend's face, the gun, the distance between where they stood and the silo exit. The holding chamber was fire- and bullet-proof, so he just had to get to it. And time was wasting.

1:08…1:07…1:06….

"Timmy, listen to me. Be reasonable. Do you see those lists of cities? There are eight of them. The first three are all United States, Mexico or Canada. But beyond that, these crazy fucks mean to kill everybody. *Everybody*. Don't you get it? There won't be anybody to come get us – they'll all be dead. Whatever this chemical is, it's not even time for the first release yet – this is some kind of pre-release and look at our numbers. Look at the atmospheric pressure. Hell, the shit's already fucking with the weather. That's how powerful it is." Steve's eyes flipped from Timmy to the countdown and back, like a fan at a tennis match.

0:45...0:44...0:43....

Worry creased Timmy's forehead and doubt clouded his eyes. Steve seized the uncertainty to drive his point home.

"C'mon, man. Come with me. Who's gonna know?" Steve edged toward the door. Less than fifteen feet separated him from freedom and death. He didn't know if, once exposed to the air, he would survive the first bout of the chemical. But he had to at least try.

"I would. And it takes both of us to engage and fire." Timmy rubbed his head savagely with the palm of his gun-free hand, trying to justify what he had to do, wishing Steve understood how important this job was to him.

Steve glanced at the computer and couldn't stand it anymore.

0:28...0:27...0:26....

"I'm leaving, Timmy. You rot down here, I don't care, but I'm leaving and you will *not* shoot me. Do you hear me? I outrank you. Now, get...out...of...my...way." Panic raised his voice a notch, but he marched toward the door.

"No." Timmy sounded decisive but weak, almost child-like.

His partner ignored him and that was the last straw for Timmy. He squeezed a round that hit the door inches in front of Steve and ricocheted throughout the chamber. Both men ducked, but the second shot nailed Steve in the thigh as he crouched. He let out a yowl and clutched the wound. He turned to Timmy, shock and anguish etched all over his face, and tried to speak. Pain and panic locked the plea in his throat.

0:16...0:15...0:14...0:13...

We're locked in here forever, Timmy, if you don't help me the fuck up.

But words unsaid had no impact and Timmy's muddled decision took away any hope for escape. In the waning seconds, all he could think about was adhering to duty and shutting up the confusion in his fuzzy brain. He couldn't get the voices to stop, but he knew how to make them.

When the numbers hit double zero, the phone rang. Timmy clamped his hands to his ears to block out Steve's blubbering, knocking his right temple with the Glock.

"Don't answer it. It's Andrews and he wants to know why the hell we didn't deploy the goddamned missiles. And now the air-tight chamber has locked us out and we're so fucked. YOU KILLED US, YOU STUPID PISSANT!" Steve screamed at his best friend until Timmy couldn't stand it anymore.

He stomped toward his partner and shot him right between the eyes. Less than a second passed before Timmy angled the pistol and shoved the muzzle into his already bruising right temple. Denial and fear of a terrifying future forced him to squeeze the trigger.

With Tony Andrews angry, it didn't matter if a chemical meltdown destroyed the planet – he was dead anyway.

Chapter Six

Nationwide
Day Two

"STOP IT! DAMMIT, what are you doin' to me, you *freak*?" A fourteen-year old girl grappled with a middle-aged man who wouldn't let go of her shirt. She tugged at the buttons and, in a panic, ripped them free and wriggled out of her favorite top. She kicked at him and finally broke free. She took off running in her bra and blue jeans. She looked like an actress in a music video.

"You little bitch. Get back here!" Then, standing in the middle of the street, he couldn't remember why he had grabbed the girl in the first place. Had he meant to hurt her? Surely not, he had a daughter of his own in college, didn't he?

No, a sinister voice hissed. *She died last night, you stupid fuck. Damn near everybody bit the bullet before daybreak. Why didn't you?*

"I don't know," he whispered, and focused for the first time on the city street. Not a soul sat outside Starbuck's and, on second glance, his mouth fell open. Starbuck's front windows were shattered and the morning hotspot – open twenty-four hours according to the sign on the door – was empty. A dog standing in the middle of Main Street barked – the terrier didn't have to worry about traffic because there was none.

"Oh, God." The evening before came back to him – his wife had been quirky, more so than usual. They bickered and he slept on the couch, but sometime before dawn an urge hit him to walk seventeen blocks to Bob Evans for a pancake.

Looking in every direction at the looted stores, broken windows, and silent streets, the former stock broker understood pancakes were a thing of the past. He headed home to hunt for his .357 Magnum.

* * *

"LADIES AND GENTLEMAN, the President of the United States."

Fifteen or twenty people gathered around the Magnavox in O'Malley's Pub. The strange news that filtered to Moscow, Idaho, by way of a local reporter made no sense. But when morning alarms went off and Moscow citizens learned the military had upgraded to Def-Con Five and moved Homeland Security to *Severe Condition Red*, they bolted out of bed. Tornado sirens whirred, and the mayor called an emergency city council meeting.

"She better have some kahunas, now, huh?" one of the regulars muttered over his coffee mug. He hadn't voted for her because he thought America wasn't ready for a lady president. Too emotional, he'd argued. A few other men snickered, but most of them looked as haggard as he felt. They may not have been affected like the fifty cities they'd heard about, but there was certainly something in the air putting everyone in a funk.

"My fellow Americans, I address you this morning from Camp David where I have been joined by several members of my staff for an emergency meeting to determine the impact of a chemical attack on the United States." Diana Cavanaugh took a breath, and so did everyone in O'Malley's Pub. She looked like she hadn't slept but had rolled around in her clothes for three or four days. Her signature stylish looks were non-existent – frizzy brown hair escaped the clip atop her head, splotched fifty-year-old skin in dire need of a better make-up job, and a missing button on her blouse exposed her bra.

"All we know at this time is that Dallas, Texas, is the point of origin, and approximately fifty cities were targeted by an unknown chemical we are referring to as X-86. This chemical causes hallucinations and other symptoms. There was a leak on Thursday afternoon that impacted these cities and hundreds more with the shifting jet stream, but then a full-blown release occurred some time last night. Thousands are believed dead, and many more are suffering from delusions and may experience symptoms.

"No terrorists have taken credit for the attack, and we have information that it may be the responsibility of American citizens. Correspondents are out in the field to keep Americans up to date. We have known nothing as cataclysmic since the dinosaurs faced extinction. Scientists are researching the nature of the chemical discovered in the atmosphere, and findings will be released as soon as they are known."

Groans erupted in O'Malley's and several patrons nodded...those who had heard the voices.

"I advise you at this time to stay in your homes. Do not travel to any of the affected cities, and be aware that many who suffer secondary exposure present a danger to anyone who comes in contact with them."

President Cavanaugh teetered on her chair, turned, and pointed to a United States map.

Crude circles had been drawn around the major cities that had been hit. When she turned back to the camera, she seemed to have forgotten what she was doing. She got up, walked straight toward the camera, and in an instant the screen went to fuzz.

"She was filmin' that by herself," the bartender said, refilling coffee cups down the bar. "And she looked like hell."

"Not to mention her shirt. Man, we don't wanna see them shriveled-up raisins."

"She ain't that old, Max. Christ, you could be her daddy."

"Shut-up," Max hissed.

"I'm goin' home, fellas. Finish up. If President C. wants me at home, that's where I'm headed."

"Christ, Boomer, you can't close. My wife left for Spokane this mornin' to see her mother. I don't wanna go home. Damn, you think she's gonna be okay?"

"I don't know, Max. Go home and call her. All I know is I gotta phone my daughter in Denver to see if she's alright. Did you see that list? It was one of 'em, so was Los Angeles, New York, and D.C. Does that mean we ain't gotta government right now?" "Boomer" Reynolds shook his head, mopped up a puddle of spilled coffee, and tossed the rag in the pile of linens that would never need cleaning again.

As his regulars wandered out the door to discover a future more terrifying than any Hollywood disaster film, Boomer gathered his things, cleaned out the cash register, and said good-bye to O'Malley's. Strange voices informed him he would never be back.

* * *

PANIC-STRICKEN TOWNS across the U.S. sat in shock after President Cavanaugh's ominous speech and reacted much the same as the O'Malley's customers. Communities went into disaster mode, building bomb shelters and air-tight chambers they hoped would resist X-86's effects.

They wouldn't.

By noon Friday, known in newspapers as Day Two, chaos erupted all over the country. Reports of shootings, suicides, and brutal attacks spread like wildfire. Major TV stations manned by skeleton crews ran on back-up generators. NBC, CBS, and ABC combined staff to have enough people to broadcast. Between the three major stations, they managed seventeen people – not one of whom had ever been in front of a camera. But news aired, no matter how few there were to watch.

Survivors from infected cities contacted family across the nation. Some ranted about the voices or the demons eating their souls, but a few shared important information. A deejay at a local radio station in Dallas received a tip at home that four people were taken into custody at Beta Tron Chemical Company – four chemists in their mid-twenties with motive, means, and opportunity to create and cultivate a chemical of X-86's magnitude.

Dusty Morris, unaffected by the chemical, couldn't believe what the anonymous caller said. *Four people in Dallas could do this? Christ.*

For lack of anything else to do, he walked to work. He was sure the streets weren't drivable. After watching the morning news, with a single reporter having to anchor and reading straight from the teleprompter, Dusty couldn't believe something of this enormity had happened on U.S. soil.

September 11th ripped my heart out – I can't fathom anything worse.

His trek to work educated him and wound his stomach into knots. The world had gone crazy, and he was witnessing it. Talking to possible listeners would be perfect therapy. Before walking downstairs into KMJC's studio, he vomited into the Rubbermaid trashcan.

Once on air, he shared with the crackling airwaves that Dr. John Basinger, BetaCorp CEO, confirmed the arrest but offered little else. *It's an ongoing investigation*, the high-powered businessman added. Dusty noted the CEO was also untouched by X-86, seeming level-headed and frustrated.

Within minutes, callers flooded Dusty's lines with additional information. One cryptic message from someone who sounded like he knew what he was talking about shared that fifty more cities had less than twelve hours before falling victim to Stage II. The informant rattled off town names, but Dusty was too shocked to pay attention. He had to play the message over and over to finish putting pins in each of the cities on his giant wall map. Seeing fifty red push pins sprinkled across the map made his skin crawl. Some capitals, but mostly large metropolises.

Ninety-eight percent mortality rate, Basinger said. Another release tomorrow and there'll be no one left.

What Dusty didn't know was that Stage III on Monday would take X-86 overseas. By the eighth day, it would swallow the globe.

Chapter Seven

Georgetown, South Carolina
Day Two

JAKE THOMAS WOKE early Friday morning to an odd sensation. He lay there in a half-sleep for five blurry minutes. Was he late for work? He reached behind him, a practiced ritual, to pull Becky into a spoon but found only cold, rumpled sheets. He forced his sleepy eyes open and tried to read the alarm clock. After rubbing them into focus, he stared but could not quite comprehend the digital 3:16 a.m. glaring back at him. He looked out the window – it was light out, wasn't it? He watched the numbers, waiting to see the six blink to a seven.

Damn thing must've stopped.

"Becky?" His thoughts, still fuzzy with sleep, segued to confusion. Some detached voice whispered to go find her.

After nearly four minutes, Jake decided the six was frozen forever in its blue world and rolled out of bed.

"Honey?" He called louder this time, his voice echoing down the stairs. He wondered if she had gone out for donuts, though that wouldn't have been like her. Her peculiar mood from the evening before was long forgotten after the escapade in bed. Jake grinned as he caught a whiff of Becky on his skin – the body wash from the bath, her perfumed salts, and the scent of her sex. He suspected showering before work might ward off the chiding he would receive from his buddies.

He rummaged through the dirty clothes on the floor and pulled on tattered Umbros well beyond their twilight years. He knew he hadn't overslept for work, but the anxious feeling got his hands moving as he shuffled through Becky's jewelry on the dresser for his watch. He was relieved to see it was just 6:45. He had forty-five minutes, plenty of time to get ready. Fragmented thoughts kept bounding in and out of his head, leaving a mild throb. He tried to pin down the strangeness overwhelming him, but that too sent a pulsating thump into his temples.

Jake called out for Becky one last time. Fridays, often slow-starting for him with her being off for the summer, had gotten tougher and tougher as the break progressed. He should have gone into education, too, he thought for the thousandth time.

Her early rise perplexed him. He usually showered and kissed her goodbye an hour before she even lumbered out of bed. He loved to tease her about teacher's pay from mid-June through early August.

"Hey, you got a paycheck! Look, honey! You don't even go to work, and they pay ya anyway! That's so totally cool!"

She had punched him on the arm. "Yeah, wanna swap jobs in November?"

"Huh-uh, no way." And then Jake remembered exactly why he *hadn't* gone into teaching.

He glanced at himself in the mirror and grimaced. He ran a hand through his short brown hair. Leaning in close, he grasped a lone gray strand and plucked it. Since his late teens, he had battled prematurely graying hair, but he fought it like a landscaper. He didn't need grief from his friends, even if Becky thought it was cute.

Becky. The only time she had gone out for an early morning breakfast without telling him had been on their honeymoon. When he woke up that day, Becky sat on the bed staring at him with two enormous boxes of Dunkin' Donuts between them.

"I couldn't decide! Besides, we might want more later, if we stay in bed all day."

She had been right.

When he let out a spontaneous chuckle, a fresh bolt of pain entered one ear and exited ruthlessly through the other. He couldn't remember a more comprehensive headache save a hangover or two.

He rubbed the bridge of his nose, squeezed the small rise between his eyes and closed them, waiting for the pain to pass. He couldn't imagine where Becky was, but he sure wished she would come massage his head and back. She had the golden touch and it felt silly to miss her, but he did. While their friends separated, fought and cheated, he and Becky continued to fall in love.

Reminiscing lightened his mood a little and gave an inkling of relief to his hammering head. He tugged a T-shirt on as he came down the stairs and began to hum. The surge of sound inside his head made him swoon. Nausea from the pain roiled his empty stomach, and Jake had to steady himself on the railing until the feeling passed.

"Jesus," he muttered, kneading his temples gently. As he rounded the corner into the kitchen, a faint odor tickled his nose, and it wasn't until then that he correlated his stopped clock with the electricity being out.

He opened the refrigerator and caught a whiff of food on the verge and slammed it shut. Power had only been out for three or four hours, so whatever packed the smelly wallop had probably begun to ruin days earlier. With the way he and Becky cleaned house, a container of leftovers could be from last Christmas. They loved the adage that a messy home was a sign of happiness, and repeated it often.

Wonder if she noticed the electricity was out. Jake stood in the middle of the kitchen. Could she... The newest galloping pain behind his eyes severed the thought.

Everything looked in order as he headed toward the living room, and then he saw the sliding glass doors half open, allowing a blustery draft in the room. The breeze had a November bite to it.

"It's fucking August," he muttered in defiance of the drums in his head and crossed the room to close the door.

What he saw instead made him scream, oblivious of the pain it caused.

Jake threw the doors open, cracked one side, and froze. He stared at his wife for only two or three seconds, but the vision it left would etch permanently in his memory with uncanny detail.

Becky sat in her favorite patio chair with absurdly perfect posture, her head straight back on the cushion. Her mouth parted as if to speak, and her pupiless eyes stared blindly toward the horizon. She seemed to be wearing a pale blue lipstick with ash gray blusher as an accent. Each highlighted the circles under her eyes.

He couldn't seem to tear his own eyes away, seeing the gray-blues he'd been so enchanted with that now looked completely alien. Aside from the facial discoloration, her vacant stare had a bewitched look, as if someone had literally scared her to death.

Jake lifted Becky out of the chair, cradled her in his arms, and brought her inside. He began to ramble about her catching cold.

"There, there, baby. Here's a cover," he soothed, tucking the afghan around her. He had to block the cool air he knew would give her pneumonia.

He laid her stiffening body on the couch and suddenly realized what he needed to do. He frantically dialed 911 knowing full well she was already dead but unable to accept the finality of it. He nearly dropped the phone when he heard the recording.

All circuits were busy? He slammed the phone down, then jabbed the three digits again. The operator monotoned the same message.

Busy, my ass! How the hell can you be busy? My wife is... is... Is what? He couldn't bring himself to think it.

Anger raged through him. Jake began to throw anything and everything he could get his hands on. He raked shelves with one arm, sweeping ruthlessly across every piece of furniture. Glass shattered, trinkets crashed into the wall, books banged to the floor with one *womp* after another. When he ran out of table tops to clear, he collapsed next to his wife. It dawned on him then what had seemed so odd earlier as he lay in bed.

As he fell silent, the clatter of his tantrum settled, he listened. There was absolutely no noise in the house or outside. Nothing. No car horns in the distance, no barking dogs, chirping birds, screaming kids, screeching brakes or whop-whopping of skateboards on the sidewalk – nothing but dead silence. Anxiety came crawling into his groin, turning his already queasy stomach.

He cradled Becky in his arms, pulling her to him like a protective shield. He refused to let go for fear she would be swallowed by the monster that had eaten the world silent. He sat in the middle of the rubble rocking his dead wife and cried for nearly ten hours.

Chapter Eight

St. Louis
Day Two

"DADDY, STOP IT! Wake up. Please, Daddy, you're scaring me. Oh, I don't know what to do! Daaadddyyy!"

Tears streamed down Jessie's face as she watched her father lying beside her on the hotel couch writhing in pain, clutching desperately at his throat. Justin's eyes bulged, and he wanted to claw away the blockage in his windpipe to make it stop.

For the last hour, he had been in a near-hypnotic state, not sure what was happening to him. Unfamiliar thoughts invaded his head and seemed to take captive any of his own. Incoherent images galloped through like lone horsemen, and confusion brought him to the brink of madness.

It took him a moment to understand why he and Jess were in a hotel – the ball game, Hard Rock, *Toy Story* – then he remembered dozing off. He woke to cramped legs and fleeting thoughts of getting to work on time. Then the air flow to his lungs simply shut off like a water spigot.

Something foreign inside his brain informed him he couldn't breathe, yet he knew better, didn't he? Justin calmed himself, attempted to swallow, and tried to expel the air as routinely as taking a pee. His lungs simply would not comply. He could feel his chest clench in panic and couldn't understand what was happening to him.

"DADDY! STOP IT!" Jessie screamed, ripping him from his quiet fall into a black hole. He heard his little girl scream that she didn't know what to do, and her cries kick-started his survival instinct. He clawed savagely at his throat again, red-whelped trails striping his neck and bloodying his fingernails. His mind reeled and swam out of focus, and then quite clearly he heard a ubiquitous voice tell him to relax. Unable to disobey the hypnotic command, he did as he was told.

The last coherent thought he understood was a deep fear for Jessie. In his dying moments, Justin Bayker seemed to grasp what was happening to the world around him, and sheer terror accompanied him into a glowing white light.

* * *

IN THE LAST frantic moments of her father's life, Jessie succumbed to hysteria. When his body relaxed, she beat his chest with balled-up fists, angry he would surrender so easily. How could he give up when she would be left to fend for herself?

After two or three minutes, the once precocious little girl was reduced to a helpless crying child. She sobbed for five minutes before realizing she should call 911. Her daddy had taught her that years ago and here she sat doing nothing.

Jessie's dexterous hands were now ten fumbling thumbs, and it took two deep breaths to calm her enough to push the correct buttons. The silence on the other end confused her. Her daddy never prepared her for an emergency where she would need to dial a nine to get an outside line. And Jessie couldn't know that, as of today, assisted phone calls were a lost concept. She punched the disconnect button four times as hard as she could.

Suddenly, it rang in her hand. She answered it more out of habit than anything.

"Welcome to the House of Horrors. What the hell are you doin' here? Don't you know the goddamned sky is falling?" a caustic voice shouted into the phone.

"Uh, I'm trying to call someone for my daddy. He's hurt, and I need a doctor. Can you help me?" Jessie's hands shook as she waited.

"Honey, this hotel is haunted by hundreds of dead people. Haven't you heard? I'm thinking of joinin' 'em, 'cause my wife…my…my…"

A deep breath gave Jessie time to wonder why this man had called her.

"My wife…DOES ANYONE GIVE A SHIT THAT MY WIFE IS DEAD?!"

Jessie dropped the phone as if it were on fire, then raced from the room. Doors stood ajar in the hallway, and what Jessie saw in the next thirty minutes running from room to room would drive fear so deep into her brain that she would forget everything about life as she had previously known it. It would never be the same for her again.

The horror worsened as she bolted out the Marriott's lobby doors onto Walnut.

"Oh, my God," was all Jessica Bayker could mutter when she got her first glimpse of the morning after.

Cars had been abandoned all over the street – some with doors open and engines running. Store and business windows sported graffiti or were completely shattered. Debris littered the streets and sidewalks; every trash can or mail drop box that could be overturned had been spilled like a paper cup. And it was chilly – not mid-August sweltering like a normal Missouri summer, but cool enough to need a jacket. Jessie rubbed her arms to warm them and looked around.

A street normally chaotic with people looked like a scene from a disaster movie – eerily silent, but littered with garbage after the storm of looters and Stage I-induced psychotics. Someone screamed in the distance, the sound echoing off the buildings.

"You be the chosen one, little girl?"

"Huh?" Jessie whipped around to see a bum staring at her. And he only had on a pair of striped boxers. "Who, *me*?"

"Yeah, you. Go. Follow your heart, little girl. Our lives depend on it." As the homeless man stared at her, his eyes clouded over. "What the hell you starin' at, kid?"

Did he mean me? Or was he just talkin' crazy? Jessie shivered. A bum pushing a shopping cart full of junk cackled that he thanked the lord for Armageddon. The ultimate salvage sale, he squealed. Then he turned toward her and grinned, revealing decaying teeth and black gums.

"Yes, he was talkin' about you," the indigent whispered and cackled. The hair bristled on the back of her neck.

Jessie back-stepped down the street, then turned tail and ran. She sprinted to the end of Walnut and wheeled around the corner. Her heart lurched into her throat at the sight of two screaming men jumping up and down on the cab of an SUV.

"YAHOO! Free DVDs, girlie. Want one?"

Before Jessie could shake her head, the taller one tossed an RCA box at her feet. It crashed and rattled with a sickening crunch. One of the guys ripped his shirt off and gave a Tarzan yell that grated on Jessie's nerves like fingernails on chalkboard.

The traffic signal blinked yellow, but there were no cars anywhere. This street was more ransacked than Walnut and just as desolate. Broken windows gaped on almost every single store and, other than a few stray dogs, not a single soul was anywhere in sight. No shoppers or business suits racing to work.

Jessie didn't understand the horrors of Stage I that had seized St. Louis, but she knew whatever killed her daddy had stolen the world at the same time. She didn't know what to do; she couldn't shake what the old homeless man had said about her being the chosen one.

And he told her to follow her heart. *What did he mean? Where should she go?* And then she knew.

Home. But without transportation, the trip would be next to impossible. Tired and hungry, she tried to find a safe place to hide that might have food she could borrow and a map to draw out her route. Her daddy didn't approve of stealing, so she would leave a note explaining how she would pay them back – she knew where her daddy kept a stash in the cabinet above the refrigerator. She hoped they would understand.

It only took two blocks to find a Texaco station on the corner of two major streets. There was a multiple car wreck in the parking lot. Jessie crouched in a doorway across the street and watched. She wanted to make sure no one was inside and that there weren't any crazies around to scare her or give her any more headaches. The screaming and strange feelings in her brain made her queasy.

While she waited, Jessie tried not to think about her daddy, Busch Stadium, *Toy Story*, or singing in the living room. Tears welled in her eyes, but she refused to let emotion get the better of her.

Follow your heart...our lives depend on it. She stood, brushed the knees of her jeans and ran across the street into the gas station.

Yes, he's talkin' about you. Had she said that out loud? She didn't think so.

Shaking the strange feelings away, Jessie scouted the aisles, ducked when she thought she saw something, and realized it was her own reflection in a security mirror. After unwrapping a burrito, she laid it in a microwave, worrying that the strange whistling and surges indicated a lack of juice. She left it to fend for itself and found a fanny pack and stuffed it with things she thought she might need – band aids, aspirin, a tiny flashlight, extra batteries, and an assortment of pens. She quickly filled two more sacks with donuts, chips, crackers and miscellaneous drinks. She nabbed a bottled water from the cooler, though it wasn't as cold as it should've been, and considered a root beer. But Daddy didn't like her to have too much soda.

Jessie packed her supplies neatly behind the counter, slipped into the cashier's cage, and locked the door. The enclosed screen wouldn't protect her from an intruder, but if she huddled in the cashier's booth near the far corner, no one could see her. Once settled directly below the cash register with someone's jacket draped across her for warmth, Jessie ripped open a granola bar and ate it in three bites.

She pulled the Rams couch throw out of her pile of stuff, wrapped it around her, and wadded the jacket to use for a pillow.

Jessie didn't know why it was cold outside, but she didn't question any of the oddities. She knew life would never be the same. She pulled out the spiral notebook and pencil and tried to decide how much to tell her Diary.

Dear Diary,

Today was the saddest day of my life.

That was the only line Jessie could write. She prayed none of the bad people she had encountered earlier would get her, but right now all she could think about was her daddy. The few words spilled onto the paper were immediately smeared by tears. She couldn't bring herself to say more.

Nothing could express the pain suffocating her.

Chapter Nine

Washington, D.C.
Day Two

TONY ANDREWS FELT like a cat with a two-pound bass in his mouth. After the fiasco with Corporal Singleton and his whiny Specialist Timmy Edwards, it had taken Tony a little time to settle his jangling nerves. Why couldn't men just do their goddamned jobs? But as further news came down the pike, he saw the nationwide crisis for what it was – a golden opportunity.

The entire debacle could be a bridge to a political career, one he was destined for. Sitting in a luxury hotel in downtown Washington, D.C., biding time before the press conference seemed fitting. And it made him antsy. BetaCorp had no weapons of X-86's capabilities, and Tony planned to clear that up first thing, right before he set out to discover if Aralco had managed it. He'd call John Basinger and have a CEO-to-CEO chat.

"Might only be bozos at this press conference anyway." He studied his reflection in the mirror, brushed his eyebrows back, and slicked down a stray black hair.

He decided food would placate his apprehension. He flipped open the massive yellow pages and dragged his finger across the restaurants. Minus a chauffeur who knew every city in the U.S. like the back of his hand, Tony was a car without wheels. He hadn't driven himself anywhere in nearly ten years until today, but a short jaunt from airport to hotel had been a piece of cake. Zeferreli's Fine Dining was another. If only he'd thought to utilize his pilot who was chilling on a private runway near Dulles International. When they'd landed three hours earlier, Tony had the misguided notion that the drive would refresh him.

Instead, dodging abandoned cars, straggling hitchhikers, and a ten-car pile-up frayed his nerves. Denial had kept fear and reality tucked safely near his waning sanity. But now he had to make a concerted effort to suppress it.

"I believe it's time for some intervention," Tony stated to the voices rambling in his head. Had there always been this many? "All the fuckers out there who think they want a piece of me are gonna get it."

Once in the hotel room, the fraying CEO whipped out his pen and started a list. It was a mission that had been brewing in his head for nearly twenty years.

"Okay...let's see. First let's start with big Willie, you stupid prick," he said, as he neatly printed the name in a notepad. Thinking about enemies from as many as fifty years earlier, he filled two pages. When he checked it over, he crossed out John Basinger's name. *Nah, he's sort of a friend – as close as I've got anyway*. He moved Brad Tavares' name closer to the top of the list. As the conscience of BetaCorp, Brad had always driven Tony to drink, not that he needed the help. But Brad constantly nagged for the company to take a more environmental approach to research and questioned every project from the do-gooder point of view. The mere idea of Brad Tavares at work irked Tony to no end.

"But I need to eat, don't I?" Tony chuckled, and his mouth watered for Zeferreli's linguini and a well-aged Bordeaux. Cook or no cook, he thought even he could handle that.

He itched to investigate, to see who survived, and to concoct a plan. He didn't bother locking up as he headed to the stairwell and the forty flights to the lobby.

Ten minutes later, the crisp evening air chilled his face as he made his way down Madison. August in D.C. warranted an extra dose of deodorant and short sleeves, not a jacket. Instead, Tony hugged his arms, enveloped in the strangeness of the moment. Time ebbed like a lazy tide around him. Not quite noticing the goings-on but embracing the oddities of the atmosphere, Andrews crossed an empty street and accepted the finality of X-86's impact. There would be no press conference – there was no one to talk to.

He stalled at an intersection, admiring the twilight sky. The scene surreal and the stress palpable, he cocked his head at an old lady thumping her head and shouting obscenities. Tony rubbed his temples. *Shut the fuck up, Lady*. He hurried down the street, trying to ignore her and get out of range. Her ranting echoed in his throbbing head.

They're weak; they're not you.

The eeriness of empty D.C. streets prickled the hair on the nape of his neck and tantalized his yearning to fry that big bass. He knew the area should be buzzing with partygoers, big shots, and a general hubbub of activity. He saw the dark sign that usually twinkled a classy capital Z and went inside. He weaved around dinner-ready tables and tried all the lights. Zeferreli's had no power and, to Tony's chagrin, there were no back-up generators.

"Well, shit." Irritated and hungry, Tony made his way back out front and noticed a group gathered in front of a store window across the street. Out of habit, he looked both ways before crossing.

In a Best Buy display, half the TV screens were filled with a tired, rapidly aging President Cavanaugh. Her shoddy make-up enhanced crows-feet and drooping bags under her sixty-year-old eyes. False eyelashes hung loosely from one, but she didn't seem to notice. She had missed a button on her silk blouse, revealing a black bra. At O'Malley's in Idaho, a regular snickered about not wanting to see some shriveled-up raisins.

Tony's head swam as he listened to her speak. *I thought they would protect you.*

"...from Camp David where I have been joined by several members of my staff for an emergency meeting to determine the impact of a chemical attack on the United States." Diana Cavanaugh took a deep breath and Tony watched, his heart thudding and head reeling. Her voice echoed, but he couldn't focus on it.

"...unknown chemical we are referring to as X-86..."

Aralco was kicking our ass. We had a contract with the military for a comprehensive chemical that would debilitate the enemy – but nothing of this magnitude. Damn you, John.

"...a full-blown release occurred some time last night..."

If one release did this and there are more, we're screwed. There won't be a White House – no political career. As much as Tony admired the conspirators who produced X-86, his respect was evaporating into good old-fashioned anger. They hadn't left anything worth salvaging.

"...in your homes, do not travel to any of the affected cities and be aware that many who suffer secondary exposure present a danger to anyone who comes in contact with them."

That is so true. He studied the onlookers staring at the many images of President Cavanaugh pointing to the U.S. map, then walking straight into the camera. Tony flinched as she reached toward him and the screens went to snow. A few seconds passed before rainbow stripes appeared with the familiar message captioned along the bottom: *We are experiencing technical difficulty.*

"Wow," a short, pudgy man muttered. "I can eat whatever the hell I want...fuck this Atkins shit."

Tony stared at the plump man and wondered if what he thought he heard had been his own loose cogs or...

"Whole country's experiencing technical difficulty. Ain't even fuckin' reruns. Where's Andy Fucking Griffith when you need him?"

"Or *Law & Order.* There's always one of them on." An elderly man chuckled, then picked his nose. He inspected his treasure and laughed again.

"President didn't even have a friggin' camera man," a former *somebody* said. He straightened his Armani jacket and gave a disgusted grunt.

"Did you see all those cities with pins in 'em? Chicago, LA, New York, Atlanta, Boston, and every city that generates programming, obviously zapped. Kaput. A shitload of people are outta jobs and got other things on their mind. I know I do." The businessman spoke with a curt realism, and Tony wondered what the man could possibly have to do – sell stock or lobby a new bill to the indigent and insane?

A wild image of a streaker racing through the Capitol screaming for supporters of the new and improved Air Breathing Rights Bill made Tony giggle.

"What're you laughing at?" A woman of obvious strength, position, and power confronted him. The rest stared at her in confusion.

"You, you skanky ass bitch," Tony hissed. Too many voices whispered, shouted, argued in his brain, layered like tortilla chips waiting to be crunched.

The lady jerked as if physically assaulted. But she didn't respond and seemed to forget what had been said. She rubbed her forehead and backed away from Tony and the rest of the group. Many of the others shared her disjointed sentiment and wandered off in pairs mumbling about an uncertain future.

Tony meant to take matters into his own hands. With silos at his disposal and no law enforcement to speak of, he had the world by the short hairs. But first he had to return to Denver, to BetaCorp headquarters and a mission to be part of something important, a milestone that would be remembered through the ages.

The CEO jogged into a hotel and spent twenty minutes ransacking rooms in search of car keys, preferably for a BMW like his own. Familiarity would help him find a car.

In the hotel's parking garage, it only took him a few minutes once he punched the panic button on the various keys in his hand. A sleek Z-4 responded with synchronized flashes and honks.

"Sweet." He slid into the sports car and breathed in the smells – leather, Armor-All, a hint of cologne.

Tony tried to digest the day as he drove, weaving through streets that looked like a scene from a sci-fi thriller. He couldn't make sense of much, but one thing he knew for sure – he meant to shove his hand in the cookie jar.

Chapter Ten

St. Louis
Day Two

LOOKING LIKE THE lone girl in a disaster flick, Jessica Bayker stood at a major intersection in a St. Louis suburb, scared and confused. Her home, she knew, was miles from here – sometimes an hour and a half drive to a Rams or Cardinal game, depending on traffic.

Cardinals' game. That fragmented thought rambled through her aching head. Hadn't someone hit a home run? The evening trickled back into focus. The irony of remembering such a recent happy time in the midst of total panic disoriented her and made her stomach ache.

She had huddled in the Texaco station and fallen asleep. Then windows had shattered over her head. In a panic, she had grabbed her things and run until she simply couldn't move anymore. Flashing recollections of bloated, stiff bodies brought bile into her throat. Car wrecks and broken buildings' windows – shattered glass speckled the streets, sidewalks, and even people. One old man's thin hair shimmered as he lay on a bench outside a coffee shop. She discovered dirty alleys, unfamiliar streets, and dangerous areas – she could hear her father's voice warn her to stay away. A craggy old bum called her a word she didn't know, but the way he shouted it scared her, and she knew it wasn't nice. Her sheltered Kirkwood life prepared her little for what she saw. After hours of drifting, she found herself back where she started – the baseball stadium and the riverfront – 'grand tourist central," her daddy called it.

She wanted to go home, to find a map and...and...*Daddy*. That's what she really wanted. She clutched the makeshift diary in her hand and resituated the fanny pack full of snacks. She refused to feel guilty for taking them; life presented her with obstacles and she proved to be resourceful. That was all – period.

Turning in a circle, Jessie sat on the soft grass surrounding the Arch. She loved this part of her home city. When her dad brought her here, she ogled the Dome, the giant Gateway Arch, the ball field, and even the casino boats.

Now all of it slammed the reality home – *Daddy's dead.* A lump jammed so full in her throat that she couldn't swallow. The last image she had of him – deep scratches entrenched in his throat, bulging eyes, gasping for air – made her ache with loss.

Oh, Daddy, what do I do now?

She fingered the new Cardinal jersey he bought her last night. *I want my daddy, not a new shirt.* The last one he bought her had been on McGwire Night a few years earlier – Mark McGwire was broadcasting in the booth, and she had been beside herself. His celebrated number twenty-five was being retired with his impending nomination for Baseball's Hall of Fame. She'd chomped into her hot dog and mustard squirted from the end and plopped right on the bat on the shirt. The yellowish spot never quite washed out, even though Daddy treated it with Spray 'n Wash. He hadn't even gotten mad; instead, he'd just grinned around his own mouthful of ketchuppy dog.

"I've gotta get home." What she didn't finish was how badly she now wanted to find that old stained T-shirt. *I think Daddy sold it in the annual neighborhood yard sale or gave it to the truck people at that Army building.*

The silence scared her. Eight years of life experience offered no background for how ludicrous the absence of rush hour traffic was, or an empty stadium parking lot only an hour before game time. It hadn't prepared her for desolate highways, the calm over Laclede's Landing, a vacant riverfront on a Friday evening.

Isolation and fear scrambled her insides. A steady thump-thump-thump in her temples made her eyes water. A voice, then a clank in the distance echoed, startling her, a reminder that she wasn't quite as alone as she felt but too alone to find help. The Jessie-of-old would have attempted to drive a car or shown some initiative to conquer the bizarre crisis. But the new and unimproved version – sticky-face, frizzy brown ponytail, watery hazel eyes, filthy Gap jeans in sharp contrast to the brand new Cardinal shirt – just wanted to go home. She was now a regressed soon-to-be third grader trying to negotiate the simple task of getting home without her father.

But home meant traversing miles that she paid little attention to when Daddy took big roads, turned off near the last Missouri exit, and weaved around the stadium searching for a parking spot. Sometimes he found a spot by TGI Friday's or Mike Shannon's, but he usually forked out ten dollars for a shoddy lot where he worried about door dings.

I'll never find my way home. As she rubbed away the tears with grimy fists, it suddenly occurred to Jessie what to do. She should call her mother in Los Angeles. Her mom wouldn't let her down, not with her daddy gone. Somehow she knew that.

Her spirits lifted at the prospect of talking to her mom; the hope eased her headache. She jogged the length of the street until she found a hotel that didn't have people lying in front of it. She couldn't handle any more vacant stares or bloated bodies. As she slipped inside the massive lobby of the Adams Mark, she tried not to look around. But giant statues – bronze horses – made her eyes go wide with wonder. The walls were mostly windows, so the setting sun made the room glow. In spite of everything, the beauty of the hotel lobby made it all go away for a moment.

Phone – I need a phone. She headed for the registration area. She dialed the number her father once forced her to commit to memory in case of emergencies. He always thought of everything. And this was definitely an emergency – the world was ending, wasn't it?

The weight of that terrifying thought reminded her of an old Bruce Willis DVD she and her daddy had watched earlier in the summer. If he could save the planet from a meteor, why couldn't he fix this?

Where were those people now when everyone needed them? She guessed someone like Bruce Willis couldn't be a hero all the time. He had done his fair share. Her favorite had been the *Die Hard* series, even though her dad argued that one man couldn't possibly be involved in that many different catastrophes.

Emotion filled her throat again. Thinking about her daddy made her head thump, like the time she let Amy Chambers time her while Jessie hung upside down on the monkey bars for sixteen minutes and forty-four seconds. Her stomach churned, and she wished she could turn the power button off on her brain. She dialed the numbers slowly, rote memorization working through her fingers before she could panic. Longer than normal clicks meant nothing to Jessie, as delayed computer terminals took seconds to reroute around non-operational systems throughout the Midwest.

Jessie swallowed hard so she could talk. When the answering machine picked up, she floundered for the right words.

"Momma, it's Jessie. I'm lost near the Arch. Duh-duh-daddy's gone, and I don't know what to do." Tears escaped, and the lump gave way as the sobs soaked the words. "Please help me, Momma. The number on this phone is um, 314...555...9880. Call me and tell me what to do. I'll wait for you, Momma." The finality of hanging up without resolution seemed fatal to Jessie.

I hope Los Angeles isn't weird like this, too.

She knew it was a long flight and an excruciatingly long drive to where her mother lived; her mom told her so all the time. Her daddy showed it to her with an atlas once. But that surely wouldn't matter now.

The precocious Jessie of Thursday would have insisted that when the going got tough, the tough kicked butt. It was, of course, a saying her father taught her. Sitting on a plush lobby bench taking careful looks around the gigantic room, Jessie thanked God she couldn't see any people – dead or alive. Both scared her. Trickling water from a sink somewhere made her suddenly have to pee.

Can I hear the phone if I go to the bathroom? She spied the ladies' room across the lobby. Uncertainty of who might be in there made her bladder clench. She willed the pressure in her stomach to subside and took to walking in tiny squares, measuring each step carefully by the fancy tiles. Heel to toe – heel to toe – heel to toe. Her shortening attention span drew her eyes back to the phone with every square lap she completed. When she got dizzy, she plopped into a high-backed chair and laid her head back. She forced her eyes closed in an effort to doze when the ringing phone woke her.

She raced to it so fast she nearly fell over a trashcan. She grabbed the receiver and shouted "hello" despite the fact that she could barely breathe and her head was pounding.

"Jessie?" A deep, unfamiliar voice seemed to reach her from the inside of a cave.

"Yes?"

"Sweetie, I'm your mom's personal assistant, Bryan. She's told me a lot about you." He paused, and Jessie wondered what her mom's life had been like for the past few years – she knew so little of her mother's world. She was supposed to spend two weeks in California in June, but that conflicted with the soccer camp Jessie signed up for. Then the week vacation in July didn't work because her mom had a flight-schedule conflict she couldn't clear. Her mom promised a few days before school started, but it wasn't looking good.

"Where's my mom?" she asked, angry that she sounded so childish.

"I haven't seen her since she left work yesterday. She was pretty down since her trip to come see you wasn't coming together."

"You know her that well?" Jessie had heard her dad and mom trying to work out a vacation. She had only been to California twice, and each time the arrangements made Momma and Daddy fight.

"Yeah, I worked for her. Made all her flight plans and that kind of stuff." Bryan hesitated, and Jessie wondered what stuff meant. *Is he my mom's boyfriend?* The thought seemed weird in her head.

"Well, can you find her? My daddy's gone, and I need her. I'm lost, and I don't know where to go." It was all she could do to talk, much less hold back the tears burning the back of her throat. The swelling lump felt like an inflatable bowling ball. She started to say something more, but no words would pass.

"Well, Jess, I'll keep looking. She was supposed to have a flight today, so if it left, she may be en route to Detroit. I've heard snips of news on the radio, but there's no electricity here. I heard part of the President's speech on my Sony Walkman. You said you were alone?" He sighed.

Jessie had a weird fleeting image of wolves circling her, snarling with spittle dripping from long, sharp teeth. She shivered.

"All I know is I keep finding dead people. And my dad," Jessie started and then went on to tell him how she had run searching for anyone who could help her, but she just couldn't find anyone. They were all dead. There was no electricity most places, clocks were all stopped, 911 didn't work, and she didn't know what to do next.

She could hear Bryan smile from the way his voice sounded. She guessed he wasn't used to eight-year-olds with an opinion.

"Listen, Jess, I want to help you. I've seen some pretty scary stuff here, too. Some of the people I've found aren't quite okay. Do you know what I mean?"

"Yeah, they're running around throwing things through windows and cussing. Some of them are saying this is Armageddon, and Jesus is coming for us. Is He?"

"I'm not sure, Jess, I'm really not sure. That might not be a bad thing given the other possibilities. I'm just glad the phones still work." He paused, and in the moments of silence, Jessie wiped her snotty nose on a jacket left laying on the counter. Disgusted, she shoved it in a trashcan. Her head thudded worse now. The more time she spent outside, the more her head hurt.

"I tell you what, Jess. I have an idea."

She liked hearing that. She wanted guidance, someone to tell her what to do. Anyone. Her father would be her first choice, then her mother. This man seemed to be her closest ally by default.

"Just help me, Bryan."

"I want you to get home, Jess, can you do that? I don't know exactly how far away from home you are, and this is asking a lot, but I have an idea that if you can get there, then I can get to you. I've not been able to find any of my friends or family, so a little travel might be a good thing. What do you think? Do you think you can make it?"

"I don't know. I'm on the riverfront by the Arch. I'm a long way away, but I saw some bikes in a store I passed just around the corner. I could take one. It'll still take me a long, long time. Dad sometimes takes two hours to get to a game. What if...if bad people bother me?"

"Well, you're going to need to be really careful. Avoid people no matter what. Some of them aren't quite right, I'm sure you've noticed. But if you're strong, I think you can do it. Now, I have your home address and I'm going to get me a map and figure out how to get to you. You just get home and sit tight."

"Okay," Jessie said and heaved a sigh. "I bet once I get the perfect bike, I can pack some food and water, then I'll study my map, too. Yeah, I'll get everything together. Should I try to start now, before it gets dark?"

Jessie's voice made it clear that the idea itself gave her a confidence boost. Bryan admitted it might be dangerous, but any amount of distance she could cover would help.

"Do you remember the road you took to get there? Think real hard about places you see when your daddy brings you to the stadium. Can you see them?"

"Uh, we usually go that way." Jessie pointed in a direction only she could see. Bryan laughed.

"Okay, that's good, and do you remember where to go once you head that way? The name of a street?"

"Well, we live in Kirkwood, and we hit Manchester Road from the highway we take away from here. I-44 is the name of the highway, I think. Or maybe that's when we go to Six Flags. Oh, God. But I do know we drive down a highway quite a ways. Then I think I'll know the rest just by being there. It will be really easy once I find the highway. I'm always excited by the time we're this close, so I don't pay as good attention as I should. Daddy always says to pay attention to details; that's what makes the difference."

Bryan coached Jessie on getting supplies, ways to chart her path, and how he planned to leave the city as soon as he could. He didn't realize how therapeutic the planning and questioning was for Jessie, but it helped her focus.

"Okay, okay. Anything else?" She was getting anxious to begin her mission.

"Plan on enough to eat for two days. I should be able to get there by late Saturday night or early Sunday. I'll be coming straight down 40 to I-44 to St. Louis. Looking at the atlas, it's a straight shot to you – a darn long one, too, but the change of scenery will be nice. Now, can you tell me what you're gonna do?"

"I'm gonna get a bike from that store I saw, then stop for food on the big road. Between tonight and tomorrow, I think I should be able to get there by dark, shouldn't I?"

She knew it was almost six and that it didn't get dark until pretty late; if she could get to the highway before dark, she would feel more comfortable.

"Absolutely. And you know what else, Jess?"

"What?"

"Be leery of strangers. I'm sure you've heard that before, but think about those crazy people you've seen and realize that some of them may try to talk to you. Don't let them. Stay away from anyone who doesn't seem normal, okay? And the X-86 has done some funky stuff. It's made people really weird, so stay away from them. I'll be there in thirty to thirty-five hours."

"Do you think my mom will come home?" Tears threatened to break her resolve.

"How 'bout I leave her a note telling her what I'm doing just in case she does?"

"Yeah, I'd like that. I'd like that a lot."

"Hey, Jess, I'm gonna start trying to call you tomorrow afternoon, okay? I'll take my cell phone, and I have your home phone number. I'll keep tryin' until I reach you. Be careful, okay?"

"Gotcha."

Jessie hung up and walked cautiously back toward the bike shop thinking about Bryan. She didn't know what he meant by assistant, but she thought he might be her mom's boyfriend, and that was okay with her. She liked him.

It didn't take long to get to the bike shop and pick out a purple cycle with tassels on the handles. She hitched a basket on back to accent the one on front. That would give her extra room for supplies. She arranged the items so they wouldn't get jostled, then plucked the notepad out for a quick note.

Dear Diary,

I'm going home and I'm really scared. But Bryan, a friend of Mommas, is going to come get me. I hope he hurries. I can't wait to look on the map and find California to measure how far away it is. I sure hope Momma comes home, but after what I have seen today, I just want company.

Diary, I am so tired my legs feel like they're gonna fall off. But the next time I talk to you, Ill be in my house.

Love,
Jessie

When she had the temporary diary tucked safely with her treasures, she wheeled the bike out of the store, mounted it on the sidewalk and took off pedaling. When the wind whipped her bangs out of her sweaty face, Jessie felt a brief reprieve from the nightmare. She felt free. The headaches came back the more time she spent outside, but they were bearable now that she had a plan.

The idea of home made her want to cry – a combination of relief and anxiety of her daddy's absence. But the desire to be there overwhelmed her.

She pumped her legs when she hit clear roads, constantly checking signs to make sure she was headed in the right direction. She was a good reader, but some of the words were big and foreign. She chugged down a double lane with anticipation of sleeping in her own bed and meeting Bryan. She was so determined she didn't notice the boy following her.

It would be nearly four miles before she came face to face with Matthew Francis.

Chapter Eleven

Georgetown
Day Two

JAKE CRADLED HIS wife in aching arms, giving her one final squeeze before laying her gently on the rubble-covered floor. He glanced down at his watch through swollen eyes – 7:50.

He crawled to the coffee table for leverage and braced against it to help himself stand. Both legs prickled and burned as he attempted to bear weight. He welcomed the pain; it validated the more permanent one throbbing in his heart. He took cautious steps until the needles subsided, then leaned against the sink when he made it to the kitchen.

"Ah, Beck, what am I gonna do, baby?" He considered the power outage, the cold weather, 911's bizarre message, Becky's death, and just couldn't make sense of it all.

He grabbed a Dr Pepper from the refrigerator, some melting ice from the freezer, and poured a soda. He drank it in four hard gulps. When he slammed the glass on the counter, he went out on his back deck and was swallowed by the silence. No shouting kids, barking dogs, singing birds, engines revving or lawnmowers. Absolutely no sound whatsoever. He felt enveloped in a sci-fi episode of *X-Files*. Perhaps he had ventured over into a parallel world where aliens sought destruction of Planet Earth.

He wandered down the stairs, around the back of his house inspecting trees, then ventured toward the front yard.

I should call Pete in Charleston. But he didn't know if he could handle talking to his brother about Becky yet. He jogged to the Griffith house and rapped on the front door.

After knocking five or six times, he assumed Sherry must be on an errand and Cooper still at work.

Or…

Too curious to return home, Jake continued his investigation at the Shaws', even though he never cared much for Bob. Their door stood slightly ajar and, as Jake rang the doorbell, it creaked eerily open. The unresponsive bell confirmed that electricity was out at least on his side of the street.

"Bob? Marty? You home?"

Becky and Marty, short for Martina, joined Sherry Griffith's aerobics class at the same time and all three became quick friends. They gossiped, exercised, and shopped on a regular basis.

Bob, on the other hand, grated on the nerves of almost everyone who knew him. Nineteen years Marty's senior, Bob was mid-forties if he was a day. She loved him, no matter how much older he was, but the generations gapped mighty wide, and Bob's personality didn't help.

Jake had several work buddies who were Bob's age but didn't possess the same pompous, seniority attitude. It reminded him of being a freshman in high school and having seniors slam him into lockers and force him to carry their football equipment at practice.

As Jake peeked into the Shaws' kitchen and headed toward the dining room, he remembered eating on their back deck earlier in the summer. Bob got to talking politics and chided the rest of them for not being alive during Kennedy's assassination. He rambled that it was the most important moment in American history, and he would never forget it.

"Hey, Bob, you ain't fifty yet, are ya?" Jake piped up.

"Not quite," Bob answered slowly. "Why?"

Doing quick math in his head, Jake quipped, "Man, you must've had an incredible memory for a pre-schooler."

The circle roared with laughter, feeling the satisfaction of putting the arrogant man in his place. Even Marty grinned in spite of herself.

"I may be twenty years older than most of you, but I can whip your scrawny ass, Jake. Any day of the week and twice on Sunday."

Jake flipped Bob the bird and told him to go screw himself. Becky scolded him later for resorting to the old geezer's tactics.

Ah, Becky.

The Shaws' house emanated much of the oddities of his own. Jake felt like an intruder as he stepped into the living room and called out their names again. He walked toward the back door but tripped over something before he reached it.

"What the...?"

Baby, the Shaws' dachshund, lay stiffly beside the couch with her legs sticking straight out. The dog had the same suffocated expression as Becky – a desperate need to breathe but the brain's refusal to allow it.

"Jesus," Jake muttered and then heard thumps above him.

"Bob? Marty?" he called as he climbed the stairs and then froze when he saw Bob Shaw clumsily dressing his wife's rigid body. Marty possessed the same Vulcan-like blue skin and strangled expression.

"Hey, Bob, man, I know what you're feelin'. It's okay to..."

To what? To let the love of your life lay forgotten on the floor like a dirty sock?

"Leave us alone...we don't need your fuckin' help. Get out. Ah, it's okay, honey, I'll help you." Bob brushed Marty's hair so gently from her face that Jake had to look away.

"Bob, I lost Becky, too," he finally said, his voice barely a whisper.

Saying it aloud brought bile into his throat. He swallowed hard, willing the vomit to stay down. He couldn't imagine what he must've looked like when he ransacked his living room and then held Becky right smack dab in the middle of it. He thanked God no one had walked in on him. It occurred to him in that instant what an intrusion he was making.

"I'll be home if you need me," Jake mumbled and slipped out the door without looking back.

As he wandered back to his house, Jake decided to be more aggressive at the Griffiths'. He had to know. He marched through their yard and reached into the flower bed for the largest of three rocks and flipped it over. He plucked the key hidden there and slid it into the lock. Inside, he took careful, calculated steps through the living room, watching for Sadie, their Cocker Spaniel.

Since crawling out of bed, the day had been a painful blur. The prospect of losing another person he cared about and facing an incomprehensible world weighed on Jake like a concrete slab. He scanned the living area and then crossed through the kitchen. He felt the chill of an open door, and the image of Becky outside slammed into him with such force that he had to brace himself on the back door before opening it. He took a deep breath and turned the knob.

Oh, God. A sharp pang of jealousy raced through him – Sherry and Cooper sat side by side in deck chairs with their hands locked in one final death grip. Their faces, too, were swollen and discolored. At least they hadn't died alone.

Like Becky.

Jake bowed his head, bade his friends a reverent good-bye, and made a beeline for the front door. He sprinted through the subdivision, chased by visions of Becky, Sherry and Cooper, and Bob trying to dress his dead wife. Looking up and down the traffic-free road, he couldn't for the life of him make sense of any of it.

And then the weird world took a strange turn.

"Ahhhhhhhh!" A man's scream sent a chill through Jake's gut. He jerked his head toward the sound and saw Bob standing on his own roof with Marty in his arms. It didn't seem so unusual after all Jake had seen.

"Where are you now, little girl? They said you were gonna save us from all the shit!"

He didn't know what the hell Bob meant, if he planned to jump or just stand there to be closer to Heaven, but one thing was for sure – surviving was a sucker-punch. And Jake wished he had been given a choice.

In the next four hours, as he explored a world he no longer recognized, Jake Thomas would make that wish more times than he could count.

Chapter Twelve

Denver
Day Two

"GREG, LAND THIS baby on field six. I want to walk to the complex and that's the closest air strip," Tony shouted toward the cockpit of the company jet.

"No problem. Radar's completely clear. Not another plane anywhere in this entire region. It's weird. I wanna hear more about who they think's responsible, but don't know what good it'll do."

Greg flipped a few switches while Tony stood in the cockpit door. The young pilot radioed the tower but didn't press the issue when no one answered.

They had listened to scraps of broadcasts en route to Denver, and it became abundantly clear to Tony that his pilot, though lucid, preferred to bury his head in the sand. It was one of the things Tony liked about Greg and why he never hired personal chauffeurs or pilots with family. Most CEOs saw it as a strange prerequisite, but it had served him well on more than one occasion.

When he spied BetaCorp from the window, Tony let out a sigh of relief. Seeing it brought a sense of normalcy to the day. The plant sat on a five hundred acre plot, a third of which was covered with the five central buildings. Tony knew four of the facilities like the back of his hand, but the fifth, Brad Tavares' Environmental Protection Division – a division required by the federal government – was of little use to Tony.

He pulled out his new list – the expendables – and eyed the top five. Even though Brad was fifth, crossing one off would be like the cherry on an ice cream sundae. *But, Willie, I'm comin' for you. Florida's my next stop.*

It pleased Tony to no end that Brad's group was no longer necessary. It amused him that a nation so intent on morality was plagued by such extreme corruption. Except Mr. Tavares, who probably dreamed of salvation and redemption. Tony would bet his life that Brad sat perched in his office at this very moment trying to save the world. The self-righteous son of a bitch just couldn't appreciate power and destruction in its finest hour.

Tony couldn't imagine such a fault. He thrived on it. He patted the notepad in his jacket pocket and grinned. He wished he could find a mirror, because he was certain he had just nailed his best DeNiro smile.

His CEO access card slid silently through the lock bar, and the foyer door clicked as the lock deactivated, though much more slowly than normal.

We're on backup generators. Power's down. Dammit, can't anything be easy today?

Tony entered the building and felt minuscule as his footsteps echoed in the massive, glass-walled lobby. The building normally teemed with staff but now loomed silent and vacant. Tony's admiration for the masterminds behind the world-altering incident increased as the gravity of it hit him. They hadn't dabbled with the small stuff.

The suffocating silence magnified his footfalls as he found the stairwell next to the elevator. He tapped the arrow just in case, but a slow whirring and a clank dashed his hopes of a light activity day. He heaved a sigh and headed for the stairs. He'd never used them in all his twenty-seven years with the company, and he didn't fancy climbing forty floors for the first time now. But loose ends had to be severed. Or was that tied up? He just couldn't seem to make sense of the thoughts and voices rumbling about in his head.

Thirty-five minutes and two brief rests later, Tony Andrews stood in the wing of Brad's departmental offices huffing and puffing. Daily workouts and evening jogs had maintained a fine-tuned sixty-year-old body, but the thinner air commanded respect from his lungs.

After three minutes of deep, lung-expanding breathing, Tony slipped into Brad's branch of offices. Andrews could see a dim light glowing in his EPD President's office, certainly attempting to save the planet.

Asshole needs a cape.

Andrews leaned against Brad's door jam for nearly seven minutes. Tony marveled at the ambiance of the office – scattered greenery accented rich paneling, city lights sparkled through three walls of windows, an original Monet hung over the gas fireplace. Tony recognized the mahogany desk, identical to his own, and felt a twinge of *you-can't-have-what-I've-got-because-I'm-more-powerful-than-you.*

Tavares, he knew too well, earned a healthy salary, obviously too much for the services rendered. Tony tried to squelch the jealousy he'd grown to view as somewhat of a third arm – at times useful but usually in the way.

Tony blinked, suddenly finding himself on the streets of West Palm as a scrawny ten-year old.

* * *

"YOU'RE JUST POOR white trash, boy," a ninth grader growled. He straightened the green jacket and smirked. "You don't belong here. Private schools are for the privileged, not wannabes like you. Jesus, look at you. Even in *our* uniform, you look like trailer trash."

A group of boys laughed, whispered, and one of them threw Little Anthony's books at his feet. He crouched down to pick them up, aware that they were staring at his Salvation Army shoes. Shame swept through him like fire, fierce and hungry.

"Willie, why do they give scholarships to pieces of crap like this kid?" a kid whose dad owned every major car dealership in the Miami/Ft. Lauderdale area asked. The ninth grader, Willie, grunted.

"Cause he's got brains – squishy gray matter that puts the rest of us to shame. But he ain't gonna amount to shit. I mean, look at him? He's a fuckin' midget. I've never seen a fifth grader so damn small. Brain's bigger than him." All the boys howled with laughter, slapping each other on the back, pushing Anthony down every time he tried to stand.

When Anthony finally made it to his feet, he brushed the seat of his pants, felt his bladder threaten to take some time off. He didn't bother with the books because he knew they would just scrap them again. But he found his voice and muttered a dangerous response.

"I'll get outta here with my brains. You'll be rich nobodies all your life." Anthony backed away but knew they would pounce anyway. But he couldn't help himself. A few punches in the gut, a kick or two, even a busted lip didn't matter. What mattered was escape – from Florida, narrow-minded people, and poverty. And Anthony Andrews meant to break free.

"Little nobody, who the hell do you think you are? Shit," Willie sniveled with such vindictiveness it usually made Anthony race home in tears. Distance required he ride a city bus, which called further attention to the fact that he wasn't cut from the same cloth. Their rancor toward him incited sores on his soul that never healed. When Willie and his buddies tossed him from one to the other, they chanted one of many taunts. But Anthony blocked out the voices by thinking of his mother.

His waitress mom cleared only flimsy tips and often drank them before staggering home. To pay rent, she hooked Little Anthony up with "runs" to make for Mr. DeFranco. He sensed these weren't legal, but he would do anything she asked. And he knew better than to cross Frankie DeFranco. What his mother really taught him was to steal, cheat, and manipulate to get what he needed and wanted. And what it all boiled down to was that between Willie and his gang and his mother's lessons, he learned well. Step on whomever necessary to climb to the top.

"Get the hell outta here, you nasty white trash. We don't need your kind here. You think you're so smart. Why don't you know when to stay with your own kind?" Willie punched his forefinger into Little Anthony's chest.

"Why don't you get out? Hell, you're so damn dumb, you don't understand what makes me so much better than you." With that, Anthony turned tail and ran.

* * *

"TONY, UH, MR. Andrews, why, I mean, I was just trying to get some information out. I…I could get out, sir, but what did you mean by that?"

Brad Tavares stammered, came from behind his magnificent desk to greet his CEO.

"Huh?" Tony's head swooned. The momentary lapse left him drained and out of sorts.

"You just said, '*Why don't you get out.*' Then you said I was dumb, sir. I've never been accused of that before."

Shit. I said that out loud? Tony felt like laughing and crying at the same time. He ached for a fleeting moment to find out where Willie was – he made a mental note to research that next.

"Uh, sorry about that. I was just, um, talking on the phone. Didn't mean you. But now that you mention it, what exactly are you up to?" Tony stifled a smile before it could betray him.

He stepped into the office, reached for Brad's laptop and turned it around to read the e-mail ready to be sent. Brad grabbed at it, but Tony held it firm and read the screen.

To: CyberSystemsWorldWideAccess

My mission is to regulate monster powers such as Beta Tron Chemical Corporation, IBM, Aralco, and DuPont/SBC and to curtail their expansion if it is not in the best interest of the majority. It is time to take control of our destiny and drive ourselves toward a common goal. With the release of X-86, we know one of these mega corporations has the ability to kill us all. We must unite, speak to the four Dr. Basinger is holding and FIND THE ANSWERS.

"How touching, Bradley. I'm sure all twelve of the surviving Americans will jump for joy when they read this." Tony hit the delete button until the message disappeared.

Brad's eyes never left Tony's. The electricity in the air was corporeal, each man's body layered in goose pimples that neither could see. In another less professional setting, the two might have settled the matter with a good old-fashioned fistfight. But Tony's list necessitated final measures.

"I think I'll control your destiny for you," Tony said, and in one fluid motion, he pulled the Glock from his shoulder harness underneath his Armani jacket, aimed it with slow cruelty at Brad's right eye, and squeezed the trigger.

Before fear could even register on Brad's face, his brains splattered chaotically on his east window. Tony watched in fascination at the gray cerebral fluid that laced an intricate pattern in its slide to the floor. Indifferently, Tony shoved Brad's body away from the desk and deleted the additional messages from the laptop. He didn't know whether they'd been sent or not, but it felt good to punch the keys.

He thumped them hard enough to release some aggression and started a search of Brad's address book. He was certain it would show him where the do-gooder had sent the e-mails.

I don't know why I care. I just want to know what the hell you've been up to, Bradley.

"Let's see, twenty-six addresses in your outgoing e-mail, you stupid mother fucker. Why couldn't you just go stand on a street corner and shout like the rest of the deranged? Jesus. You always had to be so ostentatious."

And then one jumped out like a popcorn kernel in hot oil: JBasinger@aralco.org.

"Big John. What do you know?" Not wasting any time, Tony ran out the door with only one thing in mind.

Dallas.

Chapter Thirteen

St. Louis
Day Three

WATER. IF SHE didn't get more soon, her stomach was going to revolt. Her mouth felt full of sand, and the last swallow from an Evian bottle did little to whet it. Even though it tasted warm and nasty, her cotton-coated tongue craved it anyway. Her body had been on autopilot for the past two hours and, as the sun began to rise, she could finally make out storefronts. Without electricity, it was hard to see anything.

She dropped her bike at the entrance, dragged herself into the Dierberg's and collapsed in a lawn chair displayed in front of the checkout counters. The rising sun displayed wondrous colors through the front store windows, but all Jessie could think about was home. Then, as she looked around, her heart thudded. This is our store. *Oh, God, Daddy, this is where we shopped.*

He didn't answer, but she had been talking to him all night anyway. There were other strange voices rambling in her head, and she hoped she wasn't going crazy. It sounded like radios from far away. She got up to leave the store, her body aching and exhausted.

When her legs tired too much to ride, she walked the Schwinn and told him how bad she hurt. When she had to stop for a little bit, her calves cramped. She rubbed them and cried out to him to please come get her. She had curled up in a Git 'n Go gas station's store room and slept. She didn't know how long, but when she woke, every inch of her body felt like it had after her first ballet practice.

The front display of beach towels made her cringe; her daddy had bought her a Harry Potter one with Hogwarts in the background. She tried not to look at them, but instead hustled out past the doors that had been wedged open with green bean cans. She jerked her head to the right where she knew she would see a car dealership, to the left at a strip mall with a Marshall's, a Blockbuster, and a Pier One Imports. With a sudden burst of energy, she hobbled back inside to the cracker aisle and shoved a few Ritz Bits into her mouth. Her legs felt like noodles wrapped with twenty-pound weights, but they didn't deter her from stuffing bottled water in her pants and cradling some in her arms.

She ran to her bike, dumped the water into the basket, and jumped on, already pumping her legs. She still couldn't feel the eyes watching her, nor did she realize that another bike pedaled in synchronicity with her own. The knowledge would have scared her to death. Within twenty minutes, Jessie pulled up to the Phillip's 66 that sat deserted at the intersection where she would turn to get to her subdivision. She remembered Bryan's words of caution, but she also knew how important stocking up would be.

"I can free you!" an older man screamed. "I am Jesus Christ, Savior and Lord. Come with me!"

Jessie didn't care who he was; he was wrinkled and he scared her. She ducked into the gas station, but she kept an eye on him to make sure he stayed by the road and away from her.

I'm a god, and it doesn't matter how old I am. We're all going to die in the next eight days.

Jessie jumped – had the old man talked? She had been staring right at him, and the last thing she had *seen* him say was to come with him.

Yes, little girl, I'm talkin' to you. I've heard about you.

Jessie ran inside, pushed the door closed and leaned all her weight against it.

"Oh, God." Panic raced through her – all the voices that scrambled her head, the radio sounds. Before she could stop it, Jessie vomited on a Frito display next to her. She leaned over with her hands on her knees and waited for the gorge in her throat to go down. When her stomach settled, she stumbled to the coolers on the right for a bottled water. She took a long drink and then a deep breath. When she felt better, she grabbed a sack from behind the counter, and stopped dead in her tracks next to the first aisle.

Someone else was in there.

I won't hurt you. I've been following you.

She felt the words more than she heard them, and the electricity of another body. The hair on her arms bristled as she plucked items from the shelves. She cast her eyes from side to side, studied the mirror in the corner by the ceiling, glanced over each shoulder. She filled her bag with bread, peanut butter, crackers, and a few non-essentials she just had to have, all the while letting paranoia eat at her. After the seventh or eighth candy bar, she put one back, knowing her daddy wouldn't approve. She grabbed a small notepad in case her diary at home ran out of paper.

She took another grocery sack and crammed it with juice, water, and a couple of sodas. Bryan had said to get plenty to drink. The eerie feeling washed over her again, and she looked up at the mirror in the back corner of the store.

"If you're in here, leave me alone. And stop following me."

She didn't see anything in the mirror or anywhere else, but the feeling of another person made the hair on her arms stiffen. The days of police were over. Her daddy once told her the police were her friends – that they would always be around to help if she ever got in trouble or in any kind of danger.

She felt a flash of anger at the missing help, at whatever killed her daddy and the whole world in general. She kicked a display of Wheat Thins and squeeze cheese and sent boxes and bottles flying. One box settled by her right foot and she kicked it hard enough that it exploded and sprayed the aisle with crackers.

"GO AWAY!" she screamed. She gathered her bags and set them on the front counter. She jotted a note on a sale flyer, much like all the others she had left.

Sorry I can't pay, but I want you to know I can when I get home. Please call me at 555-7628. Thank you, Jessie Bayker.

Something fell in the back by the soda cooler, and she yelped.

"Who's there?" She froze, her right hand still clutching one of the sacks. She heard someone breathing. The hair on the back of her neck stood on end and her bladder clenched.

Dammit. "Don't shoot...uh, ma'am." A teenage boy as black as an eight ball stepped out from behind the Hostess Twinkies with his hands up. A big grin filled his dark face. "Hey, name's Matthew. Whatcha call yourself?"

Girl, get over yourself. I'm just hungry.

Jessie stared at him a minute to make sure his lips hadn't moved. They hadn't. If he was so hungry, why didn't he have any food in his hands? "I can't tell you. You're a stranger. Put your hands back up!"

He had started to lower his arms, but somehow that frightened Jessie even more. He immediately put them back up. Jessie noticed his biceps – little black bulges of muscle – and suspected he wasn't afraid of her.

"Whaddya gonna do, shoot me with a twinkie?" His smile broadened even further than Jessie thought possible. She couldn't suppress the grin that pushed at the corners of her own mouth, and she smiled.

"I could, ya know. Shoot you with a Twinkie and get cream in your eye. I have good aim." Jessie tried to keep a straight face but couldn't. They both suddenly burst into uncontrollable giggles. The stress of the past twenty-odd hours sent Jessie into howls of laughter and, for much the same reason, Matthew Francis joined her.

She watched him closely when he talked and began to understand that much of what he said didn't come out his mouth. She didn't share that with him because she wasn't sure he would believe it. She wasn't sure she believed it herself.

For the next thirty minutes, the two compared survival stories, but when she tried to tell Matthew about her daddy, she couldn't get the words out. Tears streamed down her face as she tried, but Matthew stopped her.

"I know, Jessie, I lost my folks, too. And my oldest brother...he...he froze out on them apartment steps like a damn statue. And my moms, man, she laid in her bed all peaceful and Papa sat in his chair..." *like he was takin' one of his drunk naps*. Matthew looked down, his eyes full of tears and nightmares. He mumbled that he didn't know where his other brother was. Jessie wanted to console him. But she didn't. She let him finish, and when he did, the two made a pact not to discuss the pain anymore.

Jessie heard more in his head, in his voice, but she tried to tune it out. She didn't like the feeling of intruding in his brain. It made her feel dirty. All the whispers she'd been hearing made sense now.

"Here, let me help ya." He reached to gather Jessie's supplies, and loaded them in the basket of her bike. They set off for her house. They borrowed some batteries so they could listen to the radio when they got there. They took off down the street, pedaling hard. Jessie found the ride easier with his company.

"My mom's friend Bryan is comin' for me today. He's in California, but he left yesterday. He said he hoped to be here in the morning, so we'll have time to get cleaned up, rest for a bit and maybe take a swim," she shouted to Matthew as he pedaled ahead. She smelled the flowers as the crisp breeze blew in her face.

"Swim? Oh, man, girl, I'm from the projects, but I never figured you for a richie. Sweet."

Matthew grinned back at her, his dark brown face broken by stark white teeth. He slowed so she could catch up. *C'mon, girl. You too damn slow.*

Jessie grimaced and felt anger swell inside her. She had never met anyone poor who judged her, and she didn't like it when people cussed. But she couldn't tell him – *wouldn't* tell him. He wouldn't believe her anyway.

"If you wanna ride ahead you can. My legs are tired. I've been ridin' a long time."

"Ah, it's alright, girl. Sorry."

Jessie tried to think of other things so she wouldn't hear anything after, and it worked. She laughed at his slang. She had classmates who used some of the catch phrases. But most of her friends were carbon copies of her. Same upbringing, same education, same lives – and she realized how boring that had been. She liked Matthew and wondered why the world had to be so divided.

"Where are the projects? Is that downtown?"

"Girl, you're sheltered. I live on Hanley Road in government housing. You know, welfare? Nah, I don't s'pose you know what that is, do ya'?"

"No, sorry. Gosh." Jessie pedaled harder, trying to keep up but glad he couldn't see her face flush. When he didn't say anything, she changed the subject. "Hey, I have a radio that takes batteries in my bedroom. In case there's no electricity." Sweat was breaking out on her brow, so talking helped keep her mind off her cramping legs and aching side.

"Yeah. I been hearin' all kinds of stuff. Did you hear the President speak?"

"No. I've been worried about getting home and didn't really want to hear anything. I get kinda scared."

As they crested a hill and entered Woodlawn Hills, Jessie suddenly felt self-conscious about her neighborhood – the big houses, ornate lawns, and swimming pools. Matthew ogled, commenting on things Jessie had taken for granted her entire life.

Maybe after a swim, he wouldn't feel so funny about it. She hoped so. She didn't need any more conflict in her life. Not today anyway.

Chapter Fourteen

Dallas
Day Three

BIG JOHN BASINGER thrummed his fingers on the desk wishing Tony hadn't called or come to Dallas or started the final stage of losing his mind.

"Well, my list is long, John, and I really want to be a part of this," Tony was saying. "Your kids hold a lot of answers for me, you know, about the future. I need to know some stuff. I, uh, just read some e-mails about them. Seems they did quite a bit of research that you weren't privy to. And I'm so impressed with their deployment. Did you know your company was capable of this?" A giggle slipped out of Tony's mouth, and the sound made John's skin crawl.

"Tony, let me handle this. They worked for me, and quite frankly, you're not up to it."

What John Basinger really wanted to tell Tony was to get his shit together, because the BetaCorp CEO sounded ready for a strait jacket.

"Goddammit, John, at least let me sit in. Greg's got us landing at Love Field, and I'm sure we can get a car. There's a free rental program goin' on, in case you haven't heard." Tony cackled, paused long enough for John to think he'd hung up, and then added, "Fuck, John, why didn't you come pick my ass up?"

John shook his head, wishing his old friend had stayed in Denver. *Or worse.* But the thought made him feel guilty. He knew Tony's dementia had little to do with X-86; Andrews' ruthless nature had evolved in recent years. Megalomania, his colleagues and employees diagnosed, had done strange things to the old man's brain. Years of unlimited wealth and power, coupled with his poor upbringing, accelerated the mental decline. Tony seldom spoke to his underlings, even in board meetings. They consulted with him by e-mail and webcast, but listened to his speeches in the boardroom as an audience.

"Tony, take a breath. Grab a free meal. I hear they're on special, too. Then I'll talk to you about what I've learned. But until then, I'm going to pick these three kids' brains and try to figure out what the hell they were thinking. And then I'm going see what can be stopped with the next release dates. If we don't stop this, I...I can't even consider the ramifications."

"I thought there were four of them – three guys and a girl?"

"There were. Seems one of them shot the other. I don't know the details of that either. But trust me, I will."

John motioned for Haden, his Assistant of Operations, to come into the room. He jotted the beady-eyed man a note, and Haden promptly headed to Chamber Number Nine to ready the room for the interrogation and to retrieve the three employees. He couldn't defer the duties to anyone else, because to their knowledge, there weren't any more. X-86 had either wiped Aralco out or sent survivors scurrying for safer havens.

Tony hung up, and John wondered if Andrews would stay away or not. But it didn't really matter at this point. With what he had learned, the three people being brought into Chamber Number Nine held answers the whole world held its collective breath for.

John's hands tingled as he dropped the cordless on his desk. He had hired all four of the young people responsible. Did that somehow place him at blame?

For a fleeting moment, guilt clenched John's gut and groin. The idea that his wife and daughters might still be alive if...but John forced the regret away. Too many other emotions needed to be addressed.

* * *

"GREG, GRAB MY laptop. I got some research to do." Tony marveled that his pilot didn't hesitate to continue serving him.

"Sure, boss. Go ahead and have a seat in Terminal A, and I'll bring it to ya."

Less than an hour later, Tony found the information he wanted. Willie Templeton had a website for Templeton & Sons Plumbing, *Proud to serve greater Miami*. The bully who lived in his nightmares plunged toilets for a living. *How fitting*.

"I never liked Miami. Too many damned immigrants. Don't wanna run any risk of them taking a place in our future."

Tony tapped keys and realigned coordinates for a silo in Corpus Christi. Red flags would have popped up in the Pentagon, but he guessed no one there gave a rat's ass anymore. BetaCorp's military operations warranted excessive protection and now Tony had sole access to the weapons. He didn't know for sure which were operational, but it was time to find out. He had work to do. Installing missile-armed silos that would make a military man moist had been the best decision of his young CEO career. A chemical giant couldn't be deterred by a silly little national disaster.

Greg's mouth fell open as he stared at the screen.

"Sir? Are you sure you wanna do that? I mean, we're gonna need all the survivors we can use. I mean, what if someone in Miami or Ft. Lauderdale has something to offer? Do you really wanna...?"

The crack of a gunshot sounded like a thunderclap inside the airport. Greg crumpled to the carpet clutching the wound in his belly.

"I can fly my own damn plane, you sniveling little prick. No one questions my authority or my decisions. Guess everyone'll believe that now, huh?" Tony gave an indignant smirk and executed the commands Greg had seen on the laptop. He let out a howl of vindication twelve minutes later when the computer confirmed his launch.

Miami had just succumbed to his madness. And he planned to add to the list.

* * *

A GULF STREAM brought an X-86-saturated breeze drifting into Western Europe by late Saturday morning. Prime Minister George Masters feared the worst after speaking with President Cavanaugh, and he was right to. Even though the residual effect of Stage I only impacted a small percentage, the second release targeted London, Frankfurt, Munich, Milan, Reykjavik, Tokyo, and Moscow. By 2:00 p.m. Saturday in Dallas, Western Europe no longer sent messages of sympathy to the United States. Early Sunday, by Europe and Asia time, millions had perished. Try as John Basinger might, the Fab Four, as the remaining media dubbed them, had little to offer. The plan insured that nothing could stop it – not even them.

Panic swept across Asia as Moscow, Peking, and Tokyo fell. The few reporters and photographers still loyal to their jobs wired images of people fleeing an invisible enemy, bodies rigored on the streets of third world countries, and disturbing photos of families floating face down in rivers. According to reports, hundreds went into hiding, sought refuge in the hills and caves of the Middle East, retreated into the jungles of Vietnam and Cambodia. When the atmosphere became saturated with X-86, no matter how remote the hiding place, only the immune would survive. And key markers to survival didn't exist in the oppressed. Traits such as hope, faith, and optimism were common threads in the resistant.

By the end of Day 3, X-86 completed Stage II, and nearly sixty percent of the world's population suffered painful deaths. An additional ten percent experienced irreparable brain damage resulting in dementia. With three more releases scheduled, the next five days would complete a mission to rid the world of the imperfect.

Part Two
Answers

"We may be destroyed. But if we are, we shall drag a world with us...a world in flames."
– Adolf Hitler

Chapter Fifteen

Dallas
Day Three

"THEY'RE READY, JOHN. Two of 'em have diarrhea of the mouth, but the girl. Man, she's stone silent. And...and...they're either playin' it up, or they got a whiff of the X-86 themselves." Haden Compton, a bald man with bifocals perched on the end of his nose, barely cleared five foot five inches tall – but it never occurred to the Assistant of Operations to have an inferiority complex.

"I'm not buying that. They had to have run field tests on X-86. Anything you're seeing is either an act or stress. They may be going over the edge; maybe losing one of their partners is driving them crazy. Which one is MIA? And is there any word yet if the fourth member of the dream team is dead or just AWOL?"

"I...I'm not sure. I mean, I..." Haden leafed through his notes, flipping page after page on the clipboard trying to figure out the answer. "Damn. I dunno, John. But the three are in Chamber Number Nine, and we can go at them from several angles. I did call Langley and Quantico, but no one's responded to my call. That's a first. Now, do you want them all at once or separate?"

"Um, let me talk to them together. You got their files?" John stood and gathered a few papers he had been reading. He took the thick manila folders Haden handed him and raised his eyebrows. "Damn. These are thick."

"Yeah...they were your protégés. All four of 'em." Haden dropped his eyes. "You interviewed them personally, John. Jamie and Kyle never even went through preliminary interviews. You hired them on the spot. Remember?"

John did. Because no one had knocked his socks off in an interview like Kyle Spene had. Until a year later when he met Jamie Mantel, a young lady who graduated MIT before her twenty-first birthday. Nathan Kirkpatrick dazzled him several years earlier, but since coming aboard, rumors swirled about Nathan's affiliation with a white supremacist group that kept John on edge about the young chemist. Bobby Sims, Aralco's public relations guru, was quiet, often lost in the trauma of his personal life, but his work spoke for itself.

"I just can't believe these four have pulled this off. I really can't. Our contract with the government to refine chemical weaponry was years from completion. And it was nothing of this magnitude, and classified. How the hell did they get a hold of it?"

John slapped all four files into his briefcase and snapped it shut. He grabbed the leather handle, then slammed it back down on the table. "Dammit, Haden. What happened?"

Haden stared at the clipboard. Neither man spoke, and the uneasiness in John's groin tightened.

"They killed Victoria, and..." But John couldn't finish. He shoved the thoughts into the portion of his brain that dealt with personal trauma. He had work to do, and he couldn't allow himself to be distracted.

He picked up his briefcase again, squeezed it hard enough to whiten his knuckles, and heaved a sigh that blew dust from the top of a bookcase five feet away.

"Let's do this, Haden." Without another word, both men marched out of Dr. John Basinger's office and took the stairs from the sixtieth floor to Chamber Number Nine on the thirty-seventh.

John inventoried his thoughts out loud as they clamored down the steps. "There were still a multitude of questions about this project. Most of our subjects died, remember?" Memories John could do without. "The government didn't want us to rush. This was high-dollar, top-secret enemy warfare. This wasn't intended to be a play toy, which is exactly what it became. The Pentagon was funding this for a reason."

Haden didn't answer as they turned the corner toward the fifty-seventh floor. He paused before heading down the next flight.

"Okay, Stage I, we know, causes a breakdown in the atmosphere...blocking the sun's UV rays when what we really want is to enhance it. But why was it cold hours prior to the X-86's release?"

"Uh," Haden stuttered, his brain overloaded with hours of information crammed into it in only thirty minutes. "Maybe they released a little prior to the actual launch. I'm not sure. We do know they isolated certain traits for the chemical to attack. That was way beyond our scope. Hell, we still had months to go before Stage I was even in the field to be experimented on."

"How'd they do it so fast?"

"Intelligence you and I can only admire," Haden stated quickly. "And I'm sensing a serious motivation, though I'm not sure of the factors. Yet."

Both glanced at the Forty-Ninth floor sign as they wheeled around the stair rails and picked up the pace.

"Quick, Haden, tell me about the phases." They hustled down the stairs with Haden bringing up the rear talking as fast as they walked.

"Stage II had only been drawn up on paper. We hadn't even run the logistics yet. They refined a ten-year project – Operation Blue – in less than a year, so they had to narrow the original eight phases to four. In this second phase, the atmosphere is saturated and elements of the chemical are released. Stage III is addition of the chemical that makes X-86 a complete product. And Stage Four is the means by which they spread it. All this is conjecture on my part," Haden said, then stopped to catch his breath in front of the thirty-seventh floor. "You know, Tony Andrews would wet his pants to have manufactured X-86."

And would settle for the by-product now if he thought he could hand-pick his victims.

"And this isn't over, is it?" John grabbed the doorknob but didn't turn it.

"No. From what I've been able to get from the radio and the computer readouts, about fifty cities got hit. But there's a message embedded in the satellite. At least fifty more cities are targeted every forty-eight hours over the course of eight days. The next release is in less than four hours."

John bowed his head, calculating the severity of it. *This is Armageddon. These four kids have initiated the end of the world.*

"Can we interfere with the launch sequences, Haden? Surely we can figure out how to interrupt the process..." John calculated the percentages as he opened the door and didn't even bother waiting for an answer. He had lost his own two kids, his wife, and his dog. Four out of five in his own home. Eighty percent.

Victoria's beautiful smile wrenched his heart from work mode. He needed to be strong to deal with the morons in Chamber Number Nine, but separating life from work was no longer necessary.

John and Haden sped down the stark white hallway of the medical wing to Chamber Number Nine. Their shoes echoed in the empty corridor. When they reached the plain door with no numbers or letters, both took a deep breath and entered the outer room for a glimpse through the one-way window. John wanted to assess the situation before searching for answers that probably wouldn't matter.

Two good-looking men in their late twenties sat tapping their legs and gabbing away as if they didn't have a care in the world. Jamie stared at the table, but a ghost of a smile lingered on her mouth.

John peered through the one-way Plexiglas – soundproof, mirrored, and airtight. The vents along the ceiling served a dual purpose and, for an insane moment, the big man contemplated a few noxious fumes to encourage the three little pigs to talk.

He reached around and felt in his back waistband for his nine-millimeter revolver. It gave him security knowing it was there. A little pain might be a necessary incentive. Or deterrent.

He punched the code for the door, and the automated whirring was not quick enough, so John pushed past it. He was on pins and needles, ready for answers and a little justice.

"Hello, kids." John took his usual place at the head of the table.

They faced their boss with alert eyes. John got the sense that he had just entered the twilight zone. On the other side of the Plexiglas, Haden Compton turned on the speaker and the recorder. John had been clear about wanting to listen to this later. John loomed, palms on the table, back to the door. The boys sat to his left, Jamie to his right.

"Well, gang, it's time to clear the air, so to speak. Who wants to start?"

Silence. Thirty seconds ticked away on John's Rolex.

"Anyone have anything to offer, or should I begin?"

Nothing. Another twenty seconds.

"Okay then. Kyle," John said as he turned to his left. He leaned forward, elbows on the table, and had to look down to talk. He felt like a father about to scold his son for murdering a girlfriend. The whole scenario seemed ludicrous.

"You've worked for me for seven years. Exemplary employee. Top-notch chemist. UT grad. MIT doctorate, and you're only twenty-nine years old. Just had a birthday last week. You had the world by the tail. Kind of fucked up, didn't you, son?" John watched for a reaction, but got none.

Ninety seconds passed, and the only sound was John's angered breathing.

He couldn't tear his eyes away from Kyle Spene's calm face. The young man didn't flinch; his muscles were completely relaxed, a hint of a smile around his mouth.

"Kyle, an easy explanation like, 'We were shit-faced, sir, and didn't know what the hell we were doin' for twelve months...we're really sorry, sir, gosh darn it...it'll never happen again...'Any of those would help you at this juncture. Might even save your life." John's penetrating eyes pushed Kyle's to the floor.

Nathan shot a glance at his partner. A moment passed between them before John pounded his fist on the long wooden table. Only Jamie jumped.

"Operation Blue ring a bell to any of you?" John stared at each of them, one at a time, measuring their discomfort. All three employees twitched and fidgeted. John at last felt he had touched a nerve.

"Ah, a memory. I had started to wonder if you were brain dead. Because you will be, you know. Your lives are being counted down at this very moment. Tick-tock, tick-tock, tick-tock. You're obsolete now that we have broken the code and stopped the continuation of your little game. I'm not sure why I'm even talking to you."

Kyle's smile spread across his face as if to say, *Sure, old man, nice try. Fifty cities every two days, then more.* John knew he had to find their Achilles heel. Fast.

"But I can assure you, your passing will not be as easy as your victims'." John hadn't really wanted a reaction at this point. And that was a good thing, because he didn't get one.

"You have single-handedly altered life as we know it. That was your goal, wasn't it?"

Kyle cleared his throat, leaned forward in his chair, and placed his arms on the table. His face was perhaps ten inches from John's. The big man fought the urge to snarl or bark to see if the boy would jump.

"Sir, are you familiar with illegal immigration?" Kyle met John's eyes, and an uneasy sensation seized Dr. Basinger's bladder.

"Um, like from Mexico?"

"Yes, sir. Well, last month one of those immigrants, a spic, moved into my apartment complex. Just as big as you please. No papers, no residency, just came to my country without permission and started breathing my air like I owed it to him. Are you following me?"

"Uh, Kyle, is this about your little sister?" John grasped at straws.

"How dare you, sir. You don't know anything about my sister."

"Then tell me. I can't read your mind."

Chapter Sixteen

Kyle

"I SAW THAT, you stupid punk!" A fourteen-year-old Kyle Spene ran hell for leather as the lady screamed after him. *What a rush!* The bat in his hands burned from the friction, and Kyle was absolutely certain that nailing a mailbox was much more rewarding than hitting some dumb round piece of leather. Barry Bonds had nothing on Kyle Spene.

He and his buddies raced across the open field whooping and hollering as they ran. As soon as they reached the wood's edge, all four of them sprawled on the ground with exaggerated exhaustion.

"Did you see that spic's face? Man, what a dumb bitch," Bradley said with a huff, trying to suck air and laugh at the same time. He was a Nazi poster boy and a mooch. None of the other guys cared much for either image, but he was funny as hell. In the grand scheme of a teenager's world, that counted for a mint.

"Man, for a minute, I thought she was gonna chase me. She's pretty small – might be fast! I thought I was gonna piss myself when I saw her come tearin' out her front door." Kyle rolled around on the grass, holding his stomach as he roared with laughter. The other three mimicked the Chavez lady calling him a stupid punk and putting their hands on their hips.

"You guys ever see her daughter? Man, she's somethin' else. Lacy, I think her name is. Boy, howdy. I'd do her any day of the week."

"Oh, shut up, Stempy, you'd do your own momma if she'd letcha. You're a horn dog." The others tried to hold back, but "Stempy" Jones, the horniest kid on Planet Earth, was just too much, and all three burst into fresh gales of laughter.

"Oh, fuck off. All three of ya and the horses you rode in on," Stempy quipped. But he smiled all the same. Kyle knew his horny friend liked the image – it could definitely be worse.

Stempy stood a head above the rest of the boys, but his gangly body was far out of his control. Puberty had attacked him with such ferocity that the doctors fretted over his knees, and Lewisville Junior High basketball coaches frothed at the mouth over the already six-foot fourteen-year-old. Kyle knew when the coaches watched their practices with interest, they appreciated his talent, but Stempy hogged the spotlight.

"You boys are just jealous 'cause he lost his first. Makes ya hornier once ya had it. And hand jobs don't count. You ever rented *The Graduate*? That Dustin Hoffman wanted it so bad, and every time he got it, he just wanted it more. Did the mom and her daughter. I think it's kind of like an alcoholic. You get addicted. That's it, Stempy, you're a sexaholic!" Kyle sent the three of them into fits again, but Joey was immediately protesting that Stempy couldn't get addicted until he'd had it more than once.

The laughter never seemed to stop. And Stempy didn't care. It was one of the things Kyle loved best about him – that Stempy was gullible enough to believe it.

Kyle stood up and quickly declared it a go-to-the-quarry-and-swim day. All cheered in agreement. They didn't mind the fifteen-minute bike ride because the private swimming hole with the twenty-foot jump beat smashing mailboxes any day of the week.

"Let's meet there in thirty with grub and gear. Bradley, bring enough so you don't mooch. I'm not lettin' you oink my food this time. You got it?" Kyle stared hard at his gangly friend, stifling a smile.

Bradley grinned his shit-eating best, which meant he probably would anyway. The four of them lived in completely different parts of the neighborhood, Kyle the farthest away, so he pumped his legs like a maniac to make his own deadline. He bounded through his front door and winced, as always, at the biting chill in the house. Summers were cold in the Spene home and winters were a sauna. Kyle never could figure that out.

"Mom?" His deepening voice echoed in the foyer. The changes that were occurring all throughout his teenaged body freaked him out sometimes. His mom seemed to understand what was going on, but Trisha didn't. Her eleven-year-old inquiring mind and meddling nature embarrassed Kyle on a daily basis.

He adored his kid sister, though, so he tried not to bite too hard when he told her to shut-up. Since their dad had died when she was only two, Kyle had been the closest thing to a father she had ever known.

He liked that. And so did his mom. His mom would not have to worry when Trisha started dating, because Kyle would make any boy run the gauntlet if he expected to go out with his kid sister.

"Yo, Mom, Trisha. You home?" He walked through the kitchen and froze. Spoons stuck in two bowls of mostly eaten oatmeal, a box of toppled-over Cheerios, an empty milk jug laying on its side on the counter. The cordless phone sat in the middle of the daily newspaper's many sections. Plates with dinner remnants protruded haphazardly from the sink. A Minute Maid orange juice carton stood by the toaster with its spout open. A knife with butter and jelly smears on its blade rested on a half-eaten piece of toast.

A familiar pang of shame laced through Kyle. The scene triggered a dread that stirred his gut. *Hadn't Dr. Thomas given Mom new medication?* Depression occasionally seized his mother's world and the fist clenched the house in a tight grasp when it did. But nine months had passed since her last episode.

After five minutes of searching the house, the curtain of dread began to lift. Mom and Trisha weren't home. He speed-cleaned the kitchen while tossing a Twinkie and an apple into a brown paper sack, then slapped peanut butter and jelly on four pieces of bread. He pulled two sodas from the fridge as Trisha and his mom came clamoring through the front door, packages rattling and jabbering ninety miles a minute. He glanced at the stove clock: 11:45. How much shopping could they do before noon?

"Kyle, I just love a man with bubbles up to his elbows," Trisha said with a giggle.

"Bite me."

"Okay, you two, you've been in the same room for exactly ten seconds, and you're already bickering. That may be a record. And yes, Kyle, that is pretty sexy." His mom winked at him, and he blushed furiously.

His friends got all googly-eyed when they spent the night with Kyle during the normal months of the year. Kerri Spene looked half her forty-two years and had the figure of a model. Not the stick-thin kind, but the real drop-dead gorgeous ones. And to have his own mom talk about sex in any way, shape, or form embarrassed the dickens out of him.

Trisha had inherited every bit of their mother's good looks, so he was braced for her adolescence. He also recognized when he looked in the mirror why girls at school stared at him. The wavy blond hair, sea blue eyes, high cheekbones. The three of them frequented various restaurants where waitresses teased that they looked like a Hollywood family. That always made Kyle proud.

"What's with the mess, girls? Can't a man be a kid every once in a while around here?" Kyle gave his mom a quick glance to see if she looked tired, on the verge of a spell. He saw no signs and breathed a sigh of relief.

"Sorry. There was a sale at Dillard's that ended at noon, one of those midnight madness things, and Trisha needed a few more clothes before school started. You, of course, were nowhere to be found, so you missed out. Actually, I found you a really nice Polo on sale, some Levis, and a pair of Reeboks – your typical attire. If they don't fit, I'll take them back."

Kyle saw the bags on the kitchen table and guessed that Trisha had made out like a bandit.

"Who are you trying to impress, runt-face? Looks like you bought out the whole store!" He felt that funny protective feeling again and tried to act nonchalant about it.

"Yep, bought every stitch of clothes that fit me – but tight," she said with a wicked grin. "You said you were glad my tomboy days were over. Mom even bought me some make-up!"

Kyle saw his mom shoot Trisha an *I told you not to tell* glare. Trisha had obviously been sworn to secrecy but couldn't control herself. If Trisha had one fault, it was self-control.

"Over my dead body. You're not paintin' your face like some tramp!" But Kyle laughed. It terrified him that his baby sister was growing up, but pride oozed from his pores. He play-stomped upstairs and threw on his swimming trunks.

"We'll discuss this later," he said, when he came back down with a beach towel wrapped around his neck.

"Oh, Kyle, grow up. You're my brother, not my dad."

"Huh, and it's a tough job, little missy," he grumbled. He finished gathering all the food he thought he could cram into his face in four hours. "You ladies have a wonderful afternoon. The man of the house is going to go play."

By the time he pedaled his dirt bike like a maniac to the quarry, he was only twenty minutes late – early by his standards.

After hours in the sun eating, swimming, jumping off the jagged rocks, and lounging, Kyle returned home lethargic and contented. As he coasted down his street, casually observing the modest two-story homes that preceded his own, he saw a Ryder truck backed into the driveway of the house directly across the street from his. It had been for sale for a few weeks, and they had seen a variety of potential buyers. He slowed to watch. A typical slew of furniture, boxes, and junk littered the lawn. He searched for signs of teenagers, male or female. He had reached the age where either would be okay. But one thing he had learned – friends lasted a heck of a lot longer than dates.

A dark-skinned boy peeked around the van and waved. Kyle returned the hand gesture as he coasted. He didn't subscribe to all Bradley's racial mumbo jumbo, so he didn't hesitate to approach the boy unpacking boxes. The new kid waltzed up to him.

"Hey! Wanna help? Name's Manuel Hernandez, friends call me Manny." The dark hand thrust toward Kyle before he could think to reject it.

"Hey. I'm Kyle, and I live right across the street."

They exchanged basic information – name, date of birth, favorite rock band, and Super Bowl projections – and Kyle confirmed what he always suspected – a guy thought with his head, not his skin color. They spent the next hour and a half chatting about nothing important. With the ease only kids know, they laid the foundation of a life-altering friendship.

Manny and Kyle grew to be famous friends, in spite of Brad's resentment. Stempy and Kyle's other friends didn't have a problem with Manny's race since he proved himself on the field and court. But not Brad. The Nazi poster boy couldn't accept that his best friends turned their backs on him, on how he felt. That school year, Brad buddied up with other defensive linebackers and wrote Kyle off. They never exchanged blows or words, but the unspoken said plenty.

Their sophomore year, Kyle and Manny were the best wide receiver tandem in the district and competed fiercely for point guard once basketball season rolled around. As juniors, they dominated Lewisville sports, vying good-naturedly for the cutest girls. They became best buddies, completely inseparable. And it didn't go sour until their senior year – only six weeks before graduation.

The one-hundred-eighty degree turn happened in late March. Manny Hernandez's kid brother Julian – fifteen and full of gusto – made the mistake of a lifetime. A few months earlier, he had fallen in love with Trisha.

That part had been okay with Kyle. Matter-of-fact, it had been hunky-dory. His best friend's brother and his own little sister. Who could have asked for anything better?

By spring, only a few weeks before Kyle would graduate with honors and leave for Austin to play baseball, the world flipped upside down and inside-out. Julian and Trisha had dated steady all semester – movies, the soda shop, walks in the mall. They did everything as a couple, and it brought the families closer together than ever. When the "ice queen" rumors started, Kyle told his friends to shut-up. If his sister didn't want to "put-out," good for her. But it didn't stop the talk.

Kyle knew gossip, like flash-in-the-pan-bands, would fade with time.

He was wrong.

* * *

IN LATE APRIL, flowers budded, bees set about pollinating, and Trisha's resistance weakened. On a Friday night after a track meet, Julian drove to Scenic View Park an hour before curfew. She grinned, slipped out of her jacket, and reached across the stick shift to nibble his ear. Within a few minutes, they crawled into the backseat and got serious.

"C'mon, Trish," he moaned, his voice husky. "At least touch me." He buried his face in her neck, kissing, rubbing her breasts through her shirt. He slipped his hand under the soft sweater, unhooked her bra, and felt her breath hitch. She wanted him, and he knew it. He yanked his shirt off, tossed it in the floorboard, and felt the cool leather on his arms as he braced himself next to Trisha in the back seat of his Mustang.

"Slow," she instructed him. She conceded that much, but twice she rejected him fumbling with her belt. He pulled her free hand to the swelling in his crotch.

He showed Trisha the way he liked it. She was okay with rubbing him, pleasing him that way. After all, they were three days shy of their six-month "anniversary," and he was crazy about her. She unsnapped his Levis and for the first time touched him over his underwear.

"Trish, let me touch you, please." He groaned as she continued caressing him.

Only over her panties, she warned, even though she ached to say yes. Her resolve was paper-thin. She hoped conceding a little would ease some of the pressure she felt.

"Oh, God, Trish, that feels so good."

She smiled, the heat from his hand driving her crazy.

"Stop," she whispered. But his hand moved faster, keeping rhythm with his own shifting hips.

"Stop," she ordered, her voice edged with panic.

"But I know you want me." He kissed her with a fervor that sent sparks to every part of her body. He felt her squirm with desire, having difficulty maintaining her composure. She helped him tug her jeans to her knees.

"Oh, God, Trisha, I love you." He ached, throbbed with her response as she swiveled her hips at the pressure his hand provided. He pulled his own jeans down further, then her panties, and pushed himself on top of her before she knew what was happening.

And then Julian misunderstood her cries. He thought they were moans of ecstasy, but then he felt the blood, warm and sticky against his leg.

"STOP!" Trisha screamed, lashing out with her nails and clawing her way free.

Before he could get off her, her fingernails left scars his face would bear the rest of his life.

Trisha scrambled out of the car, fumbled with her shirt and jeans and, before Julian could get out to reason with her, she ran. She scampered the half-mile home, hysterical and disheveled, trying to imagine what she would tell her mom and Kyle. But she was more terrified that Julian would get himself together and come after her in his Mustang.

The sports car roared down the street the instant she yanked open the front door, her heart hammering in her chest. For a split second, Trisha considered racing upstairs and hiding in her bedroom. She could avoid a mess, wash up, and figure out what to do later. But before she could think, Kyle peeked around the corner.

"You okay?" He held a Dr Pepper in his hand, ready to pop it open when he saw the blood. "Jesus, Trisha, what happened? MOM!"

Kyle's hands trembled as he led his baby sister to the downstairs bathroom. With teeth clenched, he asked her what hurt.

"Nothing. I mean, I don't know." Trisha buried her face in her hands and began to sob – gut-wrenching crying that twisted Kyle's heart.

"Here, get out of those clothes." He handed her a spare robe that hung on the back of the door. She pulled frantically at her jeans like she couldn't get them off fast enough. He handed her a damp washcloth, his head swirling, stewing. But he knew Trisha's silence signaled something horrible, unimaginable – and he prayed it had nothing to do with his best friend's little brother.

His mother whipped around the corner into the bathroom and covered her mouth to stifle a scream. "Oh, my God, baby, what happened to you?" But before Trisha could answer, their mom shooed Kyle back and yanked the washrag from her hand. "No, don't clean anything up. I want to know what happened to you and who did this. Trisha, speak to me, now." Her mother's stern voice broke Trisha's trance.

"Oh, God, Mom, I'm so sorry. I wanted to wait, but it felt good, and...and...I wanted him to stop, but I didn't stop, and when I finally decided I had to, he couldn't. And it's all my fault and I bled all over his car and..." Sobs tore through the fourteen-year-old girl, no longer a virgin but too guilt-ridden to claim it as rape. Trisha cried while her mother tucked the bloody clothes into a grocery bag and slipped a pair of sweats onto her daughter's shivering body.

Kyle and his mom took Trisha to the hospital, filed a report and notified the police. In Kerri Spene's eyes, Julian Mantel had raped her little girl, no matter the circumstances. For Kyle, his best friend's younger brother had stolen her innocence. And he meant to get it back.

* * *

THE POLICE NEVER found Julian Hernandez. When the incident hit the papers, residents and friends speculated that he was avoiding arrest, that someone in his family must be protecting him. Many believed he had fled to Mexico to lay low for a while.

Two days after Julian's disappearance, before the Mustang was found, some of Julian's belongings were discovered at the wood's edge where once four boys lay laughing about Stempy Jones being the horniest kid on the planet. Traces of blood were discovered on a picture of Trisha Spene. DNA proved it was Julian's, so the mystery deepened.

Then the police found a note Julian had written and left in his bottom dresser drawer. They wondered why he would hide it, but the content was clear – he professed his love and apology to Trisha. It seemed an omen of a runaway or suicide.

Kyle thought it had been a nice touch. Julian's guilty conscience helped the scenario, painted the image Kyle wanted the police to see. Julian and his car had disappeared off the face of the Earth, and Trisha could finally get some peace. The town buzzed, but as days passed, it seemed obvious. Julian had run like the coward he was.

Kyle knew Manny would never give up looking. He was no quitter and several facts would bother Manny – Julian had no money and Kyle knew the two brothers shared everything. He knew Manny suspected him, but there was a loyalty they couldn't sever.

Manny finally confronted Kyle and the two came to blows. And then they never spoke to each other again.

Kyle didn't care about that or anything else, not anymore. He died a little more each day watching Trisha struggle with what had been stolen from her. She sat silently at the dinner table, talked little at school, and her grades slipped steadily until their mother broke down and hired a tutor. A month shy of finishing her sophomore year with several failing grades and permanently affecting chances at big name colleges, Trisha didn't resist the help. Within weeks, she would open up to Beth, her college tutor, who seemed to understand what she had gone through. And a deeper relationship developed – the only kind Trisha could manage after what happened with Julian.

* * *

"THOSE COPS WERE so damn stupid," Kyle hissed. But he laughed – a sadistic sound that clawed at John Basinger's insides. "That goddamned spic treated my sister like an animal, and they couldn't figure out that what I had done was justice?"

"You ever a suspect?"

"Oh, hell, yeah. The police questioned each of the neighborhood kids during the first few days after the note was found – me, Trisha, they kept a close eye on her. And they tailed me for a while – especially after me and Manny slugged it out after a track meet." He chuckled, then kicked back in the chair like he was about to put his feet up on the table. He sat up and leaned forward instead. "Each time those assholes came to our house, they consoled Trish but treated me like a common criminal. Stupid idiots couldn't find their dicks with both hands. But I knew how to talk to those jerks, especially that idiot, Detective Rodriguez." Kyle slurred the name with his best mockery of Spanish. "I shoulda won an Oscar for my performance."

John cringed and glanced from Jamie to Kyle to Nathan, but no one met his gaze.

"I knew to talk about Julian in the present tense. Dr. Brannigan, Trisha's psychologist, counseled us – Mom, me, and Trish. And I told the doc, 'You bozos should be out lookin' for Julian instead of spendin' time with me.' The bitch even admitted that I fit the profile and would have to bear the scrutiny."

"How's Trisha now?" John wanted to bring it to the present, and remind them that the Fab Four might have killed people they loved.

"She's fine. And I know what you're thinking, because you're so predictable, Dr. Basinger. She's *safe*. And she's where we would've been if..."

"HEY!" Nathan shouted and kicked the table hard enough to scoot it several inches. John jumped, and Kyle sat up as if he realized where he was.

"Must have been hard, being her older brother and not able to protect her. Probably pissed you off pretty good, huh?" Dr. Basinger watched for a reaction, but Kyle was back in control.

Nathan let out a laugh that curled John's toes.

"Record says Julian Hernandez killed himself. But I guess you know that's not true." John didn't expect any response from Kyle, so the grin startled the big guy.

And it dawned on him. The quarry. In an hour-long conversation, Dr. Basinger was able to figure out what the Lewisville police couldn't.

Not that it mattered now.

Chapter Seventeen

Dallas
Day Three

HADEN, I HOPE you're getting' all this. John cleared his throat and leaned forward in his seat. He studied Kyle, but the boy had checked out. Jamie turned her head only slightly, but her eyes told John plenty.

"Nathan, may I?" Jamie seemed oblivious that John, not Nathan, was in charge.

"Certainly, Jamie, the floor is yours."

The two smiled at one another like they were conducting a sales pitch. John's skin began to crawl, and his groin tightened.

"Okay, Dr. Basinger, sir, here's the deal. We have a population problem, true?"

John didn't need to refresh his memory about Jamie's file. She had been highly sought after by scores of companies. Her name graced the headline of hundreds of Texas newspapers as she gained national attention graduating from MIT before her twenty-first birthday with a doctorate in chemistry. John had played on her obvious desire to be close to home when his recruiters brought him her resume. He remembered the tragedies in her life and knew a little of the town she had escaped. Kingsville was allegedly the center of a renowned cult movement, and John didn't doubt it.

There was a lot of madness everywhere, he was discovering.

"Sir?" Her voice pulled him back to the present.

"Uh, what was the question again?"

"Our population problem – it's out of control, don't you think?"

"I suppose it is, Jamie, yes. More so in other countries than in the U.S. though."

"Oh, not true, sir. Not to mention the numbers you never see in the census. The illegal immigrants in this country far outnumber our Native American population. Now, does that seem okay to you, sir? And, the system by which we relegate the influx of fence jumpers from Mexico is a joke."

"So you're telling me that the Kingsville rumor is true? Is that what you're hinting at?" John's heart quickened. The idea terrified him.

"I don't have to hint, sir. Do you have any idea what growing up there was like? Kyle's story is heartbreaking, but being a kid in Kingsville was like growing up in Germany in the 1940s. You did what was expected of you."

Jamie paused and let out a sigh.

"And what was that, Jamie? What was it really like to grow up there?"

* * *

Jamie

"AND HOW FITTING is this? Last year, as an eleven year-old, she beat competitors three, four and five years older than her. This year, as a twelve-year-old eighth grader, the winner of the Kingsville Science Fair...Jamie Mantel! Congratulations, Jamie, you'll be going to Corpus Christi next week to compete in the district competition!" The principal beamed at her. Her parents and classmates cheered.

Her mom, dad, and brother came running and hugged her fiercely. She hated this part. Her dad always squeezed her too hard, but she never had the heart to tell him. She braced for his grip and grimaced as her face squished to his chest.

But, God, she felt good!

"Honey, we're so proud of you!" Bev Mantel held her daughter's face in her hands and smiled, an expression so full of love it brought tears to Jamie's eyes.

"Let me see this thing," her dad demanded. "God, this is bigger than last year's!" When teachers suggested Jamie skip grades, he had balked at first. Now he busted with pride.

She gazed dreamily at her father. Being the center of attention was not a place Jamie liked to be, except when her father held the spotlight. James Mantel stood a whopping five foot ten, but to Jamie he was a giant. Both he and Bev didn't believe in doing anything unless you were going to be the best at it.

Their children had taken that adage to heart and excelled at everything. Charlie, now sixteen, ranked third in his class academically, even got a visit from a professional baseball scout. He was being heavily recruited in football – he had blinding speed at cornerback. Texas coaches had been watching him for three years. It was never too early in a state that bred football phenoms faster than cattle.

But to the dismay of his parents and coaches, his love was baseball. Duke was his dream, but that seemed so far away. Jamie kept telling him to go for it. Escaping Kingsville would be the best thing, the only way to get away from The Movement. If it could be done.

Jamie's athletic abilities could have been a ticket out, but her love was science. She dreamed of the Nobel like most girls idolized Brad Pitt. She accepted that she was different. Embraced it, in fact, in order to fit in with kids three and four years older. Being twelve and in eighth grade wasn't exactly the easiest thing in the world.

Thank God her body had cooperated by developing early. But boys still didn't notice her. She was grateful, because she was far too smart to carry on a conversation with most of them. She could be giddy with the girls, but when the boys started acting like boys, she couldn't tolerate their immaturity. Most of her friends agreed with her attitude and liked her panache.

"Just wait till high school," they had declared. The boys would hopefully grow up. If not, they would chase college men.

"Okay, space cadet, let's go eat. Your choice, so we can celebrate."

Jamie, about to burst with happiness, left the gymnasium with her daddy carrying the heavy trophy. Charlie put his arm around his kid sister. What was he going to do when she came to high school next year? They never thought they would have to worry about that with her being almost five years younger. Now she knew he would screen anyone who even thought about asking her out, tormenting anyone who did.

Except they wouldn't, of course. Her intelligence surrounded her like an aura. The sharp features, though pretty, exemplified her genius. A girl with brains intimidated boys more than facing Michael Jordan one-on-one. And she used her intellectual prowess to breeze through high school.

By her senior year, Jamie won every science fair she entered, placed in Nationals and had her pick of colleges – all before her sixteenth birthday. While her friends worried about boys, fashion, and the upcoming prom, Jamie pondered solutions to the world's dire issues. She tried hard to understand their problems, but all they cared about was popularity and gossip.

Brianna Hambright, Jamie's closest school friend, stood bawling in the restroom one day near the end of April, and Jamie raced to her side to find out what injustice had been done to the seventeen-year-old.

"Ricky was talking to Monica. Didn't you see him? God, he's such a pig!" Brianna screamed. "I can't believe he's talking to her!"

"Does he like her?" Jamie asked, incredulous that this stirred such chaos for her friend.

"I don't know! Shit, Jamie, but he was touching her. He had his hand on her arm, that's like practically screwing her right in the hallway!" The girl wiped tears from her face and cast Jamie a *My God, are you a moron or what?* look as she stormed out of the bathroom. Jamie shook her head and wondered how long it would be before Brianna ended up pregnant.

That weekend, while Brianna shopped for dresses, Jamie and her parents visited college campuses. The first, and clearly her father's choice, was the University of Texas – his alma mater.

"C'mon, let's visit Texas Union first. Or wait, honey, you've never seen the Tower, have you?" Her dad pulled at Jamie's sleeve like an excited boy. He didn't have to look at the campus map. He knew the University of Texas like the back of his hand, even though he had graduated nearly twenty years earlier. "I wanna take you to Ransom Center and show you where I used to spend all my time flirting with your mother while she watched soap operas."

Sitting on a stone bench inspecting her own map, Jamie grinned as her mom and dad pointed to highlights on the revered campus. She humored them by visiting U of T. She had letters of application to five other colleges, four of which she would choose first. But she was holding out for her dream – MIT.

"Hon, are you with us?"

"Sorry, Dad. Where to next?" She smiled at him. He was still her knight in shining armor, the only man who had her attention. She would turn sixteen only a month and a half before heading off to college in the fall – without ever having gone out on a date. Her appearance, though young, would make her a force to be reckoned with once she got around boys of equal intelligence. Her dimples, auburn hair, and hazel eyes got second glances from boys all the time, but her reputation preceded her. She couldn't wait to escape it.

"You wanna see the Tower or Texas Union? We can get a bite to eat there if you want."

"Whichever. I'm not too hungry. You pick."

"You're not much into this, are you, honey?" Her mom wrapped an arm around her daughter's shoulders.

"I like it here, but I still want to wait to see if MIT accepts me. That'll be too hard to face if I get in there but have already decided on Austin. Do you know how few women get into MIT?" Jamie's face shone like a child on Christmas morning.

"Okay, babe. But don't mind that your daddy was a Longhorn, your mom was a Longhorn, and Charlie could've been one." Her dad giggled, but she knew deep down he was a little disappointed. University of Texas was one of the finest schools in the country. But even Charlie had known that getting away, far away, was more important. The Movement's power controlled the youth in Kingsville, and the arms of those in charge spanned miles. Jamie suspected her parents had no idea that it even existed. They likely thought all the strange things that occurred throughout Southeast Texas were just random violence, or didn't notice them at all.

But she did. And so did every other kid in town. That's why Charlie made his dream come true to become a Duke Blue Devil.

The decision had nothing to do with the countless football and baseball scholarship offers, or that the Texas chauvinism bred deep within most natives never burned within him. Or that his 4.0 GPA would get him into any college in the country. The reason Charlie had to get out of Texas rested squarely on the shoulders of his first kill at age nine. Who needed more reason than that?

If he wanted to survive, he had to escape, and he had a legitimate out. Few were allowed to leave, but when they did, technology allowed The Movement to keep eyes and ears on them for months, even years. But Charlie didn't mind. He had no intention of undermining The Movement; he just wanted freedom. His first kill, recorded and tucked safely in a Grand Dragon's safe, insured his silence. Every Kingsville ten-year-old boy had a videotape, labeled and graphic enough to keep any kid's mouth shut. Charlie's had come early.

The initiation process was legendary. Boys started hearing it from older kids, and the exaggeration only added to the effect. By age ten, every Kingsville boy got acquainted with "playing the line." When Charlie first heard the term, he thought the rumor had something to do with football.

Football and playing the line had nothing in common, except a line of defense. The object was to scout the Mexican-American border for illegal entrants. And their orders were crystal clear. "No wetback," the facilitator explained, "gets across that border and past you." He didn't have to finish the order, because every boy knew it by heart. *Not if you expect to live.*

The drive south on Highway 77 creeped Charlie Mantel out, the eeriest experience of his life. But sitting crouched, hidden in the cover of the high grasses with a semi-automatic rifle in pre-teenaged hands, made *eerie* a walk in the park. The late night hazing meant watching Mexicans climb the fence into the good old U.S of A. without an invitation. Boys lay gripping their weapons, fingers twitching on hairpin triggers, praying for nerves of steel. Or at least the appearance of it.

If those illegal immigrants happened to be crossing at one of the stakeout points between Brownsville and Laredo, it proved to be their final mistake. And if a boy failed to follow-through, he would get another try. Baseball rules applied to the game, but the similarities ended there. The third strike would be far more severe than going to sit in a dugout.

Rumor had it that "playing the line" spanned the distance clear to El Paso. The stress of being a line virgin heightened considerably with the pistol shoved behind each new boy's ear. The "three-strikes" policy made the first time terrifying, but at least there was an out. One immigrant could cross, and the finger could quiver but the brain might freeze.

"That's typical," a line lieutenant would bark. "Got two more shots, *girls*."

A second illegal jumper might come into sights, but the mental anguish, the overpowering pressure, just might be too much, and that was okay, too. Murder was stressful; the officers in charge conceded that much.

But third time had better be a charm.

Kill or be killed, or so the rumors spread. No one knew for sure, but the threat was enough – and the muzzle in the ear made more than one boy wet himself. Charlie witnessed beatings that left boys with black eyes and missing teeth. Now nearing ten, he took one boy's advice to heart – do what's necessary to survive.

What saved Jamie Mantel was Kingsville's lack of progression toward the feminist thinking. Only boys went through initiation. Girls played secretarial and recruitment roles and received warnings of having to visit the line if they couldn't make good.

Brutal stories of rape swirled around those who repudiated The Movement. And on more than one occasion, family members of vocal opposers wound up with broken legs, shattered kneecaps, even sexual assault. Very little was beneath leaders of The Movement.

Every child, male or female, was told what would be done if anyone told the police or their parents once the recruitment process started. Powerful adults were integral to The Movement. And then the recruits were shown tapes of previous performers.

"This, boys, is what happens if you strike out," Andy Witherington stated simply as he popped in a videotape and hit play. As a member of the panel, Mr. Witherington spared little drama in deterring kids from running to Mommy and Daddy.

"Do it, kid. You don't shoot that wetback, I shoot you," a line lieutenant hisses. It's dark—too dark to make out the images on the TV screen, but there's a flash of light and a sharp pop. Another boy close-by screams.

"You shot Scottie! Oh, my God, you asshole, you shot Scottie!"

"Then do your job, Marcus. NOW!" The man doesn't need to shout – he has a small microphone attached to his shirt for the video's sake.

At that same instant, a Mexican mother holding a baby gets caught on the barbed wire and nearly falls.

An adult leans into Marcus's ear and whispers: "Do it, kid." And the face that fills the camera is none other than deputy of police, Stan Waters.

The mother stumbles, pulls her baby close, and looks up at the skirmish in the bushes. Her eyes go wide when she sees the boy aiming a rifle at her. In an act of self-preservation, the kid fires – a rapid succession of pop-pop-pop. Mother and child collapse to the ground, and someone in the background shouts, "Nice shot, kid!"

Charlie told Jamie about the video. He couldn't get home fast enough that day – nearly two months before his tenth birthday. He didn't know Scottie or Marcus; they were much older, Mr. Witherington said, but seeing it acted out set Charlie's insides stewing. And his best friend was turning ten in a week.

Ten days later, Charlie came home in a state that made his parents keep him home from school for two days – *worst case of the flu I've ever seen,* his mother declared.

But Jamie knew. And five years later when she turned ten, she saw the video, too. Girls might not have to execute, but they must believe.

The fact that law intertwined with The Movement took away a kid's avenue of help. They even saw more than one uniformed officer stand vigil while boys played the line, and that knowledge struck fear so deep in all of them they didn't dare think of rebellion. Especially with the visual reminder that their act of violence – cold-blooded murder – was captured on tape. They never saw the figure looming behind them pressing the cold, hard gun barrel against their ear, and neither did viewers. All police or parents would be able to see was the boy with a gun in his hand and his disregard for the law when he pulled the trigger.

Charlie told Jamie the side she never got to see. Girls were brought in on a daily basis, but they didn't perform the duties that gave The Movement its mystique. Women wrote the newsletters that tied all factions of The Movement together. Other groups lived as far west as Arizona. Girls were also taught to know their place, to fulfill other menial tasks and some necessary ones that degraded them and kept them as fearful as the boys who committed the kills.

So most of the folks who grew up in Kingsville stayed their entire lives, fearful of retribution and hopeful someone would dismantle The Movement. But if a member possessed a gift, which both Mantels did, then leaving was accepted. Charlie knew several of his weaker friends had chosen schools far away for perhaps reasons The Movement didn't buy, had attempted to leave, and mysteriously disappeared. Their motives and loyalty had been in question. But it was no mystery to Charlie what had happened to them. He vowed not to make the same mistake.

He bragged that he was a two-sport man and boasted about his multiple scholarship offers. The big leagues called his name, and the full rides poured in for both baseball and football. It was all true, but Charlie shouted it from the rooftops. Or in this case, during a panel's circle time. The leaders of The Movement faced him in chairs covered with purple shrouds. Nearly ninety boys sat cross-legged in a cleared-out spot in the heart of the woods. Rocks outlined the circle, a small campfire crackled between the panel of men and the kids, and they were all surrounded by flaming torches. A setting sun cast shadows across the men's faces, accented by the dancing glow from the fire. Butterflies fluttered in the tummy of every boy in attendance – this was a time of interrogation and confession.

"What are your intentions, Charles?" a panel officer asked. Around the man sat Mr. Witherington, a teacher Charlie knew, and several police officers and firemen. The Grand Dragon, draped in a purple-and-gold cloak, stared hard at him with eyes meant to penetrate to the boy's core.

"Six football offers but only two baseball. Can you believe that? I'm a helluva shortstop, but they think all Texas boys prefer football. Sheez." Charlie shook his head with exaggerated disgust. His nerves prickled as the leaders of The Movement, the six sitting before him, listened intently.

"I ain't gonna be a Deion Sanders or Michael Jordan. No sirree, Bob. I'm a one-sport man."

The panel chuckled, but he wasn't done. The show had to be convincing. They had to accept his well sought after talent. And he wanted assurance that they believed it.

He needn't have worried. Charlie Mantel was one of the best athletes in the state of Texas. His name appeared in *The Sporting News* as number fourteen on the list of one hundred hottest All-American picks coming out of high school. Pro scouts had propositioned him to skip college.

"So, what's it gonna be, Charlie?" a kid from the crowd shouted. Other questions followed, but no more from the panel. The six sat stiffly in throne-like chairs and remained silent. Grins of indulgence plastered the faces of the scariest men Charles Mantel would ever know.

"I can get more longevity from baseball. Ya know, the knees don't last forever in football, not to mention that even though I'm faster than greased lightening, I'm still a runt. I'm barely six feet, and in the bigs, that makes me a dwarf."

The boys laughed, slapping each other on the arm or knee. Charlie could always play an audience.

Jamie remembered. She had been peering through the bushes just beyond the edge of the clearing to watch the show. Not that she wanted to, but because Charlie made her. He wanted her to know what went on when the women weren't around. The scene changed drastically once the female factor left the equation.

"So you'll be spending a lot of time with one of these?" An officer cloaked in his purple cape came toward Charlie and swung the bat with ferocity, barely missing Charlie's head.

The crowd moaned. The front row sat frozen, sickened by what they feared was about to happen. They had seen it before.

Behind the six leaders stood twelve Dragons. The Dragons were, in essence, bodyguards, hired guns, mercenaries. Circle Time often meant hazing for new members or a set way to dispense necessary information. Anything the panel needed the boys to know, Circle Time was the venue. Sometimes they wanted to remind the boys who was in charge.

A mammoth man stood before Charlie – First Lieutenant Ben Crowder, a growling man with a Colonel Sanders beard who was biding his time before a seat on the panel became available. And this only transpired through death.

The end of the First Lieutenant's bat loomed in front of Charlie's face, and the boy grinned with the cockiness of a prizefighter.

"You got a power swing or are you a finesse hitter?" Mr. Crowder asked, then swung the Louisville Slugger menacingly in front of Charlie's groin. The teenager didn't even cringe.

"You hurt this million-dollar body, and questions will definitely be asked. You know my lips are sealed about The Movement. I've been loyal and productive. Hell, half of you are the closest friends I ever had! I recruited tons of these guys," Charlie said, then turned around and did a Vanna White arm gesture to the group of eight through eighteen-year-olds who sat before them.

Charlie winked at one of the younger boys as he bowed to the panel. When he stood upright, he didn't see the bat coming. It rammed into his midsection head-on, hard enough to drop him to his knees with a whoof. The practiced blow would leave a colorful bruise but nothing more.

"Ahhh, shit," Charlie moaned. "You sonuva…" But Charlie saw the man's feet edge closer as he cowered on all fours, spat, and waited for the nausea to pass. He clutched his midsection with both hands, then lifted his head.

The Kingsville's Movement and its panel of officers stared at Charlie Mantel like he was a fly crawling in their soup, and it scared Charlie shitless. He had played the games he'd needed to play since he was nine. He even killed when it made the difference between staying above ground or ending up six feet under. But he had been smart enough to know the difference between himself and those around him. His casualties had been as a soldier in war. He detested it but knew how to follow orders.

That night, standing before the panel, Charlie knew his little sister sat hunkered in the woods somewhere beyond the circle. He hoped the lesson wasn't lost on her.

* * *

JAMIE SHUDDERED WITH the memory of watching Charlie clubbed and then paraded around like a trophy – she could still smell the citronella torches ten feet in front of her. After exerting their force, the panel congratulated her brother and admired his lofty future. They even presented him with accommodation – the flimsy certificate symbolized Charlie's freedom, and every boy sitting on the dewy grass knew it, envied it, thirsted for it.

The prospect of standing on a university campus thousands of miles away seemed unbelievable, too good to be true.

But Charlie had escaped, and Jamie was close behind.

* * *

"HEY, JAMIE! YOU got a letter! Oh, my God. It's from MIT!" her mom shouted up the stairs, still unloading groceries from her Saturday shopping.

It had been three weeks since they'd visited the Austin campus, and Jamie had received three acceptance letters – Texas, Notre Dame, and Harvard. All excited her, but this was what she had been waiting for.

Bev Mantel held the envelope out to her daughter and took a deep breath of anticipation. Jamie rubbed the letter vigorously between both hands.

"Well, it's not Aladdin's lamp. You're not getting any wishes, only what you deserve. C'mon, girl, open it!" Her mother, beside herself, wanted to jump out of her skin.

Jamie knew her mom was right. Whatever the answer, it would be the deciding factor.

"Maybe we should wait until Dad gets home," Jamie started, her hands quivering.

"That's up to you, honey." Her mother's eyes shone with excitement. "Oh, just open the damn thing. We can play head games with your father when he gets home. You know, tell him how you didn't get in and have him take us some place really fancy for a consolation dinner. We can get him to take us to Gregory's. We'll really play it up. Oh, come on; don't look at me like that. You're killin' me!"

The idea sounded great to Jamie. That meant her mother assumed she'd been accepted. She loved her mom more than life itself for the vote of confidence.

As she carefully broke the seal, Jamie prayed her mother was right. Her voice cracked as she began reading the letter:

"Jamie Marie Mantel, we are happy to inform you that you have been accepted at the Massachusetts's Institute of Technology and..." Jamie's eyes scanned the letter like it was a million dollar bill. "MOM! I'M IN!"

Jamie squealed and crumpled the letter in her hand as she danced around the kitchen with her mom. She quickly pressed the treasured piece of paper out before her, trying to iron the wrinkles she had just created. The two stared at it, reread it, and let it sink in that Jamie had defied the odds.

An hour and a half later, most of Kingsville, Texas, knew Jamie Mantel was Boston bound. The town had reveled in her growth and cheered the child prodigy's success. Many envied a future they couldn't even fathom. The concept of where MIT was escaped their grasp, much less the intelligence necessary to get there. But a few men with their neatly pressed red, purple, and gold robes hanging in dark closets wondered how to let Jamie go – they knew how blatantly she disapproved of The Movement. She'd said as much. She had a strong mind and a quick tongue. How many times had she spoken her piece, shown her disgust at what the panel believed and professed in their monthly newsletters? When she was thirteen, she had even written an editorial for the local newspaper that riled the panel to the point of rebuke. Jamie had expressed her distaste for the chauvinism so evident in Kingsville, primarily The Movement, even though she hadn't used the name. Her opinions stirred a fury that took her father weeks to silence.

Now that she was leaving, they agreed she needed to be warned. Something that would matter, an attention-grabber. A significant act that would never leave her wondering *what if*.

* * *

THE ACCIDENT HAPPENED only two miles from his driveway. James Mantel had been driving home from work, soot-covered after battling a three-alarm fire – an obvious case of arson – in a Mexican restaurant. And it hadn't been the first Mexican place to go up in smoke, or the first Mexican-owned anything to fall to a match.

James Mantel knew more than he was telling, but since his boyhood days with The Movement, he knew when to keep his mouth shut. He became a fireman for a reason – it was either that or a cop, but too many members of the force were embedded in the organization. He had clout in ways no one knew.

On more than one occasion, he had tipped illegal immigrants not to reside in Kingsville, not to open a business, not to be party to anything subject to public scrutiny. His advice and warnings never ended with a signature and were printed on run-of-the-mill stationery and mailed from downtown Kingsville. None were ever traced to him, but a few Dragons had him under suspicion, watched him closely, kept him in their sights.

Not anymore.

The eldest Mantel never saw the diesel coming. He rounded the corner, entering his subdivision going less than thirty miles per hour. An eighteen wheeler, bearing down on him at better than double his speed, plowed head-on into the Chrysler. The kamikaze Peterbilt mangled the car beyond recognition and ejected the truck driver, who died on impact. The Jaws of Life extricated the barely breathing James Mantel, fireman, hero to many and enemy to The Movement.

"Hey, Buchanan, we need shocks. He's flatlining!" one of the paramedics shouted. "Hang on, buddy, hang on." But the medic knew the legless man had lost too much blood and wondered if the truck driver had been on a Movement mission. It wouldn't be the first fatality he'd worked that reeked of The Movement's handiwork.

"T-t-tell my family I love them," James Mantel murmured as he lost consciousness. A piercing guilt overwhelmed him, but then a magnificent sense of relief washed over him. His dying thought was a certainty that his death was a warning to his children.

He hoped they understood.

* * *

BOTH HAD. BUT the ramifications were far-reaching. Charlie, starting his third year at Duke, fell into a deep, guilt-ridden depression. His coach and friends consoled him, each sharing stories of similar loss, but Charlie, angered by their inability to understand, knew his mother was still in danger. They couldn't comprehend what growing up in Kingsville, Texas meant. But Bev Mantel knew.

She spent the better half of her life shedding memories much like Jamie's and made every effort feasible to erase and eliminate the past in order to protect her children. She and James seldom discussed it, but the few times they had, decisions came easy. Somehow they both realized the danger of giving voice to what they felt, so they led their children by example.

James exerted pressure on the elders not to push his children too hard, but he had known he couldn't prevent Jamie and Charlie from participating. He knew because he'd tried before. His first attempt to leave Kingsville had been right after Charlie's sixth birthday. Jamie and Jennifer were less than a year old at the time, and Bev had been certain their plan would work. They told everyone of their vacation to Florida. *Disney or bust,* they had squealed with delight.

When a scout spotted them heading north into Oklahoma and not heading east, the consequences had been catastrophic.

A state trooper, followed by a Kingsville patrol car, pulled them over and the Mantels knew immediately that they would pay a dear price. A sun-glassed man jerked open the passenger door, yanked Jamie's twin from Charlie's arms, and disappeared back into the cruiser. Within thirty seconds, the incident was over. And instead of five Mantels, now there were four.

Bev and James prayed their baby's death had been painless. And they had been grateful their other two children had been young enough to forget. Charlie asked countless questions, but contrived stories placated him. He eventually accepted them.

After that, the Mantels were forced to heed all warnings and chose to push their two remaining children to a success that would give them a legitimate out. Leaking the secrets of Kingsville to Charlie and Jamie was too dangerous.

* * *

JAMIE SHOOK HER head and let the images fade. She was still far away from Chamber Number Nine, hundreds of miles south in a Texas town too real to escape, too twisted to accept.

"I don't get it. You hated The Movement. Why would you participate in this?"

Jamie laughed – a tired, lost sound of someone three times her age. She didn't speak for a few minutes, but John waited. He could see her thoughts churning, the anger flickering in her hazel eyes.

"You have no idea what my father's death did to my mom." She picked at a cuticle. "And Charlie. Jesus, he just didn't get it. He totally screwed everything up. Dad died to keep us honest, but he would have wanted us to stay free. But Charlie had to come back."

"Jamie, you don't have to rehash this. Screw this old fart." Nathan scowled.

"No, that's okay. He has to understand, Nathan. You see, Dr. Basinger, Charlie went back just in time to find my mother's body…"

* * *

CHARLIE PULLED INTO Kingsville twenty hours before his mother's suicide. He ate lunch with her, then spent two hours renting a townhouse, buying furniture with a credit card the First Lieutenant gave him, and reacquainting himself with his childhood home. Two and a half years of freedom opened his eyes to an adult world that disgusted him. They all knew what was happening to the children but did nothing to stop it.

He had called during his flight to tell his mom he was coming home, and she had begged him not to. For fear of listening ears, she couldn't come right out and tell him what would happen to him if he returned. As a mother, she wanted to protect him. But as a wife who'd lost her husband, she appreciated the company.

"Really, Charlie. You came home for the funeral, and you know how much I enjoyed seeing you. And how much I needed you. But I need to move on now. I have so much going on, and quite honestly, you'll be a distraction." She tried to sound nonchalant, to conceal her panic. She didn't want to tell him that losing the man she adored could only be worsened by the death of another child. Or by his absorption into The Movement.

"Mom, c'mon. I know you have to be hurting. Don't push me away."

A sob caught in her throat. *Push him away?* She wanted nothing more than to pull him close and never let go. But to escape once was a coup, twice a miracle.

"Charlie, I'm fine, really. You'll just make me feel bad, like you don't think I can handle life without someone else's help. I miss your dad more than you can imagine, but you being here isn't going to make that go away. I need to deal on my own. Please," she insisted, "you coming back will only make it worse."

Please don't take away the gift your father gave you. He gave you freedom.

But Charlie couldn't stay away. He knew what she was trying to tell him, but it was more for him than her. He dropped his new apartment keys in his pocket and drove to his mother's for a home-cooked breakfast fit for a king. She hugged him tightly, told him how much she loved him. The knot in her throat prevented anything more than that. The lump gelled around a million *should'ves*.

He felt good, somehow sensing that he really would be able to ease her loss. Everyone else was gone. He had come to be at his mother's side so she wouldn't be alone. And now everyone knew Charlie Mantel would be a Kingsville resident for life, because they would never allow him to leave again.

What Charlie didn't know was that his mother had become a Dragon almost immediately following James' death. She believed the adage *Keep your friends close and your enemies closer*.

Bev Mantel knew her only recourse was to rebuild what little life she had left. And The Movement could offer it. She had no reason to deny the opportunities the faction could give the widow of a former activist. She would reap the benefits now – she had earned it.

When she contacted Ben Crowder, the entire panel voted unanimously to endorse her, to embrace her with open arms. Bev would facilitate the outreach portion of The Movement. She manned the project to send a bill to legislature about the consequences of illegal aliens entering America. She justified it, knowing she would never be expected to kill. She would never be asked to compromise her beliefs or her integrity in any way. In return, she would be offered the amenities of being a Dragon – wealth, status, and safety for her children.

But now Charlie had walked right back in, had nullified the portion of her soul she had been able to sell. The rest lay in the heart of a dead man in Kingsville Memorial Cemetery.

The following morning when Charlie crawled out of his childhood bed, a little hung over after an evening reminiscing with old buddies, he traipsed into the bathroom to take his morning pee. His mother's body lay stiff and swollen in the bathtub, her blue lips frozen forever in what appeared to be a desire to speak. But there had been nothing left to say.

Her nakedness had shamed him and a chasm grew in the core of his soul that would never be bridged. Somehow, her death trivialized his father's. Like he and Jamie weren't enough to live for. He screamed, grabbed the phone to dial 911 but slammed the handset into its cradle. He knew there would be a letter. There had been so many questions left unanswered, and once The Movement learned of his mother's suicide, they would be in charge of clean up. Charlie cried as he searched.

"God, Mom, did I do this?" he bawled, wiping his blurry eyes to see, rambling as he did a room-by-room hunt. He stopped outside her bedroom door.

He ached to know but feared it all the same. It would be on the other side of that door, and he knew it. When he finally summoned the courage to open it, he saw his name printed neatly on an envelope resting against her pillow. With trembling hands he pulled out the folded papers.

"Oh, God, Mom, I can't..." The words swam out of focus, blended into a blur of ink. But before he could lose the courage, he managed to finally make sense of it all.

My dearest children,

First, do what is necessary to destroy this letter once each of you has read it. Charlie, you need to send this to Jamie by mail. Don't fax it or e-mail it. Each of those can be traced. And you must mail it before you tell anyone of my death.

I need you to understand that your father and I loved you very much. Your father did all he could to guard you from The Movement. We even attempted once to leave and Jamie's twin, Jennifer, was taken from us. We never knew if she was killed or given to someone else. It was held over our heads as manipulation, so we would never leave again.

Charlie, you were six, and we prayed you would forget. Remember the trip to Disney? But The Movement went to an unprecedented extreme to stop us.

It worked. How could we leave when they had our baby? We also wanted to protect you from it, but we really didn't know how. None of the parents in Kingsville knew how.

How do you tell a small child about a sister he would never see? By nine, Charlie, it was difficult to put into words what you would go through, and we feared repercussions if we prepped you. There are serious prices to be paid for that, and we had already paid too much for our lost baby. I'm sorry for our silence, but what could we have said that would have made it easier?

But now I have one dying wish. I would like you to find Jennifer if you can. Be careful doing this, but not knowing was an agony your father and I could never overcome. So we pushed you both so hard, teaching you everything we could, hoping you would escape. And you did.

Charlie, you coming home is not why I did this. I can't live with what I am without your father. Please understand this. I love you both more than life itself. Without me around, they'll leave you alone. They'll have no leverage to threaten you with. But you must leave. You'll only be a puppet here. You can find out about Jennifer from the outside.

I'm happy knowing I'll be with your father now. I hope to see you when your time comes.

With all my love,
Mom

Charlie Mantel laid his head down on his mother's vanity and cried until his own eyes were puffy and swollen. His heart ached with more loss than any child should ever have to bear. A murdered father. His mother's suicide. He couldn't imagine how anyone could justify stealing a baby – his sister's twin. That moment, crouched in his mother's bedroom, an obsession was born.

* * *

"HE NOT ONLY stayed, but in less than five years, Charlie was on the panel and lined up to become Grand Dragon. He was exactly what they wanted. And he found Jennifer."

Tears slid down Jamie's face, and for the first time, John saw the bigger picture.

It's an evil world.

"So how did he get to you?" It was a simple question but an obvious one. Her brother had to have lured her back in.

"When I found out about the mass grave where Jennifer was buried with hundreds of other children, it made me sick. But I had to visit it. I was shocked they let me come and go without a single word." She paused, then started to say something. But she closed her mouth and fell silent.

"You knew how much power Charlie had then, didn't you?" John was piecing the puzzle together.

"Yes. And the phone calls started. At first he told me how finding Jennifer's grave validated the truth that there was no God. Or if there was, Charlie despised Him. Then he told me of all the changes he'd made to make The Movement more proactive and less violent. He found out the Kingsville group was the largest in the country and had always been known for its extreme violence. There were others that used their numbers in a more positive way. Several in New Mexico never committed any crimes. The initiation – playing the line – was unique to Kingsville. Not a single other division participated; some even publicly denounced it in The Movement's newsletter *Our Turn Now*."

"So what turned him? I mean, why would he become so invested in something that killed his parents, his baby sister?"

"I don't know. He said he put a stop to playing the line, but I never believed him. There was something in his voice. It took him five years to get me back to Texas. I knew he was indoctrinated in The Movement, but I missed Mom, and God, how I missed my daddy. Thinking about them was the only time I felt anything warm in my heart."

"So you came to work at Aralco to be close to Charlie, to Kingsville?"

"Yes. Taking the job was a step down, but at least Dallas was within driving distance. Maybe at first I meant to save him. And when he started working on me, it pissed me off. Then he shared what the illegal aliens were doing to our hometown, how the house we grew up in had been converted into a Chinese owned laundromat that also dealt teenagers crank. *That* really irked me. And the gangbangers – God, can you imagine? Gangbangers in Kingsville. It's laughable. They prowl on the corners where I used to roller skate. Thugs with gold-capped teeth and tattoos." Jamie laughed, but John didn't say a word. He wanted to hear her out. It didn't really make sense. Racist people killed her family, brainwashed her brother – how did that lead to *this*?

"Then he started quoting statistics about immigrants costing Americans billions in tax dollars. And how The Movement planned to eliminate welfare families sucking the town dry. I got it, that's all. And when Kyle invited me to his house for a staff picnic a few years ago, I listened, and I liked what I heard, sir. Simple as that. I saw a chance to change this god forsaken country, because if someone didn't do something soon, the whole world was going to shit."

"I guess I don't see the justification. I mean, Kyle's life was affected by a tragedy that embedded racism in his soul. But..."

"You don't get it. I'm not racist, Dr. Basinger. I wanted *them* dead. No matter what it took. Five states of The Movement, and I did what Charlie couldn't. They won't steal any more little kids, and they won't create murderers. Not anymore."

Chapter Eighteen

Dallas
Day Three

JOHN STRETCHED – HE needed a break. The madness, the justifications, churned his stomach like a blender.

"I'm going to get something to drink. You three sit tight. I'll bring you a nice warm soda."

"Uh, sir, you have to let us go. Our mission is complete, and there's no reason to hold us anymore. I mean, what good does this do? This is only day three and to our calculations, there should be around twenty-one million dead in the United States and close to ten million more worldwide. By late today, Stage II will deploy and those numbers will more than double. Why keep us here?" Nathan's pleading expression belied what he had been capable of doing.

"Because I can." John left without another word.

In the outer room, he joined Haden, who had been staring at them through the observation window.

"Damn. What do you think?" John asked.

"Christ, John, they make it sound so reasonable. It's frightening, really. And did Nathan really think you'd let him go?"

"No. And I have to find out if they can stop it, so I have to hear them out. But I need something to drink. Preferably a scotch on the rocks, but I'll stick with Diet Coke for now. Think there's any ice in the staff lounge?"

"I dunno. Maybe a little. It's chilly, so I wouldn't think it would melt too fast. We should go to the cafeteria and get some from the ice maker. I'll come with you. I'm dying for junk food. I have the janitor's keys to all the machines."

John walked down the hall, watched while Haden opened the soda machine and found five Styrofoam cups. He fisted through the water for solid cubes of ice and filled each cup.

By the time they returned to Chamber Nine, they had an assortment of chips, snack mixes, and cookies plus seven cans of soda. John waltzed back into the interrogation room with the cups of ice and three Diet Cokes.

He set a cup in front of each of them and poured slowly. He watched the foam rise, amazed that some of the little things in life would never change, like his addiction to caffeine.

"Okay, boys and girls. Here's the deal. The three of you have committed the highest form of treason. If you are twisting your motives and thinking you can rationalize it as patriotism, you neglect to realize who you have killed. Murdering government officials, possibly even the President, is a violation of the most supreme law. Think of the chaos that must be occurring on our streets as we speak. Is this what you envisioned?"

Before the words were even out of his mouth, Kyle had fallen to the floor holding his stomach, laughing so hard the veins bulged in his temples. "Ah, God, that's so fucking funny!" he squealed, rolling on the floor with exaggerated hilarity.

John analyzed the act, but decided the madness was no facade. He had a vague memory of a Roadrunner episode in which Wylie dumped a whole box of marbles only to fall on them himself. Or maybe it had been Daffy Duck; he couldn't remember.

Jamie and Nathan chuckled at their friend's antics.

Desperate times call for desperate measures.

The nine-millimeter, with a life of its own, took aim at Kyle before the kid ever saw it. The instant the chamber discharged, the report muffled and died. The effectiveness of the waffled walls intrigued John so much, he fired again.

"AHHHHHHH!" Kyle's screams were not too unlike his howling laughter.

John knew Haden had to be enjoying this immensely. The small man loved blood. The two had gone to see *Natural Born Killers* together many years back, and though John had detested the senseless depiction of violence, Haden had lapped it up like a hungry dog. *Eat your heart out, Haden. This one's for you.*

"Well, now then. Where were we?" John looked around the table, pleased with the attention he was now receiving. Kyle bawled about his hip and leg, already grating on John's nerves.

Two bullets are small potatoes compared to what you did to my wife.

"Kyle, you may have a seat if you'd like. Would you care for some help?" Now it was John's turn to laugh. An unpoliced society might be a good thing, at least for right now.

Haden Compton had run into the room when the shooting started, but John motioned him to get out. *It's my turn.* John knew he had to exert the authority to let the three know that he meant to take complete control of the situation.

Kyle looked at Haden Compton with pure terror in his eyes. It was clear that Kyle Spene, the once charming and idealist kid, had just returned to the building. A spark flared in the young chemist's eyes before he passed out.

"Okay, boys and girls, who's next?" John's sneer had a maniacal Anthony Hopkins' gleam to it – somewhat plastic, quite a bit sinister.

The silence in Chamber Number Nine was electric compared to the disregard a few minutes earlier.

"Well, well, well, seems I may have to resort to some serious tactics for your attention." John waved the revolver menacingly as his gun-hand gestured this way and that. Both sets of eyes were fixed, hypnotically following the motion of the pistol. They looked like spectators at a sci-fi tennis match.

"Uh, sir, could you please put the gun down?"

"Now, Jamie, why the hell would I do that? The world, what's left of it, would thank me if I just planted one right between your eyes. I know it'd make me feel better."

"But then you wouldn't find the answers you're looking for."

"Well, welcome to the show, Nathan. Glad you could join us."

Nathan Kirkpatrick, John knew, had to be the catalyst of the troop. His tanned good looks added to his undeniable charisma. But John was also aware of the rumors that surrounded Nathan – supposed affiliation with the NAO, an organization famed for its fascism. The company had him under close scrutiny, but obviously not close enough.

"Kyle needs a doctor, sir. He doesn't seem to be breathing." The bronzed face stared at John with authentic concern.

Good... "The boy will be fine. He's just passed out, that's all. I'll put a tourniquet on the leg in a few minutes. A little bloodletting might be cleansing for him. But your sympathy is duly noted. Shame you didn't have any of that for the millions of people you've killed."

Jamie and Nathan both looked bewildered.

"You mean to tell me you don't realize the impact of what you've done?" John watched the two closely.

"Well, yes, but it was just so necessary, sir. I can't believe you don't see it. I mean, look at our society's deterioration. The violence, my God. Gangs alone have totally destroyed our way of life. What we've done is more humane, sir, don't you see? It's not murder; it's euthanasia. Our leaders were demoralizing this nation, and truly no one was making an effort to do anything about it. Dr. Edwards was right..." Nathan's voice trailed away, but his eyes spoke loud and clear.

Who the hell is Dr. Edwards? Something about that name sounded familiar. John made a mental note to find out. Perhaps a cult leader. Maybe the three stooges were only a few pieces of the puzzle. *That's all we need, another David Koresh. Or Adolf Hitler.*

"What Nathan is saying is right, sir. Bobby knew it, too, but couldn't follow through. Our mission was to free Americans from the madness and allow the strong the opportunity to start over. The homeless who survived now have opportunities they never had before, and those who died will be better off. The sick, diseased...think how much more humane this is for them. We have eliminated the concept of wealth and power. Let those who are true leaders stand up and take charge. We will follow." Jamie looked at him with an expectant expression.

"They say in a crisis it is the underestimated who have the vision to rise above and take control, not the rich and glamorous. I can't wait to see who that's going to be. It could be you, Dr. Basinger, but quite frankly, you seem a little on the edge. That might not be the best thing for people right now. The survivors need passion, hope, and motivation. We lost that much too quickly in this country. I'm the right person for the job." Nathan paused for effect. "Sure, I'm involved with what you think of as a fascist group, but isn't that what our military is? I mean, if you don't subscribe to democracy, the armed forces seem pretty fascist to countries like Iraq, Bosnia, Vietnam. And our lovely constitution supports factions like the NAO. As mutts, we forgot where we came from, but the melting pot is in complete meltdown now. Let's see what color is left standing."

"So what is it the New American Order wants from this little science experiment, Nathan? Ethnic cleansing?"

"Oh, it's so much more than that. When I was first recruited, hell, the NAO didn't have the broad reach it needed. I gave them what they wanted."

* * *

Nathan

"BUT, MOM, YOU gotta let me go. Every other seventh grader in Nacogdoches is gettin' to go."

"Dammit, Nathan. Didn't I say no to this stupid float trip once already? Why is this so important to you?" Nathan's mom cocked her eyebrow, a frown that wrinkled her forehead. He wouldn't dare share how old it made her look. He knew what the *don't cross me* expression meant – give her two or three minutes to consider his plea and then lay the bait.

"You want me to spend the weekend with Jimmy, Luke, and Trey instead?" For a thirteen-year-old, he was a master manipulator, and he liked it. He also knew how much his mother detested the "three musketeers." Jimmy, Luke, and Trey, sophomores in high school and cool as shit, liked Nathan because he contributed mightily to their Bad Deed Society. At first, as an eight-year-old, Nathan Kirkpatrick tagged along behind the older boys like a starving puppy. His size and daring made him a hot commodity. Now they treated him like an equal, and he knew why – because he was.

"Why do you wanna go so goddamned bad? Is this a trick, Nathan, because if it is, so help me, I'll..." Monica studied her son, the smile twitching at the corners of his mouth.

He sensed her beginning to concede and went for the kill. Their relationship was more of a wheel-and-deal type, and he played her like a flute. His mother had never been the maternal type, and he had been an accident she couldn't rectify. Fixing him now was not high on her priority list. Surviving until his eighteenth birthday was.

"It's no trick, Mom. All the kids are gonna be there, and I don't want to be the only one not going. You always say no without hearing me out...you didn't even read the field trip permission slip, did you?" Nathan didn't wait for an answer. For effect, he scooted his chair back from the dinner table with a loud screech.

"Well, I...Nathan, where're you going? Get back here, I'm talking to you!"

He hustled to his bedroom and grabbed the piece of paper. He hurried back to the kitchen and slapped it on the table in front of her.

"Please, Mom, just read it. Maybe this is a trip I should take. Maybe I'll make some new friends and lose the ones you hate so much." Nathan sat back down and crammed a bite of macaroni and cheese in his mouth. He kept thinking any minute he would sprout a few inches and catch up with his classmates, but he wasn't holding his breath.

"I don't like your friends because you do bad things. I know all about this Bad Deed Society, and I think it's scary. Those three boys use you, and you don't even see it. Not to mention you're spoiled, and you're always asking for something. Just because everybody is gonna be there doesn't mean you have to be. What is the purpose of this goddamned trip?"

The proverbial door squeaked open a little farther, and he took the opportunity to wedge his foot in. Once she quit preaching, he knew she was ready to listen.

"It's a camping trip. We're going to float the Angelina River, make campfires, and hang out. Mr. Goodwin, my science teacher, Mr. Meckam, the basketball coach, and Dr. Edwards, the assistant principal, are all going. All you have to do is sign," he said, pointing to the permission slip with a pen he happened to have in his hand. "There are six other adults going – parents, I think – and most of the seventh grade class is going. Boys, I mean. Girls have a separate float trip. So I don't know why you're worried." He stopped to read her expression. "It's for community building and to get kids thinking about their future. *Read it.*"

The speech had been rehearsed, and he pulled it off just as planned.

"Let me see this permission slip. God, do you see what I mean? You are so bad!" But this time she smiled as she looked down at the piece of paper. She began to read, and he itched to know her thoughts.

He knew this had to please her, that he would spend time away from his neighborhood friends and meet boys his own age. She had bitched about the three musketeers over dinner enough that he knew it was a tool for manipulation. It was one of many lectures that serenaded him at mealtime.

They didn't talk about their day, not like most families. But they weren't most families. His father had split when Nathan was born, so he didn't hold it against her that she didn't shower him with warm-fuzzies. She nagged, griped about work or preached about how he could avoid mistakes in life. Just once he wanted a *nice job* for an A paper or a simple smile to let him know she was proud of him.

But praise was not in Monica Kirkpatrick's vocabulary. As her pen hovered over the signature line, he knew she was debating – why he wanted to go so bad versus the fact that he never participated in anything. Sports, clubs, girls – none of it. Yet he was incredibly intelligent, quite athletic even for his size, and boyishly charming.

The charm scared her the most. Ted Bundy had been charming, too, he once heard her tell her best friend on the phone. It paid to eavesdrop late at night.

"Well?" He stared at her wide-eyed. When she smiled, he returned it. She tapped the pen lightly on the table as if to punctuate her permission and scrawled her signature on the paper.

"Thanks, Mom, you're the best," he said, and kissed her quickly on the cheek. He grabbed the sheet, folded it, and crammed it in his back pocket. Though he said the words and showed affection, both of them knew the sentiment was expressed more than felt. Neither would admit it, because each felt responsible.

He had been terrified as a six-year old to learn his mom had sent her first two babies to an adoption agency in Fort Worth. She'd never planned to have kids, but she could never remember to take those tiny damn pills. She and his dad got married in college, and she dropped out to let a man take care of her. His grandmother taught her the benefits of that life. When she told Nathan the story, she even shared her philosophy about life – do enough to get what you want so in the long run you don't really have to do anything. Hadn't Nathan learned that lesson well?

* * *

"MISTAKE" WAS A seven-letter word most people toss around to describe a fumble during Friday night's game or a missed question on an exam. For Monica Kirkpatrick, to call the float trip a mistake was like describing terminal cancer as a flu bug.

When Nathan returned from the weekend excited enough to invite boys to the house, something he had never done before, she had no way of knowing the ulterior motives Dr. Edwards had when scheduling the outing. Regardless of her insensitivity, she believed most people were inherently good. That adage was proven wrong in the worst way.

The Bad Deed Society had been small potatoes. Nathan knew that. He also understood that Jimmy, Luke, and Trey talked a big talk but couldn't walk the walk. They had no intention of carrying their mission through. They had been kids playing games.

But Dr. Edwards, Coach Meckam, and Cliff Goodwin were the pillars in the local chapter of the New American Order. The NAO pretended not to be racist, claiming it held no grudges against anyone except the government and believed violence held no place in society. It was a clear and well-written mission statement.

They dreamt of an America where whites ruled and everyone else had designated areas of the country in which to live, much like reservations. Otherwise, they could go back to their homelands. It could be a peaceable arrangement, but the grand old U.S. of A. belonged to the Anglos.

None of them considered the fact that Native Americans inhabited the continent first or that many of their own quite probably had multicultural blood. That was selective knowledge. What the NAO wanted now was a youth movement, so each educator had researched and made a list of potential members.

Nathan Kirkpatrick ranked number one on each list. Though many of the elders knew of some hardcore criminal types, the potential in young Mr. Kirkpatrick excited them.

Each boy had been promised many things if they could attend the camping trip, all of which had been wildly appealing to every one of them. Some of the poorer prospects were promised money or material things – dreams and wants they had never imagined possible. The only promise they had needed for Nathan was that he would be the leader of a group and would get to exercise his desire to rule other people – with force if necessary.

The day Coach Meckam approached Nathan after fourth hour, the boy couldn't believe his ears. It was like a dream come true – a hot fudge sundae with nuts, whipped cream, and fifty cherries.

Monica had been so relieved when the time for the trip finally came because it was all Nathan had talked about for days. She sent him off with her blessing and a deep gratitude that her son was actually motivated about something other than evil doings, for no other reason than she tired of hearing neighbors complain about missing pets, maimed farm animals, and punctured tires. It was no secret that he and the bad deeders were responsible for at least some of the violence that had kept the neighborhood on edge for nearly three years.

The camping trip itself began innocently enough. The group left Friday right after school, all gathering in the teacher parking lot with their gear and enthusiasm. They set off in a caravan for Tyler, Texas. The plan was to float the Angelina River all day on Saturday and set up camp at the Sam Rayburn Reservoir by five or six o'clock. They would canoe after a home-cooked breakfast and feast on hamburgers for dinner. But Friday night was the initial test. With hot dogs grilled over a raging fire, all nestled beside Lake Tyler, the stage was set.

Each boy had duties for setting up the campsite – finding wood, pitching tents, and stoking the fire. The evening climaxed with seventy kids sitting cross-legged around the bonfire listening to ghost stories. Mr. Goodwin told awesome tales of blood and gore as each boy tuned into the sounds of the night, noises foreign and frightening to many of them.

Near the high point of one story, a rabbit rustled the bushes behind them and sent the boys into a tizzy of screams. When they saw the furry bunny, they laughed with relief. But the edginess remained, and the adults preferred it that way. The kids' fear wouldn't consume them, but it would be a chain link fence of sorts. None would wander, feel the need to explore beyond the boundaries, or test the limits the adults placed on them. The sheer joy of the night air was a freedom few of them had ever experienced.

Rising with the dawning sun, all of them worked diligently to set out for the day's eagerly anticipated float.

The canoe trip down the Angelina amazed and captivated the boys with wild animals, the calming effect of nature, the camaraderie of being with a group that had a destination requiring teamwork. Each carried a pack that contained the necessary gear and supplies to survive for the weekend. That alone boosted the confidence of many who had never been asked to contribute to anything worthwhile, especially to something as basic as survival.

The May sun provided only moderate heat, though in East Texas summer could begin anytime after March and hold a tight grip through October. But it had been a mild spring and the cicadas offered an ambiance no radio could duplicate.

When the boys surrounded the second evening's campfire, bellies full of grilled hamburgers and baked beans, Dr. Edwards addressed the group, feeling the time had come to explain the trip's purpose.

"Boys, how do you feel about the way our country is going these days?" The assistant principal paused, searched the faces for someone who might have an opinion, and continued when he was sure no one did.

"Just cut to the chase, Dr. Edwards. Why are we here? You have a reason, and it'll just be easier if you tell us." That was the Nathan the three men had hoped for – get down to the nitty gritty.

The boys' faces glowed, not only from the fire but also with admiration for Nathan who had the guts to speak up. Most of them didn't really know one another. The group consisted of misfits, ciphers, and no-names. And most were only thirteen, with a few fourteen- and fifteen-year-olds sprinkled among them.

"Well, Nathan, I guess I can do that. We're tired of America not being conducted in the best interest of true Americans. Did you boys know that your moms and dads work their butts off every day only for the government to take almost a third of what they make in taxes? Does that make sense to you? This country is supposed to be about helping those who help themselves, yet when *we* work hard they take back a portion to help support those on welfare who don't do a *thing* for themselves, many of whom don't even speak English or make an effort to support our nation. How can we justify that?"

The good doctor stopped to read the expressions of confusion, agreement, and bewilderment before him. He didn't truly expect them to understand. Not yet.

"So what's the plan? I'm sure you have one." This time a few of the boys were caught off guard by Nathan's brashness. A collective *ah* followed as they waited for Dr. Edwards to reprimand him for his disrespectful nature. That would have been the assistant principal's response at school. But this didn't seem to feel quite the same as Nacogdoches Junior High.

"Well, what we have is an organization called New American Order. The idea is to take back what is rightfully ours. The Jews have native soil they have fought over since time eternal, the Orientals have countries far more productive than our own. Heck, Japan alone far surpasses our nation's productivity and it's a fraction of the size. Russians have more land than we Americans can even comprehend, blacks have Africa, Haiti, and various other small countries. Mexicans have Mexico, and Latinos and Puerto Ricans have their own islands." Dr. Edwards paused and shook his head for effect.

"Why should these people get America too? This is our only homeland, and we're sick and tired of foreigners having better jobs and taking our food and our money. Words just aren't enough anymore; it's time to take action." He paused this time for an honest reaction. This was a concept any kid could understand.

This is mine; that's yours. Anyone crosses the line – that means war.

"So we're all you got?" Nathan couldn't imagine that a bunch of teenagers was going to solve this man's problems, fulfill this grandiose mission.

"Oh, no." Dr. Edwards chuckled. "Our adult movement is strong, Nathan. It spreads across nineteen states and requires serious man hours to handle all our business. What we want is a youth movement. And you, Nathan, are the leader we envisioned to head it. Someone to take us into the future, to offer direction to those who have none, to give strength to those in our society who don't. You're showing the tenacity we need, and quite frankly, you've got the balls to do it. We need to stand up, tell people to get the hell out of our country, and show these assholes who's boss!"

The sharp intakes of breath let Dr. Edwards know his use of profanity shocked them, as he hoped it would.

"Wow." Nathan turned to look at his peers. This sounded like it made sense, but he still didn't see the big picture.

"So, boys, what we need are men like you to work with us. Come to our meetings, help us organize, learn to shoot a gun, and belong to a movement second only to the KKK. We're not into racism or hatred per se. We believe in a USA for Americans. Let's rid our country of the fear many of us live with each day. Violence isn't our primary choice; we just want to send them all packing. They have other homelands; we don't. This is all we've got, and we're tired of sharing."

Sporadic cheers and shouts of agreement signaled the tide was turning in Dr. Edwards' favor. Nathan looked around at the deer-in-headlights expressions.

Who's he kidding? Of course they're racist. Isn't that the point? It's all bred by fear.

"My mom's afraid of me." The words escaped Nathan's lips before he realized he had spoken.

The thought came to him as a revelation. He never really wondered why she kept a gun in her bedside table. To protect the family, he assumed. But she slept with her door locked. What mother does that? He sensed her discomfort. In his gut he knew she feared him, like he was capable of bad deeds against something other than lousy house cats.

Hurting people was not foreign or repulsive to Nathan, though he didn't know if he'd ever have the guts to act on the impulse. He'd suffered blows from bullies he dreamed of disemboweling. But he would never hurt his mother. She even asked him once while watching an account of the Menendez brothers' trial for murdering their parents on A & E why he thought some kids were capable of such atrocities.

"I guess they were fed up with getting molested. That's the only way I can figure why a kid would ever hurt his mom or dad, unless they're crazy like that kid who killed his parents then took a gun to school and shot a bunch of his classmates. I don't know."

He had then snuggled up next to her wishing he could say, "Hey, mom, whether you know it or not, I love you." Of course the words never came out, but he hoped she felt it.

"Why do you think that, Nathan?" Coach Meekam spoke for the first time the entire evening. He loomed over them, somewhere near seven feet tall with the bushiest hair Nathan had ever seen on a white man. And the big man's eyes were too close together, making him look like Lurch from *The Addam's Family*.

"She keeps a gun in her drawer by her bed. She sleeps with her bedroom door locked. I dunno, I can just tell. But I'd never hurt her." He hesitated, almost thinking out loud. "I guess she sees my crappy future, realizes I don't have any goals, and probably knows that my biggest dream is a Friday night party with booze and a girl to lose my virginity to."

Laughter startled him. He grinned famously and knew he could grow accustomed to all these people revering him. Having them hanging on his every word and responding to his thoughts like he was someone important appealed to him in a way he never dreamed possible.

"I guess what it all boils down to is that if you don't have money and you don't show off what you can do on a ball field, you're kind of a nobody. And that pisses me off because I don't agree with whoever made those stupid rules. I sure as hell didn't. And you're right. This is our country, yet some Wetback just got a promotion over my mom just because she says the company had to meet some minority percentage. That sucks, and we shouldn't have to play second fiddle to anyone!" He'd heard that expression in a movie once.

The boys cheered rowdily as Nathan turned to them. His right fist pumped in the air and got a continual reaction each time he thrust it higher.

Dr. Edwards, Coach Meckam, and Mr. Goodwin side-glanced each other, and their smiles spoke their approval across the campfire. Nathan's mind reeled with the possibilities, mingled with a tinge of fear. But he thrived on fear, yearned for it. And he welcomed it because at least it proved he could feel.

* * *

BY THE END of the school year, Monica Kirkpatrick was patting herself on the back, certain the camping trip was the best decision she had ever made. Nathan went from mediocre grades to the honor roll, thanks to the tutor Dr. Edwards had gotten for her son. Over the course of the summer, Nathan played Babe Ruth baseball, went hiking with his new friends, then to Six Flags, NASA, and a day trip to see the Rangers play the Mariners. Any of the boys who came to the house were polite, friendly and *normal*.

When Nathan started eighth grade, she was beside herself with joy and relief at her son's achievements. He no longer needed a tutor to top the honor roll. Making the basketball and track teams allowed Nathan to excel in sports and boosted a confidence she had never seen in him. He developed physically, growing almost six inches in three years, finally made time for a girlfriend, and seemed to have the world by the tail. For the first time in her life, she had a boy any mother would be proud of and to her relief, she was proud. Her son's transformation had been nothing short of a miracle.

Junior high success gave way to realistic dreams of college. Prep courses Monica never dreamed possible for Nathan popped up on his projected high school plan. Doors opened and his future seemed as bright as a firefly in a blackout. She splurged on a state-of-the-art computer, equipped with all the extras. It linked him to a world he ultimately would rule.

In high school, Nathan achieved every goal he set for himself. Monica ignored the rumors of the militia forming among the youth of Nacogdoches. She preferred burying her head in the sand.

The teen movement made the news, though no footage aired since all were minors. The town gossip speculated that these young people were affiliated with the radical New American Order that had arisen after David Koresh failed in Waco and Timothy McVeigh pulled off the Oklahoma City bombing. Talk of something similar to Kingsville's Movement made the entire town nervous. Secretly, many knew it had been around long before that and would outlast the flash-in-the-pan groups rising and falling yearly.

Monica feared Nathan might be involved, but she silenced the thoughts and turned from the mirror every time she faced it. Something had given him direction, motivated him, and an obvious male influence had taken over his life. She prayed it was simply a part of his growing up, responding to coaches and teachers. As long as he didn't hurt anyone, she could deal with the idea that he might have become a fascist. There were worse things – drugs, gangs, perverted sex acts. What harm could there be in a little extremist philosophy?

She often checked his bedroom for Confederate flags, swastikas, or any other telltale signs of radical worship but never discovered anything of the sort. He was too smart for that. By his senior year, Monica had evaded her mirror for three years and had stopped searching his room.

* * *

WHEN NATHAN KIRKPATRICK graduated near the top of his class from Nacogdoches High, he had been manning the helm of the largest youth movement in the country for nearly two years. The NAO required that he attend college so he could move into the twenty-first century with the intellectual tools required.

The highest-ranking officials across the southernmost five states admired the near-four hundred strong following Nathan had accrued and knew he would someday inherit the throne of his mentor. Dr. Edwards would retire from his section within a few years, opening the door for Nathan. He had leaped every hurdle and crossed every T laid out for him.

What Nathan had to offer after graduating from UTEP was far beyond anyone's comprehension. He began his work in the professional world, earning a living and making contacts, but grew miffed by the weakness of so many who ran the major corporations –

spineless men who viewed themselves as giants. Their conceit and false nobility repulsed him.

* * *

"YOU WERE THE first man of power who earned my respect, Dr. Basinger. When you interviewed me, I was thrilled. I'd heard about Aralco all my life, and when I learned of your innovative vision and the contracts you had with the government for chemical warfare – well, honestly, sir, it was my wet dream."

"And I recruited you with fervor – unnecessarily, I guess. We had the means; you had the motive."

"Yes. And once I took the biochemist position, I refined my manipulation to an art form. You'd be amazed how many of your employees sympathize with my philosophy. I mean, everyone knows the country is falling apart, with battle scars from the war on drugs, gang warfare at an all-time high, the economy floundering nationwide, terrorism an everyday threat. Actors, singers, and athletes beating their wives, molesting kids. Hell, you can't watch the ten o'clock news without getting nauseous. So I started small. You know my philosophy, John?"

Dr. Basinger shook his head. He didn't miss that Nathan went from addressing him respectfully to using his first name. Everything with Nathan was a power play, a game of tactics.

"I've got this poster on my office wall that says, *Griping about the shitty world is like sitting in a rocking chair – you expend a lot of energy, but you don't ever get anywhere.* I got tired of not getting anywhere."

Kyle moaned. Jamie looked from her boss to her accomplice lying on the floor, his blood splattered around him.

"So you recruited my employees until you came up with the four of you."

"Yes."

"So where's Bobby?"

Chapter Nineteen

Dallas
Day Three

NATHAN LAID HIS head down, the emotion evident on his face.

"This is your fault, you stupid bitch!" he snapped. Jamie jumped away from the table.

"Fuck you, Nathan. You're the one who screwed up. Don't lay that shit on me. I should be in Waco right now with my brother."

"You fell in love. God, women are so fucking weak. You and Bobby just couldn't keep your hands off each other. Jesus. This mission was too big for trivial shit."

John watched the two argue, studying their faces. To call them serial killers seemed a little like dubbing Hitler a radical. But it was a strange comfort to see them torture each other.

"Jamie? You and Bobby were an item?" John saw a glimmer of conscience, of humanity, in the girl's eyes.

"He was a nice guy. I mean, his baby sister nearly drowned right in front of him when he was ten. He thought it was his fault. He and his best friend Max were swimming in a lake in Lewisville, and his seven-year-old sister tagged along. Max got tired trying to swim to a floating dock and Bobby screamed for people to help. While they splashed around trying to save his friend, Samantha went under. They got to her finally, but there was extensive brain damage. He's taken care of her ever since. It killed their parents – they were never the same. Bobby, he, um, he had such a heart. And when we started Operation Meltdown, he...he balked. He got scared. And I loved him for that." Jamie dropped her head, but not before John saw the tears. "Then that day, Day One, everything just went wrong. But we still got X-86 launched. And now, I'm glad."

A shiver ran down John's spine at the tone of Jamie's voice.

"You're talking about him in the past tense. What happened to Bobby?"

"Huh, like you care. He was, he, I mean, Bobby...God..." Jamie stuttered, then started talking, oblivious that Nathan was trying to shut her up and Kyle had begun crying on the floor. John would have to give Mr. Spene a painkiller and dress those wounds. But for now, he sat and listened.

* * *

"YO, KYLE, YOU got the configuration ready for Stage II, III, and IV?"

"Almost, Nathan. Just about ready to blow," Kyle joked, but no one laughed.

The four of them hustled about the lab, tying up loose ends. Bobby tapped keys on his laptop and blurted countdown details while Jamie recorded the data. Kyle finalized the coordinates and smacked the enter button without fanfare. Nathan gave an "Oh, yeah!" as he finished uploading the computer virus.

"It's a go." Kyle plopped into a chair and let out a long sigh. He smiled and put his feet up on the desk. "Who's got the champagne?"

"This isn't a game, Kyle," Bobby barked. "You think our families, no matter how safe we've made them, are having fun now?"

"Our mission isn't for fun, *Bobby*. Your soft side makes me wanna puke. You got the satellite situated? My end is done. No turning back now. The only catch is that you bozos get your jobs done."

"Girls, girls, girls, quit bickering. Here's what I got." Nathan turned the Mac computer screen so the other three could see. "Uh, coordinates for Friday, 3:17 a.m. – go." He clicked on the *deploy* button. "Next is Saturday at 12:45 p.m. – go. Monday and Wednesday are both set for noon – go. Then Friday through Saturday, midnight, and they are –" Nathan typed furiously, then pecked the keyboard hard enough to shake the desk. "Go."

He let out a harsh *hoo-yaw*!

"Objectives are met, right, Bobby?" Kyle swiveled in his roller chair to see Bobby and Jamie passing a piece of paper. Both jumped.

"Uh, just a sec." Bobby palmed the scrap of paper, busied himself at his computer and printed the final details.

"Let me see that," Kyle ordered. "Now."

Nathan turned to see what was going on.

Bobby stuttered, starting to read the printout, but Nathan yanked it from his hands and read it aloud.

"Release at one hundred percent saturation, target cities, every other day until the sixth launch is completed on the eighth day. By then, the global ramifications should be complete." Nathan smiled. "Looks good, Bobby. *Now* we can celebrate."

"Not until I read that note." Kyle stood, pulled the Glock from his waistband, and walked over to Bobby. "Give it to me."

"Jesus, what are you? Mrs. Hillerby in fourth hour Spanish? Sorry, ma'am, I promise I won't ever pass notes again." But Bobby's attempt at humor didn't cover the tremor in his voice.

Kyle reached down, grabbed Bobby's hand with brute force, and pried his fist open. Kyle read the small scrap of receipt, and a cloud of anger washed over his face.

I can't do it. I embedded a back door with the code OpMeltdownStageV. We can stop this.

He'd felt this type of betrayal only once before, and that Benedict Arnold's body lay at the bottom of a quarry. Below the first message, Jamie had answered, *How?*

"Well, how quaint. Nathan, there's a back door. Get logged in, *quick*. I didn't come this far for a pissant like *you*," he hissed at Bobby, "to fuck it up. Here's the password."

Nathan scowled, read the note and shoved Bobby to the floor. Before Bobby could get up, Nathan stomped on his chest and held him there. "You sniveling little weasel. How dare you." Rage gripped the NAO leader and before he could regain control, he reached down and grabbed Bobby's head. He slammed it against the floor, ignoring Bobby's howls of pain and Jamie's screams.

"Oh, God, Nathan, stop! What're you doing? My God, I had to give us an out, just in case," Bobby babbled as Nathan clutched him by the ears.

"NATHAN! DON'T!" Jamie screamed. But in that split second, Nathan snapped Bobby's neck and then looked up at her with the most sadistic grin she'd ever seen on a human being.

"BOBBY!" She collapsed at his side and pulled him into her arms. "No, Bob...Bobby, I'm sorry. Oh, God, you wanted so much to make me happy. I'm s...sorry." Her breath hitched with the sobs.

"Jamie. Get up. This is it, and you're either with us or not. If not, get out."

She looked up at Kyle, her eyes too blurry to make out his expression. She stared, trying to make sense of what this good-looking blond man was saying to her. Was he kidding? Didn't he know the man she loved had just gotten his neck broken by a sadistic, fascist pig who meant to destroy the world? She almost laughed out loud at the drama of it.

This isn't happening. What was I thinking?

She smiled as if she had just won the Miss America Pageant, ear to ear and all paste. Her smile wavered as she spoke but both Kyle and Nathan accepted her abrupt I'm fine.

Thank God, look what that had gotten Bobby.

"Kyle, phases are all linked, launch is set, computer is now on autopilot and we're good to go. I deleted the back door, so there's no turning back now. Let's get to Waco. Everyone should be there waiting for us. God, I bet they can't believe we're really doing it." Nathan's eyes looked radiant.

* * *

"SO YOU GUYS had a get away planned. That got nipped by Jack Barnes, didn't it?" John let out a harsh laugh, pleased as punch that a friend of his had thwarted their escape.

"And you blew my chance to see the satisfaction on Dr. Edwards' face." Nathan shook his head.

"Why Waco? Have a little David Koresh envy?"

"It has nothing to do with Koresh. He thought small. But the Branch Davidians built smart. There are barracks in an underground chamber in the field behind Koresh's sacred compound. We notified ninety-one people on Tuesday to get there – no questions asked, but they knew it was serious. We have a code." Nathan smiled.

"Your mother there, Nathan? Your brother, Jamie?" John looked from one to the other.

"If she's there, she's probably madder than a wet cat, but better pissed and alive than a statistic." Nathan turned to Jamie.

"Charlie won't be there. He didn't believe me. When I tried to explain, he just laughed. The four of us agreed we wouldn't reveal any details, for security measures, so all I ended up doing was feeding his paranoia. He thinks everything's a ploy to get him away from Kingsville." She dropped her head. John suspected both needed to be pushed now, while emotions were close to the quick.

"Kyle have family and friends coming too?" John looked at Mr. Spene propped against the wall with an expensive tie wrapped tightly around his leg. Haden insisted on a dressing for the hip wound that on closer inspection had pierced at an angle an inch deep and passed on through. The gunshot to the knee was another story – the bullet had lodged near the bone and neither of them wanted the kid to die that way. That was too easy, too quick. So they fed him antibiotics to prevent infection and kept the wound wrapped and clean.

"Yes, Kyle and Bobby both. We'll still honor Bobby's invitations – we owe him that much. Kyle has fifteen or sixteen, I think. Bobby has three." Jamie made no effort to wipe the single tear streaming down her cheek.

"So did Barnes walk in and see Bobby?" John was trying to piece together the sequence of events and why no one had told him about Bobby's death. As soon as all of it made sense, he could dispense a little justice.

"Barnes is an idiot. He just waltzed into the lounge like he was invited. Shit, if the moron had accepted Jamie's answer, he'd be alive right now. Well, unless the X-86 bug bit him." Nathan chuckled.

Shit. They killed Barnes too?

"And – and we had just popped open a bottle of Dom, you know, to celebrate. Jamie was being stupid and sentimental by getting out an extra plastic glass for Bobby, so when we told Barnes that Bobby had just slipped off to the little boys' room, he bought it. Then he had to go get personal." Nathan glared at Jamie. "That asshole thought he was some hot shit. I guess I showed him."

* * *

JACK BARNES CASED the room. Nathan followed the research analyst's gaze. The bottle of Dom Perignon, four glasses – *nice touch, Jamie* – and Bobby's printout laying there for every goober and Gomer to see.

"So what're you celebrating?" Jack's graying mustache made him look much older than he was. Gaunt features and close-cropped hair gave him a military look that everyone knew he liked. His research team had no knowledge of the top secret government-backed programs the four of them had infiltrated, and that lack of access drove him crazy.

"Um, we, God, it's sort of a secret," Kyle stuttered. Barnes took another step into the room, now less than ten feet from the printout on the table with Operation Meltdown information on it. "What're you doin' up here, Jack? You solve *Farm & Home's* biggest dilemma by gettin' rid of every strain of worm known to man?"

The three of them tried to stifle their laughter as Jack's face reddened. Mr. Macho stiffened, puffed his chest out to exert himself.

"Not everyone gets a government grant to fund the newest version of Agent Orange. You four may be smart, but some of us work hard. We don't get the top secret military-funded projects you young punks do."

Operation Delta, the job they ditched to go solo, wasn't nearly as exciting as everyone cracked it up to be. But the Agent Orange comment was a little close to home for Kyle.

"Oh, kiss my ass, Jack. Just because you work with worms and bugs all day, don't take it out on us." Kyle's voice quickened as Barnes caught a glimpse of the papers.

Jamie looked from Kyle to Nathan, to the wall that Bobby lay behind and then back to the pages Jack tried to pretend he wasn't reading.

"So what's this big secret you guys're celebratin'?" Jack motioned toward the champagne.

He's tryin' to distract us so he can read that. Jamie grabbed a glass and handed it to Jack.

"Here, toast with us. I just told the boys about me and Bobby. I knew they already had an idea, but I, uh, we wanted to make it official." Jamie smiled and lifted her glass to her lips. She couldn't swallow, not with Bobby's warm body around the corner. Her hand trembled and Barnes saw it.

"So you spend a hundred and twenty bucks on a *Hey, guys, I've found me a man* toast? Do I look like an idiot? You went to dinner with me less than four months ago, so how serious could this be?" Barnes leveled his gaze at Jamie and wouldn't let go.

Neither did she. "Bobby and I announced our engagement. That was worth much more than a hundred dollars to us. And you, *Jack*, were a pity date. Sorry."

"You little bitch. You really are an ice queen, aren't you? So, where's Bobby then? Long time to be in the bathroom." He touched the champagne bottle, then tapped the edge of the table, his fingers tapping closer to the papers as if they were walking toward them.

"Uh, Barnes, do you mind? We'd like a little privacy here." Kyle took a step toward him.

"I thought your project was called Operation Delta. What's Operation Meltdown?" Jack picked up the sheet, a blunt move for someone with such limited clearance.

"Shit, Kyle, do something," Jamie whispered. "We don't have time for this. We've only got a few hours to get out of here and to Waco."

"Jack, there's a reason you don't have access to our project. It's top secret. But you're so damned nosey. Who sent you up here? Someone have you come try to get a peek of our project? You wantin' to steal our thunder?"

Jack glared from one to the other and back again. The clock on the wall ticked menacingly. Each tick-tock made Nathan's fingers twitch until he began drumming them on the table.

"You three are up to somethin'. I'm not sure what it is, but you're way too nervous for this to be just a celebration for Jamie. You've been strange all week."

Nathan stopped tapping. Kyle's head turned pointedly to look at him, but Nathan stared intently at Jack and rubbed his temples. The fine-tuning after a year of obsessive tests for the deadliest weapon known to mankind had taken its toll on all of them.

And then Jack blew it.

"Fess up, Nathan. You're a fascist and everyone knows it. This is some kinda recruiting party, isn't it? You pulling these two into your right-wing KKK? God, I just can't imagine how you believe all that sh..." Jack's voice broke when Nathan pulled the gun from the holster inside his jacket.

"You couldn't take a polite *get the fuck outta the room*, could you? Why're you so fucking nosey? Your mom ever teach you any manners?" Spittle flew from Nathan's lips.

"God, put that thing away, Nathan. What's up your butt? Can't take a little joke?"

"Ya know, Jack, you've got a big mouth. Joke, my ass. If you coulda just let it go. But no, you had to show up and butt in. Can't be left outta nothin'. Put your hands on the goddamned table where I can see them."

Jack didn't move. Nathan scooted his chair back with a screech. Barnes sensed the change in atmosphere and placed his hands reluctantly on the table. His brow furrowed and eyes narrowed.

"Bobby's not coming back, is he? What'd you do to him? I thought he was one of you...you know, part of the Fab Four. Jamie, I thought Bobby was your man?" Jack's voice hit a feverish pitch, nerves exposed and fear gleaming in his eyes.

"Shut up," Jamie snipped.

"I wanna shoot off a finger and see if you're really as macho as you put on all the time. Who's the man now, Jack?"

Kyle and Jamie stared at Nathan in disbelief.

* * *

MARCUS DEVINEAUX SAT at his security desk on the tenth floor surrounded by monitors. His eyes froze on number five. It displayed a scene so unreal, he had a brief lapse thinking it was a TV show. With frantic hands, he dialed Haden Compton's office.

Mr. Compton didn't believe Marcus at first.

"Come again?"

Marcus repeated his frantic assessment. Nathan Kirkpatrick had a gun pointed at Jack Barnes' hand.

Three minutes later, Haden stood beside him staring at the terminal. Haden still couldn't believe what he was seeing. When the bullet pierced Jack's right hand, severing his index finger, Haden and Marcus jumped even without the sound effects. Chaos ensued, phone calls pulled security from all floors to the hallway outside the staff lounge, but no one had been able to reach Dr. Basinger. He was out of town at a conference in Detroit.

Inside the staff lounge, the game played out with Nathan oblivious to the camera or the eleven security guards with their revolvers poised and ready to fire the second the door opened.

* * *

"STOP BLUBBERING, JACK, it's only one goddamn finger. Jesus."

"Shit, Nathan, we need to get the hell outta here. What's the matter with you? You're gonna get security in here, and then we're fucked." Kyle got Nathan's attention and head-nodded toward Bobby's body around the corner. "Remember?" Aware of Nathan's short fuse and how it impaired sane judgment, he approached his partner carefully. Jamie, less patient, marched toward him, grabbed the gun from Nathan's hand, and slapped him hard across the face.

"You moron, a silencer doesn't make it okay to just shoot people for being assholes. Let's get the hell out of here before it's too late."

Nathan laughed in Jamie's face. He literally let out a bellow of laughter that made her jerk away from him. She could smell the champagne on his breath.

"Oh, yeah, how silly of me to think hurting innocent people isn't okay. How about a few billion of them instead?" His smirk made Jamie think about what she had said, and she laughed in spite of herself. It did sound ludicrous.

Jack Barnes, through immense pain and an overwhelming need to pass out, took the conversation in but couldn't make sense of it.

"Let's go, boys. We're wasting valuable time. It now means life or death. We don't really know for sure if the tests on ourselves will be the same in mass doses. I'd rather not find out the hard way, how 'bout you?" Nathan swiped the gun from Jamie's hand and pointed it at Jack as they backed toward the door. "C'mon. Time to go. Jack, I hope you have, um, certain characteristics that make you immune to harsh chemicals." Nathan snickered as he reached for the door handle.

Somewhere in the hallway, he heard a muffled walkie-talkie say, "They're coming."

After that, everything moved in slow motion. Kyle opened the door and was thrown to the linoleum. Someone slammed Jamie down beside him. Nathan's gun hand came up to aim, but a sharp blow across his wrist sent the weapon flying. Before any of them could scream or resist, they were handcuffed and hog-tied face down, left to inspect the seams in the floor.

* * *

"WELL, BET YOU were thrilled that someone survived your funky little chemical or you would have starved to death in here." John smirked. To his knowledge, Haden, Kenny Jenkins, and Richard Deeks were the only executives who survived Stage I.

"I'm thinkin' we might have figured out a way to get out."

"Well, anywhere you go now is going to be with me. And I'm thinking once we get past these eight days, there are going to be some survivors eager to catch a glimpse of you. May make for an interesting trial." John cackled. He looked from Nathan who sat with a sinister grin on his own face to Jamie, still distraught over Bobby and a guilty conscience, then to Kyle half out of it leaning against the wall. The tourniquet – a four hundred dollar Versace tie – was soaked with blood.

"Or lynching," John added, and left the room to let the image fester.

Part Three
Truth & Consequences

"I saw a vision of a world about to come,
and a world about to go."
– Li-Young Lee

Chapter Twenty

Worldwide
Day Three

WHEN THE SECOND release of X-86 hit the next fifty cities late Saturday, jet streams had already dealt the initial blow to many. By the weekend, the world was in the grip of global panic.

Tokyo declared a state of emergency when over ten million of Japan's population perished by four o'clock Saturday afternoon. Other major cities – Paris, Berlin, London, Moscow, Sydney, Peking, Johannesburg, Stockholm – brought in the military, chemical emergency crews, and religious leaders to administer last rites for thousands lined up on church pews, gymnasium floors, city sidewalks. Kenya utilized a shelter once designed for starving children to house the dead and dying. Starvation was no longer the leading cause of death in third-world countries.

Friday, before X-86 crossed the ocean, television broadcasts worldwide reported the horrific terrorist attack on the world's most powerful country. For some, it was the cause for celebration. Al-Qaida reported it as "The Ultimate Revenge." Solemn leaders who once feared and despised the United States rejoiced in the powerful country's fall, no matter how short-lived. Pakistani rebels cheered in the streets on Friday, but the same area fell eerily silent on Saturday.

Headlines worldwide screamed of the injustice of how an American chemical plant could jeopardize the entire planet. Armageddon wasn't universal in language but the concept was.

Американский мертвая голова, смертный, the Moscow Times declared, reporting X-86 as Яд мировой, a worldwide poison. The *American Death* heading circulated throughout the city, but too many Russian residents had met their maker during the day to read it or understand its global impact.

The final printing of the Berliner Zeitung Saturday evening led with a single statement – Amerikaner überschatten Tyrannei Hitlers, die Welt, die durch Panik ergriffen wird – *Americans overshadow Hitler's tyranny; world seized by panic.* Only one sentence followed: Unito Dichiara ed armageddon della faccia del mondo – *United States and world face Armageddon.* There were no other stories, advertisements, nothing. The single page had been run on newsprint, but not with the expertise the world renowned press was known for. Most of the German employees had taken a permanent leave of absence.

"El pánico mundial, millones temió absolutamente," the Spanish speaking world read, but couldn't comprehend the totality of its meaning. *Worldwide panic; millions feared dead.* The Mexico City news terrified twenty-two million people – or at least those left with enough sense to acknowledge it.

Lisbon's premier newspaper, Correio da Manha, informed Portuguese residents, "Nos oito dias seguintes, o mundo terminará como nós o sabemos." A Portuguese ambassador, shocked by the American act of terrorism, fell into his chair. He read it again. *In the next eight days, the world will end as we know it.* Then came a short piece on a new phenomenon – an ability to hear thoughts on a frequency clear of radio waves and satellite communications. Not everyone possessed it, but many who did wished they could turn it off.

The ambassador didn't have the hootzpah to do it on his own, not since watching his precious daughter collapse into the swimming pool and his wife dig at her throat until the inability to breathe left her dead on the kitchen floor. He screamed, unable to help them, oblivious to the weight of what was happening to the world. Instead, he pulled the Smith and Wesson K.22 pistol from his desk drawer, checked the clip. Before he could second guess himself, he shoved the barrel in his mouth and pulled the trigger.

All over the world, the word that dominated the remaining forms of media said it all.

Turkey plastered *son* on single-page newsletters. A Croatian leader uttered *smrt* to the few left in his nation to hear him. In Sweden, a former tennis superstar repeated Död over and over until it lost meaning. The only station reporting the news said it was all they had to look forward to – *death* – courtesy of X-86 and its creators. The Pope scribbled a message in his final moments of suffocation. "Il dio li aiuta tutti," and the world shared his sentiments.

By the end of day two and the wave of fifty more cities, the Pope's prophecy couldn't reach the world's six and a half billion people. On only the third day, the population had been reduced by nearly sixty percent.

The idea that there were five more days and as many releases of X-86 boggled survivors' minds. A little girl in St. Louis and a young widower in South Carolina prayed for someone with the Pope's clout to get the attention of a higher power. The words conveyed the sense of helplessness everyone felt.

God help us all.

Chapter Twenty-One

St. Louis
Day Three

JESSIE AND MATTHEW dropped their bikes near the front porch and plodded into the living room without speaking. After nearly three days away from home, Jessie didn't have the energy to relish the moment or to miss her daddy. And Matthew didn't marvel or say a word about the size of the house, the hot tub or swimming pool. Jessie plucked a pillow and blanket from the downstairs hall closet for Matthew so he could crash on the couch, and she headed upstairs on legs that felt like lead weights.

"G'night, Jess," Matthew called out. "Or good afternoon."

She mumbled a response and hobbled to her bedroom. The sight of her things – Buzz Lightyear, Barbie's cottage, bright pink CD player complete with karaoke – made her feel like she was in a dream. Nothing looked like hers anymore. Only the pink canopy bed was appealing, so she crawled onto it without bothering to undress. She didn't have the heart to remove the St. Louis Cardinals T-shirt anyway Within seconds, despite the midday sunshine, she fell fast asleep. Overcome with exhaustion, she slipped into dreams of travelers, a small Missouri parking lot covered with tent tops, and a sinister shadow darkening the skies above it. Even deep in sleep, she shivered.

When the phone rang, it yanked her from a depth she would attempt to recall for Matthew, certain it was a vision of the future. She fumbled to free herself from covers that wrapped her like an egg roll. After nearly twenty rings, she grabbed the cordless in the upstairs office, disoriented and out of breath.

"Jessie?" Bryan's voice penetrated the fog.

"Bryan!" In her exhaustion, she'd forgotten he was going to call and check on them, and it occurred to her that he said he might be there late Saturday.

Wasn't this Saturday? She thought so but couldn't be sure. She peeked out the curtains to see the brilliant orange and red of the setting sun. She had slept for several hours.

"Hi, sweetie. It's been a heckuva trip. Tons of wrecks and just rough drivin'." His voice fell silent, and Jessie sensed there were things he wasn't telling her.

"You're still comin' though, right?" She couldn't get inside his head over the phone, but she wished she could. There were so many things she wanted to know about her mother.

"Oh, absolutely. Should be there some time tomorrow. Hard to say. Once I hit big cities, I have to navigate pretty carefully. I-44 isn't exactly a picnic anyway. Oh, well, more importantly, I guess you made it okay. Have you been there long?"

"Uh, I'm not sure what time it is. We got in this afternoon and have been sleeping ever since. I..."

"Did you say *we*?" Bryan interrupted. There was a strange tone to his words.

"Uh, yeah. I met this boy," she started, and then explained how she met Matthew. By the time she finished, Bryan understood and told her to sit tight until he got there.

"Don't take in anymore strays, you got it?"

"Yes, sir!" she answered, teasing him for being so worried and amazed how comfortable she felt talking to a man she had never met. It was the immediate comfort of an adult in charge.

"I'll call and check in this evening to let you know where I'm stopping to sleep, okay? I'm hoping to hit Springfield early tomorrow morning. If so, I'm just a few hours away. But I'll call and let you know. There's a radio station on the air you two might tune into." Bryan told her to write down the dial number and said goodnight.

When she got off the phone, she returned to her room for fresh clothes. She washed her face with the hottest water she could stand, brushed her teeth, and pulled her ratty hair into a ponytail. It was nearly dark out, and she was relieved the lights worked.

When she trudged downstairs, Jessie got her first taste of the oppressive silence. Riding on its coattails was the realization that she would not be greeted by her father. He wouldn't be scrambling eggs for what he called brinner – breakfast for dinner – and he wouldn't be razzing her about bed head the way he always did. Tears sprang to her eyes and suddenly the emptiness of her home made her feel hollow and angry.

"Matthew?" She saw the rumpled sheets and blankets on the living room couch and hoped her new friend hadn't flown the coop. She liked the company and didn't think she could stand the empty house without him. But what she really wanted right now was for her daddy to wrap his strong arms around her and make the whole world go away.

"Matthew?" she called again.

"I'm out here," came a faraway voice.

Jessie smiled. It was downright cold, but Matthew raved about the swimming pool, so she knew the odd August chill wouldn't stop him.

"Feels great. Hop in!" Matthew's glistening face disappeared as he dove for imaginary treasure at the bottom of the deep-end. Jess marveled at his swimming ability, as he slithered through the water, his dark body lacing from end to end.

With the lack of inhibition most eight-year-old girls possess, Jessie stripped off her sweat pants and plunged in with T-shirt and panties. The water, crisp but refreshing, rinsed the bad feelings away.

"Here, can you get it before I do?" Matthew grinned, his bright white teeth gleaming in the dusk. He tossed a coin into the deep end and gave Jessie a second to dive through the water for it. He dove deep and, like a fish, quickly caught and passed her. He spied the quarter, picked it up from the light blue-pebbled bottom, and glided to the surface.

For thirty minutes, they played shark, chased the quarter, and compared dives. When the moon cleared the tops of the trees, Matthew challenged her to a race for the kitchen. She didn't take the bait, but both agreed it was time to eat. Jessie sat on the pool's edge wrapped in a plush bath towel wishing someone could whip up dinner and call her to the table like in her before life. Instead she padded into the kitchen in her cold bare feet and examined the contents of the refrigerator.

"Hey, I could scramble some eggs and microwave some bacon." Jessie pulled out the carton of eggs and waited for his answer. His thoughts were cloudy to her now that she was home – maybe the open air heightened her ability. She wasn't sure, but she was glad. She didn't tell Matthew about it because it scared her and made her feel like a thief.

"Ooh, I love breakfast for dinner. My momma used to grill pancakes that would melt in your mouth. Um." He fell silent, and Jessie watched his expression change. But if pain lingered there, he hid it well. "You ever cook eggs before, girl? They ain't easy."

She had made it abundantly clear there was little she couldn't do, so she knew he wouldn't challenge her. The precocious little girl who fixed a eighty-year-old Victrola could match wits with anyone.

"No, but I watched Daddy, and it didn't look hard." She opened a fresh package of bacon and peeled off six slices.

"You're gonna burn the house down," Matthew said with a laugh, but followed her directions and grabbed the skillet from a cabinet and the bacon rack from the top of the refrigerator. He then began to fiddle with the radio but had no luck in finding a station. He asked her twice what station Bryan had been listening to, but couldn't find it. When he started to ask a third time, she threw a towel at him.

Twenty minutes later, they savored the cheesiest scrambled eggs, crispest bacon, and most jellied toast either had ever had. The occasional crunch of eggshell didn't deter their enjoyment; it made them laugh. Both burped and rubbed full stomachs when they finished, content with the first of many meals they would have to cook on their own.

"You know what I noticed?" Matthew got up and went to the back sliding glass doors and opened them. "Listen."

Jessie furrowed her brow. "I don't hear anything." She couldn't even hear him anymore, and she wondered if her powers were going away.

"Exactamundo. There's like no noise. No sounds at all. Think about how you normally hear cars, music, kids, anything. It's nine o'clock on a Saturday night."

Jessie sat and listened. Uneasiness settled in her stomach, churning the eggs and bacon with a dose of fear. She wished Bryan would hurry.

While they sat contemplating the silence, a dog's frenzied bark made Jessie jump.

"Whoa, what was that? You have a dog? He sounds close!" Matthew yanked open the screen and whistled sharply.

"No, but most of the neighbors do. Daddy said it was cruel to have a puppy if you weren't home enough to take good care of it. You see him?" Both peeked out the back door, now paranoid at the prospect of monsters.

The rapid barks shattered the silence again, this time so close that Matthew slammed the screen shut. Both knew it could be rabid; they had seen plenty of strange things in their hours on the road, including snarling dogs and hissing cats, but most they had seen were dead. As they peered into the night, a shaggy dog straggled through the backyard, stumbled near the hot tub and almost fell in. His ribs were starkly defined in the moonlight and the glow from the pool lights, and his coat was matted with mud. Drool hung from his mouth in a stream, and he turned to look at them with a movement so weak, Jessie couldn't imagine this dog barking the way they had heard. His fur appeared gray, but in the dark it was hard to tell.

"Here, boy, you thirsty for something other than pool water?" she called. The mutt had to be thigh high on her, but she didn't care. She ran around the island in the center of the kitchen, grabbed a bowl and filled it with water. The dog knew the word – she saw that he was smart like her – and came to the back door and sat down on his bony haunches. Matthew inched the screen open so Jessie could set the bowl gently in front of him, trying not to startle the dog. Before she could step back, he lapped at the water with a fervor that broke her heart.

"Oh, God, he's thirsty. Here, Matthew – eggs. Get him our plates. Throw on the last piece of bacon. And, and, and the toast, too. He might like that on his tummy."

It took the mongrel nearly thirty seconds to slather the plate clean. He looked up, eager to put on more of a show if there was anything else they wanted clean. They both laughed and raced around the kitchen. Jessie cut up a few pieces of bologna while Matthew broke open a bag of chips.

"He's had breakfast. Now let's feed him a little lunch." Jessie giggled and turned to head toward the door, but when she about-faced, the mutt stood in the middle of the dining room. "I think he's adopting us."

She scooted the plate toward him, and he obliged her by scarfing everything on it. His huge tongue got the last of the chips and then mopped the area around the plate, just in case he'd missed any.

"That's all, boy. We don't wanna make you sick." Jessie stepped carefully toward the back door so she could close and latch the screen. She felt exposed and wondered what else roamed about in the night. The thought made her shiver.

"We can get dog food at the gas station tomorrow. I bet they got some. It might not be as good as eggs and bologna, but hey, beggars can't be choosers, right?"

"Right," Jessie whispered. Her daddy said that to her all the time, and even though she didn't completely understand it then, she did now. It made her sadder than ever.

"Hey, I bet your neighbors have dog food, too. If, uh, if they're not home or too funky to ask for some." The prospect of exploring and wandering through houses hadn't appealed to either of them, but for necessities, it would be the most logical way to get food and supplies.

"We're going to call him Scooter," she proclaimed. She offered no explanation. She didn't share that once she and her daddy went to the Humane Society and there was a gangly mutt who shared the name. Now she would have her own Scooter.

Matthew shrugged and mumbled something incoherent about naming a dog after a form of transportation. She heard the word "stupid" and turned on her heel to face him.

"What did you say?" Her tone made him grin.

"I said, it's stupid transportation and a dumb name for a dog. That's what I said. Sorry, miss boss lady. I won't speak again 'til I'm spoken to."

She giggled. "Sorry, but I always wanted a dog, and I had picked the name Scooter once when Daddy and I went to the Humane Society. What would you call him? Bob?" Her haughtiness and curt manner made her seem old enough to be his mother instead of half his age.

"Bob's better than Scooter. How about Willy? Or Petey, or even Eddie, like on that old sit-com?" Matthew's eyebrows went up, and she laughed.

She would have given anything to be inside his brain now. Boys could be so stupid, she wanted to tell him, and she suspected he knew it already anyway.

"How old are you, Matthew?" Jessie's hands found her hips, and the gesture made him snicker.

"Huh?"

"You heard me. How old are you?" She cocked her eyebrow and watched him fidget.

"I told you once already. I'm thirteen and a half. Almost fourteen. Well, in January anyways. Why're you asking?"

"Only a thirteen-year-old boy would come up with a stupid name like Willy or Petey. It sounds like a man's name for his privates. There was a boy in my neighborhood who thought that was funny, too – naming his privates, I mean. The dog's name is Scooter. Either like it or lump it. You decide. I'm going to go take a bath." She wanted to reaffirm Matthew's position in their hierarchy. This was her house, her rules, and now *she* had a dog. Jessie refused to let him take charge just because he was older.

She knelt down to let Scooter sniff her hand. She flipped her ponytail off her shoulder, sending Matthew a message: *Don't mess with me; I may be young, but I am not a kid.*

Matthew chuckled. "Kids today, I swear."

"Scooter, don't listen. Boys're silly, aren't they?" She peeked at Scooter's stomach, and even though she saw the exposed privates, a canine boy didn't have the same flaws as a human one. She reached out slowly to pat the dog's dirty head. He leaned up into her hand, grateful for the human contact. When she stopped stroking his head, he whined for more.

"He was someone's baby, but we have to clean him up. He's filthy. Daddy would have a cow if I let a dog this nasty roll on the furniture. My bath will have to wait. You think you're up to the challenge?"

She turned to Matthew, who shrugged.

"Sure, why not? Not like I have anything else to do. We need to mess with the radio like Bryan said, but I guess it can wait 'til old Scooter gets cleaned up. We doin' it in the tub?"

"Yep. Grab a coupla cookies to get him up there."

Matthew furrowed his brow.

"Yes, cookies. Everyone likes oatmeal raisin cookies." Jessie shook her head. *Why do boys even bother to think?* she wanted to add. But instead she marched up the stairs to start the bath water.

Within minutes, Scooter stood in the tub lathered up, but as much of the shampoo covered Jessie and Matthew. Through giggles and much finagling, Scooter finally got clean. When they revealed his golden coat and feathery fur, they realized Scooter was not only young, but maybe just a puppy. He wiggled as he shook himself dry and ran around the upstairs rolling on everything.

"Ah, Scooter, you still don't smell so hot. Stop it." But Jessie didn't have the heart to be too stern. Her new dog raced about like a kid on Christmas morning, and all she and Matthew could do was laugh.

It felt good to have a family again. With her first dog and an adopted older brother, it was pretty cool, all things considering. She refused to replace her daddy, but she suspected he had a hand in sending her Scooter. Jessie grabbed the golden retriever mutt and hugged him with a fierceness that made him groan.

* * *

BRYAN CALLED AGAIN around ten o'clock and said the streets were treacherous with deserted and wrecked vehicles. He didn't tell Jessie or Matthew, but it seemed that whatever happened on Thursday had happened again. He didn't have tangible proof, but Albuquerque seemed to be in earlier stages of the disaster than Los Angeles. Listening to the radio told him little. Only two or three stations were broadcasting, and they spent long increments of time playing music. He was grateful for the noise.

When he crossed the border into New Mexico Saturday morning, he lost KLIK out of LA but was able to pick up the station out of Dallas again. When the DJ gave a number to call, Bryan did.

He talked with Dusty Morris, disc jockey for a classic rock station, and was relieved to chat with someone who had insight to the past seventy-two hours. Between Dusty and his assistant Melanie, they had spoken with people from all areas of the south and Midwest.

"So there are, uh, survivors from all over?" From what Bryan had seen, he worried that many were victims whether they had lived or not. But first, he just wanted to find people. He needed a plan when he reached Jessie.

"Oh, yeah, from all over the country, but some of them are a little screwy. From what I've charted, and my map is full of push pins, there are hundreds searching for others." Dusty paused and Melanie piped in.

"Where are you headed, honey?" Her voice soothed Bryan. He couldn't see her, but he imagined a blonde Catherine Zeta Jones.

"I'm going to St. Louis to meet my girlfriend's daughter. Her father died, and I guess her mother did, too. She never came home Friday morning from her flight."

"How old's the daughter?"

"She's eight, and she's met a thirteen-year-old boy who joined her yesterday. That makes me nervous as hell that she's coming across people who could take advantage of her, or, hell, you know."

"Yeah, that's the scariest part. An eight-year-old girl left alone." Melanie sighed. "I wonder how many other children are lost or abandoned. Good for you for coming to get her. You've never met her?"

"No, and her mother talks to her so little, I don't think she even knows who I really am. That's okay, though. I just want to get her and then find out where the hell all the normal people are."

"Well, Dusty and I have been steering people toward common points, trying to bring folks together. Ya'll are travelin', so you're seein' what it's really like. All we know is, ya'll need to be brought together, and that's our mission. How far have you driven?"

Bryan chuckled. "Uh, over a thousand miles. And I still have at least three hundred to go. When you get to a city, it's like driving in slow motion." Bryan didn't share the specifics, because the horrors were too difficult to talk about – kids with bloated, frozen expressions, men strolling streets in underwear screaming about the end of the world or, worse yet, those without any clothes on at all.

"Well, Bryan, drive careful and continue to tune in to us at KMJC 92.5. We're on the air to ease your tension. Keep in touch, okay? It's information that keeps me helpful."

With an eased mind and renewed faith, he skirted a wreck on I-44 and drove ninety-five, only thirty miles from the Missouri border. He enjoyed the peace of not having to worry about his speed, but the impediments kept him on his toes.

The only image that kept Bryan's foot pressed to the pedal was of what little future he could picture – Jessie alone in a house with a boy she just met, missing her father, forgotten by her mother. He was all she had left.

And he had never met her.

* * *

THAT EVENING AFTER getting off the phone with Bryan, Jessie and Matthew played Sorry!, drank Gatorade, and listened to the radio. Bryan's station played oldies that she knew her daddy would love. A DJ named Dusty kept talking about community, surviving, and a future that didn't make sense to Jessie. But for now, she had today, and that's all she could see past.

"Your turn, bonehead. Go." Jessie threw the dice at Matthew. "Bryan will be here tomorrow some time. I think he sounds real nice."

"Yeah, but remember, Jess, you ain't never met this dude. I mean, he says he's your mom's what?"

"Uh, her personal assistant. And I think you're being silly. Not all people are trying to get something from you, Matthew. You're so paranoid. Geez." Jessie rolled her eyes in her holier-than-thou way and watched Matthew reach home with another man. He had beaten her three games in a row, and she contemplated cheating. Dusty's voice broke her concentration.

"...and today, we've heard from Bryan southwest of Springfield who's going to find Jessie and Matthew in St. Louis. Good luck, Bryan, and drive careful. This next song is for you. For the rest of you, there's a light at the end of the tunnel; we just have to find it. That's a message from a small group that has gathered in Joplin, Missouri."

Jessie and Matthew looked at each other as guitar music filled the living room. The song started to play, but Jessie's head swirled with ideas. She knew Matthew was thinking the same thing. Scooter, lying in the middle of the couch like he owned the place, thumped his tail when Jessie looked at him.

"Damn. They was talkin' about us. You thinkin' what I'm thinkin'?" Matthew grinned.

"Yeah. But I wish he'd get here tonight so we could head straight there tomorrow morning. Where's Joplin?"

"Dunno, girl. Just 'cause I'm old don't mean I know everything. You got a map or an atlas?"

"Yeah!" Jessie jumped up, raced into the kitchen and rummaged through the pantry. She pulled out a Missouri map and returned, disregarding the Sorry! game by sweeping it aside.

They unfolded it and spread it out, both tracing their fingers from high to low.

"God, how does anybody ever get anywhere?" She sat up on her haunches and let Matthew continue to look. "Everything is so small."

"Here it is!" he shouted within seconds. "Down here, by Springfield. Oh, dang, it's damn near on the Kansas border. That'll take hours, five or six probably."

"No it won't. Daddy says there's no place in Missouri we can't get to in just a few hours. Branson only took us four, and that looks closer than Branson."

"You're so high and mighty, you think you know everything, don'tcha, girl? God, I'm glad I ain't never had no sister like you."

"Oh, you're so immature. And it's *never had any*. At least talk like you know what you're saying." Jessie sighed, but Matthew wasn't impressed.

"I'm an inner city kid, girl. KnowudImean? I talk like this cuz it's the damn way ev'rybody talks. Get over yourself." He pushed her by the shoulder until she toppled over. When she scrambled to her feet, she had fire in her eyes.

"I don't like it when you cuss, Matthew. Daddy wouldn't like it." She didn't say more, but she caught an angry rebuttal brewing in his head. She tuned in to what the radio was saying, to Dusty talking about places she had never seen, to people she hoped she might someday meet. A strange feeling washed over her that she would. She had dreamt about it, hadn't she?

"You okay, Jessie?" Matthew's mean streak had subsided, she was glad to see, so she decided to share her dream – or nightmare, as it had felt at the time. When she finished, he whistled through his teeth.

"That's somethin'. You actually dreamed about Joplin, and you'd never been there before?" Matthew's brown eyes were the size of quarters.

"Yeah. What do you think it means?" She fiddled with the couch cushion, certain that the strange feelings she had, the weird things the street people had said to her, all meant nothing. But with an eerie expression, she looked at Matthew and told him she needed to go to bed.

"Okay." Matthew watched her. She could feel his eyes on her back as she collected their trash and dishes and headed off to the kitchen.

She didn't mean to make him feel inferior, but her daddy had been right about boys. They were definitely less mature than girls. She rinsed the plates, grabbed a cookie, and whistled for Scooter to follow. The retriever scampered after his new mom and raced to the top of the stairs where he waited for her.

"Good night, Matthew. I'll set my alarm for seven, then I'll wake you. You're welcome to sleep on the couch again, or you can have the guest room. It's up here, last door on the left. Do you need anything else?" Distracted thoughts of a town she'd never seen jumbled her head, and Jessie wanted to know why so many people were there. She hoped sleeping would either make her feel better or answer her questions.

"Nah, I'll be awright. I'm gonna listen to Dusty a little while longer. You sleep tight, I got your back."

Jessie smiled and Matthew returned it with a huge grin. She didn't know if he knew how much she missed her daddy, but she appreciated that he didn't pressure her to talk about it. She felt his demons brewing, the fear of alone time to dwell on them and wanted to apologize to him for that. But to open that can of worms would be exhausting. She would choose the right time to discuss it – maybe he could hear her thoughts, too. That possibility hadn't really crossed her mind; it was too busy with everyone else's business.

"Thanks. I'll sleep *much* better knowing that." She chuckled and coaxed Scooter into her bedroom and closed the door. She stood staring at the room that belonged to an eight-year-old girl and wondered if she would ever feel like her again.

"C'mere, Scooter. You can sleep up here if you want." She motioned to the foot of the bed. "Or let me get this blanket and you can sleep on the floor. Your choice." She patted the bed, then pointed to the blanket beside it. Scooter promptly answered by jumping on the bed, turning three circles, then lying down with a grunt. It was obvious Scooter had been on his fair share of beds.

"You're so smart, Scooter. We make a good team. You're a good boy," she cooed, rubbing his ears. They had bathed him and brushed his auburn coat with one of Jessie's old Barbie brushes. The once gray mutt now shimmered golden.

She sat down at her desk with the small book. She had already pulled the slip of paper from the Marriott out of her pocket and stapled it to the next blank page. The tiny notebook that served as a temporary replacement was tucked in her jeans pocket, so she fished it out and added those pages after the hotel stationery. She didn't think her diary would mind if she didn't rewrite them. It was a memorial, she decided, and she never wanted to lose those pieces of paper.

Many years later, though yellowed and brittle, that first slip of paper from the Adam's Mark would never leave her with dry eyes.

The memories burned fresh in Jessica Bayker even as an adult when she chose to tell her story via computer.

The intimacy of the diary was recorded in story, recalling the moments that writing allowed her to vent, confide, and purge. About the loss of her daddy, the momma she felt had now left her twice, and the fear that no one would ever love her again the way her daddy had.

Dear Diary,

It has been a long day, but guess what? I have a dog. His name is Scooter. But I guess I should back up and tell you the whole day after my noon writing. Some of the things I saw were really scary, Diary. I don't think I'll ever forget them. I wish I could tell Daddy, but well I guess I will tell him and just hope he can hear me.

Jessie continued to write, trying to see past the tears. Scooter got down off the bed and lay at her feet to let her know he was there, just in case she forgot. By the time she finished, her eyes were swollen and her fingers cramped. She started to re-read it and decided she wouldn't do that. No point in reliving it. There would be plenty of opportunities to cry.

Chapter Twenty-Two

Georgetown
Day Three

JAKE SAT ON the curb outside Rite-Aid plugging batteries into his brand new Sony Walkman. Somewhere in the distance, he heard a whistle. He jerked his head up, but nothing else followed. He heard whispers in the distance, like a radio playing in the sky.

I think I'm goin' crazy.

In another time, Main Street would be teeming with business on a Saturday. But today, Jake had only seen three people in a town of twenty-seven thousand. And all three couldn't make eye contact with him or say a single coherent word. Friday had been different. There had been survivors like Bob. But he could tell that whatever happened in the middle of the night Thursday had hit again, and this time closer to home. He didn't know why it didn't affect him, and he wondered for the millionth time which was worst – dying a slow cruel death or being forced to live with had happened. He remembered studying it in college – survivor's guilt. A fleeting image of Becky verified that he had a full-blown case of it.

Everywhere he looked, cars sat askew on the road, shattered windows sprinkled the sidewalks where looters left a trail of destruction, and then there were the bodies. The sight of them didn't get easier; he just learned not to focus.

"Damn thing." But then the cover snapped in place over the two AA Duracells, and he was back in business. His only company had been listening to a station out of Atlanta. The DJ seldom talked, but he was playing great music. As he popped the ear pieces back in, he caught the tail end of Train's "Drops of Jupiter."

He stood, brushed the dirt from the seat of his pants, and looked up and down Main Street. Georgetown felt like something out of a s ci-fi flick, or a poorly made B movie. Even though he sensed people, he feared he was the only lucid one among them. The thought terrified him – one out of twenty-seven thousand two hundred and eighty-six. Those odds made him shiver.

"Okay, Jake. Get movin'." He tugged the keys from his Levi's pocket and hopped into his Range Rover. Driving was tricky, but he had to get around and he felt safer in a vehicle. He refused to sit in the house thinking about everything he'd seen on Friday. And passing the spare bedroom where Becky's body lay covered by a silk sheet wasn't getting easier either. He pressed his palm to the door when he woke, telling Becky he loved her. He wouldn't want anyone else to see him repeat the gesture, but it made him feel close to her.

In six hours of exploring and wandering on Friday, the body count grew, and the certainty the world was ending settled in. From what the radio said, Atlanta suffered brutal devastation between the terrorist deployment of X-86 – and those details were sketchy – to random acts of violence and massive looting. A gang took advantage of the situation and popped front-runners of a rival group. And now, the city looked like a bomb had hit, Rappin' Ray explained. The DJ said there were a few sane survivors; he even talked about a mall where they were gathering, and those were the ones Jake aimed to find once he stocked up.

When he reached the Winn-Dixie parking lot, he had to zig-zag around several abandoned wrecks. He'd seen a movie once about the day after a nuclear attack, and he imagined this must be what the world would look like – mangled metal piles, glass sprinkled on the ground like a dusting of snow, deserted streets void of any sound to speak of. It gave Jake the urge to scream.

A creeping dread knotted his stomach to see two cars angled directly in front of the store, the automatic doors wedged open by landscaping railroad ties. There were at least fifteen cars in the lot.

Did all of you die in there? He pulled the Range Rover next to the pair of sports cars – a BMW coupe and a Mazda RX-8. The prospect of more dead bodies chilled him, but the possibility of dementia scared him more. Before he got out, he dropped the earphones on the seat and turned his radio off. He felt the hood of the BMW as he passed it, but it was cool.

"Could be because it's cold out here." But he knew better. Somehow dying at home suddenly had its dignity.

"HEY! Stop right where you are!" a raspy female voice yelled from inside the store. "I have a gun!"

A loud whack sent Jake ducking. He dove behind the BMW and banged his knee on the hubcap. "Dammit!"

"Whadda you want?" the woman shouted. Whatever made the loud sound whomped the ground again. Jake pictured a massive stick, like Bam-Bam pounding his club.

Is this bitch kidding? Then it occurred to him that what had come so easily to him must have for many. An unpoliced society offered no restrictions, no limit on supplies, and no resistance for things people needed or wanted. Until now.

"I...I, uh, I need food, matches, uh, just things. I have money." Jake only had thirty-five dollars, but he knew that would get some essentials. Paying for things was already foreign. It amazed him how quickly people adapted to a strange, new world.

Free food, voices from the Heavens, dead bodies like Starbucks on every corner...

"We're clo...closed." The woman sounded tired and harried enough that if she had a gun, she might use it. Becky once told him there were two types of women to avoid at all costs – a woman home from a long exhausting day at work and women with PMS. He made it his mission to always steer clear of both.

Griffin, get over here.

Jake heard the second statement clearly, but it sounded like it came from the bottom of a well. He shook his head, fairly certain that's where it originated.

"I promise I won't hurt you. How 'bout I tell you what I want, and you get it for me? Then I'll lay the money down on the sidewalk and you can get it when I go." Jake peered over the top of the car's hood. He took out his billfold to show her he meant well.

"You...you by yerself?" she asked, the husky, Rod Stewart-like voice wavering.

You better not be another sicko.

It was her voice, but on a different wavelength. Jake began to make sense of what was happening – words said came through almost as clearly as words thought.

"Wh...uh, yeah. Name's Jake. Jake Thomas. Your voice sounds really familiar. You work here?" He couldn't see her, but he could picture the red and white checker's smocks all the employees wore. He peeked over the BMW again, trying to catch a glimpse of her. He stood now and shielded his eyes from the sun. *I'm not a sicko, honey. In case you can hear me.*

"Yeah, I work here. You shop here regular-like? You look familiar to me, too." Her southern drawl came gliding out now. Jake did vaguely remember a checker with a sexy voice that Becky called slutty. She hit him once when he asked her to talk that way after coming through Miss Raspy Voice's line. "Oh, baby, give me that dirty, sand-paper talk I love so much. You could have a sexy voice like that too if you tried."

Becky's wicked laugh sent a pang through him that noodled his knees. *Oh, God, I miss her.*

"Mister, you okay?" She showed herself for the first time, but Jake couldn't get his bearings yet. He was thankful she didn't have the same ability to hear his mental ramblings. And it was a good thing. It would be embarrassing enough to pass out cold and be saved by the only check-out-girl-turned-cop on the planet.

"You don't have no gun, do ya, Mister?"

Well, now why didn't I think of that? He knew exactly where Bob kept his .357 Magnum. He made a mental note to get it if he ever made it home.

"No gun. How 'bout you? Were you bluffing?" He craned his head but kept his hands where she could see them. He didn't want to startle her.

"Yeah, but I tell you what. I wish I did have one. There's been some crazies wanderin' around since about four yesterday mornin'. Whole town's gone to shit. You know anything more 'bout this X-86?" *It's damn confusin' to me. I don't get why they call it that anyways.*

"I know more than I wanna know. You been here since this started?" Jake couldn't imagine her stress level if so. She was his vote for August Employee of the Month – probably the only one left, but that wasn't the point. He chuckled.

"Somethin' funny 'bout that?"

She made no effort to hide her thick accent now. He imagined she thought it leant credence to hide it. And maybe she was right.

"No, nothin' funny, I was just imagining the kind of people you must have encountered the past two nights. Why didn't you go home?" He could see her now as he made his way to the metal rail next to the rubber mat in front of the door.

"I...I been too scared. And then Griffin joined me, and we seen plenty. We watched four or five folks die straight away that first night. Then it happened worse today. Folks, some pretty normal ones, had come in and just took to chokin' like it wudn't nobody's business. Really freaked me out. Them first ones just wandered away. I mean, they didn't claw at their throats or flop around in front of me. But today... Oh, you can't imagine."

A flitting image of Becky fighting for air sucker-punched him again. *Wanna bet?*

"Griffin come in the nick of time Thursday night to help me get a few crazies outta here. Thank God. Don't know what the hell I'd o' done. Freaked me out pretty good. Griffin, he took charge, but he's sleepin' now, so I gotta protect and serve like he asked."

Hearing her say Griffin's name aloud after a voice whispered it earlier – had that been hers? – made Jake shiver. As if the world weren't weird enough, the X-86 seemed to have given him ESP. Maybe he always had it. He used to tease Becky that he knew what she was thinking before she thought it. She said that was a sign of true love.

I wish you could hear me now, Beck. I need you.

"What'd you say your name was again?"

"I'm Jake. And I'm really hungry. Mind if I get some groceries?" Jake didn't want to think anymore. He craved chips and dip in the worst way, and just wanted a mental break from everything going on around him.

"Well, c'mon in then. You seem like a nice enough fella. Heck, you at least look normal –and cute, I might add. I'm Candi, by the way. I'm gonna wake Griffin so he doesn't freak when he sees you, okay? He's a little, um, careful."

"Sure." Jake entered the store slowly. The mixture of overly ripe bananas and rotisserie chicken skewered his raging hunger and coiled his stomach at the same time. An older man who looked eerily like Sean Connery squinted, rubbed blurry eyes, then leapt to his feet in a panic.

"It's okay, I'm just gettin' food. Really, chill out, man." Jake held up his hands in a peace offering.

"Sorry, but it's nerve racking trying to sleep. I was exhausted."

"Well, you're the first sane people I've come across. Everybody's either dead or got acid for brains in my neighborhood. I slept some, but I haven't eaten much. We weren't good about keeping food in the house." Jake hesitated, frozen like a boy playing tag.

"Well, that we got. We're just leery, I'm sure you understand. We've met with some strange birds ourselves. I feel like I've been here a week. Didn't even know what the hell was goin' on Thursday night. I just had my normal bout of insomnia and wanted ice cream. Imagine my surprise when Candi here nearly laid me out with her fancy-dancy baseball bat." Griffin chuckled.

Jake glanced at the girl's hands and cringed. How careless of him. She looked like she might be capable of launching his head like a melon over the centerfield fence. Candi had a gladiator's body and a supermodel's good looks. Perhaps a Barbie doll's brain, but who could have hoped for all three?

"You must be Griffin," Jake finally said and extended his hand. Griffin carried himself with intimidating authority and had the stature to back it up. "I'm Jake."

"Griffin Stevenson at your service, Jake. That nap did me a world of good." Griffin's hand engulfed the younger man's.

The two exchanged niceties just as two other women poked their heads around the corner of the entrance. Candi, still serving and protecting, lifted the bat.

"Hey," one of them greeted, not threatened by the Louisville Slugger at all.

"Rrrrrh!" Griffin purred, watching Candi interact with two Britney Spears types. He whispered to Jake, "There have been others, but they've been deficient, to say the least. Some real loony tunes. Nothing like that." Griffin nodded toward the two ladies approaching them.

"Griffin, Jake, this is Valerie and Tristan," Candi said.

"Well, hello there, ladies. You incredibly sexy women are a sight for sore eyes." Griffin cocked an eyebrow and made another purring sound, then held out his hand. Neither returned the gesture. Jake cringed and tried to apologize with his eyes.

"Well, gee, thanks, mister. We were just out for a stroll through our beautiful beachfront town. Thought we'd take in the sights, you know, see a few dead bodies, take in the dim and diluted. You know, the basic Saturday afternoon festivities. I'm about ready for happy hour. You buyin'?" Tristan laid on her best Valley Girl/blonde bimbo impression, then rolled her eyes.

The world is ending, but we still have sexist pigs, the other blonde thought, squinting coldly at Griffin.

Jake tried to stifle a grin, and she saw it. Her expression was clear. She shared the wavelength and swore him to secrecy with her eyes. *Oh, God, you heard me. I...I didn't know. I mean, I...* But the thought faded. For an instant, Jake's temples throbbed.

Griffin dropped his head and apologized for the first of thirty or forty times. When the girls relaxed, they all laughed and proceeded to make introductions.

The girls introduced themselves in detail, obviously hungry for human contact. Jake could only imagine what they had seen in the past two days.

Tristan Van Hoose taught English at Grant High School by vocation, and worked at the beach as a lifeguard in the summer. She had the white-blonde hair and deep summer tan to prove it. Jake knew Becky would belt him on the arm for staring too long at the bright blue eyes and Tina Turner legs. His wife needn't have worried; his broken heart had no intention of repairing for anyone.

I lost someone too, Jake. It's okay. Tristan gave him only the slightest wink.

Jake knew it would take a while to get used to that. He listened as Valerie Barnett gave everyone a little background on herself. She had just turned twenty-two, fresh out of college and bordering on anorexia, and she bubbled with enthusiasm about the job she had landed earlier in the week. Associate Editor of the Georgetown Daily Journal, she relished saying. Jake admired her excitement but wondered if she realized papers were a thing of the past for a while. He didn't have the heart to burst her balloon.

"You know, Valerie, there'll be Pulitzers for photographers and writers when all of this is over. You should be writin' stuff down and taking pictures."

Jake hadn't finished before she pulled a Minolta from the bag draped over her shoulder. Her chocolate brown hair framed a gaunt face that was nothing spectacular until she revealed green-gold eyes flecked with gray. They exuded confidence and character.

"Taken five rolls already. Not much for the writing part yet, but I'm all about photography. And you're right. History is being made. The scariest part is that places like the Smithsonian are free game for looters and losers. I sure hope security will protect our heritage."

"Wow, I hadn't thought about that." Jake didn't like thinking about problems outside the scope of his remedy. Matters close to home had to be dealt with before he could consider the bigger picture.

"Me either. But I do know that since round one happened in the middle of the night, security is almost as tight as the Pentagon. So maybe all is well." Griffin nodded as if to punctuate his point.

Why can't I get in your head, Griffin? You're as blank as a brand new chalkboard. Jake was only beginning to understand the odd talent – why some had it and others didn't, and why he could hear certain people as clearly as they spoke and not others.

I didn't know anyone but me could do this. I told Valerie and she looked at me like I was E.T. Tristan didn't so much as look at Jake as she communicated with him. He tried to focus, to channel a thought her way, but the headache returned. He massaged his forehead and temples and rubbed his eyes. The mental talk hurt his head.

"You know what's hard to fathom is the lack of government. I know President Cavanaugh spoke Friday, but we haven't heard a word from anyone in Congress or the White House since then. That's disturbing. And the only cops I've seen are playing with a few marbles short of a set. It seems like the heroes this time are going to be your average Joe." Valerie plucked a few grapes from a bunch and popped them into her mouth. She, too, had the bronze tan like Tristan, but her dark hair and skinny build made her look mysterious. Jake worried she would blow over in a windstorm, but her charisma and self-confidence gave her an almost tangible strength. It was one of the qualities he had noticed first in Becky, one of the reasons he'd fallen in love with her. If only her mother hadn't died.

"Earth to Jake," Tristan said, waving her hand in front of his face. He had been lost in Becky again, and he knew the dangers of drifting there.

"Oh, sorry. I, uh, never mind. This has been so bizarre, I can't imagine what life is going to be like, can you?" *And why do I even want to* almost slipped from his lips. But he did want to. If for nothing else, because Becky would want him to. She had been a fighter, too. After her mother's sudden death, Becky refused to wallow, though she'd had trouble shedding the melancholy. He sniffed his arm, remembering her bath salts on his body after they'd made love. A wave of sorrow swallowed him when he couldn't smell her.

"You okay?" Tristan whispered. She studied his expression, but Jake respected her for not pushing. He knew he wasn't much older and he was decent looking, if not a little too clean-cut for a trendy girl's taste. But Becky teased him that he didn't realize the charm he had. When they married three years earlier, both had landed their first jobs out of college and now he was a widow a few months shy of his twenty-eighth birthday.

"No, but I'll live." Jake broke from the group and listened to their chatter as he roamed the aisles collecting everything that looked good. He filled stray carts and pushed them to the front of each row. By the time he finagled all the goods he had gathered and organized the food, his stomach was in full revolt. He tore open a small package of Little Debbie donuts and ate three of them in as many bites.

"Our basic instinct for survival will take over, we'll try to find more people, and then we'll come up with a plan. As long as the strong direct the weak, I think there will always be leadership. Don't you?" Valerie looked from one face to the other. She liked quick answers, and she wasn't getting them. "Well? Ya'll aren't going to stand around with your fingers up your noses, are you?"

Griffin stood there with his hand stroking his stubbled chin. "I guess we have to identify the leaders. But then again, Valerie, where are the weak? I mean, look at each of us. Who among us appears weak to you?" Griffin twirled to get everyone's attention. "Jake? What do you think?"

"I agree. Seems the people I saw that were losing it were all people who had potential to lose it anyway. My wife was incredibly strong-willed, but she recently lost her mother. And...and..." He swallowed quickly to keep emotion in check. "I suspect stress has played a part. But what I've heard about X-86 is that it's comprehensive. You figure survivors are gonna have been your tried and true. Think about who has the lowest level of stress."

"Good thing school wasn't in session. I wouldn't have been on that list." Valerie smiled, but the expression was real.

Jake could tell she meant it, and he didn't laugh. Becky's job as an elementary school teacher rivaled any high-stress job on the planet. He teased her that her profession gave him the stray grays she loved to pluck from his scalp. They would talk about their days at work, him sharing stories about crazy people applying for loans and her replaying a belligerent ten-year-old's tantrums. He couldn't compete and didn't try. Fresh tears welled in Jake's eyes.

"I'm sorry, Jake. Most of us lost someone, I think. I know that doesn't make it any easier. My boyfriend wasn't strong. Drugs, I'm sure, finally killed him. I hope he's in a better place now. I don't feel good about it, but now I understand it a little better." Tristan sighed.

Griffin rubbed Tristan's shoulder, and Jake knew the older man was right about what he said earlier. They were all leaders, some with a little extra mental prowess. Now all they needed was direction.

"I've gotten us a little smorgasbord here. Who's hungry?" Jake pulled plastic silverware from a box, tore open the paper plates and napkins, and stacked a few of each for his new friends.

For the next hour, they ate a buffet of peanut butter and jelly sandwiches, chips, and pudding. Food in the coolers was warming, with back-up generators not providing enough energy to keep everything cold. No one officially delegated jobs, no one declared that the five would work as a team – but after eating, each set about fulfilling a role to facilitate efficiency.

Griffin and Candi formed an assembly line to pack the thawed meat into the Styrofoam coolers that had been reduced only the day before yesterday to $3.99. They were at rock bottom price now.

Tristan and Valerie collected all the charcoal, lighters, and matches, and began bagging and boxing as much packaged food as they could carry. Jake carried the full ones to the wedged-open front doors.

"Hey, girls. Let's not forget toiletries and, oh, hey, can openers!" Candi plucked two bottles of Sure, then saw everyone staring at her. "What?"

"Grab 'em all, girl!" Tristan giggled. "We don't need any of these boys stinkin'."

"Oh, God." Candi playfully pulled every bottle of every brand and dropped them into a basket. She then dramatically added all the feminine products, razors, shaving cream, and toilet paper. She swept her arm across the shelf, raking everything into the cart. Everyone laughed and Candi bowed. Her comedy was a welcome relief.

Valerie made an inventory of exactly what they were taking and instructed each of them to check off an item as soon as they used it. She didn't want to discover later that they had forgotten something important.

"That way we'll know what we need and when," she explained. Her organization would keep them focused and well directed.

When Griffin backed his truck to the storefront, they created another assembly line to pass boxes into the bed of the Chevrolet. In less than thirty minutes, Griffin's Dooley was loaded for the ultimate campout.

"Hey, let's siphon gas. We don't know if the electric pumps will work, and I'm betting most won't, so we want to take what we can now. Toss me one of those gas cans." He held out his hand as he opened his own Range Rover's tank.

Jake caught one and unscrewed the cap. In one deft motion, he pulled the plastic tube from the can, shoved it in his tank and put his mouth over the hole. He sucked as hard as he could and when he thought it wasn't going to work, gas suddenly spewed into his mouth. He maneuvered the tube into the container and smiled triumphantly.

"Yuck," Tristan groaned.

"Yeah, yuck." Valerie crinkled her nose. "You're gonna smell great. Candi, spray him with somethin'."

When Candi reached toward a box, Jake laughed.

"No you don't. And later you'll thank me. Here." He filled the first of four containers from cars in the lot, while the girls relayed them to Griffin, who situated them near the tailgate.

"Okay, gang. Let's get going. No rest for the weary." Griffin opened both doors on his side, showing off the spacious cab, and Jake understood completely why it offered a better alternative than his Range Rover.

Once the five of them piled in, no one argued when Jake asked to be taken by his house.

"We'll head to Atlanta, but there's something I have to do. It'll take me ten minutes tops. Please."

"No problem. Just tell me where to turn. Anybody else need to tie up loose ends?" Griffin had already spoken of losing his wife two years earlier and the peace he'd made as a widower.

"Um, I didn't hear from my folks, but that's three hours from here. I'll keep trying to call, but..." Tristan's silence completed the sentiment. Jake got no other signal from her and wondered if the ability was wearing off.

"My boyfriend and I were together, and I don't want to ever go through anything like that again. It was awful," Valerie whispered. Jake shivered. Others had endured a similar pain, but it didn't make his any easier. "The radio station in Atlanta, that Rappin' Ray guy, said there's gonna be another release today. It may have already happened. You don't think it can affect us the second time, do you?"

"I don't, no. I think if you're immune, all we seem to get is headaches, maybe a little nausea. Candi? Do you need to go by your house?" Griffin glanced in the rearview.

"Um, if it's not too much trouble, I would really like to see if Rudy is okay. He had plenty of food and water to last him, but...but..."

"Okay, I'll drop Jake off at his house, then we'll go check on Rudy. Dog or cat?" Griffin glanced in the mirror.

"As human a Tabby as you'll ever meet. I live out on Vermont. Is that anywhere near you, Jake?"

"Not far. Hang a left here, Griffin. Then make a right at the four-way."

Seven minutes later, Jake stood in his yard and watched his carpool drive around a trashcan and two abandoned cars in the road. He took a deep breath, climbed the front steps and opened the door to a life he could never go back to. The finality of it churned his stomach.

He looked next door before he entered, wondering where Bob went. Deciding not to procrastinate, he walked through his downstairs trying to decide what he needed. The truck was packed to the gills, so he would limit himself to a few clothes, but what he really wanted was to spend the next twenty-five years lying next to his wife. He suddenly had no energy to go on. Before he allowed pity to swallow him, he took the stairs two at a time and marched straight into their bathroom for his razor. He packed a small bag, tucked the shaving kit on top and zipped it closed. He turned to take a last glance at their bedroom and felt the weight of what was happening for the first time.

No matter what they did, life would never be the same. With that realization, he went to the spare bedroom door. He pressed his palm to it, then knew he had to say good-bye. When he stepped inside the room, he refused to let the smell repulse him.

"Ah, Beck." He collapsed to his knees beside the bed and took her hand. The cool skin felt strange as he pressed it to his cheek. He imagined his skin cells flaking off onto her arm, burrowing into hers only to bring them back to life. He brushed the hair from her pale forehead and ached to see the beautiful gray-blue eyes he'd fallen in love with, to hear her tell him just one more time how crazy she was about him.

When the tears came, Jake couldn't stop them and didn't want to. He stroked her cheek as he cried and felt the dam in his soul break.

"I love you, baby," he said around the clog in his throat. "I miss you so much."

He slipped the cross necklace over her head, picturing how she fiddled with it all the time, and clasped it around his own neck.

He stood, wiped his face, and pulled the sheet back over Becky. He touched the outline of her body and whispered good-bye. Before the tears came again, he retrieved his bag and shuffled down the stairs. By the time he nabbed a few of his favorite compact discs and the cash stash they kept in the sugar bowl, Griffin's Dooley pulled up out front.

Jake marched through the living room crunching glass into the carpet from his tirade Friday morning. He didn't glance back, didn't let himself think about what leaving meant, and closed the door on a chapter of his life he would ache to duplicate.

"Hey, Jake. Meet Rudy." Candi held a yellow fur ball in front of him as he climbed in the back. He wedged his bag under his feet and shook the cat's paw.

"Nice to meetcha, Rudy."

No one commented on Jake's red eyes. They all had their crosses to bear, and one philosophy most survivors shared was that if nothing else, X-86 forced them to start over. Baggage only slowed them down.

"Are the rest of you fine with not getting changes of clothes, or should I stop by your places on our way out?" Griffin shifted into reverse but waited for a response.

"Ah, there are new clothes out there calling my name. Why settle for old when there's so much new a hundred percent off?" Tristan giggled.

"Hear, hear," Valerie agreed. "A nationwide clearance sale."

"Okay, then. Road trip," Griffin announced as he whipped out of the driveway and barreled down the street, a pro at manipulating around debris.

"Are we there yet?" Candi joked.

"I have to go to the bathroom," Tristan countered.

"Well, I want shotgun, and Valerie stole it." Jake smiled in spite of the ache in his heart.

"Shut up. All of ya. Just suck it up, cross your legs and hold it. We've got a long drive."

Jake motioned for Valerie to turn on the radio, and she dialed it to the Atlanta station.

"I repeat, Miami is, uh, it's *gone*. News has confirmed that a missile of some kind detonated in South Beach and literally destroyed everything in a thirty-mile radius. We have a caller who witnessed it and then went into the city to analyze the destruction. The only way he knew to describe it was *total*." The DJ sighed, and the airwaves fell silent for a few seconds. A faint piano started and no one in the Dooley could comprehend what they'd heard. They listened as the Eagles began singing about a desperado and wondered if the song might be prophetic.

Don Henley sang about walking through the world all alone. But alone didn't mean the same as it had five minutes earlier. The idea that an entire city had been obliterated changed everything.

X-86 wasn't their only obstacle. They didn't know the new enemy, but he had his own agenda.

Chapter Twenty-Three

Dallas
Day Three

WITH BRAD TAKEN care of and Miami only a memory, Tony felt like a god. He helped himself to a cocktail in the Dallas airport lounge and contemplated his next move. If John wouldn't let him be part of the fun, then he would create his own. With that in mind, he flipped the battery-powered radio back on to listen to a classic rock station, the only one he could find broadcasting. He propped the small Sony portable on the bar and downed his fifth shot of Chivas.

"So if you have any information for us to share with the world," the radio announcer said, "then please call. I'm Dusty Morris and you keep us connected." Dusty repeated KMJC's phone number, and Tony scrambled for his cell phone. The prospect of that kind of access made his crotch swell.

"Who needs Viagra?" Tony cackled, a sinister sound that echoed through the bar.

He ran his hands through his softening hair and made a mental note to get hair grease. He didn't have to abandon his good looks just because of a small international disaster.

"Where the hell is my cell phone?" Tony rummaged through his things then remembered. He grabbed his suit jacket and felt the bulge of his Nokia in the pocket. When he got it out and turned it on, he had forgotten the number so he listened until Dusty gave it again.

Those little peons with their dinky-ass radio stations think they're hot shit. Well I'll show 'em whose shit stinks. He wondered if Dusty had received a quaint little fax from Bradley Tavares, the pompous asshole. His former employee had warned all the stupid people, but Tony had to gamble that he could find one who hadn't been tipped.

While the phone began to ring, Tony tried to decide which angle to take.

"KMJC," a sultry voice answered. "Melanie Stevens at your service."

"Well, you sound like someone I'd like to meet. Name's Tanner Washington, and I am a colleague of Brad Tavares'. Did you get an e-mail or fax from him? If not, I have one I'd like to send."

There was a pause on the other end that Tony didn't like.

"Um, I don't think so, sir, but let me look." Her southern accent gave every word an extra syllable, and he wondered why they bothered to live. The accent and stupidity were synonymous in his book.

"Have you been hearin' from a lot of folks? It sure is scary as hell out here." Tony slathered on the charm, doing all he could to still the tremble of his sixty-year old voice.

"Not as many as we'd like, but we're charting our phone calls, and we've heard from several hundred. We're also coordinating efforts with stations in Atlanta, D.C., and Seattle. Where are you calling from?"

Tony heard the distrust in Melanie's voice, and it irked him to have to deal with menial people with too much power.

"Um, I'm in Topeka. Just got off I-70, and it's a mess. Damn rigs flip-flopped this way and that. Drivin's like a whole new art form." Tony chuckled, trying to earn her trust and getting sicker by the second at having to do so.

"Well, it looks like there's a handful of people that'll be headin' your way from Denver. And..." A whisper in the background cut her off. "I, uh, gosh, Mr. Washington, let me look at my map again." This time Melanie covered the mouthpiece; Tony could tell by the muffled sounds that followed.

"Hey! Bitch! Get back on the fuckin' phone!" Rage ripped through Tony in a way that surprised him. Before his emotions could get the better of him, he punched the off button and stifled every urge to throw it across the terminal. The Gate E sign looked like a great target.

"AHHHHHHHH! I hate people!" Tony's shouts echoed, and somewhere down the corridor he heard shuffling footsteps. It never occurred to him that he might not be alone. He jumped up from the lounge bar and hurried out the exit. He stood in the middle of the long walkway looking to his left toward Gate D, then to the right at Gate E. A shadow ducked down near Burger King, and flaring anger bolted through him. He whipped the Glock from his back waistband and felt a little like DeNiro as he stalked toward the noise.

A lady friend once dubbed him the Italian Stallion in the throes of passion, and he'd never forgotten it. She had been great in bed, he remembered. He bet Melanie Stevens would be too, and thought he would show her what a sixty-year old who jogged four miles a day was capable of between the sheets.

"Hey, who's there?" He marched into Burger King searching for either accomplices or enemies – there would be no more Willies. He'd make damn sure of that.

When he didn't see anyone, he fired a few rounds into possible hiding places and retreated. He didn't have time for this shit.

He returned to the bar, grabbed his things, and hurried to his jet. Without Greg, and damn if that hadn't been a stupid move, he'd have to be his own pilot, chauffeur, and everything else a rich man should never have to be. He aimed to rectify that, but for now, he had a plan.

"Fuck you, Melanie, and your piddly-ass station. I have just the place for me." Tony jogged through the terminal feeling a little like O.J. in his pre-trial days. He hurdled a magazine rack someone had thrown to the floor just to show off. The acrid stench of death grew stronger when he hit the massive ticket area, but he ignored the stiff people. *Weaklings. Couldn't survive a little X-86 storm. You ain't seen nothin' yet.*

In a flourish, Tony boarded his private jet and got situated in the cockpit. It had been a few months since he'd flown, but a nice clear sky would get him to D.C. in no time. By the time he navigated the runway and got to cruising altitude, he itched to play with his laptop. He considered putting New York City to sleep, but the thought of no Metropolitan Opera saddened him. Broadway had too many fond memories for him. While he set the Cessna on autopilot, he considered his options.

So much to do, so little time.

* * *

"THAT WAS HIM, Dusty. He said his name was Tanner, but Brad warned me he would call. Do you think that means Tony got to Brad?" Melanie held the phone like the answers were inside it somewhere. Her hand was trembling. The abruptness of the powerful man's rage startled her more than she wanted to admit to Dusty.

"God, I don't know. So what did he want? To rule the planet like Tavares said?"

Dusty walked over to Melanie's desk and read her scribbles over her shoulder. She didn't know how to tell him how distracting that was. The nearness of him, no matter the twelve years he had on her, madc butterflies take flight in her stomach. She had seen some of the pixies he dated, and she wanted to tell him a full-figured girl was just what he needed. But of course she never would. In the seven years they'd worked together, she never breathed a word that gave any hint how attracted she was to him. She told Janice, her best girlfriend, that Dusty epitomized southern hospitality and the idea of a real Dallas cowboy. He even wore the belt buckles to prove it. With rugged good looks, square jaw, dimpled grin, just shy of forty, he beat any of the twenty-somethings she dated with a big old stick.

"Hmm. Wonder why he didn't press you for more info? Where was he callin' from?" Dusty retreated to a chair across from her and plopped down. He rubbed his hands over his crew-cut scalp and sighed. The crow's feet etched around his eyes deepened when he smiled, making him look even more like a young Clint Eastwood. Melanie had even teased him that with all his catch phrases, he should add *Go ahead, make my day*.

"He said Topeka, but he sounded closer than that. No breaking up or static. I guess it's possible. Some calls are a lot clearer than others." She had made contact with so many people, it was hard to keep track. She checked in regularly with only forty or fifty, but many others had called, including other stations with contacts of their own.

"Well, nothin' we can do about it now. Let's just keep our focus. You makin' your rounds yet?" Dusty laughed, but Melanie knew exactly what he meant.

Her job was to call each person every two hours to check in, to give them a touchstone and to update them on others in their area. She charted each traveler's progress and the time she last spoke to them on a poster next to her desk. It was a full-time job, much different than her usual radio operations duties.

Dusty stared at the pinpoints on her crudely drawn map. Pushpins dotted the south and midwest, a few sporadically out east and even one in Idaho. Thumbtacks marked the few stations they'd spoken with.

"We need a central location. Easy access for everyone, including us. I'd say Springfield, Missouri, but from its proximity to several cities that are primary release sites and its size, I bet it's a mess." Dusty scratched his stubbled chin.

"Or Arkansas. All these folks from Tennessee, Kansas, and Oklahoma can just meet in the middle. Those folks in Iowa, Illinois, and Indiana might have farther to go, but it's gonna be hard to make it easy on everyone." Melanie measured the distances with her pencil and considered all the factors they had discovered. She glanced at Dusty and furrowed her brow. "You cleaned up. That's not fair."

"I didn't shave, obviously, but yeah, I washed my hair with a little hand soap and wiped off a little. Sorry." He chuckled.

"I feel so grimy. I'd *walk* to Arkansas for a shower right now." She wished a little hand soap would wash her shoulder-length blonde hair, but no such luck. *Guys have it easy.*

"That's a woman thing. We men like to feel gritty in a crisis." His laughter stirred her insides. Quite a few things Dusty did flipped her stomach topsy-turvy.

"Isn't it amazing how these people are allowing us to lead them?" She brought the focus back on the map so he wouldn't see her flushed cheeks.

"Yeah, but I bet anything's better than what they're dealing with out there. People need people. It's a fact of life. And until they all come together, nothing will ever get better. It's scary that just because we're on the air, they trust us with their lives. We need to keep that in mind from now on. There may be more Tonys out there who want nothing more than to have a little power, and I guess with our connections to all these people, that's what we've got."

"I think he's had quite a bit of his own for most of his life. I remember seeing his picture when he was *Time's* Man of the Year. He's a handsome older guy, in a Mafia sorta way. But from what Brad told us, he's a megalomaniac. Like we need any of that now. Geez."

"Well, before you make your calls, let's pick a place. We need to be able to give our travelers a goal. We could bring them here..." Dusty pointed to Jonesboro, "but look how far that is for them." He traced his finger from Ohio to Arkansas. "Naw, let's do Missouri. Look how central it is to everyone."

"Umm, how about Columbia? Or Jefferson City?" Melanie measured with her pencil again and looked at Dusty.

"Actually, they're both good size but isolated. Neither is even a hundred thousand. I think we either need a bigger city or one that's close to a city. St. Louis and Kansas City are two hours away."

"Well, look at Springfield. It's big, it wasn't a primary site, and there are accessible cities from all angles." Melanie pointed to Tulsa, Kansas City, and St. Louis, then Little Rock and Memphis to the south and southeast. "How about Joplin? It's not huge, but it's in a good spot, only an hour from Springfield and not too far from us when we're ready to join them. I know it's quite a ways to the really big cities, but it's on a major highway. Doesn't look so bad from here either. We will join them, won't we?" Melanie looked up at Dusty, never considering that he might not want to leave his post.

"Absolutely. And the closer to us now, the better. You're a genius. That's what I pay you for. Remind me to give you a raise." He grinned and flashed his perfect teeth. With his bronze tan and stark pearly whites, Melanie decided Dusty would make a perfect toothpaste ad man.

"Ha-ha-ha. I think the days of paychecks are on pause for a while. A long while. God, that's refreshing, isn't it?"

Dusty nodded but his smile faded.

He likes this, but it scares him. They had talked philosophy before – how much he hated the rich ruling the poor, gang violence, and how the youth of America had lost direction.

"Speaking of food, aren't you hungry?"

She laughed at the staple of his many Dustyisms. He thought about food at least eight times a day, and anytime he was hungry, he assumed someone was speaking of food somewhere in the world. All his little catch phrases made her laugh.

"I could eat a bite. I guess there's no Chinese, huh?"

It was his turn to laugh. Melanie could eat Chinese food for breakfast, lunch, and dinner every single day of the week, and sometimes she did. She argued that it was low-carb, so it didn't violate her South Beach diet, and that she got her daily requirement of vegetables.

"I doubt it, Mel, but we could raid a store and just completely junk out. Doesn't that sound fun? Think you could wait till we get back to call everyone?" Dusty grinned again, and she couldn't help but return it. It was obvious this man was totally up to the task of saving the world.

"Sure, if you broadcast to let everyone know we haven't forgotten them."

"You got it." Dusty bounded into the broadcast booth and added a track to play while they were gone. He grabbed the microphone and hit the on-air switch. "Hey, America, we're feelin' good and hopin' your travels are safe. For those of you in contact with us, we're going to give you some classic tunes, starting with an old Seger favorite of mine. We'll be in touch in a bit; even the voices have to eat. So hold the calls, and remember, you keep us connected." He punched a few buttons and as the Stones finished complaining about satisfaction, Bob Seger's unmistakable "Night Moves" guitar filled the studio.

"Let's rock, Bullwinkle." She stole a Dustyism just to make him smile, and it worked.

"I'm with ya, Roy. But let's hurry. That's an hour-long track." Dusty led Melanie up the twelve steps from their basement studio to the sidewalk. "And don't look around too much, Mel. Sights'll stay with ya for a while."

Melanie knew. She had slept on the couch in Dusty's office Thursday night, taking the second shift to keep music on the air. But when she got cabin fever, she had migrated out early Friday afternoon, and the images burned long in her memory. She hadn't mounted those dozen steps since.

"It feels creepy, doesn't it?" Dusty looked up and down the street. "All the things lost, but then there's stuff I won't miss. It's all kind of like a dream right now. I'm glad we had a generator so we didn't lose power. I wonder if..." but Dusty paused.

"What?" Melanie prompted.

"I was just thinking of the little things we won't have, at least not for a while anyway. Like traffic jams, McDonald's, bills, infomercials, and TV. God, no *Law and Order* or *CSI!* Or *Survivor*. Dang, the world has too much reality now. But don't you wonder what famous people survived? Athletes, actors, politicians?"

Melanie shivered as they walked, not from the chilly breeze but from the thoughts rambling through her head. She didn't feel like contributing her own views because it scared her to give voice to them. As she pondered the star comment, a middle-aged woman threw a soda can toward the trashcan just in front of Dusty. They both turned to the frazzled woman. Her sprigs of hair fell loose from a clip, and make-up was smeared on her face like a drunken clown. When she saw Dusty, she ripped her shirt open and licked her lips.

"Oh, God. Uh, ma'am, button your shirt." Dusty dropped his eyes and continued to walk past. Melanie saw the wild gleam in the skinny woman's eyes and avoided the sagging breasts. She wanted to tell the crazy lady to put on a bra.

"That's the worst of it," Dusty mumbled as they put distance between themselves and the flasher.

"I know." Melanie glanced back over her shoulder at the woman, now huddled in a lingerie store's doorway, and thought how ironic that was. They jogged across the street into the Wal-Mart SuperCenter parking lot.

"Why are there always so many cars at Wal-Mart? Hope that's not proportionate to how many dead bodies there'll be. Here, let me walk ahead, Mel, just in case."

"Chivalry isn't dead. Either that or you're thinking you'll get first dibs on all the good food." They both giggled, but tension grew the closer they got to the store's entrance.

Cars sat cockeyed in the middle of Commerce Street, some with wheels on the curb, others slammed ruthlessly into other vehicles. Boxes of various appliances littered the sidewalks. Splinters of glass layered the walkway in front of them. Looters had thrown rocks through every single window in each store lining the street, and

Wal-Mart was no exception. Nothing like a sheer pane of glass to invite a vandal. The crunch under Melanie's sandals felt like she was walking on diamonds.

"Look," Melanie said as she pointed to a Trans-Am. The windows displayed spray-painted smiley faces and a crudely written sign: *Big Sale Today! 100% off! Always low prices at Wally World!*

"God. Melanie, we need to get loaded up for quite a while so we don't have to do this again."

She didn't answer. She didn't like the way her voice broke the eerie silence. No birds, no buzzing insects, none of the usual blend of car horns, squealing brakes, and shouts from angry drivers. But thankfully, few bodies could be seen. She made a point not to inspect driver's seats too closely. They had heard from countless travelers the horrendous tales of the victims' bloated bodies, the distorted expression as if a scream was frozen on their faces forever – descriptions Melanie knew she would never forget, along with the few she'd seen on her own Friday.

Saturday afternoon at Wal-Mart would normally be a stupid move, but today was like entering a time warp. Dusty neared the door and peered inside.

"What would you be doing right now, Mel?" he asked, almost as if to offer a distraction.

"Oh, me and the girls would be planning dinner and maybe going out to dance, or a few of my movie gang would talk me into something stupid at the Cineplex. A new Ben Affleck movie opened yesterday. I guess not anymore. What would you be doing?" She hung back and waited for him to signal her to follow. Prickles of anticipation made her jumpy.

"Ah, I guess I'd be catching happy hour with Keith and Sean. We usually go to the San Francisco Steak House on Saturday nights, or Vincent's. God, am I gonna miss filets for a while. No more ball games – I'll really miss that." Dusty used his foot to push food aside. There were spilled bags everywhere. Melanie saw smashed fruit laying on the linoleum without ants or flies swarming it.

Give them time, they'll be back.

"Hello!" Dusty called out, making Melanie jump. They both hesitated, listening for any indication that people remained in the store – crazies or not. She followed Dusty through the entryway, so close on his heels that if he stopped she would run smack into him. In another time, that would have appealed to her, but right now she worried about close encounters with the twisted kind.

Melanie pulled a cart from the line as they walked past them, and they weaved around spills into the produce section. She was amazed at the mess – food, broken toys, and brown soda patches that had been traipsed through so that every step she took had a sticky pull to it. And the smell. Someone had either burned books of matches or flicked a Bic while walking up and down aisles. Not enough time had passed for anything to really spoil, though she knew it wouldn't be long. Milk, meat, and bananas would soon blend into a mighty stench bouquet.

"I don't hear anyone," Melanie whispered as Dusty grabbed a few green-tinged bananas. He followed them with grapes and a bag of oranges.

"Me neither, but don't jinx us. Let's get outta this healthy shit. I want some carbs."

Dusty looked like a kid in a candy store as he piled chips, snack mixes, cookies, beef jerky, and nuts into the cart. He snickered and tossed in packages of Twizzlers, M & M's, and Starburst. Melanie countered by grabbing bread and peanut butter. For every junk food item Dusty threw in the cart, she added soup, ravioli and chili.

"You're a goof, Dusty. Your mom ever let you shop like this when you were little?" Melanie slowed the cart and peeked around the aisle before she turned.

"Shhh. Stop," Dusty whispered, grabbing her waist. Her heart jumped into her throat when someone shrieked from only an aisle away.

"Get your scrawny ass over here, Michael, you little sonuvabitch! Where'd you go?" The voice followed with a long Tarzan-like yell and a loud crash of cans.

"Let's go, Melanie. C'mon, quick." Dusty wheeled the cart around the corner away from the screaming woman and the two raced toward the front of the store.

When they whipped out the door and settled the cart around the side of the entrance, Dusty told Melanie he was going back in for matches, batteries, and flashlights.

"Shouldn't we get charcoal, too? And toilet paper, and..."

"Stop, Mel. I'll grab a sack and get some essentials. You combine all this and make room. But stay put. I don't know if that woman's all there and don't really wanna find out the hard way."

"Yessir."

Less than ten minutes later, Melanie had repacked, and Dusty returned with another full cart. The reasonable second trip made her feel better as they set off for the station. An uneventful journey back settled Melanie's nerves.

"We need to hurry. We've been gone fifty minutes, and I don't want any dead air." Dusty knew that something as simple as music gave their travelers the anchor they needed.

They hustled down Commerce Street to the small building with the odd antenna standing like a metal giant behind it. They both grabbed two bags from the cart and bounded down the steps eager for their carpet picnic in his office. Melanie's stomach growled in anticipation.

Neither saw the baseball bats in time to avoid them.

The silence was splintered by screams. Cans crashed to the hardwood floor only seconds before Dusty and Melanie did.

* * *

A THOUSAND MILES away, Tony's private jet touched down at Dulles Airport. With visions of a nice large white home dancing in his head, he pulled the plane as close to a gate as possible, amazed at all the 747s, Cessnas, and sixteen-seaters askew on the runway and surrounding areas. He would call John in an hour or so to see what the fat man planned to do with the Three Musketeers; Tony could utilize the kids' vision in a big way. If John didn't mean to maximize their potential, he certainly would. Between the four of them, they could carry out a beautiful mission – to rule right and white, as one of his college buddies use to quip.

By the time he got off his own Cessna, made his way through the terminal and boosted a Mercedes in temporary parking, his head reeled with the task before him.

If President Cavanaugh had skittered off to Camp David, the House would be all his. The prospect made him hard again. With a laptop and absolutely no morals, the world was his oyster.

Chapter Twenty-Four

St. Louis
Day Four

"MATTHEW, YOU BUTTHEAD." Jessie pulled herself up, still woozy with sleep, dropped the toilet seat and tried again. She was lucky she hadn't fallen in.

She had let the little things slide – the peanut butter and jelly sandwiches with cheese puffs crushed inside, bananas dipped in caramel, and forgave the ketchup on his scrambled eggs. But if he left the toilet seat up one more time, she was going to let him have it. Her daddy never forgot, but Matthew got a kick out of doing things that bugged her.

After she washed her hands, Jessie stared at herself in the mirror. She'd lost weight and looked like someone had colored under her eyes with a gray crayon. She had never been so tired in her life; no matter how long she slept, the feeling didn't go away.

If you were here, I wouldn't feel this way, Daddy.

"Hey, anybody home?"

Jessie's heart tripped up in her chest. For a split second she thought the deep male voice belonged to her daddy. *Bryan!*

She raced down the stairs so fast she nearly fell and then stopped ten inches before hugging a man she'd never met. After a moment's hesitation, she did it anyway. Bryan picked her up and spun her around. Scooter barked excitedly at them.

"Hey, girl. You're a helluva lot bigger than the pictures I've seen. What are you, ten? Twelve?" He grinned a goofy Bill Murray smile with two bottom teeth that overlapped a little. His big brown eyes, sandy brown hair, and animated expression made him look more than a little like Jim Carrey.

"More like thirty-two and bossy as all get out," Matthew chipped in from behind. Bryan turned and introduced himself; the two shook hands, and Jessie pulled her newest friend to the couch. Scooter followed and demanded a scratch from each of them. Jessie gave a brief rendition of Scooter's adoption and demanded that Bryan accept the mutt as part of the family. Then she paused, her face tightening with seriousness.

"Did you find Momma? Have you heard from her?"

Bryan evaded her questions, she could tell, so she pressed him about everything he had seen. She hoped other cities weren't like St. Louis. A small fire sparked in the pit of her stomach that her mother wouldn't save her – why did that surprise her? She had been deserted once for over three years.

"I can't even describe what I saw, but I took pictures. We won't look at them for a while, but I think it's important that we never forget."

"How'll you develop 'em?" Matthew furrowed his brow, trying to imagine life without all the conveniences.

"It's a digital camera. I already thought about that. But you're quick. You must be, what? Sixteen?" Bryan raised his bushy eyebrows.

Matthew nearly busted with pride, and then confessed he was almost fourteen but plenty older than Jessie to be the man of the house.

"We heard on the radio about a place where people are gettin' together, Bryan, near St. Ann. At a mall, and...and...and Matthew knows how to get there, don'tcha, Matthew?" She nodded toward the teenaged black boy who had become her best friend in only forty-eight hours. He seemed less a stranger than this man who spent everyday with her momma. Scooter nuzzled her, sensing her sadness.

"Yep. And this Dusty dude says ev'rybody's gonna travel to Joplin so we can get together like a real town or somethin'. I dunno how long they'll wait in St. Ann, but I'm all about hookin' up with people. I'm a social guy and I need a scene, knowudImean?" Matthew grinned, revealing bright white straight teeth and a contagious attitude that Jessie knew would suck Bryan in.

"Well, I don't think we should dawdle. Whaddya say we get packed up this morning and head out? We could hook up with these folks before dark. You two up for it?"

Jessie cringed for a brief instant. Leaving would be tough, because she knew once they hit the road, they'd never come back here – there would be no need.

"I...I would want some time to pack. Could I take my things? I mean, you're not gonna limit me to one suitcase, are you?" Jessie cocked her eyebrow. She knew she'd seen too many movies, but that's what all of this felt like – a gut-wrenching action adventure that could never have a happy ending because her daddy, her hero, was in a hotel room by the river.

"Hey, squirrel bait, whatever you can pack in the car is fine with me. But we'll need to stock up on food too. We don't wanna meet with these people and not be able to carry our own weight. So spend a few hours getting your stuff together. Matthew, you wanna go by your house to pack some things?" Bryan opened the refrigerator and grabbed a bottled water.

"No," Matthew answered. He didn't elaborate. A blip registered on Jessie's mental radar but disappeared quickly. She watched him, tried to read him, but he evaded her. She felt guilty, like he knew what she had been able to do. His bubbly exterior covered anything that might be lurking beneath.

"Okay, if you're sure. I'm gonna scrounge for something other than squeeze cheese and crackers, if that's alright. I don't want to just come in here and take over...so is it okay with you if I grab something to eat?" Bryan looked from Jessie to Matthew and back. She could tell he was trying not to step on their toes – it being her house and Matthew being the man in charge. She liked that he bothered.

"Well, we're gonna hafta charge ya, you know. Food's pricey these days. But go ahead; you need to keep your strength up." Jessie smiled to let Bryan know she was kidding, but she suspected he didn't get her sense of humor yet. A little mystery suited her just fine. A woman couldn't give too much away right off.

* * *

IT TOOK FOUR hours to corral everything Jessie wanted and to pack Bryan's SUV. He'd exchanged his car in Springfield at a dealership he knew wouldn't mind. He'd always wanted a Lexus, he told the kids, and now they would have the room they needed and the comfort they deserved.

"Okay, we ready?" Matthew slammed the back shut and looked at Jessie. "You forgot the kitchen sink, runt face." *And your candy bar in the freezer.*

"Bite me, Matthew. Oh, wait! I forgot something." She raced inside, yanked open the freezer and saw the half-eaten Snickers. "Hey! Who ate half my Snickers?" Like she had to ask. And the resurgence of her mental reception gave her an eerie sense of power. It occurred to her then that being outside made it easier. And then it became clear to her – *I'm breathin' the bad stuff.*

"What made ya think of that?" Matthew asked, his eyes narrowed with suspicion.

"I'm psychic, Matthew." She enunciated his name like he were the eight-year-old. "Bryan, why is it boys don't need things? At least I don't wear make-up yet. Then you'd really be in trouble."

"I think we already are," Bryan mumbled, and Matthew busted out laughing. "C'mon, let's get in." Bryan hopped in the driver's seat and keyed the ignition.

"Okay, I don't like this ganging up thing. You two are not funny and you need to get over yourselves." Jessie tucked her Diary inside her jacket pocket and climbed in the passenger seat.

"Hey, I called shotgun!" Matthew complained.

"Yes, and you also want everything that doesn't belong to you." Jessie smirked, and it was obvious her pseudo-brother didn't like the hierarchy that had formed.

"Fine," he grumbled. "But I get a turn when we stop."

"You two, I don't know how you got along before I got here, but it's a miracle we don't have open wounds. C'mon. Let's get movin'. It may take awhile with the roads and all." Bryan fell silent as he fastened his seatbelt and revved the engine.

Without fanfare, Jessie Bayker left her home and went in search of another world. By 5:30, they met seventeen fellow survivors at the St. Ann Mall – a hodge-podge of middle aged and older people, but not another single kid. Both she and Matthew decided they were lucky to have survived.

"Little girl, luck had nothing to do with it. There's an aura around you," a gray-haired man said. His clear blue eyes penetrated her like none she had ever seen. Jessie couldn't remember the man's name. They had introduced themselves to everyone – there were too many to keep track of – but she wondered what it was about her that made people say such creepy things. She wished they would stop.

"Well, what's the consensus?" a silver-haired lady with a fancy walker asked. The handful of people sat on car hoods, clearly not in any hurry.

"What about Joplin? If you've been listenin' to Dusty on the radio, he's been talkin' about people goin' there. I even talked to him while I was driving from California. These kids listened to him quite a bit, too. Sounds like Joplin is a meeting point. There's also one somewhere in Pennsylvania, Denver, and up in Seattle. Maybe eventually we can all combine forces." Bryan, by far the youngest adult, looked at every single face for a response. Jessie wanted to hug him for coming to save her and for being strong. She needed a break.

"Sounds good. I just want some information about what's happening overseas. Like, if we could get to a non-contaminated city and hop a plane, is everything fine in London or Paris or Munich?" The balding man rubbed his temples. *I need a drink.*

Jessie flinched at the clarity of the man's thought. She impulsively shoved her warm Mountain Dew toward him, but he waved it off.

I thought you were thirsty?

His eyes turned to her and a smile spread across his entire face. Not another thought passed between them, but a crackle of understanding remained. He squeezed her shoulder.

By seven o'clock, the clan had collected supplies and established a caravan. Cell phone numbers were exchanged, though only about half still worked. No one understood why; they thought it had something to do with the towers and what it took to operate them. But they agreed to quit questioning things they had no control over. Frustration was an emotion all of them had felt plenty of and could do without.

When everyone started to pile into their cars, a buzz of energy pulsed through the group. Five of the older men had been important in their before lives. Jessie knew one as Crenshaw, another as Riley, and the other three were Chris, Mike, and Tim, but which name belonged to each face was beyond her. She needed to take notes.

"These guys had clout," Bryan whispered. "They were *somebody*."

Retirement had mellowed them, they explained. X-86 would have certainly claimed them in their stress-centered youths. Three women who looked younger than Jessie's daddy had been recently married and didn't like talking about their husbands. Each had jobs, but Jessie couldn't connect them – a librarian, a florist, and a Lord & Taylor sales clerk. She felt like she was playing a twisted game of *Concentration* – and losing.

Bryan teased her that there would be a test over it later, but she reminded him that tests, thank God, were a thing of the past. She wouldn't miss her private school in the least. Too much homework and teachers with too many names. It suited her fine to have some time off.

After all the melee, maps were divvied and an order established. Their Lexus SUV led the group, and Jessie asked Bryan why no one fought to go first, to lead the way.

"You'll understand when you're older." And he offered nothing more.

"It's you," Matthew whispered. "'Member what that old fart said when we was doggin' it Saturday? And that other dude later that night?"

Jessie thought back. Yes. *He said that I held the fate of the world in my hands. But I don't want that pressure. And why me? For goodness sakes, I'm a little girl.*

When Jessie laid back, she replayed the comments in her head. It made her thoughts swim. And everyone in such a tizzy over meeting a silly DJ. He was just a man. It wasn't like he was God or something.

But then a strange sense of urgency pulsed through her. There was something magnetic about their journey, and drifting just past the feeling danced a dark, sinister shadow of fear.

Not everybody is going to be good like us.

Chapter Twenty-Five

Dallas
Day Four

"DUSTY, CAN YOU see them?" Melanie pulled up the legs of her blue jean capris and inspected her shins. Purple oblong splotches already bloomed just below her knees. She hadn't seen the bat coming, but she was grateful it hadn't crushed her kneecaps. White cords cut deep into her wrists, binding her hands in front of her, attached to a belt around her ankles.

"I think the punk went into the sound studio. God, if they figure out how to get on the air, Lord help us all. What do you think they drugged us with? I feel like shit. And, Jesus, my knees hurt. I thought they'd be numb by now. How're you feelin'?" Dusty leaned her way bracing himself, his own hands cinched tightly behind his back with clothesline. He wished his were bound in front – his shoulders screamed from the pressure.

"My stomach really hurts. I don't know what the sedative was, but God, I've got a helluva hangover. And my wrists hurt worse than my knees. These are too tight," she said, having no luck wriggling her hands free. "My hands are completely numb." She dropped her head to her restrained hands and scratched her nose. She looked up and saw Dusty's pained expression. "Oh, God. You can't...I'm sorry."

"Nothin' itched 'til I started thinkin' about it." But now he trembled. She couldn't help but laugh, even though she knew it wasn't funny.

"I'm sorry, Dusty."

"Ah, don't be. I can't even imagine how dented my wrists must be. I tried to tell that prick he was cuttin' off my circulation, but he probably couldn't think for all the lead in his blood from those tattoos." Dusty grimaced but managed a chuckle.

Melanie nodded. The skinny man's entire six-foot frame shimmered with color and lines that moved fluidly every time he did – she was sure it was why he wore no shirt. Some of the tattoos displayed radiance, others complicated black-and-white etchings. Melanie admired the professionalism of a few of the pieces with a flowing menagerie of design. Standing out amongst the studio drawings, one self-inflicted scrawling on his left deltoid declared undying love for someone named Wanda.

"Think that's Wanda?" she asked, head nodding toward their two captors. She assumed the other bat-swinging idiot must have been Wanda, but they hadn't called one another by name yet.

"You two shut up in there, you hear me?" a voice boomed from the studio.

"Right, Boss!" Dusty shouted and followed with a murmured, "Go fuck yourself."

To Dusty's dismay, Tattoo Boy appeared in the doorway.

"What'd you just say, shithead?" The boy, not a day over eighteen, glared. His face glistened with pockmarked rebellion.

"Ya know, son, I'm not sure what your plan is here. But there are only a few of us who made it, ya know? We should be on the same side. All you had to do was ask for our help, and we would've given it. What're you holdin' us hostage for anyway? There's not exactly anyone out there who'll pay any ransom for us." Dusty twisted so he could face Tattoo Boy. From the center post where they were restrained, the rooms angled out from the area like spokes on a wheel.

"I heard ya'll on the horn and thought I'd like to get a piece of the action. You wasn't appealin' to none of my kinda people. And that group headed to Joplin? They could use someone like me. But I need to get them familiar with me, sorta worship me like they been doin' you."

Tattoo Boy surveyed every inch of Melanie's body, making her cringe. Dusty met her gaze and nodded. She didn't know what he meant by the gesture.

How did a freak like this survive? Prob'ly never worked a day in his damn life. Melanie's stomach rolled. She prayed they could keep this degenerate from squelching the hopes of her contacts heading to Joplin. He was the last thing survivors needed.

Wanda slithered back into the room and hissed that they needed Dusty to get information to some of their cohorts. They had gotten separated in the night, and her man needed his entourage to lead them all into salvation. It was time to get the respect they deserved, she snickered. She ran her bony fingers through Tattoo Boy's shoulder-length greasy hair.

"Jesus had His followers; now you will." She gazed into his eyes, and they kissed, deep and throat cleansing.

Melanie shuddered.

"What's up, babe? Got a chill? I could warm ya up." Wanda nuzzled the bat against Melanie's bosom. The woman had been twirling it in her hand like a baton. Melanie kept her head down, but had noticed for the first time how ugly the woman was – gapped, crooked teeth that bucked out, a too-large nose that seemed a little off-center, and red hair that looked like it had been frizzed with a blow dryer for five hours.

"You might as well let her go. I can help you with anything you need," Dusty stammered.

"Oh, so the bimbo ain't no use? Fine, let's have some fun with her then. Ever been rode hard and put up wet?" Wanda brushed the bat along Melanie's breasts again, pulling the button-up white blouse open.

Dusty apologized with his eyes, and she knew he realized what he'd done.

"Unless you need to transmit. You know, to get on the air. Now if you plan to broadcast, she's the only one who knows the sequencing codes, all that garbage. I'm just the voice. It takes two of us to get up and running. Now I rigged that fancy generator so we'd have the power to continue on the air, but..."

A massive strip of duct tape slapped across Dusty's mouth before he could continue blubbering.

Melanie understood his motives and loved him even more for it.

"Well, Mr. Cowboy, the truth shall set you free." Wanda's clichés only added to her sex appeal, Melanie thought bitterly.

Tattoo Boy grabbed Dusty by his front belt buckle and pulled him to his feet. Melanie saw the odd expression on her friend's face at having another man's hand nearly down his pants.

"Whaddya think, Wanda, wanna do 'im before we off 'im?"

Wanda snickered her approval, striking Melanie that the two were some sadistic Bonnie and Clyde. Melanie had a sudden image of the two boneheads as Boris and Natasha, which made she and Dusty Rocky and Bullwinkle. The idea made it difficult to suppress her laughter.

"I'll do 'im if you will, big boy. You know how I love to watch that shit."

Sick fear crawled into Melanie's stomach, and she knew Dusty's steel grip on reality had to have slipped a notch. Panic blanched his face. The idea must have sunk in, because Dusty thrashed and bucked against his restraints.

"Ah, c'mon, Hoss. You ain't down with that?" Tattoo Boy swaggered toward Melanie but continued staring Dusty's way while unsnapping his black jeans. The enormous silver belt buckle fell to the side, pulling his fly open to expose frantic pubic hair. The swelling in Boy's crotch frayed Melanie's nerves – *think, girl, think*. But anything she did to distract the two would only bring their wrath on her. Or maybe not.

Men live through this everyday in prison, she consoled herself. Not that the idea made it easier, but somehow knowing men far weaker than Dusty had overcome it kept it in perspective. She had to accept it or blow a fuse. She hoped it was that easy for him.

She watched Wanda fiddle with his hands, loosening the clothesline around his wrists so she could resituate him for her nasty man. Melanie's heart galloped in her chest – maybe he could get free and get them out of this mess.

Keep loosenin', babe, keep right on workin' those trashy little fingers.

"Don't get so excited, partner. He likes a fight. Besides, you'll need to hold yourself up, ya know, like doggy style." Wanda bellowed laughter, her glee with the situation completely unmasked. She yanked the tape from Dusty's mouth, making him yelp in pain.

"He likes to hear ya moan," she whispered huskily in his ear. "Now over, on all fours like a good boy."

For Dusty, no matter his ultimate fate, Melanie knew he had to sense the sliver of opportunity with his hands and feet now free. Before she could twist around to see Tattoo Boy, she felt the muzzle of a gun jab into her head behind her left ear. The barrel traced the outline of the outer lobe, like erotic foreplay.

"You so much as twitch and the blonde loses her curls, got it?" Tattoo Boy's speech slurred, thick with sexual tension. Melanie pulled her face away from the barrel each time it neared her temple.

Dusty's legs noodled as Wanda uprighted him, trying to get him in position. She had the cords freed from his hands, and Melanie's mouth fell open when she realized the woman lifted his entire weight. Her lithe frame gave no hint of her obvious strength. Now only ten feet from his potential sodomite, Dusty seized the opportunity. He shoved Wanda hard enough to send her flying over a desk, then he dropped to the floor in front of it. Melanie twisted away from the pistol, certain the chaos would piss Tattoo Boy off.

A cacophony of gunshots, screams, and screeching furniture exploded in Melanie's head. Wanda came flying around the desk angry as a bee in a jar. Tattoo Boy screamed that no asshole DJ was gonna spoil his fun. And then a pool of blood rolled toward Melanie as she hunkered by the support beam.

"Ah, God. Dusty, are you shot?" But Melanie made sense of the scene when Wanda collapsed at her feet.

Tattoo Boy howled like he had been scalped.

"WANDAAAAAAA! OH, GOD, WAAAAAANDAAAAAAA!"

Melanie was sure windows were shattering all over the neighborhood from his cries. She tried to clamp her hands over her ears, forgetting they were still bound in front of her. She bonked herself in the nose, but all she wanted was to block out the nerve-fraying wails.

"OH, BABY, I DIDN'T MEAN TO!" Tattoo Boy cradled Wanda in his arms. "Oh, God, what have I done?" He let his lover lay limp in his lap and squeezed the pistol handle like he was trying to liquefy it. He leveled it at Dusty and snarled. Five feet away, Dusty bowed his head and waited.

Melanie hobbled two steps forward, doubled her bound fists and slammed them down on Tattoo Boy's gun hand as hard as she could. The revolver skidded across the floor only inches from the studio door.

Tattoo Boy tackled her, but Melanie kicked at him as she scampered for the pistol, bright flashes of pain piercing through her knees. Tattoo Boy grabbed her right ankle and lunged past her. Dusty tugged at the boy's loose waistband, yanking him backward, then flailed for the gun. But Tattoo Boy grabbed him and laid him flat on the floor. The men brawled, rolling and swinging fists like two schoolyard bullies.

Melanie snatched the only weapon she could reach and swung with every ounce of energy she could muster. Dusty whipped around when his leg came free, the shock on his face widening when the comprehension registered.

Melanie dropped the bat, and only then did Dusty see Tattoo Boy's face – she had nailed a crunching strike dead center across his acne-scarred nose and cheekbones.

"Wow, Mel." Dusty grinned, then felt for a pulse. Melanie wasn't sure she wanted him to find one.

"He's gonna be fine, but he'll have a helluva headache." Dusty, still on all fours, collapsed backward on the floor, smacking his butt on the linoleum. "I didn't think my knees could hurt any worse."

Melanie reached her hands out to help him up, but he pulled her to the floor beside him.

"Here, let me untie you." Dusty manipulated the clothesline, loosening the cord to reveal deep purple rivets in her wrists.

"Oh, my God, it'll take me a week to feel my hands again." Melanie massaged the bruises and then her palms, trying to bring the circulation back.

"My knees hurt too bad to move. Can you tie that jerk up?" Egg-sized lumps protruded from Dusty's shins. The color bloomed in bright circles, a layer of purple, then green and blue. If Melanie didn't know better, she'd swear it was a Hollywood paint job.

She pulled herself up and found a roll of duct tape their captors had used. She twisted Tattoo Boy around onto his stomach, wrapped his arms around the center support beam and anchored him by the wrists with enough tape to circle the building. The blood spray on Tattoo's face and shirt seemed to be drying, and the flow from his nose had stopped. He never even twitched, but just in case, she bound his ankles with the clothesline that left the imprints on her wrists. It ticked her off to look at it, so she tugged it tighter.

"Asshole. Hey, Dusty, can you tell if Wanda's dead?"

He leaned forward and scooted himself next to Wanda. Her shirt was soaked with blood from her midsection. He pressed two fingers to her neck and looked up at Melanie.

"I feel a faint pulse. But..."

"But what, Dusty? But she's not gonna make it? Shit. He killed her, so why do I feel so guilty?" Melanie ran trembling hands through her blonde hair. To say she was frazzled was the understatement of the century. What she wanted more than a pint of pork fried rice and ten orders of crab rangoon was a steaming hot bath, her leather couch, and a thousand-page novel with enough leisure time to finish it.

It felt weird to dream about an everyday event as if it were a dinosaur in outer space. It left Melanie empty and cold.

"You're human, Mel. *That* makes you different. Don't beat yourself up over some moron who jumps us, ties us up for damn near twelve hours, and when he tries to shoot us, he nails his girl instead. How can you accept any responsibility for that? You can't. What we need to do now is gather our stuff – the food, our maps, our cell phones – and get the hell out of here."

Dusty hobbled to the studio door and picked up the revolver. He clicked the safety on and placed it carefully in the back waistband of his jeans. It nestled comfortably in the small of his back. The metal insurance placated Melanie – an armed man was almost as good as her couch.

Without speaking, the two gathered the scattered food littering the floor from the ambush the afternoon before. Melanie squatted, clenching her teeth at the pain in her knees, and organized each item in a box. Her hands still shook so badly, she dropped a box of Triscuits. She heaved a sigh and started over. Dusty smiled, handed her four cans of mixed nuts and touched her hand.

The adrenaline rush plateaued. Melanie plopped back on her butt in a hopeless gesture. She couldn't keep up the bravado. Once the tears started, she didn't know if they would ever stop. Dusty sidled up beside her and held her while she cried.

"Wh…what're we gon…gonna do, Dusty?"

"Shhhh, don't try to talk, Mel."

"If this is wh…what faces pe…people, how ca…can we fix this? I…I hoped I'd wake up, and…and…" But she gave up and simply laid her head against Dusty's shoulder and bawled.

"I tell ya what we're gonna do. We're gonna load your car. Then we're bustin' outta Dodge. It's time to meet these people we've been talkin' to, and we'll take one day at a time. That's all we can do. If we try to see the big picture, it'll swallow us. But small? We can do small."

He struggled to his feet, opened the station door, and set the box of food on the bottom step. While Melanie wiped the tears away, he hustled around from the studio to the control room gathering things they might need – electronics, phones, his Palm Pilot, even the tape and baseball bat. Once everything was boxed, he collected and rolled the maps, then marched into the recording booth and made an announcement to their listeners. He explained nothing, made no excuses about the hours of silence.

"You think a three-hour track is enough?"

"It's the best I can do with the power left in the generator. Let's blow this Popsicle stand. Make like cloth and bolt."

"Hey, that's a new one," Melanie said, returning his contagious smile. She slipped the list of contacted travelers from the clipboard by her desk and folded it neatly into fourths and tucked it into her back pocket.

"You like it?" His dimples made her shiver. He rubbed his two-day scruff.

Before saying something she might regret, Melanie tossed her cell phone charger in the last box and started carting them to the steps. She couldn't imagine how much it was going to hurt her knees to add weight as she climbed them, but she faced that challenge like any other. She wouldn't think about it; she would just do it. Dusty called after her that she shouldn't leave a guy hanging, and she thought for the millionth time what a cute couple they would make, age difference or not.

Injuries slowing them, they hefted eight boxes up the dozen steps and packed them into the hatchback of her Ford Mustang. Melanie filled the back floorboards with tapes and CDs, as well as three portable radios. By four o'clock, they were loaded to the gills.

"One last run through." Dusty limped down the stairs.

"God, Dusty, we've got enough. I may never walk again." But she followed him, and both walked around the five-room radio station to see what they could use. Dusty plucked two matchbooks from a bookshelf beside one of her aromatic candles and stuffed them into his front jeans pocket. Melanie nabbed a bottle of Advil and then froze.

Tattoo Boy lifted his head and moaned. He tugged at the restraints, looking like a swimmer trying a strange new breaststroke. Melanie's heart lurched.

"Let's go, Mel." Dusty pushed her toward the door. She pulled the car keys from her pocket and never looked back.

When they stood at the top of the stairs, she breathed deep, the tainted Dallas air feeling fresh to their immune lungs. Neither could smell the poison, but the proof was scattered about them – the glass, the silence, and the smell of death.

Then Tattoo Boy's screams pierced the dead air. Moving faster than their wounded legs wanted, they hustled into the car and locked the doors behind them. Even though Tattoo Boy lay on his stomach safely restrained, it didn't stop his shouts from sending chills down Melanie's spine.

She turned the key in the ignition, drowning the final scream they would hear from their former assailant. Neither considered what would happen to Tattoo Boy, that they were dooming him by leaving him bound with his young girlfriend near death at his feet. Melanie hoped Wanda would wake up and free him. It was her nature to never see the dark side of things.

But even if a man-boy, barely old enough to vote, perished in that basement studio, she refused to feel guilty – Tattoo Boy was a casualty in a nasty war. It could've been worse.

It could've been them.

Chapter Twenty-Six

Interstate 24 Northwest of Nashville
Day Four

"I'M GONNA NEED a break soon." Jake rubbed his eyes and pressed the gas pedal to the floor. He could see a solid stretch of highway with no cars – that was his cue to cover some space. He didn't trust the black top over the horizon. It had gotten him in trouble twice.

The first time he came around a corner going ninety-five and slammed on the brakes, skidded thirty feet and crunched the front right fender on an eighteen wheeler's cab. If he hadn't been paying attention, they would've collided head-on with the six mangled cars embedded in the rig's trailer. The second wreck occurred while they searched for the Atlanta crew. A few blocks from the mall, Jake had tried to maneuver around a pile-up and didn't see a fire hydrant.

The damage had been so extensive, they had to abandon Griffin's Dooley and adopt an extended cab Dodge Ram. Jake promised they would keep an eye out for a replacement.

"I can take over, Jake. Do you wanna get through the highway changes first? I can direct you, then we can switch." Valerie examined the map, trying not to make too much noise. Griffin, Tristan, and Candi snoozed in the back seat. Each had taken a turn during the night or early morning. It was too stressful to drive more than two hours at a time, and they had been on the road for over twelve hours.

"Okay," Jake said. "I need a break anyway. We can stretch. Guide me to the next stopping point."

"From the look of the map, we gotta hit highway 57, then go south a bit. I still don't think this was the smartest route, but it kept us on the biggest interstates. Um, after we get on 57, we'll take it into Missouri, and then we're on small highways since we aren't goin' all the way north to St. Louis. I wonder if that'd be the better choice." Valerie turned the map, then flipped open the atlas. They had taken a state map each time they crossed a border, but the atlas proved the most helpful.

"Well, whaddya think?" Jake glanced at her but didn't feel comfortable enough to look away for long. The speedometer quivered just past ninety.

"We don't have to decide yet. You just have a few miles 'til 57, then the zigzag over to 55. You can pull over and we'll get a consensus."

Valerie and Jake fell silent, but he knew the voices rambled in her head just like his did. They had chatted, shared stories, but nothing substantial. Being closed up in a truck had fostered as much caution as closeness. It wasn't that they didn't trust each other; Jake just knew they all had to hold onto something of their own, to keep people at arm's length, at least for the time being.

When he saw the exit, he glanced at his watch. He had managed to saturate his thoughts with something other than Becky for twenty-six solid minutes. That was almost a record. But breaking it would wait – Becky hated St. Louis, the Rams anyway. When Kurt Warner annihilated the Titans in the Super Bowl, she cussed for days. She cheered when they later benched him and then sent him packing for New York.

Jake had laughed at her fanaticism, teasing her endlessly. But she hadn't been amused. She obsessed over the Tennessee football team almost as much as she fixated on the Atlanta Braves. It was one of the things she hated about living in the Carolinas – the only thing they had before their Panthers' expansion team was college basketball.

The memory of her screaming at the television, griping at referees' bad calls or the worst – that one yard shy of the goal line in Super Bowl XXXIV. He and Becky had only been an item for a year when the Rams stifled a potentially winning drive on the one-yard line. Despite her outraged reaction at losing 23-16, they had gotten engaged the following summer. One thing Jake learned about the woman he adored – he loved sports, but he teased her that she hated them, and that she loved hating them more than anyone he knew.

"Hey, Earth to Jake. We need to decide which way to go, so pull over. We've only got a few miles. You've been on that planet of yours again." Valerie inspected his expression, and it made him uncomfortable.

"Okay, gang," he called out as he pulled onto the highway's shoulder. Looking toward the horizon, it was a relief to see no cars, no wrecks, no carnage. "Rise and shine. We've gotta play jury again." Jake climbed out of the truck and stretched. Every joint in his body ached and popped.

“Griffin, here’s our two route potentials. Whaddya think?” Valerie laid the atlas on the Ram’s hood and traced each with her forefinger.

“Hmm. Seems like we’re goin’ a lotta miles outta the way by takin’ 55 north.” The older man inspected the map closer. “But these small roads are liable to be a serious hazard. Hell, we don’t know if they’re even open. ’Member that one in South Carolina? We had to drive down that ravine. Not sure we want to battle all that. Besides, I-44’s one of the biggest highways in the country. Even if there’re wrecks, we should be able to get around ’em.”

“Or the opposite’s true. I-44’s probably had a helluva lot of traffic,” Candi said, peeking over Griffin’s shoulder.

“Well, let’s decide. That crew from Atlanta will wanna know which way to go, and I’m not sure how far behind they are anymore.” Jake scratched his scalp, ratting the short brown hair, his head so grimy it itched. “God, I need a shower.”

They hadn’t been able to hook up with the seventeen people in Atlanta because of impenetrable traffic. When the mass exodus got stalled by X-86, it closed most major roads and clogged the city. But when they talked to Jenna Masterson, one of the Atlanta group, she shared what the Georgia capital DJ was broadcasting. Ultimately, there were three key sites – Colorado Springs, a place south of Chicago and Joplin, Missouri, each with people arriving hourly. Since Joplin was the largest gathering, that’s the one they agreed on. Jenna had stayed in touch, but getting out of Atlanta had been rough, so they were hours behind.

“Well, I think we oughta stay on a more linear path, personally. By the time we get to St. Louis, and you know it’ll be just like Atlanta, we could’ve damn near been there. Why do that? Not to mention, we could take this one.” Tristan squinted. “Um, 60, and take it up to Rolla. Then we could take I-44 on to Springfield, then Joplin. But Springfield may be a doozy. It looks bigger than I thought. But it’s not one of the first fifty, is it?”

“No,” Griffin answered. “But it may have been a second rounder. We’ve not been able to confirm all those.”

“Okay, so let’s get to 60, then we’ll decide how bad it is. If we want to drive to Rolla we can. If not, that’ll take us all the way to Springfield.” Valerie closed the atlas and looked to each one of them.

“Sounds good,” Griffin agreed. Candi and Tristan both nodded. “And when we get to Rolla, we’re gettin’ a new Dooley. This baby doesn’t have enough leg room.”

“Okay, and how ’bout a munchie before we hit the road? Who’s for a soda?" Jake hopped on the back right wheel and flipped open a cooler. "We'll need to get ice in the next hour or so."

That had become an obsession, watching for bagged ice machines. Some had lost power, but many hadn't. And in a time of crisis, all of them discovered there was nothing better than chips and an ice cold cola of choice.

"I'll take a Mountain Dew." Tristan opened her hands ready to catch it.

"Of course you will. And, Griffin, a Diet Coke?" Jake grinned.

"You betcha." Griffin caught it in one smooth stroke and popped it open.

"Val, another Diet Coke, and Candi, your signature Mr. Pibb. And, Jake, what would you like?" He scratched his chin, making everyone laugh. He had taken to talking to himself when no one would answer – now it was comic relief. He even competed with Candi for life of the party. He pulled a sack out, peeked inside, and looked at the four of them.

"Oh, just get your Dr Pepper, and let's go. You're in back. I'm takin' shotgun." Griffin climbed into the passenger seat, Valerie hopped behind the wheel, and the two girls joined Jake in back. "Divvy out the snacks before I catch a few more z's."

"Well, alrighty then." When Valerie zipped back onto the highway, Jake couldn't help but feel like they were on a road trip for the ultimate vacation. As he tossed chips, Chex Mix, and various types of candies to his friends, he thought how much Becky would have loved this.

Adventure brought out the best in his wife. A lump rose in his throat while he chewed a Dorito, and he turned to look out the window so Candi wouldn't see his tears. He glanced at his watch. That one had only been sixteen minutes, not even close to the record. He would try again after a while.

Chapter Twenty-Seven

Washington, D.C.
Day Four

"OKAY, JOHN, WE gotta get this straight. You're gonna stay there? Why? People are going to want to meet them, you know. They'll demand the right to try the fuckers and shoot 'em in the head when all is said and done. Dallas is chemical central. Hell, from what you've learned, this second release is gonna be followed by how many more?" Tony tapped the keys on his laptop while he talked. "Be reasonable, John, for once in your stupid fucking life."

"Right now, Tony, I'm getting answers. Nathan is talking. He's told us what cities are next and at least that way I can warn people. I don't know if it'll help, but it sure as hell can't hurt." John sighed.

"Tired, big guy? All that interrogating really wears ya down, doesn't it? You should let me have a shot at 'em. I don't know why you don't want me having a little fun. You hear about Miami?" Tony chuckled. "You would've been proud."

"What the hell did you do, Tony? Jesus. This isn't a game. Why're you doing this?"

"Oh, John. Because I *can*. Don't you get it? You're more uptight than ever. You used to be a lot of laughs, back in the day. Remember that night we did shooters until daybreak?" Tony cackled, a witch-like squeal that made shivers run up and down John's spine.

"Yeah, well back in the day, you were playing with a full deck, Tony." John hung up before Tony could respond.

"Fuck you," Tony hissed into the dead phone.

He sat on the bottom step of the Supreme Court building with a cup of orange juice in his hand and swallowed the last of it in one gulp. He no longer noticed the miscellaneous bodies scattered along the steps or the distorted positions many managed in death. He braced his cell phone between his left ear and his shoulder after he hit redial.

"You know, John. You really shouldn't piss me off. Check out what happened to Miami, then get back to me. You have my number. Then we'll talk. If you piss me off again, Dallas is next. I never did like Texas or their damn mottos. There's a new one now, case you hadn't heard. Don't mess with Tony. Yeah, I like it."

He clicked his cell phone off, wondering what John would have said in response. He didn't care. Basinger used to be a friend, but he couldn't afford those anymore. He had a planet to rule.

* * *

"HADEN, GET IN here." John sat up on his three thousand dollar leather couch.

"Hey, what's up?" Haden stumbled into the office doorway putting his round-lensed glasses on. He tamed the few sprigs of hair he had left. "Jesus, John, your office looks like shit."

"Yeah, well, it's not just an office anymore. It's a bedroom, living room, kitchen, and..."

"Junkyard," Haden interjected, but he laughed. "So what's wrong? Is it Tony again?"

"Yeah, and I think we need to do something about it. Who else did you say came in today?" John unbuttoned his shirt, took it off, and pulled a new one from a wrapper. He walked into the attached bathroom and took a washcloth out to clean up.

"Um, Kenny showed up, said he didn't know where else to go. Said looters tore his apartment complex up so bad he didn't have any windows. He brought two suitcases and said he was gonna crash in one of the executive offices on the twentieth floor. And Breanna Tanner has been sleeping in her office since it all started. She didn't start exploring the building until last night. That's when she said she saw your light on. Richard Deeks has been crashing in his office, but he's searching pretty ardently for his family. He was out of town when all of this hit. I think Jack Simpson is here too. Or at least he was yesterday, but I'm not sure he's gonna make it. He was sort of distracted, you know, like it had affected him."

"Okay, okay." John held up his hand. He couldn't handle any more bad news. "Have Kenny come see me when you can. I have a major job for him if he's up to it. If not, I may need you to. But this is right up Kenny's alley." He scratched his scruffy face, wished he had time for a shave, but he had an idea. "Deeks still current with his pilot's license?"

"Uh, yeah, I think so, why?"

John filled Haden in as they headed downstairs to Chamber Number Nine – about what Tony said about Miami, the disturbed CEO's frame of mind, and his plan to enlighten the three stooges.

"You gotta see this, too, John."

John's mouth dropped open. Haden held the oddest newspaper John had ever seen.

"What the hell. Haden, this is good news. I mean, at least there are people." He took the newest rudimentary version of the Dallas Morning News. The old masthead had been pasted atop a typed page with a handwritten date.

The headline screamed *Terror and Confusion Across U.S., Europe, Asia*. John skimmed the article, mesmerized by someone's elementary efforts to keep people informed. Inquiring minds.

"Did you read this, Haden?"

"Yep. People know it was either us or BetaCorp. They haven't gotten many details to corroborate the story, but someone's told 'em enough. Someone who worked for one of us."

"I think I have a pretty good idea." John didn't share with Haden all the times Tony bitched about Brad Tavares' do-gooder attitude. But he suspected a betting man could win a mint with that wager. It also crossed his mind that Bobby might have had a hand in it too. That would cleanse a troubled conscience.

"Well, they didn't make any attempts to verify their speculations. And you know whoever reads this will believe it. It's the almighty printed word." Haden smirked, but he stuffed the paper into his back pocket.

"Did you notice they got information about BetaCorp's plant in Arizona? That at least puts Tony in the hot seat with us. Like I care now anyway. They're calling Thursday X-Day." John shook his head and stormed in to Chamber Number Nine's outer room thinking of his wife and two daughters. "Not to mention, it really started on Friday."

"Except people were already suffering from the pre-release on Thursday. They planned it that way. You heard what Kyle said."

"Yeah, I heard. Now they're going to hear me." John turned the knob, then hesitated. "Find Kenny, Haden, then meet me in the lobby."

"What?" Haden's jaw dropped. "Why the lobby?"

"Just do it. Let Deeks know we're going to need him, too. Tell Kenny to meet us in the lobby as quickly as possible. In the meantime, I have a little field trip planned."

"Can I watch first? I wanna see their reaction." Haden grinned.

"Sure. You really like this shit, don't you?" John didn't wait for an answer. He opened the airtight chamber and smiled at the three inside. He'd gotten them cots, blankets, and pillows, but the trio sat at the table like they were waiting for class to begin.

"Hello, boys and girls." John mimicked his best Mr. Rogers and sensed the trio might just respond to this technique. "Did we sleep well on our cots? That's nice. Now it's time for show and tell, so get the fuck up because we're going out to play."

Kyle looked up, the haze of insanity so clear in his expression, it gave John chills. Nathan lifted his head then lowered it back onto his arms as if he didn't give a shit what his former boss had to say. Jamie stared but made no eye contact.

Losing the sing-songy voice, he turned back to them as he exited the room.

"You have three minutes," he barked. He slammed the door and watched through the one-way mirror.

All three slipped into the same socks, tied their shoes, then fingered through their hair. Kyle struggled with his Nikes, so Nathan helped him. Jamie teased that the two looked like the characters from *Dumb and Dumber*. Kyle threw a sock at her, and she picked it up and held it with the tips of two fingers then playfully tossed it back.

They had given Kyle painkillers, a moment of compassion on Haden's part. John agreed he wouldn't be reduced to their level, so he allowed it. He wanted to throttle them and scream that this wasn't a game, to stop smiling, dammit, and show some remorse. But he continued to bottle the anger, wondering how long he could keep a cork on it.

"What're you gonna do if they run?"

"Shoot them." John pulled the small revolver from his pocket and popped the clip to make sure it was loaded. He also double-checked that the safety was on. "Do you think anyone would mind?"

"Uh, no." Haden laughed. "Okay, I'm after Kenny now. See ya downstairs. I can't wait to see this."

John watched as each pulled on the company sweatshirts he'd left them, then barreled back into the room.

"We're going for a walk." John grabbed Nathan, yanked the kid's hands behind his back and cuffed him. He did the same to Jamie and led them out the door. When Haden supplied him with guns, cuffs, and other police-issue supplies, he never dreamed he'd really need them.

It took almost fifteen minutes to walk down thirty-seven flights of stairs, especially with Kyle slowing them down, but the exercise felt good to John. And going down didn't compare to climbing them. He wondered how hard that would be for Kyle and relished the thought of it.

"You three need a good deep breath of your own medicine. Being in an airtight chamber's been too humane." They stood in the massive, ornate lobby, and waited for Haden. John didn't bother with chit-chat – he was too damn tired.

Haden and Kenny came huffing out of the stairwell less than five minutes later.

Haden stopped and sucked air. John knew his friend believed firmly in avoiding exercise at all cost, but the philosophy was kicking Haden's ass now.

"What is it, sir? I need something to focus on." Kenny glanced toward the three and venom sparked in his eyes. "You assholes killed my sister, and I hope you rot in hell."

Kenny Jenkins had been a middle-level employee before Thursday, an administrative assistant in the biohazard unit. But John knew him well, because Kenny's dad, Royelle, went to A & M with him. The two played offensive line together – *Go, Aggies!* Then Kenny's dad got shot in a stick-up – a fluke that Royelle had run to the corner mart for ice-cream at 1:30 a.m. because Maribeth had a hankering for it. Nine months pregnant with Kyra, she had a taste for dairy at least four times a week, and they could never keep it around.

Kyra never met her daddy, but John tried to ease the void where he could. A six-foot eight-inch white man didn't come close to filling the shoes her father left, but John had done his best. Kenny, four at the time of his daddy's death, ended up with a basketball scholarship to Arizona State, and Kyra graduated from the University of Texas-Arlington with a degree in English. Last time John talked to her, she was ready to defend her doctorate on the social repercussions of racial typing. He swallowed the tears and said how incredibly proud he was of her. She told him she could never thank him enough for being there for them – for being the father they never had.

When Kenny applied at Aralco, he earned the job on merit, but John wouldn't have let the young man walk away without a position. John had become like a stepfather to the boy, and now Kenny was the last family he had left. The thought made his chest swell with rage, but he suppressed it – there would be a time and a place for that.

"Kenny, I have a job for you. It's detailed in this letter, but Tony Andrews is in Washington D.C. and is out of control. You've met him a couple of times at meetings and have probably seen him on magazines, but I printed a pretty recent picture, just in case. I've been trying to confirm his activity, but it seems that he has bombed Miami." John lowered his voice so Kyle, Jamie, and Nathan couldn't hear. Kenny's eyes looked like a deer caught in headlights.

"Bombed?"

"Yes. Richard Deeks is going to fly you. I tried to contact the Pentagon, Quantico, even the local recruiting office. If Tony's going to be taken care of, we're going to have to do it ourselves."

"Are you kidding? Tony's got access to his silos and can just deploy them by himself?"

"I don't kid about missiles. And with his computer knowledge, there's no telling what he can do. And I figure he's got at least four left and may be able to tap into more. He has to be stopped. You up for this?" John clapped Kenny on the back.

"Am I clear on what you want me to do?" Kenny cocked an eyebrow at his boss who said nothing, then looked down at the letter. "Ah, it's in here."

"Exactly. And keep in close contact. Take your pager and cell, and if you don't have it with you, get your charger. We need to be able to stay in touch. I want to know the instant he's, uh, neutralized." John winked at the boy, and thought how funny it was that he still saw him as a pipsqueak kid. He knew Kenny had to be pushing forty. But damned if the oldest Jenkins wasn't the spitting image of his father and ageless to boot. It made John feel old.

Hell, I'm over sixty. I am old.

"You got it." Kenny marched away like a man on a mission, and the sheer promise of Tony being erased eased John's stress.

One down, three to go.

As they stood near the circle of swinging doors, Nathan's demeanor changed. He rubbed his temples, shook his head as if the dust bunnies were loose. Haden glanced over at John, and both nodded.

"You ready?"

"Let's do it." Haden gave the emergency door a hard shove, the revolving one locked too tight to budge. He led the three into the hazy Dallas afternoon.

Nathan, the first to exit the building, didn't make it far. He sat down against the marbled granite building and closed his eyes.

"You okay, Nathan?" Jamie knelt beside him, put her hand to his forehead.

John watched the interaction from an almost clinical standpoint, though he understood it because his own head took to hammering almost immediately. The four had said they used samplings against their own DNA but obviously hadn't been able to replicate the massive dose of airborne X-86. Jamie had been unaffected, as had Kyle, when they did controlled tests with small doses in their lab, but Nathan experienced headaches even then. Nathan said it was a rare flaw and laughed.

"Get up, Nathan, we're taking a tour. No rest for the demented." John pulled the young man to his feet, watching him swoon. Kyle braced himself against one crutch and put one hand on Nathan's shoulder. The gesture angered John.

"Wish you'd have had some of that compassion before you killed my wife and kids."

The words seethed with passion. John trembled with the urge to shoot Kyle right in the face. The two stood in a stare-down for nearly sixty-seconds.

"Go ahead and shoot me. You like the power. Feels good, doesn't it?" Kyle hoisted himself forward, ignoring the twitching hand that hovered near John's pocket. Kyle's left crutch skidded against a shard of glass and nearly sent him to the pavement.

That broke the moment for John. But he was shaken by his compulsion to pull the revolver on the boy and watch the implosion of his face.

Haden stepped toward John, and the bald man's worry was clear – *Is the X-86 affecting you now?*

"I'm okay, I'm okay. Let's take a stroll to Main Street and head toward the courthouse. That should be interesting." John stayed alongside the three, allowing Haden to lead. The Aralco boss watched them closely, searching for signs that the chaos brought on any sense of responsibility. It was clear that all of them felt the X-86 – his head thudded to beat the band. And Haden kept rubbing his forehead. The three stooges looked half drunk. John could tell that Kyle tried not to look around at all. The young man stared straight forward, and John saws the direction of his eyes – they were fixed on Haden's back.

"Don't look, Jamie. Just stare forward and toward the sky. The more you see, the more you'll feel. There's no point now." Kyle took a deep breath and exhaled slowly.

John smacked Kyle's head so hard, the crutches stayed planted behind him while he propelled forward and down to his knees.

"Ahhh!" The boy howled in pain, clutching his leg.

"Shut up, you arrogant prick! What you need is a little repentance. No point now, my ass! There may not be much left, but if you believe in a hereafter, then your soul is searching hard right now, son. Don't make that decision for her. Talk again and I shoot the other leg, got it?"

When Kyle didn't respond, John pulled the pistol and leveled it toward Kyle's good knee. The greased hair and scruffy face gave Dr.

Basinger a renegade look that finally forced a reluctant response from Dr. Spene. John wiped the spittle from his mouth and lowered the gun. His head reeled with disjointed thoughts, visions of Victoria and his two little girls. And somewhere far away people were talking. Weren't they?

John looked over at Haden, an anxious look now etched on the bald man's face, too.

"We're feelin' it, John. My head hurts like a sonuvabitch. Yours?"

"Yeah. And I feel fuzzy, like I hear voices. You hear them?" John slowed, let the three get a few yards ahead.

"Voices? Shit, John, don't go losin' it on me. You had the headaches on Friday, but we've been inside so long, it wore off. Maybe we should head back." Haden hesitated.

"I'll be all right. Let's not go far." John sped up to bark at Kyle. "You better look plenty. I may just tie your asses to a sign post and leave you to rot. Or be eaten. Lots of hungry folks out here will tire of peanut butter and jelly eventually. Charcoals have been fired up, smell them? They're cooking what meat is salvageable. But give them a week or so, and you'll look like prime rib."

Jamie side-glanced Nathan, whose mouth gaped at something ahead.

John followed their eyes. "Oh, God."

A nine- or ten-year-old boy with a bloodied knife in his hand hovered menacingly over an old lady. The woman's face was frozen, contorted as if she had tried to scream. It seemed the kid had cut out her tongue and laid it in her upturned palm. Several bloody slits in her shirt outlined each stab wound, and John could count seven from where they stood. He studied Nathan, Jamie, and Kyle to make sure they were enjoying the show. As cruel as it seemed, this was exactly what he wanted them to see.

The boy's eyes gleamed with dementia. Looking up at them, he waved the knife and shouted, "G.I.P's rule, man!" He raced toward the alley annexing Harwood Street, whooping and hollering the whole way.

Jamie jumped when countless similar yells responded.

"Yikes, hope he doesn't become president someday," Haden deadpanned. His odd humor hit John like an electrical jolt. But he understood Haden's motives.

John saw Jamie's face and knew the old woman's dying expression hit a nerve.

"You did this, Jamie. You may have thought about the ends justifying the means, but did you think about people like her? Or worse yet, *him*?"

When she dropped her eyes to the pavement, John pulled her chin back up.

"Oh, no you don't. You four did this. You, Nathan, Kyle, and Bobby. If only you three had experienced Bobby's remorse, none of this would have happened. But there's no turning back now. Huh-uh. No sirree, Bob."

Tears slipped down Jamie's face. She made no effort to wipe them away. Nathan made a humphing noise, and before John could turn around, Haden slapped the NAO leader hard across the face.

"Respect, son, learn it now because it may be your only salvation." *And mine.* Distant murmurs clouded John's thinking, but he trudged along behind them.

The walk from Olive to Main brought bile up John's throat – feces, dead animals, desecrated bodies, and miles and miles of rubbish. Looting and mass hysteria gripped the city on Friday, those who survived round one of X-86 and those in the midst of its grip couldn't resist open season. Breezes brought the chemical in slowly, giving ample time for the evil to throw one last hoopla. And what a party it had been.

The three walked in silence, seeing the doom they had brought on the world. John and Haden followed in their wake.

* * *

JAMIE WONDERED IF Charlie had made it. Had he followed her plan? His high-stress life didn't make him a candidate for survival, but she had given him a heads-up. She didn't dare place too much hope in his heeding her call to safety. A lump rose in her throat – he was all the family she had left. She forced her eyes away from the boy's bloody hand, and the flecks of skin stuck to the blade clawed at her conscience.

Daddy, I hope you understand. Jamie looked to the sky, not sure she believed in Heaven but in too strange a predicament not to invest a little hope. She knew her parents would be appalled at her part in the devastation – it was the first and only time she thanked God they were dead. Had The Movement not murdered her father, she knew her direction in life would have been far different.

The bitter redemption felt good. The Movement's power didn't hold a candle to hers now. A smile twitched at the corners of her mouth at the same instant the X-86-infected boy shouted, "G.I.P.'s rule, man!" and ran.

A trickle of urine startled and shamed Jamie. For a regretful instant, she wondered why they thought this would work. She wished she could fade into the woodwork and be a nobody – a random face in a crowd of average Joes.

Or even that old woman.

* * *

AFTER THEY PASSED the boy's victim and Kyle managed to avert his eyes from the dead woman's unseeing glare, they reached the end of the street.

"Yep, this has been real educational." Kyle smirked and shook his head, sending the message to John that no matter what the big man did, it wouldn't bother him.

When he turned to see his former boss's expression, he caught a glimpse of a mongrel dog lugging a hunk of something around the corner of a building. When he squinted to see what the tanned chunk of meat was, he gagged, swallowed hard but the second convulsion couldn't be deterred. He threw up, barely missing his own feet. When he saw the rabid animal rip another bite from what looked like a human foot, he puked again.

"Ah, Jesus, what the hell is that dog eating?" Nathan stopped and bent over. He had better luck holding back his soda and chips. "Can you undo my hands? I think I'm gonna puke."

"You don't need your hands to throw-up, Nathan. You'll be fine." John glanced at Kyle, who wasn't having much luck.

"Let it pass, Kyle, and don't look that close at shit." Nathan bumped his partner with his shoulder, as close to a clap on the back as he could offer.

"Yeah, don't look at what you did, Nathan. God forbid you realize the poor animals who survived will have to find a way to eat." Haden snorted a disgusted judgmental grunt.

The five of them came to an intersection, and John paused long enough for Kyle to look up and really see. He hadn't meant to, but something tugged at his brain. The few seconds were plenty. And then his sister's voice whispered like a distant radio in his head – *Why'd you do this, Kyle? This wasn't for me.*

And then the answer became clear. He didn't have a problem with their plan, because he didn't think he would be around to see it. It changed things to witness the deaths of innocent people.

Thinking about it made Kyle itch to take off running. At least then he would hold his destiny in his own hands, but squeezing the crutch's grip, he knew his running days were over.

He hoped Trisha and Beth took his warning and reached refuge in the underground barracks the four had found earlier in the summer. But he guessed his mother would not have – he didn't grieve for her yet. She possessed the traits to survive on her own – he just wished she would play it safe. But she had asked a lot of questions, pressured him to share what he knew. When he wouldn't, she put her foot down and told him she wasn't going to fall for some terrorist threat and run into hiding.

How could he tell her it wasn't some terrorist plot? It was her son's?

* * *

"HOW 'BOUT THAT, Nathan? A little boy gutting an old lady. A dog munching on a foot. All in all, your X-86 has dumped the world into a bowlful of shit. Not quite what you expected? And I'm just wondering about your NAO or NEA or NEO buddies – think they're the type to have survived? I don't." John shoved Nathan into the street to stumble over a wrecked bicycle.

"There are casualties in every war. You may not understand, but you've never walked in my shoes. Don't presume to know what we expected, sir. Did you think we were stupid enough to believe worldwide cleansing would be merciful? Hardly. Did I want little boys cutting up old women? No. But I also didn't choose a society that sells drugs to kids, puts guns in criminals' hands, and allows American citizens to go hungry while illegal immigrants sneak into our country and steal our jobs." Nathan shook his head in exaggerated disappointment.

"So you're here as an observer, and you don't see any of this as your fault?"

Nathan studied the sun. "I'm an anthropologist. And maybe an archaeologist as well. But no matter. You'll be gone long before me, Dr. Basinger. You're what? Sixty? Sixty-two? I'm not even thirty years old. This is a hitch in the road to a better world. You don't see it now, but mark my words."

The boy standing over the woman had unhinged Nathan, but he would've puckered up on broken glass and hummed the National Anthem before admitting it to John. Maybe that hadn't been the future he had planned for, but Dr. Edwards had said that all good things took time and work. Nathan's vision had been for kids like that to perish – they were beyond recruiting – but his philosophy remained the same. There were casualties and there were survivors.

And I'm a survivor.

Now all he had to do was alter The Plan. Just because they'd gotten caught didn't mean they couldn't play that to their advantage. It dawned on him that John might just be the vehicle he needed.

* * *

HADEN SCRATCHED HIS head so hard, John could see dandruff sprinkle onto the bald man's shoulders like a flurry of snow. The walk back to Aralco had been uneventful, as much as a post-X-86 life could be. They had seen enough in the thirty-minute walk to fill each of their heads with images that would fuel nightmares for weeks. Now John just wanted to breathe less infected air for a while. His head thudded like a full-blown percussion section.

The five of them filed into the Aralco Headquarters lobby without a word. John prayed the thumping in his temples would ease once he breathed some uninfected air – if any existed. *And it's time to check in with a demented friend.* John glanced at his watch and hoped Kenny would get to D.C. soon. If Kenny could get Tony corralled, John would breathe a lot easier, tainted air or not.

"The devil's in the details, Haden," John whispered matter-of-factly as they shuffled across the lobby while Haden uncuffed them.

He didn't add that X-86 and the three who concocted it weren't the worst of their problems. A former friend hovered on the brink – likely already teetered over. And Tony still possessed the power to swat flies, as Andrews put it. To BetaCorp's CEO, most survivors were insects. He only needed a few like-minded ones to resurrect a kingdom.

"Haden, I think we're going to need a change of scenery. Where'd that DJ say everyone was heading?" John made no effort to hold the door open for Kyle. Nathan and Jamie helped their injured friend get his crutches situated to mount the stairs.

"Some small town in southwest Missouri. Don't remember the name. I can check on a map 'cause he specifically said an hour west of Springfield on I-70, right on the Kansas border. We gonna take them with us?" Haden screwed his nose up like the thought smelled bad in his head.

"I don't know, Haden, I really don't."

"You want us to head on up?" Nathan hesitated midway up the first flight.

"We're right behind you. Don't get any ideas. Just help Kyle. Those painkillers are going to wear off in a little bit, and I can't say that I plan to give him anymore." John watched his three former employees trudge up the first of thirty-seven flights.

He didn't glance back at the towering lobby with the glass-sculpted centerpiece, but he considered the finality of what he was doing, where he was going.

He flipped open his cell phone and pulled up his menu of numbers. While he punched buttons, he and Haden climbed the first steps to keep Kyle, Nathan, and Jamie in sight. The last thing he needed was more drama.

"Hey, Jack," he shouted into his static-filled Nokia. "It's John. Haden said you've been around today. Do me a favor. When you get this message, give me a holler. I've got a job for you." John snapped the phone shut and used the handrail to heave himself up the next few steps.

"Damn elevators. Do they really take that much energy? Shit." John lowered his head and stomped up the second flight, almost on the heels of their prisoners.

By the time they made it to the thirty-seventh floor, all five were sweaty and exhausted. John led Kyle, Jamie, and Nathan back into Chamber Number Nine, left them with snacks and soda and checked Kyle's wounds. Both oozed infected pus, but the antibiotics would relieve that in a matter of days. The shots went through the flesh cleanly and exited without hitting any major arteries. The bullet-hole in the knee had been close, but the shattering patella rerouted the slug, partially deflecting the shot. John rewrapped each, applied a fresh bandage and dressed them with salve. To keep things in perspective, he refused to give Kyle any more painkillers. He felt too damn soft as it was.

"John!" Haden poked his head in as his boss finished cleaning up Kyle's wounds. "Jack Simpson is on the phone."

"You kids get some rest. We've got a long day ahead of us tomorrow." John winked as he closed the door, then took the phone from Haden.

"Hey, Jack. Thanks for calling. Would you mind firing up the chopper and getting it on pad one?"

Haden dropped the magazine he was holding and stared at John.

"Great. Thanks, Jack. Think you can have that done by eight?" John looked at his watch. "Oh, okay. Well, if you're going to be much later, just give me a ring."

When John dropped the cordless onto the cradle, he didn't even have time to sit down before it rang again.

A slither of unease gripped his privates. He'd given Kenny strict orders to communicate via cell phones to keep the other lines open. This was what he had been waiting for since taking the little field trip. A nice chat with an old friend.

Chapter Twenty-Eight

Washington, D.C.
Day Four

"HELLO, JOHN. I'M sure you know all about Miami now, right?" Tony snickered.

"Tony, what's this all about? You can't schmooze high-powered politicians and get your face on the cover of magazines now, so you have to find another means of entertainment?" John plopped down on the stiff leather couch and contemplated two or three fingers of scotch. But he thought he might need a level head for this conversation.

"No. I just plan to have a little fun, that's all. You noticed that you can hear what some folks're thinkin'?" He stood at the penthouse window of the luxury condo, the same one he'd been in only days earlier when he witnessed a variety of bizarre activities.

"Yes, I noticed. It's weird, and I'm not sure who all can do it. I...I don't get anything too clear from everyone, how about you?" John sighed. It disturbed him beyond belief that Tony put into words what he was just figuring out – and that it meant his old friend must be able to do it. He caught snippets of Haden's thoughts but hadn't been able to admit the ability. It seemed so invasive.

"Oh, yeah." Tony cackled, no longer firing on all cylinders.

"Do me a favor, Tony. Meet with me. I could come to...to D.C., right? We could have a drink. I mean, like old times. Not shooters, I think I've done all the shooters I can handle, but maybe a martini or a scotch. How about it?"

"No dice, big man. D.C.'s my town now. You can have your stupid Texas chauvinism. But surely you don't plan to just sit there with your genius kids, do you? Maybe that's the question of the hour. Why are you talking about meeting me when you have all the answers at your fingertips?" Tony pulled up a chair to spy on any potential survivors and thrummed his fingers on the armrest.

"I've gotten all the answers they have to offer. The next four or five days will tell the tale." John held his breath – Tony could hear it.

"Hmmm. That's interesting. Almost as interesting as some of the things I saw this morning. Wanna hear about them? Of course you do." Tony took a deep breath and shared how at 7:05, thousands of District of Columbians took a deep whiff of X-86, stopped in their tracks, and stared at the sky. Tony's sinuses had immediately swollen, and the headache that originated in his sleep became thunderous in response to the chemical. He confided in John that it gave him a painful erection.

"They all stared at the sky like someone up there was either talking to them or going to help them. How come no one ever looks down?" Sitting at the enormous window, Tony laughed aloud, his antics not so different from those below him on Massachusetts's Avenue earlier that morning.

He went on to describe how the screaming started around 6:45. Passersby bellowed sweet nothings, while one older man shouted that the world was ending. Tony suspected Grandpa might just be right, but he certainly wished the old geezer would put on a shirt.

"John, if I look like that old fart in twenty years, I'll friggin' blow my head off now. Anyway, where was I?"

Tony continued his story, unsure if John was still listening but he liked the sound of his own voice. He tried to depict how ridiculous the few looked who simply plopped down in the middle of the street and then got plowed by erratically driven cars. Tony didn't flinch one millimeter. He'd never had much compassion for people in general, much less the fragile-minded. What kind of moron sits down in the middle of the road, for God's sake?

Those who clawed at their throats intrigued him. What thoughts came when the inability to breathe overtook them? He wanted to know, in a God-envy sort of way.

He had never witnessed human suffocation. Even a disturbed megalomaniac couldn't observe that kind of suffering and not be moved by the excruciating sight of it. Yet the reality of it, seeing it up close and personal, resurrected memories he had squelched for fifty years.

"Tony?"

* * *

"GET UP, ANTHONY! Now! We've gotta go." His mother yanked him out of bed to do the midnight, ditch-the-rent move to a new trailer.

"I'm comin'." In a panic, a nine-year-old Anthony Andrews scrambled around his bedroom for his most prized possessions.

He knew she would find a slum somewhere in town because of his schooling – the city was big enough to skip around unnoticed for years. He knew his mother prided herself on being able to give him the chance at success, and he hated her for it.

It wasn't until he was in college, two years after she had died in a single-car collision with a telephone pole, that he realized she had freed him. The prison of poverty no longer held him captive, though growing up an outcast was its own sort of punishment. He regretted never thanking her.

The next morning in a new neighborhood, a local yokel discovered little Tony to be a private school snob.

"Jesus, how does p.w.t. like you get into that school? You too good to go to mine, piss ant?" The overgrown thug glowered at Anthony with a mouthful of broken, greenish black teeth. The boy stood head and shoulders above Anthony, but only had two or three years on him. Anthony remembered thinking Mr. Smartypants needed a dentist worse than a life.

"Eat shit, loser," he said through gritted teeth. "Looks like maybe you already did once."

The fist into his gut didn't take away the satisfaction of pushing the bully's button.

I may be smaller, I may be as poor, but I am not like you, Greenteeth. Not in a million years. People like you make me wanna puke.

He clawed his way out of those slums, and he would never go back.

* * *

THE MEMORY FADED, but Tony subconsciously rubbed his abdomen where it had weathered the punch so many years earlier. Then abruptly he felt the phone sweaty against his ear and switched to give that one a rest.

"You got what I want, John." Tony's thoughts segued to an image of him on the cover of every newspaper in the country, the universe. And three shadowed faces hovered just behind him.

"You're a mess, Tony. You really need help and I want to help you. We used to be friends, remember?"

"John, you are so full of shit. So where do you plan to take them?" He saw a dead suit face down in a mud puddle.

Tony remembered watching him bite the dust that morning. Dressed for success in his triple breasted Armani, the lawyer-type dropped his thousand-dollar briefcase in a muddy storm drain to clutch his collapsing throat. In a lame quest for air, he took the time to pull the leather briefcase out of the water. Either he hadn't realized he was dying, or Tony thought maybe he wanted something from it. He imagined the yuppie pulling out papers and finding someone to sue for what was happening to him. Tony cackled – he felt like he was watching a cruel lawyer joke being acted out before him. *Whaddya call a lawyer at the bottom of a swimming pool? A good start – hahahahaha.*

Tony hadn't felt sorry for this young man. He detested lawyers, though his had gotten him out of a pickle or two.

He heard John say something, but he became transfixed watching a heavy-set lady waddle toward a bench clutching her dysfunctioning throat. Their eyes met. She stared at Tony so many floors up, perhaps wondering why she was airless and he was not. He wondered the same thing himself. John's quartet had perfected a warfare chemical his company could only envy. Jealousy mingled with the resentment somewhere in his subconscious for the third or fourth time.

"Tony? Hey, man." John's voice tried to penetrate the haze, but again, the woman somehow made perfect eye contact with him through the reflecting glass. Her eyes glazed and retreated toward the top of her skull, but the look of anguish gave Tony a blip of sympathy for her. He didn't know why he was spared. Had he sold his soul and he couldn't remember doing it? It seemed possible, even likely.

Tony imagined himself at the pearly gates, and St. Peter telling him to enjoy the flight south. He shuddered.

No one ever consoled him when he was in pain. No one gave a shit how he felt. When he was a boy, the patterns repeated weekly, monthly, even annually, like clockwork. The whole lunch money gig, supplying stolen materials. They ordered it; he swiped it – the actions of a survivalist.

And the teasing never ceased, it seemed. Supplying stolen goods felt like it served a higher purpose. But the taunting that started in first grade and lasted through junior high left scars he cut open now and again, to keep the venom close so he never lost his edge. By high school, his twisted sense of power became evident to those around him. A total disregard for rules and life made classmates keep their distance, and that suited Tony fine.

"Yo! Tony." John's voice sliced through the fog of memory – the big guy too much like many of his tormentors.

"Sorry, just resurrecting some demons. What'd you say?" When had John called? *Why* had John called?

"Shit, man, you asked me a question then checked out like a two-bit hooker. You've got to find some meds, Tony. Local pharmacies can hook you up with Prozac or Valium, even Zyprexa. You're not sick and you're not God. You've got to calm those voices; if you don't, I'm worried you're going to be..."

"Fuck you, you prick! You better go, 'cause I'm done runnin' your scams, stealin' for you, I'm finished. I'm not anybody's bitch anymore! I QUIT!" Tony punched the off button on his cell phone, then threw it as hard as he could against the window he'd been staring out. The phone bounced off with a *bonk*.

He stormed across the room, grabbed his laptop, and slammed it onto the small round hotel table. The explosion in his head made him clench his teeth, double his fists, and take a deep breath so he could see.

"Goddamned asshole. Fuck them and the horses they rode in on." Tony typed in coordinates so ruthlessly the Macintosh trembled. His impressive executive career had been sprinkled with fits of rage that he had managed to channel into savvy business-decisions and aggressive takeovers. But now his willpower had diminished with the ozone.

Miami had been the tip of the iceberg. He had seven more silos, seven more opportunities to emit justice, seven ways to silence the voices. All those sons of bitches who had laughed at him in grade school. The pricks who had beaten him up in junior high. Anyone who had ever laughed at him for any reason at all. His hand was at the top of the bat in the deadliest game of one-upsmanship.

"I hope every sonuvabitch who ever looked down on me still lives in Florida – no matter how fucked up you are now!" He thumped the enter key with enough force to crack it.

Somewhere in Denver, the Earth opened and made way for Florida's annihilation. Four missiles fractured the state, leaving large islands as stark as the Sahara.

"Oh, John, you should be so fucking scared. Now I am God." And hadn't it been John he was talking to? Dallas would have to wait. The three little treasures couldn't be harmed.

He decided he liked the way that sounded so much, he picked up the hotel phone since his cellular lay in pieces on the ugly blue carpet. It took John nine rings to answer, long enough for Tony to worry that he had missed a date with destiny.

"Hey, John, heard any big booms lately?" Tony's demented laughter made John jerk the phone from his ear. Before the click, John jumped up from the couch and raced to Chamber Number Nine dialing his cell phone and screaming for Haden.

After the brief, albeit entertaining conversation with the good doctor and taking his pent up aggressions out on the Sunshine State, Tony exited the penthouse by way of the stairs and emerged onto a desolate street. He looked around the high-dollar district and tried to orient himself. Though he'd spent hundreds of hours in D.C. at boring meetings and ending the days at expensive bars, everything was different now. No traffic, no buzz of energy from theatergoers, name-droppers, and spotlight-seekers. It was what he loved and detested about Washington, D.C.

Tony headed toward Pennsylvania Avenue. He remembered thinking Friday how this had been the big fish he'd always wanted to fry. He knew now that there might not be a frying pan left for the cooking.

"Hey, handsome, gotta dime?" A beautifully exotic middle-aged woman snickered as she tossed a tin cup at Tony. He watched her wander past him, aimlessly traverse the street from side to side, and then she sauntered into the FBI building like she owned the place.

Had she been someone? A senator? An actress? Maybe a judge or a doctor? She had that air about her. He decided thinking made his head hurt and he couldn't care less who the hell she was – she was fucked up. *That* separated her into the other of the three neat categories – the dead, the sick, and the survivors.

The question lingered – which one was he?

Chapter Twenty-Nine

Springfield en route to Joplin
Day Four

DUSTY ROUSED MELANIE from a fitful car-sleep.

"Look, Mel." Dusty slowed the Mustang to a twenty-mile-per-hour crawl down Glenstone in the once booming city of Springfield. Missouri's third most populous metropolis suffered from a recent bout of chemical-itis.

"God. It looks more recent here."

"Yeah. I gotta pull over. My back's killin' me." Dusty stretched, bracing his arm against the steering wheel. The rough drive, the detour into Arkansas to skirt jammed highways, and north on tiny two-lane roads grated on his nerves.

Two SUVs blocked the oncoming lanes while a bronzed thirty-something man sat cross-legged on the cab-top of one.

"Hope is gone!" he bellowed through a megaphone. He caught Dusty's eyes and held them. "Turn back, you two, don't proceed into the future. It's not what it appears to be. Doom lies ahead, his evil hidden beneath gold cuff links, a Rolex, a Ferrari. And the little girl can't save us from it all. He will be her downfall."

Dusty and Melanie couldn't tear their eyes away from him – tanned good looks, lucid eyes, and level head. And in a bizarre moment of clarity, Dusty heard the man tell him to get the hell away. *The devil's coming.*

"Did you hear that?" Dusty glanced over at Melanie – she stared at the clean-shaven man dressed in blue jeans and a Polo shirt.

"That doom lies ahead? Think he meant Tony?" Melanie squinted at Dusty, and he wondered what X-86 was doing to his brain.

"Uh, I dunno. Maybe." But Dusty hadn't even thought about that. He knew this guy wasn't the same as all the others. For a fleeting moment, Dusty locked eyes with him and knew the wires buzzed both ways.

"Dusty, he's so normal, he..."

"I know." Neither spoke another word, but he knew what rambled through both their heads. *A survivor without hope.*

"We need gas." Melanie peered over at the instrument panel of her Ford. "The gauge doesn't go all the way to E, just so you know."

Dusty laughed, shaking off the strange encounter. "Same with cars as with people. We all have our little quirks."

The mindless chatter allowed Dusty to pass the preaching man without looking back. For some reason, the tirade of a sane man scared him more.

"Let's gas up, grab a bite, and switch. You feel like drivin', Mel?"

"Sure. Get us farther down the main drag. From the looks of the map, Kearney is the last intersecting street before we hit I-44. Then it's a straight shot southwest. We're about an hour away, depending on the roads." Melanie refolded the map and sighed.

"Watch for an older gas station so we can work the pump, unless you happen to see one running. That kid you talked to a little while ago said a mechanic had electricity working at a station in Tennessee, so you never know. What was his name again?"

"Austin, and he wasn't a kid. He has to be nearly twenty – not that much younger than me. He was in college." Melanie glanced over at Dusty.

He could feel her eyes, but he wouldn't take the bait. He knew how she felt about him, and the age difference didn't bother him at all. But he cared about their working relationship, and back when there had to be one, he didn't want to jeopardize that.

"A kid isn't always about age. It's the attitude, and he sounded like a kid. He used all that slang, you know, like *aiight, dude.* Geez. Now what he said about Miami, that was scary." Dusty stopped for a massive pile-up and didn't know if he could get around it.

"Remember what Brad said about Tony? Worrying about X-86 poisoning isn't our only problem. We'll be looking over our shoulders for a madman – and I don't even think I'd remember what he looks like. I only saw his face on the cover of *Time* once. He was in the news a lot, but I didn't pay that much attention."

"Melanie, there're going to be lots of crazies – Tony may be the worst, but there'll be more where he came from. And God forbid he starts recruiting. Are any of your contacts close to us? Check your little map there, girl." Dusty laughed. He loved that she spent much of the eight-hour road trip staying in touch with their many contacts. It made him feel part of something big and important.

A flash of memory tugged at Dusty – Tattoo Boy unsnapping his jeans and pulling at Dusty's belt. *Do 'im, baby. You know how I love that shit.* Wanda's voice brought shivers down his spine.

"Dusty, you okay?" Melanie rested her hand on his shoulder. He shook his head, mumbled that he was all right and wound around the entangled cars. "Austin would be the closest one. Actually, he could be here by now. He might even be ahead of us. It's hard to know, as congested as some of the roads are."

"Well, we'll know soon enough. Let's put a call in for everyone to start the chain. We're in Springfield and about to hit the last leg to Joplin."

"Gotcha." Melanie dialed quickly and jabbered away while Dusty weighed the new voices rumbling in his head. He wasn't sure all of them were his own anymore.

He slowed the Mustang to a crawl. Less than a mile from Kearney, Glenstone became a wall of cars. Some slammed into a hotel on the left hand side of the thoroughfare and formed a dam of metal all the way into a parking lot on the right. Dusty reversed the sports car, pulled into the parking lot and saw two men standing at an Amoco gassing up.

"Mel, look," he whispered, not wanting to interrupt her conversation but he wanted her to hurry and hang up. He didn't like approaching strangers unprepared.

"Okay, Bryan. I hope you all can be here soon. Talk to you later." She punched the off button. "You think they're okay?"

"Only one way to find out. We need gas." Dusty eased the Mustang around a Saturn to another pump and popped the gas lever. Both he and Melanie hopped out without hesitating.

No one spoke for a few seconds. They all seemed to be sizing each other up. Dusty grabbed the handle, popped it in his tank and raised the arm to start the gas. The familiar hum was music to his ears.

"Hi," he said simply to the kid getting gas behind him.

"Hello. I'm Austin Kinsey. I look grimy, I know, but I've been on the road for a while."

Austin fingered through his sandy blond hair, trying to tame the chaotic waves. Dusty thought the college boy looked a little like a skinny John Goodman with too much hair.

"I'm Dusty, and this is Melanie. We're from..."

"Dallas! Oh, my God, you're the DJ!" Austin clapped Dusty on the shoulder and hugged Melanie. "I've been talkin' to you, Melanie. Austin, from Florida! Remember you talked with me right after somebody bombed the hell outta the sunshine state."

"Oh, hey, Austin! It's good to finally meet you. I tried to call you a little while ago and got your voice mail." Melanie grinned from ear to ear, and Dusty knew she liked finally meeting one of the voices.

"Yeah. My battery's dead. Billy and I were talkin' about finding a cell phone supply store. He thinks there might be one in the North Town Mall just ahead." Austin motioned to the lean guy standing next to him.

"Name's Billy Ferguson. Just met Austin, and, boy, am I glad to finally talk to some real survivors. There are some doozies out here, ya know."

Everyone shook hands and spent a few minutes comparing stories and sharing insights. Dusty liked Austin right away – the college boy planned to save the world by solving every economics problem on the planet.

That's a big job now, Austin.

"Yeah, it is," Billy said, and winked at Dusty.

Confusion riddled Dusty's face. He looked at Melanie, who appeared as shocked as he felt. They had discussed what the X-86 might do to sane people, but he never considered anything extrasensory. It made him replay what the man standing on the SUV had said.

"Sorry, Dusty. But your signal was powerful just then. Most of your thoughts were cloudy until that one. You're confused, I can tell, but don't be. The air is free of interference – all those phone lines, internet mumbo jumbo, radio waves. Whatever it is that clogs the atmosphere, it's gone now. Leaves us wide open to really listen. I suspect X-86 has cleared the air, so to speak. You know, enhanced our sixth sense. Think about it. If it kills some people, those who survived must be the select few who are stimulated by it. And this isn't the first time for me; it's just much easier now. Maybe it's because I'm a writer." Billy chuckled. "I'm also a mechanic, so I multi-task well."

"Wow, a literary mechanic. That's a twist. Dusty, he probably likes all your NASCAR stuff." Melanie shook her head as soon as both men began bantering about who would've won the Winston Cup. Billy's deep tan rivaled any Texas man she'd ever seen. The dark brown hair spiked on top was speckled with gray, but it seemed premature. She guessed him not to be a day over thirty-five.

"Wait a minute. What do you mean, this isn't your first time?" Dusty liked the mindless chatter about sports, but he was still pondering Billy's earlier comments..

"I've always done those doo-doo-doo-doo kinds of things," he said, adding the Twilight Zone jingle. "My mom read that Stephen King book where that little boy had the shine, and she and I used to tease that we had it. Well, I think some people do."

"Like that kid in *Sixth Sense,*" Austin piped in.

"Sorta. Except he wasn't real, and he saw dead people. Well, damn, I guess we all do that now, but they're right in front of us." Billy laughed, but he stopped when he saw the disgust on Melanie's face. "Sorry, ma'am."

"Well, I don't subscribe to any of that crap. All I know is I don't like any of this, and the fact that someone nuked Florida has me pretty freaked out. Do you think the same people who released the chemical have decided to speed up the process?" Austin looked from Dusty to Billy, then over to Melanie standing on the other side of her Mustang.

"I think we have more than one problem," Melanie started, then tossed the mental shoe to Dusty by raising her eyebrows at him.

"Yeah, we've been in contact with a guy who worked for a CEO who's a few cars short of a train. The bombings might be his handiwork, but we don't know for sure. We heard a rumor that the folks responsible for the X-86 are in custody, but who with, I have no clue."

Dusty fiddled with the pump, clearly addled by the telepathy prospect. The handle clicked several times, but he managed another gallon and a half to top it off. He returned the nozzle and screwed the cap back on.

"Any gas tanks in there?" He nodded toward the small booth that served as a payment window.

"Nope, already looked. But there will be at those stations." Billy pointed at a Phillip's 66 and a Conoco station near a hotel. "There's been some crazy folks runnin' around, so I've stayed put for the time bein'. Just been waitin'."

"For what?" Melanie asked.

For you. But Billy just smiled and Dusty wrinkled his forehead in confusion again. Had Billy listened to them on the radio? When Billy winked at him again, Dusty shook his head and laughed nervously.

"Let's get this show on the road. If we're going to explore for cell phone batteries, let's make sure everyone has enough food and supplies to last for a while. We don't know how many people will be in Joplin and what's available. I'm thinking kerosene lanterns, batteries, matches, charcoal – all that kind of stuff." Dusty motioned to Melanie to get the lead out.

"I guess the pre-season game between the Chiefs and Bears won't be on, huh?" Billy play-kicked a candy wrapper like a disappointed kid.

"Huh, Dolphins were gonna whoop up on the Saints today," Austin said, glancing from Billy to Dusty.

"Don't ignore me, boys. Ask Dusty. I know more about football than all of you combined. The Steelers are due, and it's their time.

Shame you'll never know how dominant they were going to be. Won their pre-season opener last week forty-four to *nothing*. Against the Patriots. Put that in your pipe and smoke it." Melanie gave a satisfied *hum!* and all three guys laughed.

"She's right, boys. She can quote damn near any stat you wanna know, not to mention she's a Cowboy specialist and doesn't even like them." Dusty rolled his eyes, always miffed how she could be such a Steelers fan living in the heart of Texas. She claimed that since Cowher had been a Cowboy, it made them okay by association.

"Aw, Parcells couldn't even do it for the Cowboys. Kept gettin' 'em to the playoffs and they'd choke." Austin put hands around his throat to illustrate his point.

"Careful, Austin, Texas chauvinism is everything you ever heard it was. I'm a Lone Star boy through and through. Rest of ya'll wouldn't have a team if it weren't for Texas. All the best come from there. You should know if you're a Dolphins fan. Hell of a running back you used to have. A Longhorn, you know." Dusty finalized his point by nodding his head hard one time.

Melanie knew the signal well. Sometimes he even added his famous Forrest Gump Dustyism, "And that's all I got to say about that."

"Well, my Chiefs have made it to the AFC Championship last two years in a row. Vermeil's gonna hang on 'til they win it. Mark my words. After the Bucs won it, AFC's dominated ever since. Peyton Manning, Tom Brady, stick a fork in the NFC, 'cause they're done. Now baseball, that's another story." Billy twisted the cap closed on Austin's gas tank and slapped the cover shut.

"Whatever," Austin said, waving his hand like he'd heard it all now.

"Boys, I'd like to debate sports with you, I really would. But I have calls to make. We've gotta get on the road. We only have an hour, so I have at least twenty-five more people to get hold of. Do you mind?" Melanie looked to each of them. *Light a fire under your asses, boys, we got things to do, places to go, and people to call.*

"I know, Melanie, twenty-five of them in all." Billy winked.

"Ugh. I don't like that, Billy. Get outta my head."

Dusty laughed. At least he wasn't the only one uncomfortable with the violation of privacy.

* * *

AFTER FORAGING THROUGH the North Town Mall for over an hour, Billy helped Austin load his Saturn while Dusty and Melanie repacked their gear to fit as much as possible.

"Okay, I'm carpoolin' with Austin. We good to go?" Billy smacked the roof of the car before he got in.

"Yep, let's boogie." Melanie hopped in and led the entourage onto the ramp heading west on I-44. Within only ten miles, the Mustang and Saturn caught up with several other vehicles driving in the same direction. Some of the wrecks had been cleared by motorists or looters, but traveling fast went in spurts.

"Dammit." Melanie slowed while a brand spanking new Dooley in front of them navigated around a six-car pile-up. After giving up trying to make phone calls and driving, she resorted to cussing.

"I like seein' all these cars, don't you? I count eight now." Dusty glanced at Melanie and then back at the Dooley. Doing eighty on I-44, he itched with anticipation. At this rate, they were less than twenty minutes from a reconciliation with civilization.

* * *

"BRYAN, LOOK AT all the cars!" Jessie sat up and leaned against the dashboard. Her heart raced. The last few smaller cars disappeared over a hill, but when they crested the top of it, she counted.

Twelve!

"Yeah, I see 'em. They're quite a ways ahead, and with all the wrecks, I'm gonna just keep my pace. We're almost there anyway." Bryan glanced in the rearview. The few who had joined them in St. Louis kept a fair amount of stopping space between them.

Jessie grinned at Matthew snoozing in the back seat. Scooter lay sprawled across the boy, literally on top of Matthew like he thought he was a lap dog.

"Oh, God. Poor Matthew." Bryan chuckled.

"Poor Matthew. What about poor Scooter? He's the one havin' to share space with a boy." Jessie sighed dramatically, and Bryan laughed again.

She liked that there were no weird voices in her head from Bryan, and only a few when Matthew had been awake. The strange talent ebbed and flowed like the ocean, and she wished it would stay away permanently. It occurred to her that many might have the ability and introductions in Joplin might be interesting because of it.

"Why don't you lay your head back, Jess? We've only got about twenty minutes, and with all these cars in front of me, I'm not gonna need you to help me with the map. I think we're all goin' to the same place." Bryan smiled and Jessie liked seeing it.

"Okay. Let me write a quick note to my diary."

Dear Diary,

We're almost there, and Im real excited about meeting all the new people. I keep dreaming about meeting them but Im sort of nervous about a few from my nightmares. Its so cool to know that everyone's been listening to the same radio guy and that maybe things are going to be okay.

I just wish Daddy could be here with me. Momma too I guess. Im kind of mad at her but sad too. Do you think she is dead, Diary? I hope not but then again I guess it would'nt change things much. I've been dead to her for a long time.

Well, Diary, I'll talk to you tonight - I cant even imagine what Joplin is going to be like! I'll tell you all about everyone then.

Love,
Jessie

Chapter Thirty

Washington, D.C.
Days Three and Four

KENNY GAWKED AT the sight of planes askew on the runway. Richard Deeks maneuvered the company jet as close to the terminal as he could.

"I'm gonna open up and let you out, Kenny. I can't get any closer. I'll wheel this baby around by the TWA tarmac. Let's get the emergency exit open. That'll be easier." Deeks ducked his head as he gripped the exit door and helped Kenny drop down the inflatable chute.

"Hey, toss me my bag." Kenny waited while the accounting executive threw the duffle down to him.

"I'm gonna steer wide and just leave this down. Don't know how we're gonna get it closed, but we'll cross that bridge when we come to it. See ya in a few. I'll meet you, um, by the first Burger King."

"Gotcha." Kenny turned and made his way into the luggage area of the airport. He'd always watched the little truck-trailers wheel around dispensing suitcases and such, but he'd never been in that part of the airport. It took him nearly thirty minutes to find his way to their meeting point.

Standing near Gate B, Kenny listened for signs of company. Goosebumps erupted on his arms as a shriek filled the terminal, the following echoes making him shudder.

"I do not want to hang out here, Deeks, come on." Kenny paced, glancing at his watch wondering if somehow Richard had beaten him there and gone looking for him. He felt the beginnings of another headache and grabbed a couple of Advil from his pocket and dry-swallowed them.

"Hey, Jenkins! Down here!"

Kenny whipped around and saw the balding Mr. Deeks waddling his way. He didn't know the branch vice-president well, but with the strange ways of the new world, every casual acquaintance became an automatic friend.

"Thank God. I got worried you beat me here. I had a helluva time finding my way from the loading docks. I thought we'd go to the Hertz counter and find us some keys." Kenny shook hands with Richard as if he hadn't seen the plump man in ages.

"Better yet, let's just head to the main concourse and grab a car in short-term parking. You know there'll be something with keys in it." The middle-aged man toted his leather bag, brushing the sweat from his slick forehead. Kenny wondered how he could be hot, but the added insulation and exertion couldn't help. One of the phenomena about X-86 had been the chill – bizarre for a Texas August. He knew D.C. should be cooler with the proximity to the Atlantic and northern location, though he knew summers in the capitol warranted open fire hydrants.

"Sounds good. This place is creepin' me out. And I've not seen very many, um, people, have you?" Kenny slowed as they walked toward the concourse, aware that the chubby man couldn't keep up.

"You mean dead bodies? Not many. But that doesn't mean we won't, so try not to focus on them. Don't care to see maggots oozing in and out of eye sockets." Deeks made a snorting noise, and Kenny frowned.

"That's nasty, man." Kenny's screwed-up face made Deeks laugh.

"Sorry. You don't know me well enough. I'm one of those people that just says what's on his mind, Kenny. Always have been. You can't be a savvy businessman high up on the food chain and worry about reactions. It's one of the things Dr. Basinger likes about me. Didn't mean to gross ya out. The world's gonna do a fine enough job of that without my help."

Deeks didn't look his way as they walked, but Kenny thought maybe the man's thick neck would make the gesture difficult. And it would be a long look up. Kenny barely cleared six feet, but Richard Deeks had to fudge to list five feet six on his driver's license.

Conversation subsided as they pried open the automatic doors leading outside, averting their eyes from the frozen bench-sitters waiting for rides that would never come. It only took three tries to find a vehicle with keys in the ignition – a BMW with its trunk open ready to embark on a vacation and getting a permanent one instead.

"Want me to drive?" Deeks offered as they tossed their bags in the trunk.

"No problem. Get us to a really swanky hotel, then I need to call John. You think this baby will start?" He wondered with the trunk being left open for days.

"Ah, these cars have all kinds of back-up systems. Trunk lights probably go off automatically. I'm going to hit the top-dollar places near Pennsylvania Avenue. Isn't that where you think Andrews will be?"

Kenny nodded, and before he could get his seatbelt fastened, Deeks whipped out of the parking space and sped toward the highway.

"God, I can't wait to take a shower. I haven't gotten cleaned up since Thursday. Yuck." Kenny thought he might do that before calling his boss.

"Yeah, me, too." Deeks didn't add more, but the air in the car reeked. Kenny suspected his thirty-year-old athletic body wasn't nearly as ripe as his new friend's.

Two hours later, they pulled in front of a magnificent grand palace of a hotel. A valet counter stood silent, and non-operational revolving doors had been bypassed by the massive swing of a bat or crowbar. Huge plate glass windows, jagged and missing, allowed them to carefully step into an impressive lobby the size of a gymnasium.

A few people were sleeping on couches; a few rigored ones twisted in chairs. A fireplace crackled with a dissipating flame. Kenny wondered if the napping were of sound mind.

Reaching the counter, he saw many keys missing, most of which probably lay in jacket pockets of big wigs who had flown the coop. He was certain some might be new residents, so he decided to steer clear of lower floors and removed the only remaining penthouse key.

Neither spoke as they climbed stair after stair to the 28th floor. Exhausted and grimier than a kid after making mud pies, each hobbled into one of the bedrooms. Kenny started the water in his private bathroom and considered all they had seen – the scores of wrecks, vandalism, and the overall feeling of doom that enveloped the city. He had hoped Washington D.C. wouldn't be as bad as Dallas, but no such luck.

While he soaked in the enormous tub, he checked in with John. He updated his boss about plans to locate Tony before dark and get the job over with quickly.

"Be safe, Kenny. Don't wander around without your gun. Times are different now and survival is the name of the game."

"Got it, sir."

"Kenny, call me John. I think the 'sir' days are over for a while." John laughed.

"Uh, you got it, s...John. Sorry. That'll take a little getting used to. Deeks has crashed for a little bit, so after I get cleaned up, I'm going to explore. Anywhere special you think he'll be?"

John laughed again. "Uh, yes. One pretty white building will be like a magnet for Tony."

"Oh, duh. Okay. Well, I'll keep ya posted."

After hanging up, Kenny finished bathing, put on clean clothes, and left Deeks sleeping on the couch. *Ugh, go shower, man.* He thought he might not sit on that couch, that they might be best off to burn it.

Once outside, Kenny breathed deep, ready for his adventure. Jogging down twenty-eight flights of stairs, afraid to close himself in a generator-powered elevator, made the chilly breeze a welcome relief. He pulled out the street guide he'd found in the lobby and oriented himself.

The sun had dipped below the horizon and much of its glow was blocked by the silhouettes of buildings. Kenny hastened toward Madison Drive. He abandoned the notion of driving for fear he would lose the surprise advantage. A car would be noisy in the oppressive silence, and Tony would hear him coming from blocks away.

He enjoyed the pleasure of walking now more than ever, even if it was getting dark. That would provide even better cover.

"Yo, my man, whatcha hangin' in these parts fer?" A mammoth street man rose from under newspapers, watching Kenny approach.

"Uh, just lookin' for a place to crash," Kenny lied, startled by the giant's sudden appearance and his own recklessness. "Ain't no place in doors for ya with all the recent, uh, vacancies?"

"No desire to sleep where I can't feel the air. Stuffy indoors, even with thuh winders open. Know what Ah mean?"

Kenny really didn't. He imagined sleeping on hard concrete or street benches while crazies ran around everywhere with knives, guns, and whatnot. It seemed a dangerous way to rest. It actually made his skin crawl with a raving case of heebie-jeebies.

I guess if he can survive D.C. streets, he must be a special breed. Big as a house, anyway.

He reminded Kenny of a prisoner he once saw in a movie – a high-tech film that enhanced a man to make him seem bigger than he actually was. But this guy had to be bigger than Shaquille O'Neal.

"Whaddya say?" The man's eyes and teeth were all Kenny could see in the darkening street.

"Huh? Oh, nothing, why?" Goose pimples rose on his arms.

"Thought I heared ya say I's as big as Shaq. Rightcha are 'bout that." The old man sniggered through gaping holes where teeth once lived.

"You heard that?"

"Yep, air's lot clearer these days. Not as much 'lectricity to block my waves. And some says that the funny air makes us better at it." An enormous grin gave Kenny another flash of yellowy-white in the midst of all the blackness. His night sight was beginning to adjust.

"So are there a lot of people 'round here with thoughts worth catchin'? I'm searchin' for a guy who's probably got some pretty dark ones rumblin' in his evil little head." Kenny figured it was worth a shot.

"Him an' a thousand others. One idgit took his Uzi earlier today and shot up every glass winda and anybody who got in his way. Kilt prob'ly ten people. They wasn't in they right mind, but hell, ain't no reason to shoot 'em up, know what I mean?"

This time, Kenny did.

"Well, catch ya some z's, my man. I'm gonna find a really good scotch. Know any good spots?"

"I'd try the White House. 'Course ya might get shot if they sees a colored man comin'. But nobody's been there since the President left yestidy." The old man chuckled, reclined again, and covered himself with his papers.

Kenny looked east where he knew the White House stood and headed for it. No point in putting off the inevitable.

A pistol John loaned him pressed hard into his spine. Another strapped tightly to his left ankle gave him a sense of sneakiness. Kenny felt like a Mafia impostor heading undercover. His nerves twitched and his heart lurched every time a voice rang out or something crashed close by.

He saw no one else throughout his walk toward the Ellipse, but that didn't mean they weren't there. He picked up faint whispers in the dark and replayed in his head what the giant man had said about catching others' thoughts. That could be a liability, and Kenny knew it. Or maybe Tony would mistake Kenny's for the many others that lumbered around in his head.

Bodies littered Constitution Avenue closer to the museums, but as he neared the White House, only a few had collapsed in the sacred area. Almost as if they knew better than to die on the revered ground.

A man sat on a bench cradling a bloated baby in his arms. The blank expression, vacant eyes, stared right through Kenny. *God, I'm sorry, man.*

For the umpteenth time, Kenny wondered about his kid sister. Kyra inspired inner city kids to love reading books. Not just through traditional education, but by living them, devouring them, experiencing them. Her teaching strategies made her an icon among her peers and a god to the students, not just for her style but her non-traditional classroom. Her middle school room consisted solely of couches or chairs of garage sale quality. Often, teenagers would plop into one and dust would billow out like a stink bomb. The entire class would chant in unison, "Ms. Jenkins, Febreze it!"

"You all quit sweatin' on my furniture, or I'm gonna have to buy stock in Febreze!"

Kenny swelled with pride with each of his sister's successes. One Friday toward the end of the school year, her students pooled their money and bought her five bottles of Febreze. For many of the inner city teens, that meant chipping in allowances or selling aluminum cans in order to donate.

Twice she'd been honored as Best Inner City Teacher of the Year in Dallas. Students often returned to tell her what a difference she had made in their lives. That, to her, was the ultimate reward for teaching.

A nearby popping sound yanked Kenny forward to the X-86 aftermath. He'd been standing at Zero Milestone facing the White House for nearly fifteen minutes lost in thoughts of Kyra, the kids, and a lost past. Kenny quickly jogged to the corner and huddled next to a bush to watch.

If Tony had chosen to come out during his reverie, the stakeout and his plan would have gone up in smoke. He was grateful no one emerged.

Unsure whether Tony had hung around after the threatening call to John, Kenny knew it was a long shot to stake out the White House. But John's instincts usually proved worthy, and where else would a power freak like Mr. Andrews most likely want to crash? Could he pass up such an opportunity?

Kenny hoped not.

* * *

HOURS PASSED AND still no Tony. Kenny gave up and allowed himself to slip off to sleep, knowing where he hid would shelter him but might also block his view if someone approached quietly. But his eyes were too heavy.

What felt like minutes later, sun streamed across Kenny's face, jerking him awake. He sat up so fast he got a head rush, and then he tried to make sense of his watch.

"Christ, it's seven o'clock." Another reckless move, and he chided himself for not just sleeping at the hotel and starting fresh this morning. Deeks had to wonder where the hell he was. He pulled the cell phone from his pocket, turned it on to check for messages, and wasn't surprised to see four from his travel partner.

The frantic feeling of oversleeping reminded him again of his college days – missing eight o'clock classes because he worked late the night before or chugged one too many beers with his buddies. Those years long gone felt like another life in his brain now.

Kenny gnawed on an apple nearing its deathbed, but the sweetness tasted like heaven. His stomach rejoiced and grumbled that it could do with a little more.

That's it. Maybe the old man'll come out to feed. Kenny's vision blurred from staring at one place for so long when something caught the corner of his eye. Coming up behind him was an older man carrying five or six plastic shopping bags filled with groceries.

Is that Tony? The thin, athletic build of an aging man fit Andrews, though the geezer had lost some serious weight since the photos John showed him.

He couldn't be sure. The scraggly dark-hair, baggy jeans that seemed so unlike Mr. Andrews, and a Redskins T-shirt didn't fit the normal Armani attire or beloved Broncos' sportswear that John described.

As the distance closed between them, Kenny thought quickly.

"Yo, Mister, gotta dime?" Kenny tried to roll his eyes back in his head and thumped the heel of his hand hard against his forehead.

The Redskin fan neared him, leery of the beggar.

"Man, I gotsta call God, tell Him I'm comin' home. C'mon, man, spare a little change for a nigga, won'tcha?"

The elderly gentleman stepped deliberately past Kenny, dashed toward the enormous white building, and sprinted up the stairs into the front doors.

That's him. The sonuvabitch just raced past me right into the fucking White House like he owned it.

Kenny's slamming heart took ten minutes to slow to a steady lub-dub. Had the old man been suspicious? Kenny worried. The fact that Kenny was clean and clear-eyed should have tipped Tony. The question was, were there too many loose marbles rolling around in Andrews' head?

Well, I blew round one.

Kenny continued surveillance, but he wandered, tried to look convincing as an X-86 victim. He ripped his shirt, then took dirt and ground it in to his clean jeans. He circled the area again, all the while keeping the front of the White House in his sights. If Tony left through any of the other exits, Kenny would never see him, but would the old man feel the need for caution? Kenny was banking against it.

Around seven, the spying paid off. He spotted someone waltzing out the front and plopping down on the front steps. The man pulled out a cell phone and starting punching buttons.

"Hello, John, still manning the helm, I see. Jesus, why don't you get the fuck outta that hell hole? It's the Sabbath, ya know. On the seventh day, He rested. So anything new on your end?"

Tony listened for a moment, then let out a maniacal sound that must have been a laugh.

"So no confessions or deep insights to stopping it, is that what you're sayin'? God, what the hell are those three talkin' about, the weather? And now that you mention it, that X-86 has wreaked havoc on the atmosphere. It's downright cold here. I wanna know how the hell they managed that little detail." Tony popped open a silver beer can. Kenny couldn't tell from where he sat what kind it was, but the foam that sprayed let him know it was probably warm. The idea of tepid beer sounded about as good as snot to Kenny.

Okay, do I make my move while he's on the phone? Kenny measured the distance between the old man and him – twenty yards, maybe thirty. While he watched, Tony braced the phone between his right ear and shoulder so he could peel an overripe banana.

This is a great window of opportunity...

Tony jerked his head up, dropping the cell phone and his banana. He looked right at the bushes where Kenny cowered. *Shit.*

Tony clearly thought he'd heard something. Kenny froze, not moving a muscle. He consciously tried to cloud his thoughts, to *not think*. Tony picked up the phone without ever taking his eyes from the sidewalk ahead.

"Sorry 'bout that. So how'd they like seein' a kid kill somebody? That'll test the weight of their gonads." Tony barked laughter again, the edge in his voice unsteady.

Kenny thought the old man might be operating without a full tank of gas.

Tony jumped up and while he talked, he strolled down the steps to check out what kept rattling in his head. Kenny knew if he didn't make his move, the old man was going to turn the tables on him.

"So are you gonna keep them there? There's all these lovely little communities joining forces – one in Pennsylvania, another in Seattle, and I think there's one in the Midwest somewhere. I keep listenin' to this station out of Atlanta, some loser named Rappin' Ray, but damn if he isn't playing some great music." Tony popped the last mushy piece of banana into his mouth.

Kenny watched him smear his fingers on his jeans with a methodical back-and-forth motion. Stripes of yellow spotted the denim.

The conversation paused on Tony's end. Kenny couldn't imagine what his boss was saying to the mentally challenged Mr. Andrews, but it distracted Tony enough that the old man stood still in the middle of the plush green lawn. Kenny knew the two once claimed to be friends. They often played month-long chess matches on the internet. John seldom won, and it drove him bonkers. Now his boss just wanted to put the BetaCorp CEO down, to euthanize a man struggling to keep his bearings. How many lives would they be saving? After what Andrews did to Florida, Kenny couldn't even venture a guess.

"I can't do it, John. I understand what you're asking, and I'm not even sure what I have left to do here. My other silos are longing for action; they want to be free, free at last. I promise I won't do Dallas, though I had ya worried before, didn't I? But we've been friends a long time. I plan to beat your ass in the football pool again someday. If there's ever football again. God, how depressing." Tony's head hung as it truly mourning his beloved Broncos.

Kenny's heart raced as he contemplated his move.

"Ya know, John, I could solve your problem with the three stooges. Leave the city, head to the Caribbean, relax, enjoy the surf. I'll take care of the rest for ya. You'd never even have to know."

Another shorter pause.

"Okay, okay, it was just a thought. Well, I'll check in with ya when I see Diana. I'm planning a lovely dinner when she shows. Talk to ya soon...bye-bye now."

The ancient man on the bench had told Kenny that President Cavanaugh left. He wondered if Tony was bluffing John or if he was really that out of it. As far as Kenny knew, the President addressed the nation Friday and hadn't been heard from since.

Kenny expected Tony to stand and walk back toward the White House, but instead the deranged man stretched dramatically and wandered across the perfectly trimmed lawn. Kenny's stomach seized in apprehension.

He's comin' right at me. He's gotta recognize me from this morning. Shit, I'm 0 for 2 now.

He hunkered in a ball and pretended to be asleep. Footsteps neared him, slowed, unlike the pounding in his chest. And then he felt a foot press against his top leg.

"Well, what do we have here? Don't you have some projects to sleep in? Maybe a whore house to haunt? You people make me sick."

You people? Kenny's insides twisted with loathing. *Fuck you, you arrogant prick. You're as fuckin' crazy as they come.*

"What was that?"

Oh, shit...

"Yeah, I'd say that's about right. Thoughts are speech if you know how to tune in, wise ass. Get the fuck up." Tony loomed directly over Kenny and had his legs spread like he was ready to spar.

Kenny tried the not thinking routine again. He pictured blue sky, imagined white fluffy clouds, like those he'd seen on a Caribbean cruise.

Picture the water, blue, pristine...

"Nice try, ass wipe. I don't give a fuck what you think about, just haul your lazy ass away from my house."

Slowly rising, Kenny's hand gently rested on his ankle. Maybe he should wait.

"What's on your ankle you're thinkin' about, shithead?" Tony stepped back, but then planted his left leg and caught Kenny off-guard with a solid kick to the chest. Kenny splayed backward, tried to catch himself but landed square on his butt. Tony was in his face with a Glock pointed right at his left eye. Kenny's insides coiled. Fear, metallic and acrid, burned his throat and nostrils.

"Do I know you?" Tony's eyes narrowed and cleared momentarily. The senility waned for the briefest moment. Tony Andrews, CEO, business tycoon, shimmered just below the surface.

"Uh, I don't think so, man. You white folks all look the same to me." Kenny let out a nervous laugh, tried to make it sound unsteady.

Oceans gently beating against the sand, the surf. Snorkel the waters, starfish settle just below me...

"What are you hiding, son? Who the fuck are you?" Tony's eyes burned. He grabbed Kenny's chin so he could study the kid's face.

This time Kenny shut his brain down cold. No thoughts, blank slate, tabula rasa.

"WHAT IS YOUR FUCKING NAME! Tell me or I blow your miserable brains out," Tony hissed, over-enunciated through clenched teeth.

The moment of anger seized Tony, and Kenny could tell his opportunities waned. He needed a distraction. But Tony pulled the muzzle back hard and quick, popping one in the chamber. Kenny trembled as the barrel pressed into the side of his nose, less than an inch from his eye. Peering down the pipe, a friend once told him, is the truest way to discover who you are and what you're made of.

Kenny believed it. Kyra flitted through his mind.

"Who's Kyra, homie? That your chick, your woman, your fuck buddy?" Tony cackled.

With one fluid movement, Kenny rolled, pulled the pistol from his back and got to his feet with his revolver leveled at Tony. The two stood face to face, man to man, Glock to .38.

"You should've pulled the trigger the minute you aimed it, because now if you shoot me, my jerk reaction will pull the trigger. And visa versa. No one wins here, homie. You had a clear shot and you blew it. You could've kept rolling, popped off a few rounds, and I'd have dropped like a sack of potatoes." Tony smiled, almost as if he respected the move but was disappointed in its execution.

"Don't call me any more names, Tony." Kenny smiled. The confusion on Tony's face gave some satisfaction, no matter the verdict.

"John sent you." Lights went on; somebody resided there after all. Maybe not the slickest silk shirt on the rack, but soft all the same.

Thirty seconds passed. Neither said a word or moved a millimeter.

"I'll be a son of a bitch. That prick. I will blow him into a million tiny fucking pieces. You better kill me, son, because if you don't, all your little friends in Dallas are history. I can't believe it. I was just fucking talking to him, and he..." But Tony stopped. He stared at Kenny and then seemed to look right through him. "You were listening. You've been here all day. Why didn't you just cap my ass?"

"Because I'm not a murderer. I'm just here to talk." Kenny knew the next move was his. Checkmate or die.

Trying not to mentally picture his intentions, Kenny made his move. He dove to his right and rolled toward the lawn, firing six shots as he spun. Two or threw went wild, but he knew he landed at least one.

"Sonuvabitch!" A bullet grazed Tony's leg, sending him to his right knee howling in pain. Another caught his right shoulder, ripping away a half-inch of flesh.

But Tony looked like the terminator getting blasted and getting right back up. Anger flared in the older man's eyes, and he squeezed off rapid rounds before Kenny ever knew what hit him. The first two pierced his chest; a third shattered his kneecap.

"Ahhhhh, God." Kenny grabbed his chest and curled into a fetal position to hug his leg, to ease the fire bolts of pain in his knee.

"You goddamned sonuvabitch. YOU SHOT ME!" Rage reddened the tanned face, making Tony's eyes bulge. Grasping his own bleeding shoulder, he hobbled over to Kenny and aimed his pistol at the boy bawling with pain on the White House lawn.

"Tell John when you see him in Hell that friends don't play dirty. And he will *never* win a fight with me because I...don't...have...any...fucking...morals."

With Tony's deliberate declaration, Kenny squeezed his eyes shut and waited for the bullet that he knew would end his life. He refused to look, and he would not beg for mercy. He would not give Tony the satisfaction.

"Look at me, you pig." Tony smacked the barrel of the gun against the young man's head, but Kenny refused to comply.

You can't make me. You can kill me, you can blow my brains out, but you do NOT control me.

"Fuck you." Tony fired three shots straight into Kenny Jenkins' head. He released four more rounds directly into Kenny's belly just to prove the boy wrong.

"Rest in peace, ass wipe."

Kenny didn't have any dramatic dying thoughts. Tony's quick and painless execution saw to that. In the grand scheme of life after X-86, Kenny's exit beat the hell out of the alternatives.

Chapter Thirty-One

Joplin
Day Four

"WHAT THE HELL is that?" Dusty leaned forward in the passenger seat.

"Um, I don't know, but I guess I'll have to stop at it." Melanie slowed her Mustang as she exited onto Joplin's main drag. Rangeline had once been a booming street with hotels, restaurants, and every variety of store imaginable. But on the fourth day of X-86 in the Earth's atmosphere, the only beauty was glass twinkling in the hazy sunlight.

In the middle of the opposite lane sat a black-and-white striped roadblock, a wooden barrier designed to keep newcomers from avoiding the crudely built tollbooth. A Ford Windstar was parked perpendicular in their lane blocking their path, so Melanie had nowhere to go but to the booth's window. The wide lanes had been narrowed by a deliberate mass of mangled cars.

A burly man leaned out with a shotgun perched across his arm as if he didn't plan to use it, but he certainly wanted drivers to see it. When they got close, his right hand gripped it a little tighter.

"Howdy," he greeted, then peered into their car, into the back seat and then at Melanie. He ducked down so he could see Dusty.

"Uh, hi." Melanie was dumfounded.

"Well, you two look kosher, so that answers one question. Second one is your names. Then I'll need to know where you're from." The bushy haired man – beard, mustache, unibrow, and head covered with brown curls so wild Melanie wondered how he washed it – held a clipboard and waited for a response.

"Uh, I'm Melanie Stevens and this is Dusty Morris – we're from Dallas."

"Oh, my God! You're the DJs! From...from 92.5, right? Wow, we've been expecting you. You'll be impressed with what all we've gotten done. And lots o' folks have gotten here in the past few hours that've been listenin' to ya'll. We're sure glad to have ya. I'm Chuck Keeler, but I've been dubbed Checkpoint Charlie." Chuck grinned, revealing a set of perfect teeth. If not for the wild hair, Melanie thought the heavy-set man might be handsome.

"Wow," was all Melanie could manage.

"You had a need to build this? I mean, you have trouble with people?" Dusty leaned over Melanie to talk.

"And how. We've had some strange folks, so to deter the crazies, I've had to zap 'em." Chuck held up a small square device and pushed a button. When he did, a blue jolt of electricity buzzed from tip-to-tip. "But I've had to do worse. One guy jumped me when I was just set up with a table and chair, and we hadn't put up the roadblock or nothin'. Gave me this," Chuck explained, pulling his plaid shirt sleeve up to reveal a nasty gash on his left forearm.

"Man, that needs stitches," Melanie said, curling her lip in disgust.

"Yeah, that's why I also gotta know what you did before, well, you know. Before X-86."

Chuck picked his clipboard back up after buttoning his cuff. "But since I know you two, I can just fill that in. We're really hopin' for a doctor soon. We've got former cops, business types, preachers and retired folks – we got plenty of them. But you're our first DJ. Heard about one in Atlanta though."

"Well, we're here. Is the gathering easy to find?" Melanie looked ahead, as much as she could see around the mini-van.

"Yep. We marked the turns with balloons and blocked most other roads. You can't miss it. You're looking for Seventh Street. We've given jobs to folks, so they may not all be around when you get there. There's still a ton to do, but there was only about twenty of us until this last stream of cars. Three just rolled in ahead of ya. We've not tackled the Hall itself yet. Thad will explain that to ya when you get there. It's gnarly." Chuck grinned again, then scratched his beard hard enough to make Melanie think of brillo pads.

"So how many are there now?" Dusty asked.

"Um," Chuck tapped his sheet and counted. "Looks like near forty. But I suspect with your message repeating on the radio that more will be here. I guess it just depends on how many survived. How many *sane* ones survived. We gotta weed out all the rest."

"Are you...you killing them?" Melanie wished she hadn't asked as soon as Chuck dropped his head.

"Only if I gotta, ma'am." He looked up, motioned for someone, and like magic the Ford began to back out of their way. "Glad to have ya, Dusty, Melanie," Chuck said with a wave as the Mustang eased past.

Glass and metal glinted on the pavement, but wrecks had been removed. Piles of smashed cars lined the wide thoroughfare. There were no bodies that they could see.

"They've done a lot of work here." Melanie sped up, watching for the street and balloons.

"Yeah, they have. That tollbooth is a pretty cool idea. Sad though."

"Really sad. Can you imagine him having to shoot people?" Melanie shook her head, then looked around at the destruction. Timberline Restaurant's shattered windows, a McDonald's lost battle with enough baseball bats to leave it windowless, and a Taco Bell with two motorcycles rammed into the front door. Puffs of smoke spiraled over a charred strip mall, a blackened shell of stores once frequented by eager shoppers.

"Yes, I can imagine. If we hadn't been so naïve, we wouldn't have nearly gotten killed by Wanda and her thug boyfriend." Dusty rubbed his knees as if the thought of it made them hurt again. Melanie's last dose of Tylenol kept the sharp pain in her own shins at a dull throb.

"There!" Dusty shouted, pointing to three colored balloons bobbing from a pole at a major intersection.

Melanie turned left and slowed to a crawl to navigate around fender benders that covered half the road. She saw more balloons, and five minutes later, they found it. The sign in front read "Memorial Hall," the building itself tucked beyond a parking lot full of cars.

"Wow." Dusty gawked at the packed lot as Melanie turned in. "That can't be good."

"No. I guess maybe there was a concert or something. The place is sure bigger than I thought it'd be. I don't know what I expected, but this is a nice-sized town." Melanie found an empty spot on Wall Avenue and parked. Along the front, a stone fence guarded Memorial Hall. Situated between Wall and Joplin Avenue, the Hall and its parking lot took up the entire block.

"Yeah. Should be plenty of supplies." Dusty waited until she killed the engine, then climbed out and stretched. He massaged his sore knees again, and for the millionth time, Melanie thought about Tattoo Boy fastened to that center beam.

"Dusty, do you see any of the people?" She craned her head trying to see over the larger SUVs and trucks. Then she saw a spiral of smoke dancing over a row of canvas tops along the side of the building. "Hey, look over there!"

Dusty followed her pointing finger and saw the tents lining the far side of the building.

"C'mon. Let's meet our new friends." He hobbled to the front of the car, stiff from the brutal attack at the studio. They weaved their way around sports cars, trucks, and SUVs toward the new community.

"Weird seeing a campfire out here in the middle of all this, isn't it?" Melanie turned a circle as she walked, trying to spy any new arrivals, and then thought to touch the hood of a few cars as they passed. "They're all ice cold. These cars have been here a while." *And I can only guess where the owners are. I'm tired of dead people.*

"Yeah, I'm sure Chuck and his crew have a plan for that, don't you think? I don't want to come in and step on any toes. And I'm tired of dead people, too." Dusty saw a group of people on the Joplin Avenue side of the building. Some sat on metal picnic tables while others milled around the crackling fire.

"Don't do that; it creeps me out. And don't flaunt that ability in front of strangers. It'll make them not trust you. The world may be full of Wandas, you know."

Dusty grinned. She knew he could be careful, but she wanted to remind him just the same. A car door slammed somewhere behind them, then five or six followed.

"Well, good grief, it's Grand Central Station." But Melanie sighed with relief after she said it. She didn't want to greet a group of people as the only newcomer. There was comfort in numbers.

A young, good-looking guy walked a little girl toward Melanie, and she knew instantly who they were. A lanky teenage boy followed them rubbing his eyes.

"You must be Bryan!" Melanie stuck out her hand, and a Dooley full of people came up behind him. Before anyone knew what was happening, introductions flew like confetti.

Jessie shook Dusty's hand like she planned to woo him into a business deal. "I'm Jessie, the sleepyhead is Matthew, and this is Scooter. We're just now unpacking our stuff. We just went to get something to eat. That's Jake. He's from South Carolina. That's over by Georgia, and they've driven a long ways."

"Well, Jessie, this is Melanie. We're from Dallas and you may have heard us on the radio. Hi, Matthew." Dusty stooped down to rub Scooter's ears. The retriever-mixed mutt wagged a mile a minute, letting Dusty know he could do that all day if he had the time.

"It's good to meet you, but I need my beauty sleep, know wud I mean?" Matthew grinned and dragged his feet toward the campsite.

"Yeah, we listened to you on the radio, but you play sad music. We had to put Nelly in just to cheer us up. No offense." Jessie smiled, and

Melanie knew instantly the precocious girl would be a force to be reckoned with.

Yes, I will.

Dusty met her gaze and smiled. Melanie watched them and knew they were communicating on a level she couldn't reach, and it made her feel left out.

"So you folks have come all the way from the East coast," Melanie said, shaking Jake's hand.

"And we're tired." Jake motioned to the gray-haired man and three women beside him. "This is Valerie – she's taking pictures of everything so she can win the Pulitzer when they award it again. And Tristan, Candi, and God forbid I forget Rudy – he's our mascot and damn eager to clean your ears if you let him."

Melanie laughed and stroked the cat. Scooter growled, just to let Rudy know his place on the food chain.

"I'm Griffin. I always play second fiddle to beautiful young women and their adorable pets." The older man who Melanie thought could be Sean Connery's younger brother chuckled and shook hands with Dusty, Melanie, and Jessie. Bryan waved from behind Scooter, holding tight to the leash just in case Rudy decided to get frisky.

"Griffin will woo you with his sexist charm, Melanie. Watch him like a hawk. He may be fifty something, but he acts like a teenager." Valerie whopped the tall man on the shoulder. "We have to keep him in his place."

Melanie glanced Dusty's way, but played along with Griffin's flirtatious game.

He had to have enjoyed the long road trip with Valerie, a little plain and too skinny, but gorgeous green eyes. Tristan's blonde, tanned beauty had to be hard to ignore, and Candi had it all – great sense of humor, fabulous body, and the sharp features of a beauty queen. Her throaty voice reminded Melanie of Lauren Bacall.

"How did you girls survive with him?" Melanie giggled.

"Are you kiddin'? He's wonderful for the ego," Tristan said, and then explained that flirting with Griffin was like playing hard to get with her brother. It was harmless and for show, nothing more.

Melanie wondered why some men were like Griffin, consumed with women and attentive to everything about them. But then Dusty was so clueless.

"What'd you say?" Dusty asked, turning to her like he'd heard his name. His questioning eyes and ornery grin made her blush.

Oh, God. I've gotta watch what I think! She turned fiery red all the way to her eyebrows. *That's not fair, Dusty. You don't get to play if I can't.* She ached to know what he was thinking. When the subject came up in a tighter-knit circle, she was going to ask if someone could teach her or if that was even possible.

"I'm never going to remember everyone's name," Dusty complained. He glanced at Jessie and winked at her. *You're one of the easy ones.*

"Yep, I'm an easy one. The youngest, cutest, and smartest," she said, showing off the biggest grin north of Texas.

"God, can everyone do that?" Dusty shook his head, rubbed his temples and chuckled. "Damn if that doesn't blow my mind."

"Hey, folks. Welcome to Joplin," a muscle-bound man greeted, followed by others from the settlement to the right of Memorial Hall.

"Hey, Austin! Billy! I wondered where you two had gone off to." Dusty hugged the two from the gas station as if he'd known them all his life. Melanie did the same and then helped Dusty introduce everyone to the young men they had met on Glenstone Avenue.

"It took you bozos a long time to get here," Austin teased, then admitted they'd beaten them by maybe ten minutes.

"It's 'cuz Melanie had to pee again," Dusty deadpanned. She slapped his arm, and she knew he would never admit it was *him* who had to stop by the side of the road. A girl can hold it for an eternity, she teased. "She put us behind as usual. So fill us in."

"Well, gang, this is Thad Anderson, and we'll let him give you the lowdown. They've been waiting on the rush from your broadcasts, Dusty, 'cuz there's some big jobs."

"Hi, Thad. Chuck said we'd be meeting you." Dusty stepped aside so everyone could meet the mammoth WWF look alike.

"Well, folks, it's sure good to meet all of you. Gosh, this is what we've been waiting for." Thad scratched his head, motioning for a middle-aged woman to bring him a clipboard. "I'd like to share with you all the details of the past three days, but I think we ought to wait for the bulk of it until sundown. Give more folks a chance to get here. Over there, beside the building – on what little grass we have – we've built a fire. Tents run along side the building and a few are already pitched on the other side. Let's meet at the fire at say, ten o'clock. That'll give us time to get the info from you, Dusty. Who all you been talkin' to and so forth. Sound okay with everybody?"

Heads nodded and many made immediate plans to grab a nap.

"Can you fill us in on your security measures? I like that checkpoint station. That's a good idea. Anything else we should know? Any more roads closed if we go exploring?" Jake addressed the question to Thad but then turned to the other original campers.

"Well, here's the biggies. We focused on protecting ourselves first by setting up the barricade off I-44, where all of you met Chuck, and another one at the next exit. Then we cleared Rangeline and Main Street of the bad wrecks and then took to burying bodies. Felt that was the most reverent thing to do, and most sanitary." Thad pulled a thick square of folded papers from his back jeans pocket and pressed them onto the clipboard. "These are the names of the folks we could identify from purses or wallets. We tried to give people proper graves with monikered wooden markers. But for the ones we didn't know, we just put a white cross, kinda like at Arlington."

Dusty ran his hand over his short, spiked brown hair. *I feel like a grease pit.* "So how many you buried so far?"

"Countin' the ones on I-44 west of town, six-hundred fifty-two."

"Oh, my God." Melanie couldn't comprehend the time it took to dig all those graves, much less to collect the bodies.

"Yeah. Two jobs need done in the worst way, but it was just too damn big for us." Thad nodded his head toward the front entrance of the Hall to Dusty's left.

"Shit. Was there a concert?" Dusty glanced back at the sea of cars in the parking lot.

"A comedian. And it was sold out, according to the sign at the box office." Thad shook his head. Melanie marveled at his soft features, deep dimples, and pale complexion. For such a muscular man, there was nothing foreboding about Thad Anderson.

"Jake, let's go take a look. Thad, you been inside?" Dusty started to walk toward the front, but stopped when the big man didn't answer.

It's carnage I can never describe.

Dusty grimaced, and Melanie knew they transmitted mentally.

"Okay, then, let's see for ourselves what we're up against." As the two men marched toward the stone ramp, Melanie thought of what Thad had said.

"You said two jobs. What's the other one?"

"We haven't gone into houses. Those six hundred bodies were in cars, on streets or in stores. We'll have to find Joplin's forty-five thousand residents. I'm not from here, so I don't know how accurate that census is, but you get the idea." This time, Thad's eyes glistened with tears.

"Yeah." Melanie couldn't say anything more. The mental picture boggled her mind. She turned to her new friends. They seemed to be dealing with the same images.

Jessie scrunched up her face and pulled Scooter's leash from Bryan. "I've seen a lot of dead people. I don't wanna see anymore."

"Me either, Jess, me either. How 'bout we unload?" Valerie led them to the Dooley, and Melanie rousted Matthew to help carry boxes from her Mustang.

When they had most of their cargo stacked on two picnic tables, Dusty and Jake returned without a word.

"Okay, that's who the cars belong to." Bryan scratched his head. "And Thad says they've not done a house-to-house, so we've got some hard work in front of us. But we can't rebuild Rome in a day. How about we eat – I'm starved – then we delegate jobs afterward?"

"Sounds good to me. We've got a lot of meat in our coolers. Let's stoke that fire and grill some burgers." Jake started rooting through the boxes next to the picnic table, pulling out plates, napkins, plastic silverware, and cups. "Hey, Bryan, you guys, help me get the coolers from the back of the Dooley."

The prospect of a barbecue cheered everyone up. They gathered around the dying fire while Jake delegated duties. People hustled about getting cords of wood Thad and two of his buddies had loaded into the back of a truck. Others pattied the meat, cut up whole chickens, and pulled out various sides in deli containers – baked beans, coleslaw, and potato salad.

Billy popped the lids on each and took a whiff, just to make sure they hadn't spoiled. The new wave of the future, Melanie noticed, was caution – and rightfully so.

Chapter Thirty-Two

Joplin
Day Four

AT TEN O'CLOCK, people pulled chairs, blankets, and pillows to sit on to meet and greet all the newest Joplin residents. The camp buzzed with energy – too many people crammed in a tiny space eager for direction and duties. A granite Korean and Vietnam memorial separated the cookout area from tents that ran all the way to a graffitied building behind the Hall.

"I'm gonna start, then I'm going to turn the floor, so to speak, over to Dusty. He's kept lots of you informed over the radio, so he's got the inside scoop to the broader impact of X-86. First," Thad started, and then went on to share all the details of what the twenty-three original campers had focused on – safety, sanitation, and supplies. He admitted they had avoided dealing with the cars in the parking lot because that job would require manpower. Since listening to Dusty on the radio, they knew that help was on its way. When Thad finished, the crowd clapped, motivated by their ingenuity.

Before Dusty could even begin, a squatty man standing on a folding chair asked, "So who do all these cars belong to?" He motioned behind them at the sea of abandoned cars. Every head in the group turned to the lot, then back at Dusty.

"Well, while I was eatin' that wonderful burger – thanks, Thad – a lady over here says there was a comedy show. She didn't know for sure if it was Thursday or Friday. But the box office says 'sold out', so there were a lot of folks here. Melanie, was Springfield one of the first fifty?" Dusty glanced beside him while she looked at her map from the radio station.

"Uh, no, but Kansas City, St. Louis, and Little Rock were. Could've been a show Friday night. With the breeze comin' in, that would probably be about the right time." Melanie slid the map back under the notepad.

"Oh, my God, does that mean...?" Austin gestured toward the indoor arena.

"I bet that's exactly what that means," Bryan finished. "Has anybody gone inside?"

Heads shook throughout the crowd, but Jake stood and recounted a little of what he and Dusty saw inside Memorial Hall. Melanie shuddered at the mention of digging a mass grave.

"Well, we're going to have to divide into teams," Dusty said. "This is the kind of thing we're going to have to do a lot of. They'll have to be buried. We're going to have enough problems without disease and contamination."

"You know, Dusty, there might be a more sanitary way. It might not seem that way at first, but that place has gotta hold several thousand people. We can't bury that many people properly – you know, a casket, etc. So we have to consider animals digging them up and all that. I think we have to consider burning them – a mass cremation, if you will." Griffin stopped when moans from the crowd expressed dissent.

"Now wait a minute, folks." Jake held his hands up. "Maybe Griffin's right. Do we have a doctor here?" It was hard to see past the glow of the campfire. Someone had set lanterns on top of a few cars parked on Joplin Avenue. Five or six citronella torches burned near the back, but they didn't provide much light.

"Back here, Jake," a woman called out. "I'm a pediatrician."

"What's your name, ma'am?" Jake walked around the campfire and people parted for him as if he were Moses.

"Sarah Adams."

Melanie scribbled the name on her pad and jumped up to see who the woman was. If Dusty, Bryan, and Jake wanted minutes, she would have to be thorough.

"Well, Dr. Adams, I remember meeting you earlier. Do you practice here?"

"Uh, actually I'm an intern at Barnes Hospital, and I am fully capable of performing any task you need. What are you thinking?"

Melanie judged the doctor's age to be comparable to her own and added a few physical details to match the name with the face.

"Thad, Bryan, Billy, and I discussed the dangers of handling dead bodies after, you know, several days of ripening." Another collective groan came from the crowd. "We'll need you to help us do that. Do you mind?"

"Not at all. And maybe we should get to that Wal-Mart SuperCenter on Rangeline and gather all the medicines so we'll have them for potential infections and illnesses. The last thing we need is for all those *other* people to get hold of depressants and stimulants and the like." Dr. Adams shook her head with disgust. Melanie figured out right away that their intern rated high on the snob-o-meter.

"What other questions or comments do you all have before Dusty starts?" Thad waited for the murmur rippling through the crowd to subside.

Everyone had a story – they all discussed that during introductions – but first they needed to take care of business. Dusty had even told Melanie to write it at the top of her tablet – *Record facts only; emotions cloud objectivity.*

She smiled, and for the first time she considered the promise of a future.

"Well, I'm Dusty Morris, for all of you I haven't met yet." Dusty had been leaning on a picnic table, but he stood and addressed the Joplin crew who sat cross-legged before him. Most had tossed blankets on the ground, a few lounged in camping chairs, and five or six men at the back leaned on the tables where they had eaten. Their space alongside Memorial Hall was narrow, cut in half by the pitched tents, so meetings would eventually move inside when the current inhabitants had been dealt with.

"I know you all have questions, but maybe some are things I can answer before you ask. First, let me introduce someone who's been able to share some frightening news. This is Austin Kinsey." Dusty motioned for Austin to stand, and the young college student turned and waved at everyone, gracing them with his trademark goofy grin. Melanie couldn't help but smile looking at him.

"This young Miami boy escaped shortly before the city became an island. And then information we've gotten tells us the whole state is now a whole bunch of keys, mighty small ones if the missiles did the damage we suspect it did."

Melanie's mouth fell open. *Dammit, Dusty. Where's your couth?* She watched the faces and knew the sharp intakes of breath meant they hadn't known. Did Dusty think they had?

He turned and apologized to her with a wide-eyed expression.

"Whaddya mean, an island?" someone shouted from the crowd.

"Just what he said," Austin interjected. "Seems several missiles hit in timed intervals across the middle of the state. Just below Tallahassee is now a canal and the rest is surrounded by water. For now, that's all we know."

Austin had done just as Dusty instructed on the jaunt from

Springfield. He called radio and TV stations and then friends to find out what happened to the Sunshine State. Twenty-odd calls, and so far, that was the gist of it.

"I...I don't understand," one elderly lady began. "The chemical is somehow now triggering explosions? I have a home down there. Does that mean it's *gone*?"

Murmurs of *yeah, I don't get it either* filtered through the crowd like a wave.

"No, ma'am. The explosions are the work of, um, someone else. We will investigate it, but we hate to speculate." Dusty glanced at Melanie. She knew he intended to get on the internet and find as current a picture of Tony as they could. If they could get a server, then existing information would still be available. Or so they hoped. Tony's face on *Time's* Man of the Year cover had been a decade earlier, but it would suffice.

"So we're sitting ducks waiting to be blown up?" A panicked voice vocalized what many hadn't t considered yet. Another ripple of conjecture rolled across the camp.

"First things first – we have no idea why this man is doing this, but as far as being sitting ducks? I don't think so. He's got bigger fish to fry. Right now, we do too." Dusty took a deep breath and continued. "We know a group of either three or four scientists concocted a time-release chemical they've called X-86. It will be released in at least fifty target cities every two days over the course of eight days. Estimates range near ninety-eight percent loss by the time all is said and done. We don't really know why we've survived; we just know a common thread is lower-stress lifestyles or maybe something as simple as immunity. We've heard these chemists are in custody, but we don't know where. They might be in Dallas, because Aralco is there and that's who they worked for, but we don't have confirmation from anyone."

Dusty paused and waited for Melanie's signal to continue. She recorded the facts as he shared them. When she finished, she stared out at the faces of survivors and measured the strength she could see in their features.

"It first chilled the atmosphere, then a computer virus interfered with electrical currents and other systems. X-86 also caused disorientation and headaches in those it didn't kill. It remains potent in the jet stream for nearly twelve hours, allowing it to travel up to five hundred miles before dissipating. This is all from an inside source at another company and a few phone calls we received on Friday. Beta Tron Chemical Corporation – BetaCorp – and Aralco Chemical

Company are both somehow involved, though we're not really sure of that alliance, if indeed there is one.

"Nuclear missiles hit Miami, then central Florida. Early speculation was that al-Qaida terrorists were bombing us while we were unable to fight back, but we now have confirmed reports that the missiles are American." Dusty waved his hands for everyone to quiet a moment as the questions and fears filled the night air. Questions overlapped, forming a bizarre conversation.

"How come there ain't hardly any kids? When I look around us, I see a couple up front, but most everyone is early twenties and thirties, then fifties and up. And has anybody noticed there ain't hardly no animals?" Benson Neuheisel looked at his buddy and nodded like he'd thought of something no one else on the planet ever would. Melanie wrote but dropped her head so her hair would block her face. Something about him cracked her up.

Dr. Adams shot her hand in the air. "May I answer that?"

"Absolutely, Doc." Dusty motioned for her to stand.

"Well, as for kids, their immunities battle constantly against germs they encounter twenty-four-seven. They don't wash their hands, and they're around other sick kids all the time. There are probably more survivors out there, but one reason we might not be seeing them, too, is that they're scared. They may be hiding, or they may be in their homes with dead parents and not know what to do. That's just a guess, but most children aren't going to know what to do in this kind of crisis."

"Hell, neither did I!" someone shouted. The crowd tittered.

"And I speculate animals may be the victims of circumstance," Dr. Adams continued, not pleased with the interruption. "How many of you had pets at home that you didn't retrieve? Their horror will be finding a way out of their prison or scrounging for food. I can't even think about that, but we'll have to deal with it. I can also bet we'll see more animals emerge. They're smart. They've gone into hiding because two-legged animals are scaring the hell out of them."

Everyone attempted to speak at once, but Billy, Jake, and Bryan jumped up and started delegating who could speak next.

"Does anyone know the motive of the group that did this? Was it a militia group, terrorists, or what?" A middle-aged man stood off to the right of Dusty.

"Well, at this point, we just don't know. That's top on our list. We will be very forthcoming when we get information. I have phone numbers for Aralco that we finally got hold of. We'll call them tomorrow."

Melanie knew Dusty had no knowledge of the guilty parties – the primary goal here was to keep people from the lynch-mob mentality.

"How do we find people who may not have heard the radio? I mean, there may be lots more survivors out there, right?" Matthew Francis's eyes shone like enormous marbles reflecting the light of the crackling fire.

"Well, um, Matthew, right?"

Melanie knew Jessie and Matthew both made an enormous impression on Dusty, so he repeated the teenager's name for everyone else. She also knew Dusty was terrible with names, but those were two he wouldn't forget.

"Yeah."

"We found a radio station we're going to continue to broadcast out of a few miles from here. But I think one of our first orders of business will be to organize task forces to search for survivors – people holed up in their homes, businesses, and maybe in their cars. These are our hopefuls. That's how we're referring to those who lived but didn't suffer brain damage. I'm sure many of you witnessed those who were, shall I say, *not right*."

"I...I...just kinda wanted to go back to U City to look for my brother. My mom and other brother didn't, uh, make it, but Marcus wudn't there when I left. I dunno if he'll listen to the radio or not."

"Hopefully, if he's okay, he'll find other people. Just because he isn't here doesn't mean he's not alive. We'll try to find out, Matthew, okay? Have you tried callin' your house lately?"

Matthew whipped his head around and looked at Bryan like that was a fantastic idea.

"How about up north? It sounded like the way the jet stream moved that northern cities weren't affected as much, that maybe a lot of people headed into Canada to avoid populous areas and potential hit sites. Could there be a substantial population up there waiting for news?" A thirty-something lady with a southern drawl caught most people's attention with her knowledge of the situation.

"Honestly, we don't know. But it's a real possibility. Again, we have some connections we're going to explore tomorrow and try to find out more. Melanie, did you speak to anyone with information that far north?"

"Uh, the group in Seattle talked about heading south, but my notes indicate that Vancouver and Juneau were both hit in the initial blast. They were the only northwestern cities in the first round that we know of. But the jet stream there moves rapidly and many suffered in the second-hand manner. Then Saturday we believe there were several hits to the northern areas – Helena, Boise, Bismarck, and a few Canadian cities. So if they rushed up there, they may have been in for a rude awakening. With the panic in the southern half of the country, I'm sure TV stations were still broadcasting up there and may even have shown footage if they were able to get it. That's a facet of this disaster we can't know until someone finds out. My guess is that yes, there may be pockets of large numbers up north." Melanie sat down and noted the woman's question and indicated her clothes so she could find out her name.

"Who was hit yesterday? We passed through Springfield, and it had obviously just started all over again there. That's when many of us realized this wasn't a one-time thing."

"Well, according to a guy who worked for BetaCorp, another fifty cities were targeted – smaller cities, some international and widespread. It looks like the second deployment's mission was to cover all corners of the United States and introduce it to Asia, Africa, and Europe. To our knowledge, Australia has not been attacked yet. We hope to find that out tomorrow."

"How exactly do you know all of this, and if we didn't die the first time, we shouldn't be affected if we get exposed again, right?" A mother or adoptive guardian wrapped her arms around a tired, scraggly five- or six-year-old girl. Melanie craned her head, excited to see another child.

"We believe if you've survived the initial dosage, you're immune. It doesn't mean you won't get headaches, some funny psychic phenomenon or suffer some post illnesses that we're not aware of yet. Only time will tell. And we know all this because a BetaCorp executive named Brad Tavares figured out what was going on and sent a mass e-mail to radio and TV stations. We owe him a lot." Dusty sighed, and Melanie could only imagine what he was thinking.

"What about the explosions in Florida? Who the hell is doing that?" Faceless voices launched questions, so Dusty answered toward the vicinity.

"Well, I can ease your minds by saying we don't think it's any kind of terrorist group. We think it's one man, but again, this is information we plan to confirm as soon as we can."

"When will we have full electricity? And do we think we're gonna need to stay clumped like this long or will we spread to other towns to search for survivors?"

"Thad, you were talking about things you all had done. This one's for you."

"Well, hopefully we'll have all power on by mid-week. Those systems are all computerized, so we simply need to find the central controls in Joplin and figure out what's what. We already know about the water sources, so running water will be available soon, maybe tomorrow. We want to make sure there are no, um, well, we have work to do first. I figure once we clear homes of the deceased, we can begin all other processes. We'll discuss that tomorrow too." Thad smiled and backed up to let Dusty take the lead. The muscular man didn't seem too keen on being the center of attention.

Sporadic cheers and sighs of relief made many realize that modern comforts were top priority.

"So, what now?" Ben Neuhseisel asked, and Jimmy, his traveling buddy, smacked an approving high-five.

Heads turned in Ben's direction. Melanie hopped up because that was her cue. She was relieved the conversation hadn't turned to the enhanced sixth sense, because that conversation could last forever.

"That's a great question," Melanie added, as she walked to a huge piece of cardboard stapled to a tree. "Let me show you our initial plan."

Outlined on the flip side of a Gateway computer box were branches looking like a goofed-up tennis tournament bracket. Two more just like it were attached to neighboring trees. On the top line of each box was either Bryan, Billy, Melanie, Jake, Griffin or Dusty's name printed in block letters. Below each name was a row of blanks.

"These blanks are for your names," Melanie instructed carefully. "We've broken down our needs into categories like computers, carpentry, plumbing, mechanics, electricity, and so on. You get the idea. As soon as we finish here tonight, please read the categories carefully and sign up for an area you feel you can contribute to. Whatever your strengths are – what you're good at, hobbies you enjoy, maybe some of you don't have a lot of talent in any of these areas but you're a hard worker. There are jobs all of us can do. For instance, first thing in the morning, we're going to clear the Hall." Melanie turned to make sure everyone understood. "Anyone have any questions?"

Several heads shook – the scores of people, restless to get started, shifted, stood, and began to whisper.

"Um, just one. We gonna go after the assholes who done this?" Ben nodded at those around him.

"Not yet. We have work to do here, and this isn't the old West. Hopefully, we'll hear from someone." Dusty parted the crowd as he asked if anyone else had questions and made his way to where Melanie stood.

Moments later, they steered people toward the posters. People chatted, jotted names, and joked that they felt like high schoolers signing up for classes.

"Well, I think that went okay, don't you?" Dusty asked Melanie, glancing over at the mass moving from poster to poster.

Austin pushed his way toward them. "We sure got our work cut out for us. Notice how many senior citizens we got here? We're gonna need some muscle, some more whipper-snappers like me." Austin grinned like a goof, making Melanie laugh. Dusty punched her playfully on the arm, and butterflies all over the planet took flight – at least the ones in her belly did.

Maybe he's jealous. As juvenile as it felt, she squeezed Austin's arm and oohed over his biceps. No matter how young Dusty thought the college boy acted, Austin wasn't much younger than Melanie. She was willing to do whatever it took to get Dusty to take the bait. She'd waited long enough and now he was everyone's hero. The competition warranted action.

"Yeah, but some of them – like Griffin and the St. Louis crew – I can tell are gonna be able to handle their own. You should've seen Griff loading the truck when we started out. He'll be fine. And Ben, he may be a dork, but he and Jimmy will give us some muscle. Plus Thad and Chuck. We'll wait and see what we've got. There are people still trickling in." Jake scratched his stubbly face.

"Wow, you're right. I hadn't really noticed," Billy muttered. "They just get here?"

"Yep, nine or ten of 'em. Dusty, weren't you surprised by the questions? I think I would've wanted to know more about what happened, what the casualties are, that kind of thing." Bryan scratched his scalp and shuddered. "God, I'm filthy."

"Yeah, aren't we all? I think the questions are typical for people trying to get a grip on the whole thing. Plus, you've come cross country, and you have a little more insight into the totality of it all. Some of these folks are like Billy. They're from around here, or at least close by. Most of them are actually doing the right thing by just looking toward tomorrow. That really impresses me, personally. I hope it stays this easy." Dusty walked away, heading toward the cardboard posters.

"I like his attitude," Austin said as they watched him go.

"He's a great guy," Melanie said and stopped herself from adding, *There's plenty more to like about him than that.*

"That's obvious," Billy whispered in her left ear making her jump.

"Stop that!" She smacked him on the arm and grinned in spite of herself.

"Does he know how you feel, Melanie? It helps sometimes to know that someone cares about you. The two of you are heroes. I can imagine what a perfect pair you'd be."

"Oh, I'm not the hero, he is. Besides, hush. He might hear you. I don't know. He's real hung up on the age thing, I think. He's like eleven years older than me, and well, he sees me almost as a little sister."

"I don't know about that. Then again, who knows what that man is thinking. He's got a cloudy thing goin' on. I can't read him much because he doesn't transmit the same. You heard how much it frustrates him. But that may be a good thing. And, it's got to intrigue you about him even more, doesn't it?"

"God, Billy, are you a matchmaker, or what?"

The philosophical mechanic grinned, and she couldn't help but notice how attractive he was. He had a ruggedness that she had always liked in men. The few stray grays made her wonder if she had a thing for older men.

"I'm only thirty-seven, Melanie. That doesn't count as older." Billy's wicked smile made her heart beat fast.

"Oh, my God, I'm going to have to learn to turn my brain off. This talent some of you have is going to be unfair for those of us who don't. It'll certainly take all the fun out of dating. And it is older if you're only twenty-one." Melanie flashed her own grin and laughed. She always vowed she'd never lie about her age, but if they thought she was young, then she might as well play it up.

"Hey, we can really do more than be matchmakers," Billy offered. "We can manipulate our future by pairing the right people. I mean, think about it. Our society was going down the toilet, if you don't mind me saying so. All the gangs, drugs, violence. Don't you think most of those people are gone?"

"Yeah," Melanie muttered, sobered by the idea of the uncertain future but excited at the prospect of a new beginning. "I think we have a wonderful opportunity to make life better. We saw the mistakes we made, and now it's our chance to improve ourselves. God, I hope we don't blow it."

Just as those words passed her lips, Tony Andrews stood over Kenny Jenkins, the blood still spreading beneath his warm, dead body.

Jessie grabbed Melanie by the waist and trembled.

"You okay, hon?" She stooped to see the fear in the little girl's eyes. The ponytail had more escapees than not, and the disheveled expression scared Melanie.

“The bad man is coming,” Jessie whispered, too frightened to say it louder. She gripped the nice lady’s hand and pulled her journal out of her pocket with the other. Even with Matthew and all of her new friends, she wasn’t so sure it was going to matter.

By tomorrow, X-86 would be the least of their worries.

Chapter Thirty-Three

Washington, D.C.
Day Four

"HEY, YOU FUCKING asshole. Nice try," Tony hissed through clenched teeth.

John cleared the sleepiness from his throat with a cough.

Tony. Oh shit.

"What're you talking about, crazy boy?" Queasiness stewed his insides.

"That black hobo you sent me. What a trooper. Took the bullets like a man, though, I have to give him that." Tony clapped, a muffled sound through that phone that sent chills down John's spine. "But the asshole shot me."

Oh, God, Kenny...I'm so sorry. How do I respond to that?

"You don't have to answer, John. You fucking prick. I haven't blamed you for any of this. Your kids created this. This is all your fault, remember? How dare you send someone to kill *me*. That nigger shot me – twice! We had honor between us. Friendship. Now your homeboy out there is buzzard food, and that's on your shoulders, too. How's it feel, John? Enjoy the guilt while you can, asshole, because it's all you have left. Your measly fifteen minutes started three minutes ago. That's all the honor I have left – to give you enough warning to know you're gonna die."

"Tony...I..." But the line hummed before he could beg for his life.

"Up! Haden! Get the hell up! We've gotta get outta here. Find Jack – he can fly that Huey on the roof. I'm getting the kids. Go...*go!*"

"Shit," Haden snapped as he barked his shin on a chair and stumbled out the door. "How long we got?" he called back as John followed him.

"Ten minutes tops. Maybe less."

"You should leave those three to fry." Haden jogged to the stairwell, but didn't wait for an answer.

You know better than that, Haden. I want them to suffer. Quick would be too easy.

Six minutes later, John and Haden raced to the launch site accompanied by six remaining employees. The all-call over the intercom rousted people John didn't know were there. That many people, plus the three prisoners, necessitated a second helicopter.

"Shit, Haden, we need another pilot." John shoved his buddy toward the launch pads. The three company choppers sat on their designated x's, one whipping loudly, ready for flight.

"Everyone, get your asses in here. GO!" John steered the four men and two women aboard. Each looked only vaguely familiar – one was a front-lobby secretary with a dazzling smile that greeted him every morning. "You three are with Haden and me. Jack, take everyone to our plant in Amarillo. We'll rendezvous there. That should be a safe distance from…well, from whatever the hell he's going to do." Smacking his hand on the side of the loaded chopper like a horse, John yelled for them to go.

He stood waiting for Haden to get off the phone.

"No dice, John. No other pilots made it. We shoulda thought of this earlier."

"Uh, sir…"

"Shut up, Nathan. Glad to see your headache's gone, but I'm in no mood." John motioned for Haden to go ahead and get on board. "I guess we can try to fly it. That's the only thing I can think of. But we're wasting time. We'll die for sure if we just stand here."

"But, sir, I can fly that thing." Nathan's eyes met John's.

Haden turned to face them. No one moved for twenty precious seconds.

"You sure about that, Nathan?" *What the hell am I thinking?*

"Positive, sir. In the NAO, I learned to fly small planes, copters, quick getaway type aircraft. It was an important part of our training." Nathan's own self-preservation brought stares from his partners.

"Then let's go! We don't have time to argue," John shouted as he jumped into the chopper. He motioned for the other one to go. Their clothes and hair flapped harshly under the helicopter's rotating blades. Nathan jumped into the pilot seat and started flipping switches.

Jamie smiled, grabbed Kyle's crutches, and followed him on board.

Eleven minutes from the dead phone falling from his hand, John Basinger, Haden Compton, Jamie Mantel, and Kyle Spene held tight as Nathan Kirkpatrick performed his first good deed since well before his Bad Deed Society days.

Thanks to Tony's lack of preparation before the phone call, the blast didn't hit for another nine minutes. A moment of collectively held breath, a jolting tail spin followed by a lurch that sent them all spilling to the floor, and all was right with the world.

In a crisis, you come together. But what the hell're we going to do now?

Kyle and Jamie held hands so tightly their knuckles were white. Haden glanced at John and eye-pointed to them.

John bowed his head and prayed. He didn't know if there was a God, but he couldn't risk the alternative. Not anymore.

He thought of his family, his home, and Kenny. Voices overlapped in his head, bantering thoughts of those captive in the chopper.

Though no one spoke, plenty was said as they rode silently to Amarillo.

John didn't try to sort any of it and didn't care – for now, he was just glad to bc alive.

Chapter Thirty-Four

Lancaster, Pennsylvania
Day Four

TONY EASED THE Cessna down on a tiny runway overrun with weeds. The airfield looked as if it had been used maybe five times if ever. Not a single plane sat alongside the landing strip. He consulted his list to make sure he hadn't forgotten anything – he needed the plane to be safe and sound when he returned. He opened the hatch and studied the drop.

God, as a kid, that would be nothin'. But Tony wasn't a kid, and he had a bullet in his knee to think about. He knew to jump meant agonizing pain.

He measured the distance between his dangling legs and the ground – fifteen maybe sixteen feet. He looked up at the hangar yawning in front of him. It stood sentinel along the edge of the field, but sun-bleached paint, an unhinged door, and an eerie screeching sound as it waved back and forth told him airline staff probably last saw the place during the Reagan administration.

There was no tower, no air traffic control, no runway lights to guide a plane down. Had he not had the remaining twilight, he would've never been able to land. Airline travel would be rudimentary for a while – maybe a *long* while.

"Okay, old man, let's do it." Without procrastinating, Tony tossed his duffle bag onto the ground with a *plop*. Then it occurred to him that he could throw out all the safety gear to cushion his fall.

"And then I'll twist my ankle on it and lay there writhing in pain for the coyotes to get me." Tony let out a nervous chuckle. *Coyotes?* He hadn't seen an animal in four days. Before he could make it any worse, Tony jumped.

He hit, bearing most of the weight on his good knee, and then rolled, the way he'd been trained centuries ago in Vietnam. It couldn't have looked pretty, he knew, but it worked. He let out a howl with the jolt to his bad leg and then a flash of pain to his shoulder.

"Ah, God." He pressed his palm to his right shoulder to stop the pulsating throb. Even though the bullet had ripped away muscle and exited cleanly, he knew it would need an antibiotic cream and continual redressing. His left knee had only been grazed, thank God, or he knew getting around would be a bitch. He touched it gingerly and then laughed. He had come to rest on his butt, and imagined his little show would have been wildly entertaining for the media. *Former Time's Man of the Year hops out of plane in grand fashion!*

At sixty years old, he wondered how many men his age, coupled with two gunshot wounds, could've done any better. Tuesday racquetball paid off. And quite a few painkillers.

"Good God, I'm in the middle of Podunk, USA." He pushed himself up with his good arm, brushed the dirt from his pants and sweater, and pulled his duffle bag toward him. He put pressure on the shoulder again, waiting for the pain to dull. The bleeding had stopped but his whole upper arm hurt like a tetanus shot multiplied by a wisdom tooth extraction without nitrous oxide. As long as he had an unlimited supply of Tylenol with codeine, which he had stocked up on in The White House – he surmised someone dulled a lot of pain there – then all was kosher in his kingdom.

Just for safe measure, he pulled the bottle from his pants pocket and popped two and dry-swallowed them. He grimaced and then hobbled toward the office.

"Anybody here?" he called out, his voice echoing inside the empty hangar. He limped to the door with *Lancaster Airfield* printed on it – the ink almost too faded to read.

Tony slipped inside the deserted building hoping for one thing – keys. There might be supplies he could use, but what he really hoped was that someone had bitten the proverbial dust and left a car out front. Once outfitted with a vehicle, he had a mission.

He would consult his map to find the camp of people he'd heard about on the radio, but first he had to clean up. Blood had soaked through his cashmere sweater, and he had a maroon patch across his entire left knee.

"Well, let's snoop and see what turns up." Tony liked the sound of his voice, a break from the consuming quiet that smothered the world. At twilight, there should be crickets, the hum of power lines, dogs barking in the distance. But there was nothing, and it made Tony's skin crawl. All the mental voices in the world couldn't splinter the suffocating silence around him.

After thirty minutes of fumbling through drawers, on desks and in cash boxes, Tony gave up.

"Shit." He stood out front of the private airstrip and looked up and down the deserted highway. He braced himself on a walking cane he'd found hanging on a hook and made his way to the road. He stepped onto the blacktop, uncertain which way to walk, and did a quick *eenie-meenie-miney-mo.*

"Okay, if I go the wrong way, at least I'll surely find a car." Tony situated the duffle bag strap across his chest and turned left. His knee didn't hurt much now, but he knew with too much walking, it would.

It didn't take long for the throbbing to start, but the muffled world maddened Tony more. He took to humming for a diversion, and when his leg began to hurt, he sang.

A highway sign corroborated that he was headed in the right direction, straight into town, and that eased the monotony. The physical exertion and the codeine-numbed pain – after he downed two more pills with a fruit punch he'd found in the hangar's refrigerator – lifted the fog in his brain. For a few fleeting hours, Tony Andrews wondered why he had come here and if his energies wouldn't be better served helping John. Then he remembered that he had blown Dallas into smithereens. A twinge of conscience startled him, but madness subdued it quickly.

Certainly he had no intention of joining this piddly-ass group. From the gist of the radio DJ, there might only be forty or fifty people gathered in Lancaster. And even if there were more, did he really want to scare them? To recruit them? To maybe even kill them?

Tony didn't know. In another time, he would've joked about ruling the planet – now the possibility sent shivers of delight through his veins. The brief sanity dissolved in the wake of images of returning to the White House as the real deal.

And without all the obstacles and hurdles, who would stop him? While he considered his limitless future, nearly two hours into his excursion, he spied a car lurched headlong into a shallow ditch. The old Toyota looked banged up but drivable. He didn't fancy the idea of someone decaying behind the wheel, but aching feet, a rumbling stomach, and a knee that felt like it had been wedged in a vice for a month forced him to navigate carefully down the ditch to the driver's side door.

"Oh, thank God," Tony mumbled at the sight of the empty car. He studied the position of the Camry and decided he might be able to rock it back and forth over the hump. If he could get it forward enough to drive it through the ditch and into the field, he figured he could get up some momentum and get it back onto the road.

"Easier said than done." With the car in neutral, Tony braced himself against the bumper and ignored the spurts of pain in his knee and shoulder. He shoved the car forward and then let it roll back, then pushed again. When he had the Toyota rocking nearly a foot backward, he heaved with all his might. The clunker lurched over the small hill and rolled ten feet into the open field, the weeds almost swallowing it.

"Hot damn!" Tony thrust his fist in the air like Peyton Manning after a touchdown pass. Everything hurt again, so as he limped to the car, he swallowed two more Tylenol. Maybe it would ease the chemical-induced headache as well, though he wasn't betting on it. In D.C., nothing had worked for that.

Ten minutes later, Tony revved the Camry and kathunked it through the ditch and back onto the highway. He felt like a teenager joyriding on a Friday night as he sped down the road with nothing standing between him and his first stage.

It neared midnight when he entered the township of Lancaster, Pennsylvania. The city redeemed itself with a small but beautiful golf course on New Holland Pike. Tony made a mental note to check it out in the daylight. Nothing would please him more than eighteen holes of bliss – shoulder injury or not. He pulled into the downtown square and parked to have a better look around. He couldn't explore while driving, especially in the dark.

When he got out, he stretched his sore muscles – some that ached from compensating for his injuries, others from getting the car out of the ditch. The moon, nearly full, gave him enough light to make out store names. A street lamp would have helped, but the darkness that blanketed the square let him know there would be no electricity to aid his hunt.

"Okay, kids, I need a flashlight." He caught a glimpse of a sign for Franklin and Marshall College and thought that might be the location he'd heard about on the radio – the campsite.

As he made his way down the street with the help of his cane, he tried to ignore the gruesome sights. Though on a much smaller scale than D.C., the dead, bloated bodies made Tony queasy. Hunger and death didn't mingle well on his stomach.

You ain't gettin' my Chivas, old man.

Tony jerked his head toward the thought-speech and chided himself for being so reckless. He hadn't even bothered scouting for resident loonies.

"Hey, I don't want your stinkin' Chivas," Tony called out into the dark, though the idea of a scotch on the rocks made his mouth water. "I just need a flashlight and some food. Any ideas?"

"Down to yer right. Military supply store. Been picked over pretty good, but should be some stuff for ya. And then a coupla shops over is a café – lots o' good shit to eat there. Made myself a banana and ketchup sandwich earlier."

A shrill sound that Tony supposed was laughter followed, then a shadowy whisper about potato chips came next. Tony couldn't decipher it.

"Thanks," he offered instead and headed in that direction.

Before he could get turned around, he noted that he had come straight in on New Holland and then turned on Franklin. The last thing he needed was to get lost. He made his way around the square and spied two more street people huddled in doorways. He steered clear until he found the supply store.

He thought briefly of John. Sending a fucking hitman to do him in. He never dreamed a friend would do such a thing. Guess he'd shown the fucker. His thoughts skewed more without someone around to ground him, so he would miss conversations with John. But now he had no sense of loyalty to anyone except himself.

Military Surplus, the storefront read, as Tony slipped through the large broken window. He rummaged around for over an hour, packing a flashlight, batteries, a hunting knife, and his own tent. The idea was preposterous – him sleeping outdoors, on the ground, in the cold.

Stupid people could be in a fucking hotel.

When he finished, his next order of business was the right car. A leader, a master, someone of his stature must arrive in proper style. Seven minutes later, Tony found a brand-new Porsche Boxster.

"Now that's more like it." Even better, the keys lay under the driver seat's floor mat.

Without fanfare, Tony peeled out of the square and followed the signs to the college. He could be wrong about the location, but he didn't think so.

Twenty minutes later, his heart pounded at the sight of a fire's glow. He whipped into parking lot A, reminded of his long ago college days, and pulled alongside a group of hard-traveled vehicles. Bugs spattered the front grills – had he seen any bugs in the past four days? – and an engine or two even ticked as though recently parked.

He saw the roaring fire and felt a pang of remembrance. A camping trip with his Boy Scout troop when he was seven.

"Shhhh, he'll hear you."

He knew they were close, but he was still climbing the ladder out of his deep sleep. When he was nearly there, his bladder suddenly relaxed and released. He realized his hand rested in a shallow pail of warm water.

"Look at the loser, he did it! He wet his sleeping bag!"

The two eight-year-olds scrambled out of his tent just as others came running.

He explained to his scout master what happened – splotches of red hot on his cheeks.

"I...I was having a nightmare, sir, and uh, I, uh, I wet myself." He hung his head, unable to make eye contact. He made no mention of the two boys.

The memory brought a fresh rush of anger and humiliation. He also recalled the second night when he reluctantly slid into his still-damp bag only to immerse his feet in shaving cream. The laughter that echoed in the night and filled his head from that long ago September still resonated in his calloused heart.

Tony Andrews entered the Lancaster camp with the memory burning fresh in his disintegrating mind.

"Hey, mister, nice to have ya. I'm Maggie," a redhead chirped, then shoved her hand toward Tony and wavered when he didn't take it immediately.

With a chauvinist touch, he shook only her fingers.

She cased him; he could feel it. He could only imagine her thoughts, because reception was down. He had walked several miles, but he didn't have the wear of four days outdoors like the rest of them. He had changed into a clean pair of Hugo Boss pants and a heavier sweater he'd bought on a Paris business trip last January. It covered the gauze-wrapped shoulder injury. Though a little sweaty, he had shaved that morning and showed only a hint of stubble. The bandage that bulged the knee of his pants could be the result of an X-86-induced wreck. Or a sign of survival – which, in a way, it was.

I wouldn't trust me either. Then he drew the curtain on his thoughts, just in case. Seven or eight people had wandered over to greet the newcomer – Tony felt his audience gathering.

"Folks, I'm here to pass on some important information." He paused for effect and to make sure he had everyone's attention. "I'm the advisor to the Secretary of Defense. Name's Anthony Parker. I've been traveling from camp to camp to keep survivors informed. We want you apprised of what President Cavanaugh is doing at Camp David, the direction we're headed and what all of you can do to prepare for the future. We all have pertinent roles, especially now."

A surge of excitement burst into the darkening night air along with the sparks from their fire. Their expressions humored him, fed his ego, and begged for more.

He didn't need Viagra when he had a crowd.

"Seems there are massive numbers of you scattered throughout the U.S., and we can either rebuild in small sections, or you can join larger settlements and branch out. The choice, obviously, is yours. I have a lot to share with you, but to be real honest, I'm starving. I've been in a plane or a car for over eight hours today." Tony relished the glowing faces gathered around him. They, too, were starving, but for more of him. The surge of power squelched the memory that had rersurfaced only moments before. "If there's anything you can spare, I'd love something to eat. I can even pay for it."

Several clamored toward the fire and the mess of pots and pans gathered there.

A man laughed. "Don't think money's gonna be much of an asset for a while. But we would be happy to feed ya, uh, Mr. Parker. Do you have a title? I mean, like, what's your rank?"

Tony grinned. He had considered that a Secretary of Defense's right-hand man would certainly be a high-ranking officer. He hoped no one knew the real advisor – that would certainly throw a wrench in things.

"General Parker, son. Three stars earned through the course of my thirty-one year tenure with the Armed Forces of the United States of America, at your service."

With great pomp and circumstance, Tony hitched his legs stiffly together and saluted as though he'd done it a million times. He had rewrapped his knee, now swollen and showing signs of infection, but the jerk sent a shriek of pain all the way down to his ankle. He had forgotten to get an antibiotic, but he would make that a priority. He still managed to get pants over the wrapped knee. His shoulder was covered with a wad of gauze and several large square band-aids.

He had, in fact, served two long grueling years in the bush of Vietnam, and loathed every single moment of it. He never saw action, never made it to a battle site. He served his time cooking, cleaning, and kowtowing to maniacal officers.

"Wow, a general. No grunts to travel around to the camps?" An elderly gentleman who looked old enough to know a thing or two about Vietnam made Tony a trifle nervous.

"No, sir. Only a few of us survived the X-86. Two others, a captain and a lieutenant, are midwest and southwest bound. We'd like to form some kind of communication band between all the groups, but really the goal is to get you folks with more people. Your numbers aren't broad enough to get a lot accomplished yet."

"Yeah, we heard about that big group in Missouri. Talked to a fellow who headed to a location south of Chicago, too, then he called and said they were migrating to Missouri. Seems a huge settlement is being formed near Springfield. Guess you probably know that already, though, huh?" The condescending question from the same old geezer angered Tony, but he covered it up well.

"Yessir. I have a man, the lieutenant, Tavares is his name, been talking with him all day. Seems that one's got a large draw due to its central location." Made sense to Tony as he said it, and he wished he *had* known about it. But better to start small.

"So, General, join us before Martin bends your ear off. Here's some soup. Made it myself. All canned vegetables, but beggars can't be choosers, eh?" The redhaired greeter handed him a hot Styrofoam bowl with steam curling up from it.

"I'm not doubtin' that one bit," Tony said with a polished smile. He took his first bite and oohed and ahhed for the lady. He savored the wonderful soup and nestled up to the fire with the forty-eight grouped there. He avoided conversation with the elderly Martin Kemp for fear of war talk.

Tony's glossy speech won him accolades. They hovered over him like crows circling roadkill. When he departed from the campsite, claiming he didn't sleep well in a tent, he imagined they would contemplate all his news and consider what to do next. But then he thought he might be giving them too much credit.

He revved the Porsche and drove off into the night. Less than fifty yards down the road, he turned around and circled back, letting the car coast as close as he thought he comfortably could. Like the snake he knew he was, he slithered between cars and tents until he could hear their voices floating toward him.

"I don't know. Think he's right, Martin?"

"Don't know, but typical that the powers-that-be can still feel good about separatin' themselves, even at times like these," Martin Kemp added, shaking his head. Tony could barely see the old fart, but he could picture the wrinkle-ridden face.

"I suppose they got a lot weighin' on 'em though."

"Ayuh," one man agreed. "But where you think he run off to?"

"Reckon he's gotta plane or somethin'. Probably holed up in the Westchester penthouse."

"I'm glad we didn't. Bein' around all those dead bodies is too much for me. When we get everybody organized, then we can do it the right way. I don't fancy bedding with ghosts."

Groans of agreement flitted through the group.

"Let's turn in and we'll decide tomorrow what we want to do. No sense in hurrying these days," said one of the leading members. "I spent thirty-seven years making quick decisions. This humdinger of a stock market crash put me out of work and on a long vacation. I intend to take my time from now on."

Everyone agreed and wandered toward tents.

General Anthony Parker, aka Tony Andrews, sneaked off into the night, raced down the road in his sports car, and returned to the army surplus store.

Who do I really wanna be?

He didn't have to be a CEO or even a general. He could be all he could be – and more.

He stepped out of the Boxster, waltzed up to the store, and slid back inside. He found a gas lantern and lit it so he could explore. He rummaged through the mustiest clothes he'd ever smelled and smacked the dust from his hands after every item. He sorted through stacks of different sizes, styles, and ranks of army wear. He ultimately chose five pairs of officer's pants, still neatly pressed, three green shirts with a nametag embroidered on the right chest, and a dress uniform decorated with two stars across each shoulder. It was the highest rank he could find.

He folded each garment into a government-issued duffle bag and then scrounged around for the more important things. The shattered glass case was strewn with random bullets, and on a whim, Tony lifted the bottom. Tucked underneath was a row of guns – a Glock nine millimeter, a Saturday Night Special, two twenty-two pistols, and a .357 Magnum that warmed his heart. Jerking the heavy revolver recklessly through the glass, Tony cut himself on his right middle knuckle. He didn't care – he embraced the gun as if it were a young woman's breast. He rubbed it, caressed it, and finally set it gently on the cabinet next to the glass case until he found a shoulder harness. The pistol he'd used to snuff Kenny Jenkins didn't compare with this fine piece of weaponry.

Before leaving, he strapped on the handgun shoulder holster and picked two expensive pair of sunglasses from the pile next to the register.

As he exited the store and stood on the sidewalk of Lancaster, Pennsylvania, General Anthony Parker paused. He had stuffed his pockets with clips for the Magnum, shouldered the military bag over his good arm, and fingered the hat with fancy gold markings on the brim.

The only thing wrong with this picture, Tony knew, was the absence of a limousine with the U.S. flag on each side of the front end. His limp added to the image.

"Damn, I'm good." Tony strutted to the Boxster, satisfied with the new him, and slid behind the wheel. He wished it were daylight so he could sport the new Oakleys and race off in style. Instead, he sped off into the night with a glint in his eye and the last remnants of his sanity waning.

When he reached the Cessna, his treasured Silver Bullet, he slid into his own cushy bunk without undressing. The new garb lay on the table beside his bed, and he slept better than he had in months.

At six a.m., he pulled out the maps he'd pilfered and charted his course.

"Missouri bound, baby. My audience awaits." Tony proceeded to hum as he toasted two pieces of wheat bread, spread them luxuriously with grape jelly, and inhaled them before firing up the plane.

He had once been criticized for the extravagance of his private jet's amenities. But now the Bullet allowed him the comfort to travel and live in style. And it could only get better.

He dreamt of a throng of people chanting his name, placing him on shoulders, and seating him on a throne in front of them. The size of his grin didn't compare to the bulge in his crotch.

God, this is going to be such fun.

He inspected his new wardrobe and began to change. And change he did. The last of Tony Andrews, CEO, seemed to be shed with the day-old clothes.

General Anthony Parker donned his hat and saluted the reflection.

Pleased to meetcha, Sir.

Signature Andrews laughter filled the Cessna.

Chapter Thirty-Five

Amarillo
Day Four

BIG JOHN BASINGER fingered the plush grass of the football field waiting for divine intervention. The two choppers escaped the Dallas explosion by mere minutes and now he didn't know where to go, what to do, or how to stop Tony. He wondered if they should even try. What the hell was the point? They held onto life by a thread, and even that grip was tenuous.

John stared up at the stars – the same that reigned over Dallas even though the city had been obliterated. In West Texas on a chilly August night, one thing had become abundantly clear – the X-86 couldn't reach the heavens and no matter how God like the three thought they were, *they weren't*.

The CEO was glad to be alive, but he didn't know what he was living for. Two days ago, he cursed the same God for taking his family and leaving him to fight alone. Now he couldn't understand why He saw fit to spare the killers who nearly destroyed everything it had taken seven glorious days to create. John didn't get the bigger picture – not yet, and maybe not ever.

"Okay, big guy, what now?" Haden's arms crossed behind his head serving as a pillow.

How could anything be wrong on a night like this?

Bitterness lingered on John's tongue, itching to be unleashed. Instead he stared at the gorgeous sky. The pitch-black night cloaked everything with an inky oppressiveness that made him claustrophobic.

A twinkling star winked and seemed to mock him.

"We can head on to Plant 24 and stay there for a while. When I saw the stadium, I just told Jack and Nathan to land. I needed to think, and I knew we'd gone far enough. I think maybe I was getting air sick," John added and chuckled. But the laugh died in his throat when the soft music from the chopper changed to a tinkling of piano.

A familiar singer's voice added to the mystique of the midnight hour, singing about riding fences and tugging at John's heart. It was one of Victoria's favorite songs.

I'm so sorry, Victoria. Somehow all of this is my fault.

John let tears slip down his face. Victoria used to sing the song to him after his mother died in '95. He eased his tired mind continually after work each night with soothing music, but the tune always reminded him of his mom. She often drank herself into oblivion while wallowing in the depressing lyrics of soft rock. For the longest time, John couldn't bear to hear various James Taylor, Carole King, or Eagles' songs.

Turn it off. The song, my heart, my brain. Can't somebody turn any of it off?

The piano echoed in the night. The song melted into a Seger tune that perpetuated the deep nostalgia. Other than the faint music, silence surrounded the helicopters and those who lay staring at the sky. The darkness pressed down on them adding to the incredible solitude John felt.

As the guitar faded away, a familiar voice suddenly filled the air.

"Hey, that's the mornin' guy on 92.5!" Haden sat up, grabbed John's sleeve, and yelled for Jack to turn it up.

"...so if you're out on that lonesome highway feelin' the way I'm sure you are after the tunage I just laid on you, give us a holler. We're comin' at you from the mighty metropolis of Joplin, Missouri. If you're in the vicinity of the Show-Me state, give me a buzz on my cell phone at (417) 555-7766. I'm Dusty Morris and you keep us connected."

"Write that number down, somebody, quick!" John yelled while Jack and Haden scrambled for a scrap of paper. Even Jamie, Kyle, and Nathan cheered to hear Dusty Morris' voice channeling through the airwaves, giving them all a sense of home and normalcy. The morning show so many of them shaved to, laughed with, and spent hours sharing their daily jaunts to work with spanned the distance like a welcome bridge.

Joplin? Where the hell was Joplin? But John had been to Springfield enough times to know the small city was situated somewhere near there. His heart pounded at the prospect of speaking with someone in the know. Haden tossed John a cell phone with the number punched in.

"Just push talk."

All of them stared at John as he waited. When the phone began to ring, he turned and gave a thumbs up.

"Uh, hi, is this Dusty?" John's voice shook with excitement. He nodded as he introduced himself and then listened.

"That's great. I'm here with some of my colleagues out of Dallas, and we've barely escaped an attack on the city. We just heard your broadcast and wanted to know where you're located." John fell silent again and listened.

"Oh, we can explain the explosions – all of them. I think I have answers to a lot of the questions you might have." John paused. "I'm, um, the CEO of Aralco. Are you familiar with the company?"

Everyone stared at John, and he stared right back. He saw Jamie's face fall, and Kyle closed his eyes.

We're being presented as an offering.

John nodded at Kyle's accurate thought. The chemist shook his head and grunted. No one spoke of the ability, because only a few of them had it.

"I'd rather not go into it on the phone. Let's just say I have three young chemists your group will be eager to meet." John stared at the ground this time. He didn't owe any of them anything. Theirs were the most heinous crimes against humanity. He shared a little more, and then listened.

"God, that's great. Okay. Yeah, that seems about right. I'm going to pass you off to one of the pilots to let you give him directions, okay? I can't wait to meet you, Dusty. And I can't thank you enough for going to the trouble to get on the air. You're the answer to our prayers." John tossed the Nokia to Jack and turned to Haden.

"There's over a hundred of them there. And from the sound of it, they're getting things done." John turned to the Jamie, Kyle, and Nathan. "You three will get a chance to speak for yourselves, to cast a vote for your punishment. It's only fair. We still support the Constitution, and you will receive the fairest trial possible."

The accused three sat speechless. Maybe emotion overwhelmed them, he couldn't be sure, but none of them said a word. And what was that expression on Kyle's face?

Uncertainty? Apprehension? Superiority?

"Don't judge us, John." Kyle held the CEO's gaze and then smiled.

"You haven't earned the right to call me John."

"Yes, I have. Without us, someone here wouldn't be alive." Kyle stared at the confused faces. "Who would've been picked to stay behind? You?" He pointed to Haden. "Doubt it. You?" He raised a finger to Breanna Tanner this time. "Perhaps, or most likely *her*." This time he directed his attention to the lobby secretary.

John looked down, grateful he wasn't forced to make that choice. "But you're here and not *there*."

It was Kyle's turn to wrinkle his brow. *What the hell does that mean?*

It means you keep having this thought about Waco, but you weren't able to make good. No matter what you think you accomplished, your mission was a failure. Because you're here, not there. John watched Kyle's eyes go wide. The CEO felt a rush of adrenaline, and it became crystal clear to him in that instant.

The four of them had designed an escape, a place for their loved ones to hide and be protected from the X-86. But the Fab Four –three by then – had gotten caught instead.

Are they there now, Kyle? All your worshippers? Wondering where the hell you are? And they know what I know – you're a failure, a loser, and a murderer.

"Kyle, are you all right?" Jamie rubbed Kyle's back then tapped Nathan's shoulder to get his attention. Both looked at John and back at their friend. "What'd you do to him?"

"*I* didn't do anything to him. This is all your doing. It's not my fault you don't have a fucking clue." John smirked, then snapped for Haden to get the ball rolling and for Jack to round up the three stooges. "Get them out of my sight. Breanna and this wonderful secretary – for the life of me I can't remember your name..."

"Kathy." She grinned, and revealed dimples as deep as the Rio Grande. Her perfect white teeth had been one of the things about her that always captivated John. He had told Victoria that he had a secretary who could be a Crest girl.

"Well, Kathy, you and Breanna are with Haden and me. The rest of you, and I'm sorry about this, but you're with them." John shook his head, brushed the seat of his pants and helped the women on board.

"Uh, John, why don't you let me ride with *them*. One of us needs to be on Nathan's chopper." Haden stood between the two helicopters, and as soon as John thought about it, he knew his friend was right.

"Okay. Here, you take this." John made sure the pistol's safety was on, then handed it grip-first to Haden. "Here're the keys to their handcuffs – fasten 'em to the chopper. And let Phillip stay with you. I'll take one of the other ladies."

"Will we be light enough?" Haden counted heads.

"Jack, will that be evened out?" John shouted over his shoulder at the account executive who looked right at home as a pilot.

"Should be fine! That's about how it was before – all ya'll were in one with only four left over for Nathan's. It's all good. Let's boogie." Jack flipped switches, had the blades whipping their hair as everyone held on to flapping shirts and jackets.

The last of them piled in, and within minutes, the two birds were Midwest bound.

Chapter Thirty-Six

Joplin
Day Four

"DUSTY, HE'S SURE it's them? I can't believe it."

"I know, Mel, but it's them. John's been interrogatin' them for days, he said. And when they had to rush out of Dallas, he couldn't leave them. There were too many unanswered questions, and frankly, that would make us like them, ya know? So now we're gonna need a place to lock them up."

Jake jumped into the conversation, scratching his head. "Hey, Griff! Didn't we see the city jail?"

"I think so," Griffin answered, as he ambled their way. Dusty mopped his forehead with a handkerchief, still in a sweat from racing back to the sight after John Basinger's phone call.

"Uh, Jake?"

Jake looked down to see Jessie tugging at his arm. Scooter wagged a mile a minute and nudged his hand for a pat or two.

"Hey, Jess. Hang on a minute, okay?" Jake gestured for Dusty to flip through his notepad for the conversation's details. "You said John mentioned *the three*. I'm betting the fourth we heard about must've escaped or gotten killed, and he..."

"One of his friends killed him for trying to back out," Jessie said. "But the other three want to escape to some hideout in Texas. That's their plan – to get away and join all their friends. And I know what we're supposed to do with them."

Dusty and Jake turned and stared at Jessie like she had just spoken Japanese. Their mouths hung open until Melanie walked up.

"You two all right?" Melanie squeezed Jessie's arm and then furrowed her brow as she glanced back at the two men. "You two are catchin' flies."

"Jessie? What're you talkin' about?" Jake squatted in front of the eight-year-old and remembered what Bob had screamed while standing on his roof. *Where are you now, little girl? They said you were gonna save us from all the shit!*

"Bobby didn't make it because Nathan killed him – he's bad, but I don't think he's the bad man in my dreams. That man is old." Jessie stopped and rubbed her forehead.

Jake studied the little girl's face and saw her distant expression – she appeared to stare right through him.

"What's she talkin' about, Jake?" Melanie grabbed his arm.

"I...I think our little Jessie is something else," Dusty said, and shared how he remembered a guy saying a little girl would save them from all of this.

"Wow," Jake muttered. *Could Jessie have been that little girl?*

Melanie's eyes went wide. "That guy standing on the SUV in Springfield!" She looked at Jessie.

"*And the little girl can't save us from it all.* But he also talked about an evil man." Dusty shook his head, then dropped to his knees in front of Jessie. "Do you know who the evil man is, Jess? It's important – try real hard."

"Good grief, I'm not psychic, Dusty. These are dreams, and I don't even know if they're real. But I've been having them a lot. They're really detailed – ask Matthew. I've told him about most of them. But the ones I haven't, I've written in my diary. You guys need to relax a little – you're too uptight. Lots of people have said weird things to me like that, but I'm just me."

Jessie grinned and Jake caught a whisp of thought, but the little girl was able to mask her signal.

"How'd you just do that?" He cocked his head.

"Do what?" This time Jessie's mischievous smile told him that this eight-year-old had more than just a gift.

"You know what I mean. You shut me out," Jake whispered. None of them had spoken about the telepathic ability, so he didn't know if the others would think he'd lost his marbles.

"Oh, that. It's easy. All you gotta do is close the curtain. C'mon, Scooter, let's find Matthew." Jessie turned to march away when Melanie ran to catch her.

"Jess, you think we could read your diary?"

Jake nodded – *yes! That's a great idea.*

"No, it's not a great idea. It's personal. But I can rewrite parts for you if you want. The dreams. But there is stuff about my daddy that I don't want anyone else to read." Jessie dropped her head and looked eight again. Melanie put her arm around the little girl.

"Jessie, what if we sat down and you just read us those parts? That way we can hear them now. This is all real important." Melanie brushed Jessie's hair from her eyes and Scooter nuzzled his young momma's ear. Jessie glanced up to see Dusty and Jake hovering over her.

"Stop it, Scooter, you big goof," Jessie said with a giggle. "All right, I guess. But I'm tired now. Isn't it real late?" Since all the chaos of reaching camp, no one slept normal hours, Jessie included.

"Yes, it's late, almost one a.m. How 'bout first thing tomorrow? Melanie, why don't you get Jessie tucked in and we'll meet before breakfast. How's that sound?" Jake rested his hand on the girl's shoulder and felt slimy for manipulating her. He tried not to think it, because her power was intense. Being around her was like feeling the surge of exposed power lines.

"Okay. C'mon, Scooter. Let's find Bryan and Matthew." Jessie led Melanie away, and Jake let out a long sigh.

"Damn."

"Yeah, damn. Jake, I think we may have some problems comin'. Oh, wait...HEY, JESS!"

From the other side of a tent, the little girl yelled, "What?"

He jogged toward her. "You said you knew what we're supposed to do with them, the three. What was that?"

"Build a cage and put them right here. With us. Don't put them in a cell because we have to watch them. You all are going to clear all the dead people's cars in the parking lot tomorrow morning, and we'll pitch our tents there because there'll be too many of us to fit on this small strip of grass. But you can put the cage here, under that tree in front of the wall. I saw it in a dream. G'night." Jessie twirled on her heel and zipped off without another word.

Jake laughed and Dusty joined him. "Yeah, damn. So if our little girl says that's what we're supposed to do, I suppose we shouldn't mess with fate, huh?" Dusty raked a hand through his grimy brown hair.

"I'm not one to buy into all that shit, but these days, I say we do what's best for the group. And Jessie seems to be, um, *powerful*." Jake didn't share his brain speech with Dusty, because the DJ's signal was fuzzy, untuned. Nothing like Jessie's. Hers made him nauseous, almost stronger than his own thoughts. In a way, she made him uncomfortable.

"Bringing those three here really makes me nervous. How 'bout you?" Dusty led Jake past the circle of tents around to the other side of Memorial Hall. It separated them from the others, but for now, everyone was trying to stay on soft ground until they had more comfortable sleeping arrangements.

"Yeah. But what she said about a bad man…that makes me *more* nervous." Jake unzipped the front flap of a small domed tent that he wasn't sure he would fit in.

"And I think I've heard about him, too. The guy in Springfield, the one who prophesized about a little girl also talked about an evil man with a Rolex. And something else, but I don't remember. You don't think that could be John, do you?" Dusty crinkled his forehead.

"Oh, God. No. I don't think…I mean. I guess that would fit, but it doesn't make sense. Wait – John said he knew who was doing it. We'll know tomorrow." Jake's head swirled with the possibility of two choppers coming to their camp with answers or every intention of killing them all. It made him shudder.

"Yeah, you're probably right. But I don't like it. What're you doin'? You're not goin' to sleep, are you? We've gotta get a fence." Dusty buttoned his jacket and pulled the collar up to block the late night – or early morning – chill.

"Well, crap. No rest for the weary. Fine. Let's get Bryan, Griffin, Billy, and Austin to help. This is gonna be a big job. Sure you don't want to sleep first?"

But Jake didn't wait for an answer. He closed his tent and trudged back toward the eighteen other campsites with Dusty following him.

When they came to the newest outcropping of canvas houses, Jake motioned for Bryan, Billy, and Austin to join him.

"Where's Griffin?" Jake peeked inside a large eight-person tent and saw a sleeping bag groan and stretch.

"Asleep, which is where I'm headed." Austin rubbed his eyes. "It's late, even for a college boy."

"Huh-uh, not yet, kid," Dusty teased, and then proceeded to discuss what tools and materials they needed.

"What's the plan?" Austin furrowed his brow. His mussed hair and red eyes made him look drunk. "I am *so* tired."

"A dog kennel," Jake said, filling the others in on the finer details of John's phone call and Jessie's prophecy.

"There's a fencing company not far from here. We'll hold them where we can see them, but we can make it plenty big for three people. We'll need three extra cots or air mattresses since we're gettin' all those tomorrow. We'll bolt it into the ground with something they can't pull up and fasten it to that tree with bike locks." Dusty scratched a crude design on a yellow legal pad. "Like this."

"Yeah, and I was thinkin' if we also wire the corners to those trees, that'll reinforce it," Jake said, as they walked around the massive oak tree now surrounded by tents.

"So we're gonna put it together tonight and then clear everyone out of these in the morning?" Bryan peered toward the sea of canvas shelters.

"Yeah. I don't think they'll be here for a few hours – not in a helicopter. So that'll give us time to get the stuff. When they get here, we'll tell them what we're doin'. They'll have to wait while we finish it, I'm sure. Depends how efficient we are," Dusty added. "But we've gotta get this done. There'll be plenty of time to sleep next week." He barely cracked a smile.

"Well, let's divide duties," Jake suggested. "Me, Bryan, and Billy'll go get the stuff if you and Austin want to move these folks to the other side. Then we'll follow Jessie's lead and clear the lot tomorrow."

"Gotcha." Dusty dragged a sleepy Austin to the first row of tents and began the unpopular task of uprooting canvas homes.

Billy and Bryan made their way to Griffin's tent. This would require a good-sized truck and his Dooley fit the bill. Jake hoped the store might have a company truck with easy-to-locate keys to help haul materials. Fifteen minutes later, the three headed off into the night while Dusty and Austin rousted people out of much-needed sleep.

When John arrived at three in the morning, the cage was a work in progress, already taking shape under the tree. The choppers lit on Seventh Street in front of the Hall's parking lot, and a band of twelve joined the Joplin community, three of whom would be like sharks stirring the waters come Monday.

Jake introduced his cage crew to John and Haden, the only passengers awake when both helicopters landed.

"Where are they?" Jake asked while Dusty and the rest scrambled to get the cage functional enough to house the criminals.

"C'mere." John led them to the other chopper and pointed to the three young, good-looking kids. Nathan was scrambling around his sleeping mates for the cooler, grabbing a Sprite and an apple.

"Jesus, they're my age." Jake didn't know what he expected, but the word scientists and the peers he stared at didn't mesh in his head.

Kyle shifted in his seat, his head leaning against the outside window. He opened his eyes, startled.

"Who the hell're you?" he slurred.

"Your worst nightmare," John answered for Jake.

Chapter Thirty-Seven

Joplin
Day Five

WORD BUZZED THROUGH the camp at daybreak that the *three* had joined them. Outraged, many refused to accept that they would share space with terrorists.

By ten o'clock, a slew of workers pitched in to get the cage finished. Jake and his crew had stolen a few hours' sleep, but they didn't have enough hands. While the prison was under construction, Dusty, John, and Haden cuffed Nathan, Kyle, and Jamie to a wire that wrapped around another smaller tree.

"Well, kids, whaddya think?" Jake, with tired hands on his hips, studied their expressions – Kyle smirked, Nathan remained guarded and emotionless, and Jamie was horror-stricken. "Dusty, I don't think they appreciate their accommodations."

"Well, they should. We worked hard on it. These old knees have had about all they can handle." Dusty rubbed his battered shins. Melanie groaned, massaging her own knees.

Nathan whispered something to Kyle, and the two snickered. Jamie smiled but said nothing.

"What's the problem, boys? Don't like the idea of being on display?" John grinned. Humanely, the odd-looking jail was being built apart from the future campsite, but close to the entrance to Memorial Hall. They wouldn't be the center of attention, but they would be easy to watch from different vantage points. And every single person approaching the new community from Joplin Avenue would see the prison first.

Matthew Francis and another teenaged boy were digging furiously for what appeared to be a hole for a latrine.

Jamie grimaced. *No way am I going to squat in front of God and the whole world.*

"You gonna hold it for the rest of your life?" Jake stared her hard in the eyes. "I don't think so."

"Boys, cat got your tongue?" Dusty wanted a response, and Jake figured he would keep asking until Nathan and Kyle answered.

"Huh? Oh, our new home? It's lovely. Nothing like braving the elements with these wonderful Midwestern yuck-yucks staring at us." Nathan laughed and turned so Kyle could tap an upturned palm with his own cuffed hand. A crude low five.

"You self-righteous sonuvabitch. Did it ever occur to you that these *yuck-yucks* are who you designed to survive? Jesus, Nathan, you're not nearly as bright as I thought you were." Haden shook his head, clearly at a loss for what was housed inside Nathan's skull. Jake caught the bald man's garbled afterthought about a blown chance to shoot the motherfucker in the face instead of the leg.

Yeah, what did happen to you, Kyle? The crutches, bandaged knee, none of it had registered with Jake until now.

"He got shot," Nathan whispered. "Big John took that nasty revolver of his and plugged two rounds into him. Very humane treatment we've received thus far, don'tcha think?"

It startled Jake at first that Nathan had been in his head, and he hadn't felt it.

"To my knowledge, Nathan, war criminals are entitled to due process, but there's nothing in the Constitution about those who orchestrate Armageddon," Dusty said. "And by the way, not all these folks are Missourians. The group that arrived from south of Chicago, most of them were from up north. So most of these folks don't qualify as Midwesterners, son. Sorry, you lose that round." Dusty made a buzzing deep in his throat signaling the loser sound from game shows of his past.

Nathan didn't appear to be amused. Kyle leaned on his crutches and rubbed his sore hip. Jamie had her lip curled, disgusted by everything and everybody.

Jake didn't care. He hoped they rotted in hell. It would be more compassionate than what they had done to Becky. For that, they deserved to suffer.

* * *

"FOR ANYONE WHO arrives, give them one of these, then we'll do another one tomorrow. But for now, this will catch them up to speed, make them aware of our near four-hundred population. It'll answer many of their questions. If you need anything else, Melanie, I'll be with Dusty in the Hall, okay?"

"Sure, Austin, thanks." She looked down at the flyer and smiled. Valerie and Tristan had done an amazing job on their new paper.

It would help keep all newcomers informed. On Monday alone, over two hundred new arrivals had streamed in. Two college-aged girls helped Melanie hand out the one-page newspaper.

"Kim, when they grab the paper, have them sign this, okay? We want their names and their license plates. That way, as Griffin and Jake tow all the cars away, they don't take a new one. Make sense?" Melanie held a chart in front of the Vanderbilt junior. Her caramel skin had Matthew swooning, thanking God he wasn't the lone dark face in the crowd. And her doe-like eyes and flowing auburn hair didn't hurt.

"Hey, Storey, you seen that babe? Dang, she's hot. And that girl with her, she ain't nothin' to sneeze at neither." Matthew clapped his new friend, a fifteen-year-old boy from Chicago, on the back.

Jessie rolled her eyes and practiced her fist-on-the-hip image. Both boys told her she had it mastered better than either of their mothers ever did. Jessie had hoped Storey, a boy named after an astronaut, might have more class.

"Storey, don't fall under his spell. He's a charmer." She turned and flipped her ponytail dramatically as she left.

"God, she'll drive ya nuts, huh? She sure is bossy." Storey shook his head, and he had just met her a few hours earlier.

"I heard that!" she called over to them, helping Kim divide the stack of paper so Melanie could deal with the eight older people walking up.

"Hey, don't cut on Jess, man. She's like my kid sister. Besides, she's about as smart as anybody I ever met. And I'm pretty doggone smart myself."

Jessie was proud to hear Matthew openly admit his own intelligence. In the grand scheme of things, there was no point in upholding the macho image he once had in the inner city.

"Quite a setup you folks have here," a gray-haired gentleman complimented as he leaned against the table to catch his breath. Jessie turned to see what he meant and realized the man was right. Their new camp was impressive. She was also glad Thad and about twenty people had spent the morning removing all the bodies from the Hall. Knowing they were gone and soon to be cremated made her feel cleaner somehow.

The large parking lot, now nearly empty of cars, was speckled with two or three dozen different smaller groups – each with five or six tents surrounding a fire, a grill, and a canopy with chairs under it. The sea of canvas separated Seventh Street from Memorial Hall, with all their cars lining Joplin and Wall Avenues on either side. It looked like a giant Girl Scout Camp, and Jessie was proud of her role in it. The greeting table was situated on the sidewalk in front of the Hall itself.

"Yep, we take your names here, then after we get your info, we send you in there." Melanie pointed to the ramped entrance of Memorial Hall. "One of those folks will get ya all your supplies – a tent, a sleeping bag or cot, whichever you prefer, and a site. You can set-up with people you came in with, or if you're on your own, we connect you with a smaller group. Are these three with you, uh," Melanie said as she glanced down at the clipboard. "Mr. Reeves?"

On your own. An image of her daddy alone in a hotel by the river chilled Jessie. Melanie and Kim steered Mr. Reeves and his three friends into Memorial Hall, chatting about their progress. But Jessie remained frozen by the thought – her daddy in that hotel room with bloody scratches down his neck – alone. She shook her head to get rid of the mental picture, certain that people could tap into her brain-waves when her guard was down. She didn't like that others could do it, but it sure helped her know what was going on. Otherwise, she knew adults had a tendency to shelter little kids. They couldn't fathom how much she knew.

"Okay, Matthew, if you're gonna gawk, get yer booty over here. Storey, you too. Help Kim categorize who's camped together, okay? Put numbers by them and chart a map with the numbers on top of the boxes to indicate the tents. Can you do that?" Melanie didn't wait for an answer because three more women had walked up. "Boys!" She snapped her fingers.

"I'll help," Jessie offered. Thinking about her dad in that hotel room four hours away made her heart ache. The more involved she stayed, the less she dwelled on the bad memories.

"I know why you two wanna help," she finally managed. "You can't fool me, I know better. I'm not a kid, you know."

"Ah, Mom, c'mon. Cut us some slack." Matthew giggled, but it was clear that Jessie was not amused. He looked her in the eyes and asked if she was okay.

"I'm fine." She leaned in closer to the boys, and she sensed Storey fighting the urge to shout boo in her ear. His immaturity was testing her nerves.

"Well, get outta the way then," Storey insisted. "You're blockin' my view."

She scowled at Matthew's new friend. "Your secret's safe with me, boys. I'll never tell Kim you think she's cute. And by the way, Storey Roberts," she smirked. "I wouldn't have jumped."

This time, Storey *did* flinch, and his mouth dropped open. Confusion spread across his face and Matthew nearly busted a gut laughing. Storey popped him hard on the arm, but the younger boy couldn't control his cackles.

"Kim, can you manage here? Jake gave me some changes for tomorrow's paper, so I'm heading over to the Office Max to print and copy. You three want to come since you're holding up progress here? You probably have some computer expertise to offer." Melanie flipped through her legal pad, clipping a hand-written note from Jake to it.

Office Max had become headquarters for the upstart newspaper, stocked with paper and ample printing supplies. Tristan and Valerie had worked hard to get the first edition out in only a few hours. Information was what new arrivals craved most.

"You betcha! I've had computers every single year. I even learned how to use all kinds of publisher programs. We can make some awesome graphics."

"Actually, Storey, that is exactly what I was hoping. Right now, our paper looks pretty elementary. You big junior high boys are just what I need! Valerie's busy setting it all up and writing the copy. If you three could help Tristan with all that computer stuff, it'd be a big help. And then we're going to get you all ready to distribute the second edition, like dispatchers." Melanie grinned and Jessie caught a trace thought about keeping them busy.

"Them especially," Jessie whispered, then smiled.

"Stop that! It makes me feel like I've got spiders in my brain. So you're game?"

"Yep, we're all yours."

"Kim, Jenny, we won't be gone long. And when we get back, hopefully we'll have a new paper. Hold down the fort. Austin is inside if you need him." Melanie motioned the kids to follow as they made their way to her Mustang, now parked nearly a block away.

A senior citizen with a young child got out of a beat-up Chevrolet parallel-parked behind Melanie's car. The elderly gentleman gripped his cane and gave a radiant smile as he saw Melanie and the kids approach.

"Howdy. I heard Dusty on the radio talk about the settlement."

"Well, you've found us," Melanie said, shaking the man's hand. "I'm Melanie. I worked with Dusty at KMJC in Dallas, and you'll definitely want to get to know these young folks. This is Jessie."

I hate it when you parade me like this.

She's not parading you, young lady. You're special, and you know it.

Jessie peered into his baby blue eyes, surrounded by a sea of wrinkles. The ancient gentleman caught a glimpse of the paper in Melanie's hand.

"Ah, news. That's a sight for sore eyes." He winked at Jessie, and she felt a powerful surge of warmth in her heart.

"They've got the current edition over there. This one will be back shortly. Matthew and Storey here are going to spice it up a bit."

"I'm Sanford, and this young lady is Melissa. I saw people venturing into houses, was that a clean-up crew?"

"Yessir. We've devised task forces of all sorts. An electrical co-op, a housing unit, but the clean-up group is over eighty strong. As sad as it is, burying the dead is incredibly necessary for sanitation, and once the homes are checked, we can all begin claiming a house of our own. I can't wait, personally. I want to sleep in a bed more than I want to breathe." Melanie smiled so genuinely, Sanford couldn't help but reciprocate. Her good nature was refreshing, Jessie knew. She felt another rush of energy as she stared at him.

The five-year-old looked up at Jessie and tugged her arm. "You that girl Sanford says is gonna save us from the bad man?"

Jessie's breath caught in her throat. She stared at the small blonde child, only three years younger than her.

"I'm Jessie," she said simply and shook the little girl's hand. "It's nice to meet you. This is Matthew. He's my best friend, and that's his friend, Storey. They're boys, so you'll wanna watch out for them." Jessie grinned while the boys shook Melissa's hand, but she never took her eyes off Sanford. Something in his craggy face drew her to him like an orbiting moon.

"She's just jealous 'cause we're cool."

"I don't know you. But I know her." Melissa stared at Jessie, her large green eyes full of wonder.

Jessie stuck her tongue out at Matthew, making Melanie and Sanford laugh.

"Well, nice to meet you, Melissa. And you too, Sanford. We'll be back shortly with a new paper. Just wander over there, and Kim or Jenny will get you hooked up."

"Thank you. I'm sure glad to be here. I can't wait to take a load off, eat a bite, and then take a snooze." His fancy cane's gold handle, a magnificent lion, caught the morning sun.

"You'll have lots of time for that. Hope to see you at the fire tonight!" Melanie unlocked her car with the button on her keys, and all three kids piled in. Matthew didn't complain when Jessie called shotgun.

"Is that an every night thing? The fire, I mean?" Sanford called out as he shielded his eyes from the sun.

"Yeah. So far, it's just been a way to meet the new arrivals, touch base, and keep us updated on everything going on. Fire's gettin' bigger as the group grows!"

"Well, good. We'll see ya tonight, then." Sanford and Melissa walked around a tent close to the street, immediately greeted by Kim. Jessie craned her neck as they pulled out, and felt a swell in her chest when he peeked around a tent and gave her a finger wave.

At Office Max, everyone kicked into business mode. Tristan set Storey and Matthew up at a computer doing tedious searches for certain types of graphics for the next two editions. Jessie helped Valerie arrange the page and mastered the copy machine. Melanie retrieved the printed pages and stacked them in sets of twenty, criss-crossed so they could track how many they distributed.

When the kids finished their duties, they gathered around the table to see the final product.

"Well?" Matthew danced around like he had to pee.

"Whaddya think?" Valerie turned a copy around for all of them to inspect. "Impressive, isn't it?" She high-fived Tristan, who joined them at the table. Both young women looked like they hadn't slept in days.

"Wow." Melanie pulled another one from the stack so she didn't have to look over Matthew's shoulder.

"Yeah, *wow*." The kids couldn't believe they had helped with the impressive paper.

Caged three set for interrogation. The headline caught Jessie's eye. *And then there's the bad man.* All of them began to read – Storey to catch up on current events, but the rest of them to fill in the gaps.

The Tribune

Volume 1 Issue 3 August 14, 2008

Caged Three Set for Interrogation

Today talks begin with the three we now know are singularly responsible for the events plaguing our nation and the world.

Dusty Morris, colony leader, along with Jake Thomas, crew coordinator, will create a forum for Kyle Spene, Jamie Mantel, and Nathan Kirkpatrick to be questioned. This inquiry will determine whether a trial will take place, or if sentencing will be passed without trial.

Various colony activists feel the trio's admission of responsibility is a guilty plea, thus allowing sentencing to take place without a lengthy and pointless trial. To date, we have not re-established judicial processes, so this hearing will be led by the colony panelists.

Bryan Saunders, heading the clean-up commission, commented, "What these three have done is an atrocity against mankind. They will take a special place in world history that no one else will replicate. Yes, we are an America that believes in swift justice, but likewise they are entitled to a fair trial. Do I think they can get one? No."

Other sources agree. The hearing can only create further animosity toward these individuals. The temporary jail has some citizens riled. There is discussion of a vote as early as Friday.

"Let's just find the local prison and lock them up. No point in all of us

staring at them 24-7. I'm sick of looking at them." Candi Brookens, a former resident of Georgetown, SC, went on to say she hoped the majority of the population of Joplin agrees that seeing the case day to day has been mentally taxing and an unnecessary reminder of a painful past.

> *What these three have done is an atrocity against mankind. Do I think they can get a fair trial? No.*
> *– Bryan Saunders*

Electricity, Plumbing Priorities

A small crew of ten set forth today to get full electricity running by week's end.

Sources say the power outage was a break in computer connection so the problem is minor. We can expect complete restoration of all electrical capabilities by next week.

Plumbing will also be restored within a day. Although we have had this luxury already, the town will be fully operational by Friday.

Election registration deadline: August 20
Speech forum: August 21
Election: August 23

Housing Project Making Headway

"Plans to acquire homes released soon," says Jake Thomas.

Plans to get the ball rolling on the Housing Project started in full force Monday. Ten crews of five were created to sweep the city in an effort to lay the dead to rest, chart living areas, and determine the best possible scenario for "purchase" of new homes.

"Purchase" will entail duties comparable to the once famed Habitat for Humanity Project. Each potential homeowner will sign a document agreeing to meet monthly duties, area cleanup and maintenance, and will adhere to community standards set forth by the commission.

Sources say citizens of our new colony are excited by the prospect of finding new homes, creating some semblance of normalcy, and getting back to the idea of real community.

Elections Set for Aug. 23rd

You may have thought we avoided the good old presidential election with this unprecedented international disaster, but we will have our own.

As of now, all title-holding citizens are panel-appointed. Therefore, to hold true to our Constitution, anyone who wishes to run for office should register with Melanie Stevens by Sunday, Aug. 20.

Chapter Thirty-Eight

Joplin
Day Five

"HEY," A GRUFF voice whisper-shouted, startling the trapped trio.

"Yeah?" Kyle whipped his head around trying to make out shapes in the dark. A shadow passed in front of their cage, eclipsing the glow of a faraway fire. The miniature door rattled close to him. The small passageway had been used earlier to slide plates of sandwiches to them.

"Got some food for ya. Melanie said no one fed ya'll, so here's some beans and cornbread. There should be plenty for the three of you. Sorry, we'll try not to forget you tomorrow."

Kyle searched for brainwaves but found none – only the slippery feeling he'd just missed an overthrown pass. Dusty limped away in the night barely catching the last few words as he headed back to the campfire.

"Thanks, man. Appreciate it."

Nathan swung his feet over the edge of his cot, sniffing the air. "Do you trust these morons, Kyle?"

"Hell no, but we don't have a choice right now, Nathan. I'm so hungry, my stomach hurts. Hell, that sandwich for lunch was just a snack. These people don't realize how much I eat. I'd meet buddies at the quarry and bring enough for three people. 'Course Brad mooched off everybody. Anyway, is Jamie asleep?" Kyle rubbed his head, aware that the X-86 fuzzed his thoughts the longer he stayed outdoors.

"I think so. Let me check." Nathan took baby steps toward Jamie's cot to make sure he didn't stumble on anything.

"No, I'm not asleep," she slurred. "What's for dinner? It smells scrumptious."

"Cornbread and beans. God, it's my wettest dream come true."

"Yuck. Kyle. Leave the macho visualization alone, would ya? I don't know why everything guys experience has to be compared with something sexual." Jamie grunted as she reached for a Styrofoam cup.

Nathan and Kyle both chuckled around mouthfuls of delectable white beans that dripped down their chins. Kyle dipped his cornbread into his and appalled Jamie further by wiping his chin with it before shoving it into his mouth. Now that they had their night sight, the dark seemed less oppressive.

"God, it's like living with cavemen. You know, in the year we've been working together, I never saw this side of either of you. You both seemed so civilized, even watching football. I might never have agreed to partner with you had I ever seen you eat beans." She grinned, but Kyle wondered if she about half meant it. He knew she had an older brother – *surely he farted around her.*

"Just eat, Jamie. For once, enjoy something without taking the fun away for the rest of us." Kyle handed her the third cup of what smelled like fresh-squeezed lemonade – it reminded him of Trisha. Was she in Waco? Not knowing made him ache with worry.

After the midnight meal, the three of them huddled in the space between their cots to talk so no one could hear them.

"I wonder what they're going to do if we refuse to answer their questions," Jamie whispered.

"Is there any point in telling them anything? I mean, really. What's the benefit? There is none. If they want to persecute us, they will anyway. When I told Jake they could never understand why we did what we did, that was as good as admitting it. They're just too damn dumb to get it." Kyle shook his head trying to read his two partners – their expressions and their thoughts – but signals were weak.

"Kyle, their mission is to stop the deployment of future launches. Can you blame them for tryin'? It'll be a moot point by Friday anyway. By then, our mission will be accomplished, and reversal won't matter." Nathan squinted at both of them. "You don't have regrets, do you?"

"You know mine," Jamie said, and dropped her head. "I miss Bobby, and I don't know if I can forgive you for that, Nathan, but what's done is done. I've been dealing with death all my life. So if you don't want to tell them anything, God knows I can keep secrets with the best of them." Jamie fiddled with the hem of her jeans. "Keep in mind we might frustrate them to the point that they may kill us. Are we prepared for that? We could say, 'Uh yes, we installed a back door, but we gotta return to Dallas to do it.' We have to manipulate this so we have opportunities to escape. Or hell, even if a little remorse convinces them not to kill us, I'm all about that. But saying nothing won't cut it. I don't think so anyway."

Nathan glared at Jamie, and the air suddenly became electric. Kyle caught the volleying snips between them.

I shoulda sent you with him. Two for the price of one. Nathan may have thought it, but Kyle didn't think his friend really meant it. They had talked about how much she meant to the both of them. Bobby, too. If Sims hadn't gone soft – but Kyle knew it had been more than that. Nathan would've killed his own mother in that instant just as easily.

You're a fascist pig, and you don't know shit about the world I grew up in. Your NAO crap doesn't hold a candle to The Movement. Jamie sniffled, and Kyle caught a fragment about her dad and a Peterbilt.

Kyle had asked questions about Jamie's childhood, about Kingsville and the rumors he'd heard growing up, but she was as evasive as water in the desert.

Jamie and Nathan sighed, each oblivious to the other's thoughts. Their tolerance of the chemical, though very different, left both of them without the ability to hear the mental ramblings, as far as Kyle knew. He had practiced his talent on others around him – several people tuned in to him without knowing who rumbled around in their head. But if Nathan could do it, he hid it well.

Kyle read them both loud and clear, and recognized that Nathan would have to be harnessed. His dangerous attitudes and ruthless nature had been Bobby's biggest fear. And rightfully so.

Jamie, on the other hand, had the right idea. Don't just roll over and die, play the games. Sit up, beg, rollover, whatever it took to get the right kind of attention.

"Well, both of you are bitter, that's obvious. This isn't a competition – the NAO is a bad ass operation that can whoop The Movement any day of the week and twice on Sunday. Or vice versa. Who cares? We gotta come up with a plan, Jamie's right about that. If we go in with an obstinate attitude, then we're cutting our own throats, and I personally don't want to die. Not like an animal in this God-forsaken place." Kyle paused, waiting for any mental resistance. He realized how beneficial his talent was going to be, especially if he was able to keep it under wraps.

"They're not gonna let us go to Dallas, Kyle. Don't be stupid. You're as naïve as Jamie." Nathan picked at the ground and tossed a rock through the fence roof.

Kyle had studied the way they fastened the panel of chain link on top, frustrated by the padlocked corners and soldered seams. There would be no escape from the cage – opportunities to get outside the twelve-foot by twelve-foot prison hinged on their captors.

"You're an idiot, Nathan. All that hatred crap isn't going to get you anywhere here. You're on their turf now, so you have to play by their rules. And we have to be smart. What's our goal here?" Kyle gave

Nathan an *I'm fed up with your bullshit expression* – furrowed brow, a roll of the eyes, shaking his head.

"Don't condescend to me, Kyle." Nathan started to say something else, but fell silent instead.

"Well, we can't just be sitting ducks, boys," Jamie said. "We have to come up with a plan. We can even come clean for all I care. It's not like it matters. Hell, we never planned to be appreciated for this by anyone except our crew in Waco. Our first priority should be to get word to them. Let's appease these bozos and bide our time. Then we'll make a move to get the hell outta here. We have designated cell phones to use – anybody remember the numbers? If so, all we gotta do is get to a phone, and maybe we can get someone to come to us."

Nathan and Kyle considered what Jamie had said, though Kyle wondered what move they could make to get out of there. No response from the fascist group leader could only mean one thing, but right now, Kyle had to look out for himself.

"We have them in an underground airtight chamber for a reason, Jamie. Coming out too soon could kill them. We told them we would be in there for months, remember? Whose life are you going to jeopardize to save your own?" Nathan scoffed at her, not making any bones about his feelings or their stupidity.

Kyle stifled a grin. *Dissension in the group might not be a bad thing at this conjecture. If Jamie and I come across as cooperative and repentant, they might cut us some slack. We can show our desire to rectify the situation. It may be our key to survival.*

At that very moment, Tony Andrews' moved his rook for checkmate in his final chess match against John. Tony didn't even care that John hadn't been playing for several days, should in fact be dead – winning was the point now.

Jamie, Kyle, and Nathan sat with their heads together saying nothing, surrounded by their chain link prison. In the game of life, they appeared to be in their own symbolic checkmate.

But, of course, they hadn't met Tony Andrews.

Yet.

Chapter Thirty-Nine

Joplin
Day Five

"HELLO THERE." KIM stuck her hand out. "It's a real pleasure to meet you. Are you with the government or something?"

"Or something," the man replied. He massaged a wound on his shoulder but offered nothing more. He looked around at their swelling community and sported a strange grin. Lanterns hung from metal stakes with hooks, but the majority of light came from the huge bonfire crackling in the middle of the pavement. Scores of tents surrounded smaller campfires, but it was clear the group centered everything around the bonfire.

The man's cool demeanor caught Kim off guard, but she went through her spiel anyway. "Well, I'm Kim, and this is Matthew. We're part of the welcoming crew, sort of the resident greeters. This is a publication we're handing out to new arrivals to inform you of some basics going on day to day. Here's yesterday's. They each have pertinent details about the chemical hazards, what we feel is happening, who we've been in contact with, and other various information. What's your name?" Kim poised her pen on her clipboard to record their next citizen. "Or you can record it yourself and give us your license plates."

The man's resistance disquieted Kim. Matthew didn't like him right away. Something about the dark eyes made him uncomfortable.

"Anthony Parker, at your service. What a divine creature you are to meet a man who's not seen a beautiful lady in days. Perhaps none as exquisite as yourself. And you, young man, must be one of the gentlemen in charge, no?"

Kim blushed furiously, reveling in the wonderful attention, but Matthew didn't bite. He knew a schmooze job when he heard one.

"Well, Mr. Parker, I..."

"Actually, it's *General* Parker, but, darlin', you may call me Tony," he cooed, though to Matthew it sounded about as slimy as the slugs he used to salt on his porch back home.

Matthew looked around for Dusty, Jake, John, Billy or Bryan – any of the men in charge so he could get them to meet the first military man to join the community. But he also wanted someone else's opinion about General Parker. The smarmy words were wrapped in intonations of *I'm kissin' your ass, is it working?* The teenager worried that Kim might be playing right into the man's hands.

"Okay, Tony," she said. "Billy is right inside those doors at the top of the ramp. He'll check you in and give you everything you'll need. But if I can be of any service, I'll be right here." Kim winked at Tony. Matthew studied the exchange and wished he had the weird telepathy so many talked about. Even without it, he felt some strange vibes from this Mafia-type.

As Tony sauntered into the Hall, toward Billy sitting at the first table in the carpeted lobby, Matthew slipped in the door behind him.

The teenager lingered far enough behind so the older man wouldn't notice. General Parker went through his routine with Billy, who returned the greeting with a warm smile.

"Hey, a military man!" Billy said, with too much excitement for Matthew's crawling skin. "I'm Billy Ferguson. Nice to meet you, sir. Where you from?" The two shook hands.

Matthew wandered to a table parallel to Billy's, plucked a pecan twirl from a plate and nibbled on it as he watched Tony. He didn't know why he felt so suspicious about the man, but he planned to keep an eye on him.

"Well, I'm from Washington, D.C., sir, General Parker's my name. Kim said something about you checking me in. What exactly does that mean?" His silky smile caught a moment, and Matthew wanted to shout for Billy to wake up and smell what the guy was shoveling.

"Well, sir, it means I have some basic supplies for you. Right next to the table is a sleeping bag, though that's only temporary, and here's a list of what we're gonna give you. That way, when we ration out things, you can keep track of what you've used and what you need. By the weekend, we're hoping to be housing all these folks. We know everybody prefers a bed over a cot, so we're humpin' it to get the houses cleaned out and ready for new residents." Billy's tone had cooled a little, and Matthew sensed a mental struggle between them. No one had stronger mind control than Billy, Jessie said – and a senior citizen named Sanford.

"Thank you, sir. Anything else I need to know? This little newspaper seems pretty advanced already. You folks are working hard. How many of you are camped out in this community of yours?"

Matthew caught Billy's eyes. *He's talking about us as "them," not us.* To a teenager, that's as clear as a line in the sand.

"Well, by noon today, we were three hundred eighty-seven strong. We've only added eighteen today, so we might be tapering off. I don't know. There's another scheduled release of X-86 tonight, so it could be that. But we plan to welcome everyone who wanders into our humble community!" Billy grinned, then faltered as he saw Matthew shaking his head. "Um, here's, um, your news...newsletter," Billy stammered, and Tony turned around to face Matthew Francis.

"Kid, you need somethin'? Or are you just nosey?" Tony stared cold and hard at the teenager

"Nope, just waitin' around for Jessie." Matthew's head thudded, and he knew the old man was clamoring around in his brain. But he took everyone's advice and slammed the door, pictured a curtain closing on a window – all the images that shut out prying eyes.

When Tony turned back to Billy, General Parker was all smiles. "Well, everybody seems real hospitable here. Good to see such an advanced camp. I'll be sure to pass this news on to my colleagues. This...this is incredible." Tony peered through the doors that led into the arena. The floor covered with tables, a buffet of food, and music playing on a radio somewhere. People wandered around with plates in their hands talking, smiling, and sipping from cups. Voices echoed in the massive room, bouncing from the high rafters above them. Matthew watched Tony study the auditorium, an odd smile spreading across the general's face.

The seats were empty now, but the stench lingered. It had taken twenty-five or thirty adults hours to clear the Hall. The count was near fifteen hundred – all dead, rigored, and in various contortions of suffocation. It made Matthew shiver to think about it.

"Yeah. We've worked real hard. There was a show in here Friday night. Seems they hadn't been affected 'til then. But when they turned the air on in here during the concert, it happened fast. It was pretty gruesome. It's sure good to hear there will be some military to facilitate clean-up." Billy's responses had now cooled considerably. He pointed at the news page in Tony's hands. "Take note of the elections. We could sure use some strong people to head our offices. Anyway, go on in and grab a bite to eat. They've fried some chicken, got baked beans, rolls, and all sorts of drinks. Whatever hits your fancy. One of the elderly gentleman makes a killer homemade stew." Billy clapped the general on the shoulder, warming back up to him but Matthew could tell it was guarded.

"Thank you, Billy. I appreciate it. I'll read my literature here, get me some grub, and maybe grab a nap." Tony gave Billy a casual salute and limped down the steps to the arena floor and the buffet tables.

Matthew noticed that the general walked away without picking up a sleeping bag, but he did keep the pack of necessities.

He's too damn good for us.

* * *

OH, DO I have such plans for this place.

Tony stood in the middle of Memorial Hall's floor, staring at the small stage with a surge of come-uppance. *They will worship me.*

He glanced down at the bottom of the flyer. *Elections: August 23rd.*

Oh, I have found my niche. When they get me into the biggest mansion here, then I'll cohort with these hicks. But I'm not sleeping in a goddamned sleeping bag on the fucking ground. Ingrates.

Tony grunted. But standing on that floor, he took it all in. He could be the Sam Walton of the new world. Or Bill Gates. Or God. Whichever. He just planned to be the cornerstone of whatever developed, and Joplin had Lancaster beat by a mile.

Tony felt Billy watching him. He tried to pry into the young man's head, but one thing Tony had to give these folks – they knew how to drop the curtain, so to speak. And it pissed him off. He detested paranoia – it was a sign of weakness, as far as he was concerned. The teenager skulked away, and Tony decided he best keep an eye on that one.

A cacophony of thoughts clawed at his deteriorating mind, random snippets of those mingling in the auditorium. Mundane aspirations of the ingenuous. Their eyes followed him, as well they should, as he worked the room.

It made him hard, anticipating their worship.

* * *

BILLY MOTIONED MATTHEW back to his table in the lobby with a finger hook.

"What's up, Matthew? You don't think he's on the up and up?" Billy kept a view through the doorway to follow Tony's migration through the people.

"No, he's slimy."

Dusty and Austin entered the Hall, wearing the scrubbiest clothes Billy had ever seen.

"Whoa, you homies look downright skanky," Matthew said, holding his nose.

"Thank you sooo much, Matthew. We're thinkin' we can find you some scrubs so you can join us. It's been fun so far." Austin rubbed his forehead with the back of his gloved hand.

"Oh, man, you guys reek." Billy covered his nose. "Sorry."

Dusty laughed, then picked up the clipboard. "We've got over a hundred houses ready, thanks to a hard-working team. Any good new additions?"

"A general," Billy offered, while Dusty scanned the list.

"And," Matthew whispered, keeping an eye on General Parker, "He's funketated, knowudImean?"

"A general? You're kidding. Whaddya mean *funketated*?" Dusty and the crew had seen their share of kooks impersonating everyone from Cleopatra to President Cavanaugh. It wouldn't surprise them.

"I mean the dude ain't right. He's puttin' on a show, tryin' to schmooze and stuff. And he's *strange*. Ya know, funketated. Man, you guys need to expand your vocabulary." Matthew shook his head.

"I want you to meet him, Dusty," Billy suggested, and pointed into the arena at Tony chatting with two older women near the punch bowl. "If we don't want it to be obvious, you can meet him at the fire tonight. But you should probably talk to him before you introduce him to five hundred hungry people."

"I'll try to bump into him this afternoon. Nonchalant like. If not, it'll be okay. Don't sweat the small stuff. I mean, what's the worst thing this guy can do? I mean, really? He's just a guy, maybe he's military, maybe he's not. Maybe he's a...a, you know..." Dusty fumbled for the right words.

"A poser." Matthew raised his eyebrows.

"Sure. But if we're wrong, we can't alienate someone who may have a great deal to offer. Right?"

"Oh, Dusty, I hope you're right, man." Austin watched the old guy laughing it up with a group of gray-haired women buying everything Tony had for sale.

"Hell, if he's like most military men I've ever known, he'll try to take over by nightfall." Dusty dropped the clipboard on the table and tugged Austin to follow. "It's time to clean."

"Have fun," Billy said with a chuckle.

But the aura of the day had evaporated around the general's

arrival. For the first time since all the clean up and rebuilding started, Billy's stomach churned.

"Billy, you seen Jessie?" Matthew popped the last bite of a cookie in his mouth.

"No, but it's fire time. Let's close up shop."

* * *

"THE SONUVABITCH AIN'T answerin' his phone." John thumped the off button on his cell and leaned over the small popping campfire. Behind him, people streamed out of the Hall heading toward the bonfire.

"It's Circle Time. I'm curious to see who's joined us. Aren't you? Let me get my jacket and we'll go." Haden drained the last of his coffee and slipped inside his tent.

"Yep. Jack and Breanna should be back any minute. They ran to Office Max to get Tristan and Valerie. They work harder than most of my employees. Uh, former employees, I guess." John leaned over to pull his shoes back on as Tony Andrews, aka General Anthony Parker, waltzed by behind him.

Had Tony looked off to the right of Memorial Hall, he would have seen the metal cage; instead he was drawn to the bonfire like a magnet.

* * *

TONY WORKED THE clumps of people like a calculating grifter. All the average Joes with a penchant for control sickened him. With no political gibberish to cloud the issues, to slide in some hidden agenda, the yahoos thought they could facilitate a government of the people – truly *of the people*.

As he played his role of government liaison, he suspected their wish would never come true – there would always be people like him to spoil the party. Most of the little clones embraced his ties to the White House with open, gullible arms. The comfort of a ranked official in charge lent integrity to their community. And his smooth tongue made him a god with the women. Even though he was obviously older, his elegance and charm overwhelmed everyone he met – he took pride in his work.

Except a lady named Cindy Timmons who, much like Billy, slammed the door on his thoughts and clamored inside his head with an ability he'd never felt. *I need to stay away from her.*

The idea humbled him. He heard about an eight-year-old girl, Jessie, and knew he needed to steer clear of her, too. He didn't need to meet her – he'd felt her in his brain for days.

Ruling the masses warranted caution, and Tony knew Jessie wouldn't trust him, that maybe her power was beyond his control. So he would have to win her over later. He pondered how to do that while he kissed some fat lady's hand.

The things he'd been reduced to.

* * *

CINDY TIMMONS' MIND abilities packed a punch, only comparable to a few – Jessie, Billy, and Sanford Grimes, the elite trio. While General Parker milled through her campsite, she studied his chiseled Italian features, and red flags popped up like teenage acne.

He's excited about the big fish. What the heck does he mean by 'give 'em a Florida exhibition'? Other random thoughts, darkened by shadows and a tangible anger, iced her insides.

I need to tell Dusty.

Could she make Dusty understand what she felt when peeking inside the general's head? The sensation of spiders clawing over one another to nest? It made her shiver in disgust as he left her sitting by a stoked fire. He was wary of her, that much was obvious – he glanced back at her with raised eyebrows, trying to read her – she felt him pry at her, but she had mastered the controls to a proverbial garage door in her mind.

After General Parker finally left, Cindy set off for tents nearest the bonfire – it was time to consult with Jessie about the man she couldn't shake from her thoughts.

If anyone would understand, it would be Jessie.

Chapter Forty

Joplin
Day Five

JESSIE'S STOMACH STEWED, making her sick all evening – something hadn't settled well. Or – but she couldn't consider the *or*. It made her head hurt worse than her stomach.

Matthew tried to roust her, told Melanie he really needed her to get up, but she couldn't lift her head or settle the boiling acid in her tummy. By 10:30 Monday night, she dragged herself out of her sleeping bag, tugged her unruly hair into a ponytail and plodded to the bonfire. She patted Scooter on the head and nudged him out the tent door. The cool breeze washed over her. She closed her eyes and let it erase the bad feelings.

"Movin' everybody inside for Circle tonight. Figured might as well keep warm and dry and have plenty of light. Besides, that way folks aren't sittin' on their butts. Dusty was looking for you earlier, by the way. And so was Ms. Timmons." Kim shuffled papers and dropped half of them.

"What for?" Jessie steadied herself with a trembling hand on Kim's table.

"Don't know, but I'm sure it can wait." Kim knelt down to scrape together the pages littering the sidewalk.

"Here, let me help." Jessie could tell the tanned girl all the boys had gone googly for was nervous about something. "You okay, Kim?"

"Yeah. I guess. I've just had some doozies this evening." Kim gathered the stray sheets, took Jessie's stack and straightened them.

"Anyone, um, really mean-looking? Or...I don't know, just *bad*?" Jessie's heart beat fast – she had dreamed about the bad man, hadn't she? Scooter whined and pushed his head under her hand. Cockroaches skittered around her brain.

"Oh, no. Just male chauvinists. Don't ever get married, Jessie. Matter of fact, don't fall in love. They're not worth it." Kim grinned, and the two of them headed up the ramp toward the entrance with Scooter trotting along behind them.

"We're inside!" Austin shouted, letting everyone in the parking lot know the venue had changed.

As they entered the Hall, Jessie scanned the tables in the lobby – cookies, bowls of mixed nuts, snacks and pretzels of every kind and drinks galore. She plucked a brownie from a plate, broke it in half and gave a piece to her tail-thumping dog.

"You're so spoiled, Scooter. Geez. Ooh, hot chocolate. Maybe that'll feel good on my stomach. You want some, Kim?" Jessie grabbed a Styrofoam cup and filled it to the brim, excited by the dull roar of voices, scooting chairs, and someone tapping on a microphone.

"Yeah. That sounds good. It must be packed in there – we may have to grab a few extra seats. We're about the last ones." Kim took a steaming cup from Jessie and the two went down the steps into the auditorium. The empty seats in the upper sections were a stark contrast to the floor where there was a buzz of activity – people dragging folding chairs closer together, Dusty at the podium in front of the page shuffling papers, and enthusiasm brewing at the sheer number in attendance. It made Jessie's head thud again.

Too much interference...Cindy said my receivers were the strongest she'd felt, but that it opened me to all the other stuff. That must be why it hurts so bad. The pain swooped over her like a hawk after its prey. Jessie's eyes watered and her stomach cartwheeled and somersaulted. Wobbly knees made it hard to stay upright.

As Kim led her to a chair near the back corner, voices bombarded the eight-year-old.

I shoulda brought my bottle in if...

Oh, my God, that guy is so adorable, Leslie, look at him!

...and if we get a house near the...

Lordy, you don't mean that, Jake is the smartest of all the...

That general, he's a charmer and handsome for an older man, did you hear what he said about...

Jessie tried to latch on to the last one. *A general?* Tiny sparks of electricity brought the hair on her arms to attention. She stood, ignoring Kim's plea to sit because everyone was getting quiet, and climbed to stand on her chair. She could see the panel's chairs, six of them to the left of the podium. On the other side were charts on dry erase boards and easels with crazy markings that made no sense to her. A bunch of posters were taped to the edge of the stage. She couldn't read any of it from the back.

Hey, are we gonna ask who's interested in the elections? Ya' know, like who's gonna run? Might be kinda neat to let people speak up for candidacy positions. She couldn't have heard Jake better if he'd spoken directly in her ear, despite him being forty rows and four hundred people away.

Dusty's signal, cloudy and fragmented, annoyed her.

We got....registered today... city council seats and...on another...tag board...then I'll get on the air in the mornin' to...

From somewhere beside her, she caught a snippet about the caged three – *What I wouldn't give for a chance to knife a toe or finger for posterity.*

Yeah, and that babe, Jamie? I'd like to...

She clamped her hands over her ears, but realized that wouldn't stop her from hearing. She hopped down and teetered

"Kim, make them stop." Jessie jerked forward just in time to vomit on the floor. "Uh, I can't breathe. There's...something...wrong." She raced up the auditorium steps, through the lobby, and into the fresh air – X-86 or not, it felt better than being invaded.

Vomit spewed from Jessie's lips again, no matter how hard she fought to keep it down. Melanie and Kim both knelt beside her saying something, but too many other voices clouded the girl's brain. She couldn't think, couldn't stand, couldn't stop her dinner from rebelling. For almost four minutes, she breathed and intermittently spat vomit onto the concrete in front of the Hall.

"Honey? Are you okay?" Melanie rubbed Jessie's back, disturbed by the suffering in the little girl's eyes.

Baby, what's wrong?

"There...there's a bad man. And...and I...I th...think may...maybe he's *here*." Jessie couldn't explain and didn't really know how she knew that. But she felt it in her gut – that the churning was him. "I gotta get back inside. To see."

"Okay. Let me help you. God, you threw up breakfast, lunch, and dinner. C'mon. Easy does it." Melanie lifted Jessie to her feet, both of them held her from either side so she could get her bearings, then they headed back inside.

Jessie practiced her door-closing methods even though that shut her off from voices she might want to hear. With a mental drop of the curtain, her head cleared and the swirling in her stomach subsided. She settled in the seat next to Kim, while Melanie headed toward the front, after asking Jessie one last time if she was okay.

"Kim, did they decide who's running for the jobs?" Jessie had so many questions, but there was really only one she cared about right now. *Where is he?*

"We're hoping Dusty goes uncontested for mayor. Jake hopes someone runs against him just so people have a choice and it's their decision. *You* even get to vote. How's that for democracy?" Kim patted Jessie's leg.

"Is Jake runnin' for something?" Her throat, sore from the burn of the vomit, made her voice weak.

"Yep. He's running for Police Chief, John's proposing a barter system and wants to be the county financial advisor, and Bryan and Jack Simpson are both running for something. I'm just not sure what. Austin wanted to, but everyone agreed they had to set an age limit of twenty-one for elected office. I guess you'll vote for Bryan, huh?"

Jessie managed a weak grin. Bryan was like a pseudo-father to her, but she still jokingly called him Uncle Bryan – the name had stuck for Matthew. Quite a few of them felt like family to her. Especially Matthew, though she wouldn't admit it to his face.

"Uh, ladies and gentlemen, we'd like to get started." Dusty thumped the microphone and asked the crowd if it was loud enough. He sighed, a long ragged breath, and Jessie felt his brainwaves tug at her.

Taking control without being controlling is wearing me out.

"We hear ya, Dusty!" someone in the middle shouted.

Without hesitating, Dusty called the meeting to order, and a hush rippled until everyone fell silent. The chairs in front of her were all full, as far as Jessie could see. She looked up at the middle and upper levels – hundreds of empty seats – and shivered with the thought of all those dead people. But tonight, the entire floor hummed with energy.

"Good. I want to wrap up some business from last night. A couple of you asked about banks, and we've decided we want to propose an alternative to money for the time being. It'll keep it less complicated and give no one a leg up. Money shouldn't equal clout anymore."

Cheers erupted from the crowd before Dusty could finish.

"We will devise a committee to organize and resolve the issue, and though Jake had banking experience, he abstained from the nomination. Now was his chance to do something he liked and to make a difference in a way he had never been able to. So we have other people on the ballot for that position. We also want you to know the Housing Project should be complete by Wednesday. It doesn't mean when you choose a home that it will be clean, but it will be, uh, body-less. Does anyone have questions regarding that or any other small matters before we discuss the elections?"

"Are you gonna introduce all the new arrivals since last night? I see a ton of new faces."

"There've been over fifty since midnight last night, and since that's so many, we're going to just have them stand. Hell, who'd remember all their names?" A titter of laughter followed until Dusty continued. "We can get acquainted with their faces tonight. In case you see someone you know, then you all can introduce yourselves after."

When no one offered anything further, Dusty asked the new arrivals to stand and be greeted.

Seats screeched, a murmur followed, and people stood, waved or saluted, and turned for everyone to see them.

Dr. John Basinger, three seats down from Jessie, dropped his coffee cup when Tony Andrews gave a cocky head nod to everyone around him. John ducked to retrieve the cup as Tony turned his way. *Shit.*

Jessie bolted upright at John's mental panic. She watched the big man crouch unseen until people took their seats. When he thought it was safe, he looked up ahead ten or twelve rows at the man who had startled him.

...once an old friend. Jessie watched John watch the man. The three laurel leaves on the shoulder – *a three-star general. How fitting.* She didn't understand John's thought, but she sympathized with the hammering in his chest and acidic taste in his mouth.

Cockroaches infested her head again, and she threw a mental blanket over them.

John turned to his friend Haden back by the entrance, but his right-hand man was still handing out leaflets to late arrivals.

"Okay, let's continue then. Welcome, everyone. We're glad you joined us. I guess all of you got the new paper this evening. Valerie, Billy, Austin, Tristan, and Melanie worked really hard on this, and I..."

"And Matthew and Storey," Melanie interrupted, sitting in a panel seat beside him. "They did all the graphics. Made it very impressive!"

A few laughed on the front row. "For those of you who couldn't hear Melanie, apparently Matthew Francis and Storey Roberts, our resident teenagers, added all the graphics and spiffied it up. It looks great, guys."

Matthew stood up, grinned and bowed to the crowd behind him. Storey did a half-stand and sat back down before anyone could see his cheeks flush.

"Now to highlight a few things, we need to finalize our decision about the three we have locked up out there."

Several new people asked questions about the caged three, offered advice for the inquiry, and then began arguing about removing them from the grounds.

"Put them in jail! I'm sick of lookin' at them!"

"Hell, no. I wanna spit on 'em ever' time I walk by 'em," Springfield Jimmy shouted.

"But we're givin' them a chance to talk to folks. What if they lure someone onto their side?" A new resident stood as she spoke. "I mean, c'mon. Let's put them somewhere that doesn't give them access to us. If..."

"Screw that! We have a right to face our demons, don't we?"

"Okay, let's not argue." Dusty quieted everyone with his hands in the air. "The panel will be assembled in two days, and the inquiry will be Friday. We don't have to have an argument every time the subject comes up. A decision will be reached then, and you all get to vote for the panel members and the final decision as well."

They moved on to boring business by eleven, and Jessie couldn't focus anymore. She wanted to meet the man who had startled Dr. Basinger. Exhausted, she closed her eyes and listened.

"Okay, folks, listed up here are fifteen positions we feel are very important to be filled. We'll have a majority election for each office, and anyone can run. Money is not an issue. Any posters you want printed, Valerie and her team will set you up at Office Max on Rangeline. Computer printouts can be made. Whatever you want. So, let's open the floor for any declarations. Now, you can decide later, but this way we'll have an idea of who's interested in what." People fidgeted in their seats. Postures straightened, so everyone could get a glimpse of raised hands.

"Is there anyone who plans to run for Mayor?"

The crowd stirred, two hands shot up, and Griffin Stevenson shouted, "I'd make a damned good mayor!"

Jessie bolted up from her slouch and grinned at the gentleman she thought might be the smartest man on the planet.

"Well, Griffin, you'll give me a run for my money. We'll have fun, and I promise not to cut on your age," Dusty chided.

The crowd laughed.

"Wisdom comes with age," Griffin countered and beamed as the people around him cheered. The two chuckled good-naturedly.

"I think I might want to join that race," the other raised hand's owner shouted.

Everyone's head turned to see who had spoken. John shuddered.

Melanie Stevens frowned.

Cindy Timmons furrowed her brow and jotted something on her flyer. Sanford Grimes glanced her way and nodded in agreement with her thought-speech.

Various other people smiled and applauded. Jessie watched them all and tried to get a better look at the man. Cockroaches clawed at the suffocating blanket.

"Uh, General Parker. Well, we welcome you to our race. Now I can't make any promises about giving you a hard time, because I don't know you well enough yet. Give me ten minutes."

Dusty brought laughter back into the Hall, but not into John Basinger's heart. Jessie felt Dusty cringe – a sensation that troubled her, though she couldn't see the uniformed man to measure her stomach's response to him.

By the time the meeting adjourned, the atmosphere was palpable. People buzzed about the new houses that could be chosen Friday and speculated about the hearing Friday night.

Lines formed for those who wanted to declare candidacy for an office, and a few suggested other offices.

John hung to the side, waiting for Tony to leave. He motioned to Dusty and Jake. When the men gathered in front of the stage, Big John trembled.

"We have a problem," he managed, but any other words died in his throat. The big man was as pale as a piece of paper.

Jessie sat in the front row trying to listen but didn't want to hear. Kim and Melanie had drifted to the exit to chat with a few of the new people.

"What's up, John? You look like you've seen a ghost." Jake wrinkled his forehead.

Jessie looked to each one of them, strange images flashing and disappearing before she could make sense of them. The sensation of insects scrabbling at her brain made her squeeze her eyes shut.

"I have, I think. Your General Anthony Parker. Did he talk to either of you? Because I'm betting he didn't socialize with anyone in charge very much, but schmoozed with the regulars. Networked, brainwashed, if you know what I mean. Did either of you meet him?" John leaned against the stage, and Jessie thought he might throw up like she had. Her own stewing stomach was out of ammunition.

"Haden, didn't you see him at the door?"

"Huh-uh. He must've come in a side entrance and not gotten a flyer. Maybe he read someone else's. Damn. I can't believe he's here." Haden rubbed his bald head, then his eyes.

"Who? God, don't be so cryptic. Melanie already said he gave her the heebie jeebies. She said he's been working the camp all day, hitting on the women, talking war stories with the men. Who is he?" Dusty's voice rose a notch, annoyed and impatient.

"It's Tony Andrews, Dusty. That's the bomber himself. My old friend and rival CEO – of BetaCorp. And this falsifying his name, and the whole general thing, that's just creepy. Scary as hell if you think about it." John's expression clouded.

"Oh, my God," Austin muttered. "That's the sonuvabitch who nuked Florida and nearly killed me."

"Yeah, that's him. And God may not be able to help us here. I'm thinking we need to play this out very carefully. Do we blow his cover, John, or do we wait until he really develops the lie and then show his true colors?" Jake looked from face to face for a response. He had heard plenty about Andrews but couldn't believe the BetaCorp boss had the nerve to impersonate a military man. But then again, it served as the perfect lure.

"We need to find his plane and Greg. Tony's obviously not sleeping here, he'd never manage that, not even for cover. Second thing to consider is that the longer we allow him to manipulate the people, the more allies he gets. But if we piss him off now, he might just blow us to B.F.E. And he may anyway. That may be his plan." John sighed. "He's surely seen the three out there. He's got to know I'm here."

Jake, Billy, and Dusty pulled up chairs. Bryan lifted himself backwards to sit on the stage. The sudden weight on their shoulders made it a concerted effort to think, much less stand.

"John, let's just kill him. He knows we're here. I mean, how did they get here if we didn't survive his blast in Dallas? I know that's not the way to start things, but he has murdered hundreds of thousands, maybe millions, of possible survivors. Hell, parts of Florida might not've been contaminated yet. Blowing up an entire state is insane. And what he did to Kenny, well, John, I'm sorry. I don't see any other choice." Haden looked at Dusty and Jake. "What's to stop him? I mean, he has no scruples. He enjoys killing. You always knew Tony was on the edge, and that made him good at cutthroat corporate business, but he's lost it, John. Please." Haden's pleading eyes said what the rest of them were thinking.

Melanie drifted over after putting away all the posters and materials.

"What's wrong?" She looked at their bewildered faces and then over at Jessie. None of them had noticed her expression until then. They saw her ashen face, and she trembled like an epileptic in the throes of a seizure.

"Oh, God, honey." Melanie grabbed Jessie and held her.

"Why don't you take her to her tent, Mel. We'll be out there in a minute." Dusty managed a smile, but couldn't bring himself to stand or walk over to them.

"No." Jessie stared down at her hands, the flyer crumpled there. "I'm not leaving."

No one rebutted. They all seemed caught in a bizarre game of freeze tag.

"Someone tell me what the hell is going on." Melanie's voice hit a pitch Jessie had never heard.

"Remember Brad's e-mail, his warning? Well the good general is Tony Andrews. God forbid he figures out who you are. Remember hanging up on him and pissing him off?"

"Holy Mary, Mother of God." She sat heavily in the chair next to Jessie.

"John, you're our only hope. You two were friends. There's a bond there, something that can be of use to us. And I think we need to decide by morning. This can't wait. The longer we put this off, the more damage he'll do. General, my ass. What the hell made him decide to go military?" Haden grunted and kicked at a pen cap on the floor.

"Was he ever in the army or navy, John? Did he serve time in 'Nam? He'd be about the right age." Dusty held out his fingers like he was counting.

"Yes. Not long, maybe even got drafted. He hated the Army, despised it with a passion. It was another place where he was treated like a subservient peon. He didn't talk about it much though. I spent a lot of time with Tony, but he didn't share much about his personal life. I know he had a shitty childhood, grew up dirt poor. That's what drove him. Talked about his rags-to-riches story quite a bit, but the memories, I could always tell, must've been tough. Grew up in Florida, small town outside Miami, I think. God, this is making my head hurt." John massaged his temples.

"Well, that makes sense," Austin mumbled. "Probably thought he was blowin' all those idiots up."

"He's a general. That sure makes sense, too," John added, thinking out loud. "If I know him, he's scouting, seeing what we have. He's probably wooing friends. He wants to be mayor, then president, then king. That's what he's evolved to. And I don't think it's X-86 poisoning. I think it's called psychosis. He has no morals, you guys. He'll kill however it serves him best. If you sneeze and it scares him, he'll shoot you. If you're ugly, he'll shoot you. If you get in his way, he will shoot you. He's beyond saving now. I figured that out the hard way."

"Maybe if you confronted him, John. You're his equal; maybe he'll respect what you say. Especially if he sees you were savvy enough to escape him."

"I don't think so, but let me think about all this. I've got to let it digest and try to figure out what he's after. He can't want to be mayor and have to work again. That doesn't fit. My guess? He's planting a seed in our heads that he's a man of power, then he's going to fly right back to D.C. and take office. *The* office. He'll gather people from other sites if he feels we're too much of a threat. But with his arsenal, how can we stop him? And we have to find his Silver Bullet."

"His what?" Melanie's face registered how all of them felt – shocked, confused, and more than a little pissed off. Surviving X-86 shouldn't be compounded by this lunatic.

"His Cessna – that's what he calls it. And I bet that's where he's holing up. It's like a fricking luxury hotel."

"Well, let's do that now. It's late; he's probably already headed there, but at least we can do it discreetly enough to just see where it is. Then we can come up with a plan. What else do we need?" Jake jumped up.

"Prayers. God help us all."

Dusty mumbled, "Amen."

As they turned to go, they saw Jessie stooped over in the chair with her head down.

"Jessie? Are you okay?" Dusty sat beside her, and Melanie put her arms around her from the other seat. Bryan stooped in front of her, cupping her face in his hands.

"No. He's the bad man, Dusty. The one I've dreamed about since...since...I think since I was six. I thought all this started with the chemical stuff, but I'm not sure anymore. He's not here to be mayor." She looked up, her eyes glistening with tears. "He doesn't even want to be president anymore. He wants to kill us and save those three. That's all he wants. Because they have friends somewhere in Texas. And somehow, he knows that."

"Shit." John dropped into a chair again.

"What?" several of them asked.

"He knows because I told him. I don't know where they are, but Kyle or Nathan, I don't remember which now, let it slip that they have a bunker for their families and followers."

Moans and questions erupted. Jessie slapped her hands over her ears again and screamed. They all stopped and stared at her.

"He just shot someone," she mumbled. "And he...he has a lady. I don't know her, but she's scared. He shot her friend, too."

Jessie burst into tears as Bryan and Dusty held her. The others' mouths fell open, not sure to believe her but too afraid not to.

Chapter Forty-One

Waco
Day Six

"DID YOU HEAR that?" The young man leaned in closer to the radio.

"What?"

"They just said something on that Joplin station about the *caged three*. Details are coming up. Shit. It's gotta be them." Charlie Mantel's face mirrored what most of them felt – desperation. The idea that Jamie could be trapped with no way to join them made his skin crawl. The *not knowing* was almost unbearable, and seven days of being cooped up with sixty-one total strangers had him climbing the walls. The concrete barracks that entombed them fifteen feet underground had worn out its welcome. It may have saved his life, but now he wondered what kind of life it was going to be.

Charlie felt Dr. Edwards studying him. He knew his reputation preceded him; the doctor had said as much when they met last Wednesday.

"You're immortal in Texas." But it was what Dr. Edwards didn't say that worried Charlie. *You're a smug thirty-year-old with no idea what power you had.* Charlie suspected thoughts like those, but he could only guess. He lacked the mental telepathy.

"What's your gut say, Charlie?" The NAO leader raised an eyebrow. In the dimly lit great room, Charlie couldn't see Edwards well, but when he heard the others start mumbling, he speculated that Edwards was fanning the competitive flame. Their struggle for alpha dog was taking its toll on everyone.

"Well, Jimbo," Charlie said, swaggering toward the doctor. "I think Jamie never dreamed I would come here in the first place. But when she said not to ask questions, to trust her, I knew something had to be up. Then she e-mailed me that it was life or death. I couldn't ignore that. And my guess is the three they have in Joplin are probably three of our four. One of them must be missing. Maybe the fourth got away and is headed here now. That would explain why none of them showed – they got caught." Charlie took a breath and scanned the sixty-one faces.

The group had been imprisoned for almost a week, since early last Wednesday. Jamie insisted he be there, explaining that they would seal them in at five o'clock that evening, and there would be no turning back once they made that choice. To avoid possible X-86 poisoning, it was imperative they understood that. The underground chamber, airtight with its own heating and cooling system, had been designed for the select few – those the four listed to survive and play a role in the re-establishment of a pure American race – a dominant people who would rule the world. The bunker was a giant room with small round lights on the stone walls, a few dangling bulbs over mismatched couches and chairs, and a TV in two of its corners. DVD players with a stack of movies served as entertainment, coupled with a stereo and plenty of music to meet all preferences.

But all they had done was listen to the radio in hopes of getting information. Right away, they rejoiced to hear Dusty Morris broadcast, keeping them informed and connected – not that their cell phones worked in the concrete tomb.

"Well," Jim Edwards started, and sighed. "My guess is you're right. Which one escaped, I can't speculate, but I'm sorry to say for most of you folks, I hope it's Nathan. His vision is why all this came about."

Trisha Spene sat back and refused to let the slimy man bait her. She wanted to claw his eyes out and pluck what little hair he had left one strand at a time. Instead, she crossed her legs, still parked at one of the kitchen tables from lunch, and listened.

She hadn't been able to come to grips with Kyle's part in this horrific incident. She and Beth had read the invitation over and over again, trying to make sense of it. They called him and his curt response of *Forget about Julian; just follow it* confused and angered them both. But when push came to shove, they were too afraid to ignore it.

As Charlie and Dr. Edwards speculated about who was being held captive in Joplin, Trisha tried to untwist the pretzel in her brain. What had Kyle been thinking?

One thing was crystal clear – Kyle had been responsible for Julian's disappearance. He had to be. What else could have driven him to this totalitarian thinking? She felt it in her gut, and it skewered her heart. She couldn't sort that out in her head, didn't want to hate her brother for it, because he had done it for her. For years, she believed that Julian had run away because he succumbed to Kyle's threat – *I'll kill you if I ever see you again.*

But Manny and Kyle had knockdown drag-out fights. One left Manny with stitches and Kyle a chipped tooth. Other heated arguments led Manny to cooperate with the police because he believed his best friend had killed his little brother and wouldn't own up to it.

The friendship ended like a bad marriage. If Kyle entered the locker room and Manny was there, he turned and walked out. If Manny came over to borrow an egg so his mom could make brownies, Kyle stomped upstairs in a huff.

Neither would discuss it – they were beyond that now. Kyle's face reddened at the mention of Manny's name, so in the Spene household, it was a taboo topic.

And now here she sat in an underground town. That's what it seemed like – the great room, cement hallways that gave way to a score of small rooms. Each housed four bunks, a toilet, a sink, and a mirror with a tiny medicine cabinet above it. A small chest of drawers stood at the foot of each bed.

She felt like she was in a stony, damp single-floor dormitory, and she hadn't been allowed to choose her roommates. Two Nazi-wannabes kept flashing knowing grins at one another and pounding their chests with fingers manipulated into some kind of hand signal. One of the thugs had more tattoos than bare skin, and teeth so green she suspected he ate grass. His eyes – flat and cold – were framed by greasy brown hair pulled back into a frizzy ponytail. *Aren't white supremacists supposed to have crew cuts?*

The other Nazi-boy wandered to his and Green Teeth's room every hour or so, leading several to speculate they had stocked up on drugs. She was grateful that, despite the four-bunk rooms, most of them only had one or two roomies. Plans had obviously been for more than the current inhabitants. When she calculated it, Kyle equipped the safe house for one hundred people, more if they needed to use the couches in the huge living space.

The cement central room gave way to a kitchenette. Five long dining tables, eight couches, five easy chairs, and a radio filled the room, and there were plants everywhere – fake plastic ones trying to give the illusion of life. But for Trisha, it didn't work. When she woke every morning, she and Beth prayed it would end – that miraculously someone would tap on the hatch and tell them it was all a big joke.

Instead, devastating news marked each day. Friday they received staggering statistics of deaths across the United States. On Saturday, the Dallas DJ delivered the mind-boggling story that a bomb had obliterated Miami. Sunday they learned that Florida itself had been fragmented by missiles, turning the Sunshine State into a slew of new island keys. Monday, Dusty informed them Dallas had become the latest to suffer at the hands of a demented bomber the day before.

When they woke on Tuesday morning, electricity flickered and died for a fleeting moment, leaving them entombed in darkness. But when it returned, Dusty's voice boomed with Tuesday's news – perhaps the worst of all for everyone confined.

"There will be an inquiry this Friday to determine the fate of the caged three. We invite all listeners, whether they've joined us in Joplin or not, to come be part of this historic event. If..."

But frantic questions and comments drowned Dusty's voice. Trisha grabbed Beth by the arm and led her into the kitchen, not hidden from the others but at least out of earshot.

"I can't stand this. These people, they're not like us. And I can't believe Kyle would do this. We've only been in here for seven days. Can you imagine a month?" Trisha poured them both a glass of Chardonnay, and they looked up to hear what Charlie was saying.

"We may have to spend more than a month in our cement coffin if some lunatic keeps nukin' cities, especially as close as Dallas." He shook his head.

When Dr. Edwards spoke behind her, she nearly dropped the bottle. He pulled a fifth of scotch from the cabinet above the refrigerator, filled a tumbler, and dropped in two cubes of ice while he talked.

"We don't know it's nuclear. Our real fear is the X-86. We've heard the death percentages from exposure to it, the numbers dying from shifting winds, and that yuck-yuck says there are going to be releases over the course of eight days. If in eight days the chemical can kill over ninety-eight percent of the world's population, it's not going to dissipate in a matter of three weeks. Hell, Agent Orange affected the Vietnamese for years. We may climb into that vacuum chamber, then open the hatch and die on the spot. Without Nathan here to guide us and let us know how to measure its affects, I don't see an end." Dr. Edwards walked around, as if to exert his authority. Few of the tomb residents were over thirty-five years old, so he stood to reign just by age. One couple in their late forties didn't look to challenge his influence one iota.

The neo-Nazi poster boys who made Trisha's skin crawl flashed wicked grins at one another. They both made that same hand gesture similar to a surfer's hang ten.

"Who invited you here?" Trisha stared in disdain at the two men, surrounded by ten or twelve skinhead types.

"Nathan Kirkpatrick did, gorgeous, and you better remember that name, because he's going to be the next president of the United

States." Mr. Greenteeth spoke like he thought someone important might be listening.

One of his cohorts piped in, "But we may change our country's name, of course. We're not exactly united anymore, are we?" Brendon Highsmith winked at Trisha. At least he had better teeth than his buddy and the right kind of haircut – buzzed with a swastika notched into the back.

He had another swastika tattooed on his right biceps, and it twitched each time he flexed, which Trisha noticed he did every time he looked at her. She suppressed the urge to hold Beth's hand because she suspected he was the type to do more than condemn them. He might be one of those who thought he could convert her. She felt their lifestyle might be a secret best kept to themselves.

"You may not have heard of Nathan," Greenteeth continued. "But damn if he doesn't have the balls to see this thing through to the end."

"I know who Nathan is," Trisha snipped. "My brother and him were pretty tight, I know, but Kyle would never have thought of any of this on his own. I don't really understand what's going on, but I'd say Nathan is behind most of it." She sipped her wine, measuring the expressions of the more normal looking residents.

"I sincerely hope so, honey. But you're wrong about Kyle. I met him, and he's an NAO endorser all the way. He may not have been one of us yet, but he damn well did his part, and did it well, I might add. Kyle and Jamie were the masterminds. Nathan's got brass to think it up, but the genius work came from those two." Brendon winked again and flashed straight white teeth.

You should've taught your buddy to brush. Trisha had the wild urge to giggle but thought those teeth might sprout fangs – *the better to eat you with, my dear.* Her imagination was getting the better of her now.

"No way in hell Jamie did this. I couldn't get my sister to come to Kingsville to be part of The Movement. Why would she do something this extreme?" Charlie shook his head, obviously bewildered. "This was my league, not hers."

"We all have our buttons. Nathan knew how to push them," Brendan added with pride. "Who was the fourth person?"

"Our son," spoke a small voice from the other side of the room. Everyone turned to look. The fortyish couple Dr. Edwards dismissed earlier huddled by the radio, appearing as meek as they sounded.

"Who're you?" Charlie directed the room's attention to a man and haggard woman sitting on the floor with their backs against the wall.

How metaphorical. Trisha swelled with pity for the two before they even said a word. Until now, everyone had been satisfied with names without affiliations. For Trisha, congregating with the sleazy NAO members made her feel dirty. Like being caught in a pornography store after dark.

"Bobby Sims' father. My name's Robert. This is my wife Tabitha. I knew something strange was going on starting about eight months ago. He got secretive. He was seeing a girl named Jamie, so she must have been your sister," he said, nodding at Charlie. "He was stressed all the time, and he occasionally missed visits with Sam, which was totally not him. Then he started talking crazy about our government not being a true democracy. Socialist talk. We got in some huge arguments about racism, and he expressed views I never knew he had. Maybe they weren't all his own."

Tabitha, frail beyond belief, locked eyes with Dr. Edwards.

"Something awful happened on Wednesday," she murmured. "After dinner we went for a walk, and when we got back, there was an urgent message on our machine. Grandview Homes needed us to come to the facility ASAP. Needless to say, we panicked." Sobs muffled the last word and forced Tabitha Sims to cry into the nook of her husband's shoulder.

"My wife and I raced there," Robert said. "When we arrived, they told us Sam, our daughter, had died. The bizarre part is that a nurse said she sat straight up in her bed, screamed bloody murder, and then died from a massive brain hemorrhage." Robert paused trying to maintain composure.

"My God, I'm so sorry," Trisha soothed. "Was she ill?"

"Our daughter had been in varying stages of a coma since she was seven years old. She nearly drowned when she went swimming with Bobby and his best friend Max." He seemed to get lost in the memory for a moment. "Max did drown that day, and Sam might as well've. Bobby never really got over it."

Robert Sims hung his head so low, no one could see the tears dripping straight to the concrete floor. Trisha believed Bobby wasn't the only one who hadn't dealt with it.

"So what are you saying, Mr. Sims? About Sam's screaming before she died?" Trisha leaned forward, to somehow show the couple she sympathized.

"Yes, please share your divine wisdom with us." Dr. Edwards took a long slug of his scotch and smirked. Trisha wanted to smack him.

"I'm saying I think our daughter died because something happened to Bobby. They were, how do I say it – *connected*. Bobby always knew when Sam had bad days no matter where he was. He would call from conferences in New York City and say, 'Sam didn't respond today, did she?' He could sense it. I think Sam felt something Bobby experienced. We tried to call him all day Wednesday before coming here. We decided we better listen to the invitation just in case he might be here, but I think we both knew better. My wife didn't get her hopes up, and I shouldn't have."

"I've heard of things like that happening. Twins have that connection a lot. They must have been very close," Trisha consoled. She caught Charlie's pained expression from the corner of her eye.

He's haunted by something horrible. Maybe we all are, that's what ties us together.

Tabitha nodded.

The conversation lagged. The talk of death disquieted many of them, and Trisha fought images of her mom – when they received Kyle's message, their mother left for work Wednesday morning and never came home. Trisha and Beth had driven into Plano to get her, but after going to her office, back home and then to her favorite restaurants, they gave up.

Beth speculated Kerri Spene had driven into Dallas to straighten Kyle out, to speak to her son face to face and find out what the hell was going on. Trisha listened and wondered if her mom had gotten the answer she wanted.

"Okay, gang, who's turn to clean-up?" Charlie went to their chart and laughed to see his own name as one of the self-appointed three. By nine-thirty, the dishes had been cleared and cleaned.

The chart designated a trio to have kitchen responsibilities every evening. Five others prepared each meal, rotating to a new five from breakfast to lunch to dinner.

Dr. Edwards opposed such menial work, but majority ruled, and men, as well as women, did the daily chores. Trisha could tell this was definitely not what he had envisioned in a new world where the white *man* would rule.

* * *

WHEN WE GET out of here, there will be a new order of things. Where are you, Nathan? You did the deed, now we must succeed.

Dr. Jim Edwards smiled at the catch phrase the NAO created for Nathan Kirkpatrick. They would chant, "Do the deed, and we succeed," over and over and over. As a seventeen-year-old, Nathan responded with untethered enthusiasm.

Could we be wrong for wanting a perfect world? The good doctor didn't think so. Theirs had so many faults already, and to have to deal with the pettiness of Trisha Spene and the wilting conviction of Charlie Mantel irked him. How could The Movement's Grand Dragon not aspire to the real possibility of purity, of taking their vision worldwide?

Nathan's plan could mesh so beautifully with The Movement's. Perhaps if Mr. Mantel couldn't see fit to mastermind it, someone of Brendon's motivation could. Nathan's vision outlined everything, from the fusion of government and military to more efficient schooling for America's youth. He designed many public schools to be converted into specialized educational institutions – schools of technology, fine arts, and masters of weaponry – and military training in a more regimented fashion. People would specialize in a way they never had before.

White people.

The prospects were endless. Julliard would no longer be a cut above the rest. It would play second fiddle to many of these. Dr. Edwards was certain of it.

"Hey, turn it up!" someone shouted as Dusty's voice broke in after a long stream of classic rock.

"...as the caged three decided today that they would be willing to speak at an inquiry. The process will begin Thursday, at which time the community's panel will determine who will sit on the jury for the interrogation. We plan to hold the inquiry Friday if all goes as planned."

No one in the tomb breathed or spoke as they listened to Dusty Morris shuffle papers.

"Also today, the housing project has almost completed its mission. Clean-up teams led by Bryan Saunders have confirmed that all victims have been buried and sites are ready for claim. Death toll in Joplin is near ninety-seven percent of the city's population. The remaining three percent are unaccounted for. The home acquisition procedure will involve scouting the neighborhoods, pulling the flag, which has stars to indicate the number of bedrooms in that house, and then bringing it back to the New Home Commission table. Once all the papers are signed and new homes are documented, the house is yours. If you are on the road and haven't joined us yet, don't panic because there are still only five hundred of us and plenty of houses to choose from. We have been in contact with two other large camps that have designed the same procedure using ours as their guide. There will be a vote on how businesses will be restarted and what our means of bartering will be. Obviously, we have chosen to destroy our old monetary system to avoid robberies and theft. Many banks have already been cleaned out. For this we will take suggestions, and then put it to a vote.

"If you're out there wondering about gathering money, which we know many were doing, stop. Enough damage has been done. Your skills will be your equity for right now. We will accept your handshake as commitment, and from there, we will deal.

"This will be an America truly run by the people. We hope you can join us in our quest for a better way of life. Enjoy another ninety minutes of your favorites on the new 97.9, previously on 92.5 out of Dallas. I'm Dusty Morris, and you keep us connected."

Everyone sat in complete silence for about sixty seconds, then the dam broke.

"...but without money, it will be chaos. You can't..."

"...of the inquiry is a joke. Those three can't get a fair hearing. My God, they'll be..."

"...if we can't get out for months, what will be left, I mean..."

"...clean-up concept is great, but with hundreds of thousands of towns and cities, how..."

"HEY!"

Everyone froze. Charlie stood in a chair with his hands up about to yell again.

"People, listen up! We can deal with all of this, but we can't panic. Some of you want to leave, I feel it. But you can't!"

"Who died and made you boss, son?" Dr. Edwards looked hard at Charlie, and barely controlled the desire to knock the kid off the chair and be king of the mountain. Timing, the fanatical doctor knew, was everything.

"Nobody did. I'm just trying to stop anyone who's getting desperate from killing me by opening that hatch. That's exactly what will happen. Anyone susceptible to the X-86, which by Dusty's calculations is about sixty-one of us, will die. That means out of all of us, one or two survive. Is that what ya'll want?"

"No," ten or fifteen voices replied. But several didn't answer. Charlie shook his head.

Dr. Edwards felt the surge of the competitive beast well inside him.

"I'm willing to take my chances. I'm tired of being a prisoner when I haven't committed a crime. We've got cabin fever already, and it's only been seven fucking days. What about come September and we can't decide when to open it? What then? The note said four weeks should be long enough for the atmosphere to clear, but *what if*? I know, we've got gas masks, but do you want to live with a gas mask on your face? Give me a fucking break." Dr. Edwards' reddened face matched the feverish pitch in his voice.

No one responded to him. No one spoke; they didn't move but stared at him with no expression whatsoever. He fought the urge to rip off his shirt and flaunt the Confederate flag tattooed on his chest – anything to get their attention and channel it in the right direction.

"C'mon, folks, how many of you are already claustrophobic? Maybe eight or nine of us will make it. If I don't, then it's God's will. But I'd rather go that way than sit here for another thirty, forty, even fifty days. *And it may happen anyway.* We don't know."

The wicked gleam in his eye didn't catch, and when they turned and looked at one another, Dr. Edwards knew it was win or lose. Draw wasn't an option.

* * *

"SO YOU'RE WILLING to die? Good soldiers can withstand their time in the pen, sir. You trained us for that. POWs suffer all the time, and they're innocent. This is why we will overcome, sir – you said it yourself. You even recognized that the weak would crumble in seclusion, that the walls would close in on those not strong enough to outlast it. What are you saying now?" Brendon Highsmith's voice had risen to a nervous pitch, Trisha noticed. She gripped Beth's arm.

"I know, Brendon, but don't you see what we could be doing now? Being here is going to cloud our vision. Listening to people rationalize our world. This Dusty character is talking about an America run by the people and the new order of things. I am the new order of things. *Nathan* is the new order of things, and they have him in a fucking cage. The New America Order is designed for times such as these, and we will rise to power. But we can't sit back for a month while these people gain power and revive civilizations in which we play no part. We are destined to rule. Right, men?"

Sporadic cheers peppered throughout the group. In a campsite long ago, Nathan Kirkpatrick had been in awe of everything the doctor said. Back then, Dr. Edwards epitomized what the youth hungered for. Now the fifty-year-old fascist seemed to be losing his grip; Charlie recognized the symptoms.

"So who's with me? Let's vote! We can use democracy. There are sixty-two of us. A majority will decide. Do we stay in captivity for another month? Or do we let the sun shine on our faces and take our chances? All in favor of leaving this hellhole, say aye and put your hand to the sky!" The gleam in Jim Edwards' eyes allowed many to see that cabin fever had a firm hold.

Not a single voice replied. Not even Brendon or his buddies.

Without waiting for the rebuttals, Jim Edwards pummeled people as he raced down the hall for the hatch. Several followed trying to grab the flapping tails of his Polo. Charlie was the first to catch him. He tackled the man and both crashed to the concrete. The doctor's glasses crunched under someone's feet.

"My glasses, goddammit! Who just broke my fucking glasses?" Spittle flew from his mouth.

As everyone looked around for pieces of the crushed spectacles, Dr. Edwards pulled a pistol from his ankle harness.

A collective groan from those swarmed around him got Charlie's attention a split second before the bullet to his left shoulder spun him around. The piercing pain brought sulfur burning in his nostrils. The gun's discharge was metallic in the air. A smoke cloud hovered just above the barrel of the pistol. Charlie grabbed Edwards by the foot as the doctor scrambled for the ladder to freedom. They all knew how imperative it was for a person to enter the holding chamber then lock the hatch behind him before lifting the cover in the middle of the Waco field. If Edwards didn't, they would all die, not just him.

Charlie yanked the older man back as hard as his throbbing arm would allow. A dark blood splotch spread quickly on the left side of his Hard Rock T-shirt.

Dr. Edwards swung around, flailed the gun and fired. A scream splintered the air behind Charlie, followed by angry orders. Someone barked for towels and bandages, while another moaned in pain.

Before Edwards could fire again, Charlie had the man's trigger hand pulled straight up toward the cement ceiling. Charlie's daily strength training at Gold's Gym guaranteed that the aging doctor was no match.

When he shoved Edwards' gun hand around until the barrel pressed hard into the man's own neck, Charlie struggled to get his finger on the trigger.

Trisha screamed for them to stop, and Brendon Highsmith scrambled to stop Charlie from executing the founding father of the NAO. Robert Sims tugged the Nazi boy around and punched him as hard as he could right in the nose.

"You will not kill us," Charlie insisted as the gun aimed straight up under Edwards' chin. The blast would blow the top of his head off, if Charlie could press the old man's trigger finger hard enough.

Everyone froze – Trisha saw something flicker in Charlie's eyes.

"My little sister would beg me not to kill you," Charlie snarled, his voice so low and commanding that they all held their breath. "Kingsville ruined our lives. It killed my mom, my dad, and I guess it killed Jamie inside. 'Be stronger than them, Charlie,' she once pleaded."

The gun shook violently in their hands. Edwards' eyes were wild with panic. "Do it," he hissed. "You prick, do me. DO ME!"

But Charlie wavered. Trisha wanted him to kill Edwards because the doctor symbolized terrible things for the underground inhabitants, and for the rest of the world if he got out.

"Shoot him!" someone shouted.

"Kill the sonuvabitch! He just shot my wife!" Robert Sims screamed above the rest. The agony in his words squeezed Trisha's heart.

But Charlie tugged the gun away from Edwards throat and yanked it from the man's hands. "I will not control with violence. Not anymore."

He turned to the others. "I'm sorry. I can't. It's not right." He shook the pistol from his finger like a stubborn bugger, but Edwards overruled the decision. The wrath of the good doctor propelled him toward the hatch, hell bent on getting out of the prison. He pounded a balled fist into the side of Charlie's head, nearly knocking the young man over.

Charlie grabbed the revolver and released Edwards from his prison by firing a single shot right between the eyes. Jim Edwards crumpled like a limp scarecrow.

Several screamed, but more groaned with relief. A few clapped Charlie on the back. He collapsed to the floor and dropped the gun again. His left shoulder throbbed.

"He's losing blood fast," Trisha shouted. Beth raced to the kitchen for towels while another lady hopped up and grabbed the first aid kit.

Hands pressed a cloth firmly on the wound, sending Charlie into a pain-induced faint.

"Look, Trisha, there's an exit wound in the back. See it? That's good. At least the bullet's gone."

"Yeah, I see it. Hey, Brendon, can you get me another bandage? And Scottie, some more water? What's your name?" she asked the young woman helping her. Scottie stumbled over them, the young boy eager to follow her directions.

And so developed the group guided by a recovering Charlie Mantel. Daily information from Dusty gave them the strength to survive and to plan. They elected a scout to exit first, to wear a mask, to call Dusty, to test the air. And then they listed details of what would need to be done when they escaped.

They filled two notebook pages and attached names to each duty. It signified the unity they now felt. Without Dr. Edwards to skew their thinking, even Brendon Highsmith and his friends believed it could be done.

Freedom of speech, Charlie reminded, didn't have to be a crutch people used to incite violence and hatred. The amendment was intended to allow voices of progress to be heard, not screams of fascism. As he healed, his presence strengthened.

"If you truly believe America can't operate by the people, by us, when we get out of here, please...go find a country that endorses that philosophy. I want a better world for my children – a place where I can walk down the street at eleven o'clock at night and not worry about gang-bangers shooting me. I believe we have the right to expect a safe world to live in. I've never known that in my lifetime. Not from where I come from, not from where I've been. But by God, I plan to find it where I'm going!"

The cheers of approval said it all. Even Brendon Highsmith's swastika shook as he clapped his hands.

Tabitha Sims smiled. She would bear the scar on her leg of Dr. Edwards' bullet, but the pain woke her to a new world. Trisha guessed all of them bore wounds of some kind, but with hope, she knew they could overcome anything.

Charlie Mantel's transformation proved that.

Chapter Forty-Two

Joplin
Day Six

Dear Diary,

Tonight me and Matthew listened to the three people in the cage talking. I know they did real bad things. They killed my daddy. But the girl Jamie told the boys they were going to talk to our board on Friday at the hearing. We're not going to lie anymore, she said. There's no point. Then Matthew crunched a stick with his shoes and they heard us. We ran but they saw us anyway. When we got back to our camp, something real bad was going on with the army man. I could hear what he was thinking and he was staring at this real nice lady thinking about spiders and rats and snakes. I did'nt know why, so I hid and listened. He was saying mean things to her because she would'nt let him sit with her, so he told her she had one more chance to get in good with him. He said, "I always keep my enemies and rivals close to me."

She called him a bad name in her head, Diary, and he heard her just as clear as I do. I'm not real sure what he meant, but then his voice got real yucky, and he said he was going to be the leader of our little town (except he used some big word I did'nt know but I knew what he meant). He pulled her off with him, holding her arm real ruff. He put his hand over her mouth cuz she was trying to scream. Me and Matthew tried to follow but the man turned back and saw us.

We ran and told Billy what we saw. I dont like that man, Diary - he's bad. When I'm around him, my stomach and head always hurt. I dont know why. Austin and Billy ran to see for themselves, but they could'nt find nothing. Mrs. Davidson, the woman he walked to the back of the building, hasn't been back since but Austin told us maybe Tony and the lady were taking a walk. He whispered something to Billy and then they left. I think they were going to find Dusty and Uncle Bryan.

Diary, that man is going to hurt us. I just know it. He's creepy.

Other stuff is going real good - Bryan says we're going to get a house, Diary. And Melanie, my newest friend, hopes to get one with Dusty, but she says he doesn't feel the same way about her as she does. I'm going to have to tell her that was'nt what I heard in his head. She's way nice - I hope they get married. And, Diary, Matthew is real nervous about us getting a house. He dosen't know if Bryan will let him live with us. I told him he's just like my brother, and I'll tell Bryan that. He hopes if Bryan doesn't want him to live with us that he can live with Storey Roberts - the butthead who picks on me. Jake has been taking care of Storey, so that would be okay, I guess. But, Diary? Matthew is like real family to me and I hope he gets to stay with us.

So I can't wait until Friday. I don't know if we'll get a pool or not. Me and Matthew are going to ride our bikes and look at houses ~~tamarow~~ tomorrow. (I usually don't spell that one right! I looked it up, and its way different than I thought!)

Well I'm tired, Diary, so I'm going to sleep now. In the morning me and Matthew are going to try to find Mrs. Davidson before we go look at houses. If that man hurt her, I hope Dusty locks him up. He scares me. Well, goodnight, Diary. Goodnight, Daddy, goodnight Momma. I love you.

Love,
Jessie

"KNOCK-KNOCK," MELANIE said, as she slipped into the giant tent looking for Bryan and saw Jessie tuck the journal under her small pillow.

"Hey, Jess, whatcha' writin'?" Melanie sat on the small chair next to Jessie's cot, then saw the tears.

"I'm okay, Melanie. I – I was just writing in my diary." Jessie wiped her cheeks. "And I miss my daddy." She sniffled, and Scooter jumped up from in front of her cot and came to nuzzle her face. He licked where the salty tears had been until she giggled.

"I used to have a diary. Wrote in it for eight years. Never missed a single day," Melanie remembered, though she suspected that might not be completely true.

"Really? I'm going to need a new one soon. I only have seven more pages. I've been writing in it a lot, telling what all's goin' on here. I got it for Christmas last year, but I've used some temporary notepads when I was downtown. Before I got home." Jessie fell silent, remembering the horrors that seemed like months ago, not five days earlier.

"You were downtown when this happened?"

"Yeah, Daddy had taken me to a Cardinals' game, then we stayed at a fancy hotel by the Arch." Jessie didn't offer more, and Melanie could tell the little girl had seen her share of trauma. She didn't press the issue.

"Well, I'll help you find one when you're ready, okay?" Melanie patted Jessie's shoulder. "Get some rest, honey. After that ordeal with Tony, you must be exhausted. I'll see you in the morning, okay?"

Jessie's long face lingered for a moment or two longer, then she recovered before Melanie could leave.

"Hey, I saw that cute little girl, Melissa, hanging with you. Are you taking care of her now?"

"Well, Sanford doesn't seem to know a lot about five-year-old girls, so he asked me to help. You think you might be able to play with her some? I know she's younger, but you could sort of babysit." Melanie knew Melissa had seen her mother and father die, perhaps not too different from what happened to Jessie. And friends would certainly help speed the recovery process.

"Yeah, sure. Matthew might take some warmin' up, but he'll like her, too. But Storey's a real butthead. Me and Matthew are gonna go looking at houses tomorrow. You should come, and we could all live next to each other. Will you and Dusty have Melissa live with you?" Jessie's innocent expression made Melanie laugh.

"Well, now what makes you think Dusty and I will live together?" Melanie's stomach did flip flops at the prospect of it.

What dreams may come.

Jessie smiled. "Why wouldn't you? You love each other, that's the dream you want, isn't it?"

Melanie shook her head. It was clear there was something special about Jessie, that the little girl possessed a magnetic force – many who called the radio station spoke of a little girl they had dreamt about. But at times, she was just an eight-year-old girl – it was what Melanie loved about her.

"Well, love's a funny thing, Jess. He and I are just friends right now."

"But you want him to be your boyfriend. I hear it in your thoughts all the time – he makes butterflies go crazy in your stomach. He's hard to hear sometimes, but I caught him thinkin' bad thoughts about you yesterday."

"Bad, whaddya mean, bad?" Melanie panicked. She had negligible abilities, caught occasional thoughts that she wasn't even sure had happened. And from what everyone told her, Dusty's mental frequency was cloudy. But obviously not to Jessie.

"You know, Melanie, sex," Jessie whispered.

"Ahhh." Melanie suppressed a giggle.

"He's thought about kissing you, and...and...other stuff I can't tell because it's downright embarrassing. Daddy always told me that was a big people thing, and he'd tell me when I was older, but I know what it is. What Kelley Habersham didn't tell me when I was younger, Matthew filled in the gaps. Boys like weird things, Melanie. Yucky things. But one thing's sure, Dusty thinks you're hot!" Jessie grinned from ear to ear, mischief gleaming in her eyes. The ache from her father's absence had climbed into the backseat of her heart for a little while.

"Okay, Jessie, time for you to catch some z's. I'll be glad when we aren't sleeping in tents. Can't wait to curl up in a comfy waterbed."

"You're changing the subject, and that's okay. I understand. Adults are complicated, Melanie. Very complicated." Jessie enunciated the big word carefully. "And *actually*, I don't think I want to be one. I'm going to stay a kid forever, because people treat us better. I'm tired now. Goodnight." Jessie flipped over with her back to Melanie, pulled the cover over her shoulder, and let out a long sigh.

Melanie laughed, amazed at the insight of an eight-year-old, and made it a point to remember that statement.

Jessie snuggled into her covers, nodding her head. Melanie mussed the little girl's hair. "Sleep tight, Jess."

A hitching snore startled Melanie as she got up to leave. She peeked around the partition and saw Matthew sprawled on his cot, flat on his back, and passed out to the world. The eight-person tent was large enough to sleep more, but comfort and convenience allowed many to spread out. Scooter scrambled to the side of Jessie's cot, within closer reach. His own little nest of blankets spanned the foot and side of Jessie's cot – she spared no expense for her son. His eyes remained intent on his little girl. He wouldn't lay his head down until her breathing evened.

As Melanie zipped the tent's door closed behind her, she saw Tony, the infamous Mr. Parker, swagger by. General Anthony Parker, as he insisted being called, was still unaware John had joined the Joplin camp, though the presence of Jamie, Kyle, and Nathan had to tip that Dr. Basinger had at least been there.

"Fuckin' bitch," he hissed, his shirttail flapping, half-tucked in his pants. His tie hung loose and askew. A long scratch down his right cheek shone like a rust-colored trail. He ran his hands over his head to straighten his disheveled black hair. Melanie ducked beside Jessie's tent as he headed away from her.

He glanced over his shoulder – *he feels me watching him* – and jogged along the back line of tents. When his shadow disappeared, Melanie sprinted in the opposite direction for the campfire in the middle of the parking lot. Clusters of tents, ten or twelve of them, each centered around a perfect low burning flame – even on pavement, the community managed to create a campground. They were now so large that as many as fifteen fires burned well into the night. But what she wouldn't give for a streetlight or two.

That man gave her a bad feeling. And seeing him prowling off into the pitch dark made her skin crawl.

It would have been worse if she had known he was doubling back.

Chapter Forty-Three

Joplin
Day Six

"JAKE, DUSTY," SHE started but sucked air, still shivering with apprehension. She took two deep breaths while they stared at her. "I just saw Tony come from the back of the parking lot with his shirt untucked and a nasty scratch on his face. I...I knew you were looking for him a little while ago when Jessie and Matthew came to you about seeing him with Karla Davidson. Well, he's back, and I have a bad feeling. I know John said tonight we'd be safe and that he was laying low until morning, but maybe we should speed things up a bit." Melanie looked from one face to the other and could tell she had interrupted a similar conversation.

"Mel's right." Dusty bowed his head. "Valerie, call John and Haden. Let's meet at Office Max in an hour. It's time to get this ball rolling. There's no reason to wait until daylight – that just gives Tony more time to plan. Or fester. And, Billy, call Chuck – tell him whatever car General Parker drove in that he's to let us know if it leaves. The *second* it leaves."

"Gotcha." Billy raced to his tent for his cell phone, followed by Valerie already punching numbers into her own.

Melanie scoured the area to make sure Tony wasn't hovering, ready to pounce on them like a wild cat.

"What'd Jessie and Matthew see?" Austin finger-brushed his hair from his face. He'd taken an early-evening nap and missed the brouhaha.

"Well, she and Matthew saw Tony pulling Karla Davidson over toward the middle school. I wasn't sure it was anything. At first I tried to follow, but I couldn't find them. I figured it was a little hanky panky, with how smitten the women are with him. I suspected the kids just didn't understand what they saw. But if Melanie just saw him with a nasty scratch on his face – that can't be good. Her friends haven't seen her for two hours now." Dusty looked down at his watch.

"And his clothes were a mess. If it was a lover's tryst, he would've either tucked his shirt in or not bothered putting it back on."

Melanie tried to remember his expression – he'd been wild-eyed. But it was dark. Maybe she imagined that part. "Oh, and he had a tie on, half pulled off."

"Jessie said when she saw him, he was fiddling with his belt but gave up when he heard some people coming." Dusty stopped, seemed to think of something but said nothing.

"Let's go see if Karla showed up. If he's back, she might be, too. We can talk to her friend again. What's her name?" Dusty had met her earlier the day before, but his difficulty with names had gotten to be a communal joke.

"Tonya? Or Tina. Shit, I don't remember." Bryan glanced at his watch. "If we're going to meet John, we need to hurry. And I think we need to include Thad in this. A little muscle might be an asset."

"I agree," Dusty said. "We've gotta be quiet, though. And remember, if we see Tony, act nonchalant. We're just visiting folks. We don't want him suspicious. Not yet, anyway. Tristan and Bryan, you two go that way. Jake, you and Valerie take the center, and Mel and I will take the left side." Dusty pointed directions and everyone scattered without further deliberation.

He and Melanie wandered through the next circle of tents, inspecting shadows to make sure no one was following them. They met in the back of that campsite and made their way to the farthest left – the one Karla Davidson shared with eleven other people. The woman whose name evaded Dusty unzipped her door and came out, almost bumping into them.

"Have you seen her?" Her graying hair hung limp around her pale face. The absence of make-up revealed the wrinkles she tried so desperately to conceal. Age spots dotted hands that nervously caressed her sagging neck. "I'm just a basket case."

"No, but we're worried about her. Did you see her leave with Mr., uh, General Parker?" Melanie detested the false title, but she didn't want to dispel the myth just yet.

"No! And she loathed that man. Said he gave her the willies. He hung around here for a bit, asking her how many grandkids she had, stuff like that. Then he left. She took her make-up bag to the Hall to wash her face and get ready for bed. Oh, God. You don't think..." Tonya/Tina shook her head, rejecting what seemed to be dawning on her.

She continued to stroke her neck.

Nervous habit. Melanie wanted to say something but didn't want to give her false hope.

"I'm sorry...uh, I forget your name." Melanie reached for the lady's hand in an attempt to console her.

"Tina. Tina Dobbins. Karla and I met in Columbia. We both lived there but never met. Different sides of town, opposite sides of the world, ya know?" Her voice trailed.

Melanie did know. She sensed the dynamics between various groupings that arrived at the settlement. She noticed Tina and Karla when they joined, because it had been like Daisy Duke and Jackie Kennedy – Tina in her mid-fifties sporting a cheap halter top, pierced belly button and hip-hugging shorts that barely covered her rump, and Karla who defied age, in dress khaki shorts with a tucked in Liz Claiborne or Anne Klein or Tommy Bahama top. Something name brand. She had worn Tommy Hilfiger plain white shoes. Melanie tried not to look at Tina's dirty bare feet.

"Karla's husband was an anesthesiologist at the University. He also had a shop downtown. My ex robbed one of the stores a block from theirs, and, well, was in the county jail. Ya know, I didn't even go check to see if he was alive," she muttered. "Damn. But she was my friend. She helped me deal with losin' my kids, Trevor and Jonathan. She tried to call hers – they lived all over the world. One is, was, in Italy. Another lived in New York City, an artist I think she said. My Trevor and Jonny were only fifteen and seventeen. And..."

"Ma'am?" Melanie grasped Tina's hand to stop her.

"Huh? Oh, sorry. Can you help me find her?" She rubbed her neck, staring at them as if she noticed Dusty for the first time. "Please?"

"C'mon. Let's go look," Melanie coaxed. Tina, Melanie, Dusty, and two others from around Karla's campfire headed off in the direction Jessie had described earlier.

An owl hooted – Melanie had noticed a few the night before. And she had seen a cockroach in the Hall that afternoon. Not even X-86 could combat roaches. A car crunched noisily on glass somewhere down Joplin Avenue.

That may be Tony.

Campfires popped. Voices murmured in quiet conversation. Two or three crickets hummed a ditty, a welcome return to the Missouri population. It was a sparse buzzing of insects, but it indicated the resiliency of life.

Their footsteps crunched and scraped glass shards as they hit the sidewalk on the backside of camp.

"Space out a little. I'm going toward those stores over there. He might be sleeping in his car, so be careful. We're looking for her, not him. And stay within eyeshot of each other. The cars all up and down the street, those yards down yonder – check it all out. And remember we're due at Office Max in less than forty minutes." Dusty headed off to the left toward Wall Avenue, while two of Tina's fellow campers trotted back to Seventh Street. Tina followed Melanie as they angled right, walking toward Memorial Middle School.

"What's at Office Max?" Tina asked as they left the dim lights of campfires. It felt creepy skulking off into the dark night.

"I'll explain in a little bit. You can go with us," Melanie offered. She didn't want to go into detail just then but thought the lady deserved to be in the know. Especially now.

They crossed the road and headed straight toward the front of the school, ducking under a low-hanging branch. Wrecked cars had been lined up on the street, so Melanie casually wandered closer to see between and under vehicles.

My God, I'm searching for a body. It hadn't dawned on her until then that she assumed Karla Davidson was dead.

An unfamiliar sound bristled the hair on the back of her neck. Melanie froze in her tracks, her heart racing. *What the hell kind of animal was that?*

A rustling next to the school, under a clump of decorative bushes, brought a scream into the base of Melanie's throat. She swallowed hard to suppress it.

"What is that?" Tina whispered.

"I don't know." Melanie realized it might not be smart for two women to challenge whatever made such a noise.

She whistled a sharp *whippoorwill*. Seconds later, someone answered it. She repeated it, and within a few seconds, Dusty's hushed *where are you* eased Melanie's fear.

"Over here," she whispered back.

Dusty came under the same low branch and stopped when Melanie held a finger to her lips. They listened and something rustled next to the school again. Dusty got down on all fours, wincing at the pain in his knees. When he got a foot from a classroom window, Melanie and Tina held their breath. He took a stick and pulled up a section of the bush and a tabby cat came flying out and darted past him to the yard next door.

"Shit! Scared me to death." Dusty fell back on his butt and howled with laughter. "God, I 'bout wet my pants."

All three of them cackled, partly from being startled, mostly with relief at not finding Karla's body.

"Let's head back. It's too dark, and honestly, this is dangerous. We don't know what crazies are loomin' around out here." Dusty gestured for them to go first, and he followed.

"We'll find her, Tina. I bet she's off exploring. Hell, she may have decided to drive around for a munchie. Everybody gets their hankerin'." Melanie managed a laugh.

"She doesn't have the keys – I do. And we're pretty stocked up on munchies. I just don't know why she would do this." Tina massaged her throat again, tears brimming in her eyes.

"We'll hunt for her first thing in the morning. She's not out here anyway. She'll be someplace silly. Hell, she may be in the Hall. Did anybody look there?" Dusty looked at each of the women as they crossed the street. The crackling fires and hodge podge of smells made Melanie's stomach growl. Someone was cooking, even at this hour.

"No, actually I didn't even think of that." Tina's face brightened. They hustled up the stone entrance ramp, casing the perimeter of the parking lot campground as they went. Tina didn't talk, and neither Melanie nor Dusty knew how to combat her silence.

They explored the Hall and a few of the camps closest to the front, but no one had seen Karla Davidson. There was no sign of the woman who befriended Tina Dobbins; it was as if she never existed.

"We've gotta go, Tina. I promise we'll search in the morning. But I bet *she's* back when *we* get back." Exasperated, Melanie, Dusty, and Tina loaded into Melanie's Mustang. They followed Austin's Saturn and Griffin's newest Dooley. Upon scouting in Joplin, he'd upgraded again.

"What's at Office Max?" Tina asked again, and this time Melanie told an abridged version of a man they were worried about. She refrained from sharing who she meant – there was no point in frightening Ms. Dobbins with the true identity of General Anthony Parker.

"Dusty, when Chuck called, what car did he say Tony was driving?" Melanie noted that a snappy Lexus she'd parallel parked behind earlier was gone.

"Um, a Lexus sports coupe. LSI, I think he said. White. Why?"

"Because it was parked in front of mine this afternoon and now it's gone."

"Shit," Dusty muttered and stared out the passenger window.

"Yeah, shit." Melanie revved her Ford down Main onto Seventh, following the Saturn.

"Ya know, what's he doing driving something like that? Doesn't exactly fit the persona, does it?" Melanie glanced over at Dusty, trying to talk in code. She knew he understood what she meant. Someone trying to emulate a general would drive a Dodge Ram or a

Ford Expedition or a Cadillac Escalade. Style with a sense of masculinity. Tony was all about that.

"A Lexus LSI does nothing to complement the, um, image, do you know what I mean?" She didn't want to tip Tina that she was talking about Tony, aka Anthony Parker.

Nothing about Tony Andrews seemed right.

Dusty turned to her and said, "That's exactly what I was thinking."

Melanie grinned. She hoped Tina didn't share their talent, but when Melanie glanced in the rearview, Ms. Dobbins stared out the side window lost in her own thoughts.

She pulled in front of Office Max, and parked in a handicapped space Jake and Austin had left empty. *Habit.* It amazed Melanie that Jake continued to drive Griffin's Dooley and hadn't gotten one of his own.

She hopped out to let Karla crawl out of her small back seat. While the woman walked past her into the store, Melanie furrowed her brow and cocked her head as if to say something. John's new Chrysler pulled into the lot, breaking her train of thought.

"What is it, Mel?" Dusty caressed her arm, sending her stomach into somersaults. She glanced around to see if anyone noticed. She also made sure the door closed behind Tina.

"It doesn't jive, Dusty. He pops in, he's obviously worked hard at this image, even announces intentions to run for mayor. People respect his title, they like him, they trust that damn uniform. Why risk losing what he spent all day creating? It doesn't make sense."

She popped her knuckles until Dusty grabbed her hands and made her stop. She blushed but continued. "Hell, if I hadn't known who he was, I would be excited to see someone important join our crowd. Why blow your own cover in less than twenty-four hours?" Melanie shivered in an effort to shake the feeling that something evil just slithered across her back.

"Because he's certifiable, that's why," John stated matter-of-factly. He'd walked up and Melanie hadn't even noticed. "He really is, plus he's a control freak. I think he's past being able to stop himself. He has to be to blow up a city just because I pissed him off. Granted, I did try to have him killed, but still."

"Uh, yeah. That could be why," Haden added, and laughed. "You know, he had mistresses all over the country and used to joke about his satisfied customers. He wasn't just a sugar daddy. They loved him. I suspect he was supporting a harem. God knows he has the money. And the Viagra."

"Yuck." Melanie grimaced.

"I don't think there's any reason not to take him into custody now, personally. I know there's no evidence about Karla's disappearance. But we know for a fact he's responsible for bombing all those cities. And he killed Kenny." John's voice cracked, but he coughed to conceal any emotion.

A cell phone rang, making everyone jump. Valerie turned away to answer while they continued to talk.

"We gotta get rid of Tony, we deal with moving forward and not getting caught up in this crap. I'm so tired of assholes who shouldn't have survived the X-86." Dusty let out a frustrated growl.

Melanie dropped her eyes. She hoped no one would want an explanation of who the other asshole was.

"I assume he's gone back to his plane, but we can hardly sneak up on the Silver Bullet without him hearing us," Haden added.

"Jesus, that damn Silver Bullet. The Marriott with wings, he used to say. I remember when he named her." John rubbed his stubbled face. "Anyone have suggestions? We can't wait until morning. We have to do something now. There's no telling what he's apt to do."

Valerie returned to the group, her expression making all of them freeze. No one said a word. Tina had walked back out to see what was holding them up.

"They just found Karla," Valerie said, tears filling her voice. "And another woman who'd been shot in the head."

Tina Dobbins' knees noodled, and Jake barely caught her in time. He shook his head to let Valerie know not to say more. They led Tina inside so she could sit down.

"Oh, God, tell me. Please tell me she's not dead. Tell me some lunatic didn't kill Karla. Oh, God." Tina sobbed into Jake's shoulder, her whole body shaking.

"Oh, Jesus," Tristan muttered, and Billy's eyes went wide.

"What? Jake, take her over there and let her sit," Melanie directed. As Jake walked away, leading a trembling Tina, she turned back to the rest of them. "God, tell me. I hate it that ya'll can do that, and I can't."

Valerie lowered her voice to a barely audible whisper. "That was Matthew. Seems a few senior citizens were going to their cars to replenish their supply of booze and found her stuffed in a trunk. Matthew said from what he could figure out from all the blubbering is that she was cut up pretty bad, and she was naked. They found another lady in a tent who'd been shot. We've gotta get back. He says the whole camp's in a panic. People are threatening to form a lynch mob."

"Shit. Well, I think that makes our decision easy. Let's get back," Dusty said, as he shook his head. "Let's do a full search of the camp, tell everyone we know who it is, and we wait until morning for him to return to camp. Then we lock him up. Not much strategy, just brute force. Any objections?"

"No, I think that sounds great," Billy added, already heading for the door.

"Me, too." Austin ran his hands through his reddish-brown hair and rubbed his eyes. "I just want to get a peaceful night's sleep."

Bryan and the others nodded. "I hope Jessie slept through all of it. I wish I hadn't left her."

"Well, we need to be aware of the fact that he probably has a gun. In fact, unless he's lost his, I know he does. Brute force may be fine, but we can't go in blind. Macho may not serve us best here. We have to use our heads. He can read your thoughts almost as well as Jessie and that Sanford dude. So use the method to close yourself off to him. If not, he'll be tipped before he ever gets to camp." John looked at Haden and both let out a sigh.

"Okay, here's where we hand out the paper, near the wall. And here's Melanie's post," Dusty explained, drawing on a piece of card stock he'd ripped from a package. Then he jotted a big X where he wanted people on lookout. When he finished, there were eleven spots indicated.

"We need a way to communicate…cell phones?" Jake suggested.

"Huh-uh. They make noise when you push the button. He'll hear it," Candi said, shaking her head.

"Damn, okay. Well, then someone will just have to be here," he said, pointing to one spot near the sign-in table, "and sneak out when he's not looking. Who's small enough for that?" Dusty looked up, adrenaline pumping through him so fast, his hand trembled.

"I am," Valerie offered.

"Okay, good. And here, by Kim, you two can be hanging out with her. Make it look like you're flirting, or something." He motioned to Billy and Austin, and they nodded.

"Bryan, you and Griffin hang back by John's new truck here." He circled an X on a side street. "And let's grab Cindy Timmons and Sanford Grimes for some mental power – don't tell them much. Just position them at the table with Kim. That won't look suspicious. Groups hang out around her all the time to get a glimpse of the incoming people."

"He's gonna be paranoid if he truly did hurt that woman."

Tina moaned from a few aisles away. Jake held up a hand, then put a finger to his lips.

Melanie didn't like John's use of *if*. The alternative would be worse. The idea that someone else, another murderer, lurked in the shadows of their camp, felt like an old slasher movie. The stupid kind where the skimpily clad college girl always opens the front door to see who's out there. *Dumb bitch.*

"Sorry," Dusty whispered, then turned and stared at Melanie. "Who?"

Melanie let out a nervous laugh. "No one. I was just – oh, never mind. Finish. We've gotta get back."

"Okay. Let's apprise Chuck and Thad of the situation. Bryan, when you see him, signal by getting out of the truck and slamming the door. That'll be our cue. I'll be hiding around the tents, just in case he gets past."

"Here, you might need this, because I'll have to hang back, and it won't do me any good." John handed Dusty his pistol. "There are only a few bullets left. I, uh, I've used two."

Dusty took it, released the clip, then shoved it back into the handle of the gun, startling Melanie. She had no idea he knew a thing about revolvers.

"I suggest anyone else with a gun arm themselves to the teeth. John, if you have another one, use it. And you're right – you and Haden have to be out of sight. No matter how confusing it is that the three are here, he's not seen you and we want to keep it that way. Valerie, you need to pack the materials under the table a little tighter, to really conceal you. The worst part is, we have to get set up early enough so he doesn't surprise us. And you have to not think about it. If he catches even a blip, he'll know and he'll run. We can't compete with the Silver Bullet." Dusty looked to everyone for feedback. Heads nodded agreement.

"Billy, you scouted the police station yesterday, didn'tcha?" Jake asked, an idea dawning on him.

"Yeah, why?" he asked Jake, confused.

"Get some of that stuff out when we get back. Candi, you help him. The cuffs, stun guns, billy clubs – we might need them. I know it sounds paranoid, but if each of us has a weapon of some kind, I'll feel much better. Evens the odds." Jake nodded like the idea made him feel better.

Melanie had a flash of Tattoo Boy hovering over Dusty. Her stomach clenched with the memory, the acrid taste of primal fear in the back of her throat.

"A bicycle chain lock," Candi offered.

"Come again?" Griffin asked. *A sexy thing like you ain't supposed to be mysterious.*

"Stop that, Griffin. You know, the kind of chain with a plastic coating on it. Has a swivel combination. We can chain him to the cage. Even if he's inside, I'd chain him down. Let those four bond. Shit, he'll be like the father figure the two boys never had. Well, let's give them a daddy. They're made for each other," she finished in that husky voice that Jake loved. *Sorry, Becky.*

John laughed. "That's perfect."

The three might not agree, but it seemed perfect to Melanie, too.

"Hey, and there's a Spokes and Spandex bike shop on, um, Rangeline, I think," Austin said, excited enough to run to the counter to look for a phone book.

"Good. Bring it with you, Austin," Jake said, motioning for everyone to get moving.

With the intensity of a group on a mission, they marched outside and piled into their vehicles. Melanie was halfway down Rangeline when she realized they'd left Tina sitting at a desk with her head down. Melanie did a u-turn and raced back to get her.

When they returned to the campsite, they circled the perimeter, then Valerie, Billy, Candi, Bryan, and Jake spiraled their way inward, inspecting every campsite and filling the four-hundred residents in on the fact that they had apprehended the killer. It seemed safer than just saying they knew who it was.

Even if it angered people later, they hoped everyone would understand that their thought-speech could have tipped him off.

They staggered sleep time, agreeing to meet at five a.m., in less than three hours. They synchronized watch alarms and tried to relax a little. For most it didn't work.

* * *

THEY HADN'T SEEN Tony slip into camp around one a.m., about ten minutes after the panel returned from Office Max. He wanted to know where they had been. From the road, he watched the three cars leave around midnight but lost them when a deer darted out in front of him and then froze in his headlights.

Almost as if it had known.

But he waited for them to return, his Lexus parked on the other side of the school. When the Dooley, Mustang, and Saturn pulled onto Seventh Street and found various parking places along Joplin Avenue, he watched them bail out of the cars. A brand-new Chrysler of some kind parked on the far side of the parking lot along Wall Avenue, a sea of tents between him and it. As two people emerged, he squinted through his binoculars. But it was too dark. Their shapes disappeared among the tents.

You folks are up to no good. An inconceivable memory threatened to break free – a flitting image of cars without headlights peeling into a parking lot with him in the back seat, gagged and bound. A thirteen-year-old Andrews had repressed that night for forty-seven years, but it hovered just below the surface of his evaporating veneer.

They don't know hell – but I do.

He waited for two hours, watching them flit around like insects. *What're they doing?* It occurred to him that they might have found Karla's body, her luscious, firm body that pleasured him so much he hadn't wanted to kill her. But ties must be severed and leads erased.

He had such plans for this place.

At four a.m., with an aching back and a raging hard-on, Tony slinked across the street and lounged in a camp chair behind Tina Dobbins' tent. He laid his head back and listened to her breathe, knowing the skank couldn't measure up to her friend, but why not compare notes? He drifted off, a grin the size of the White House plastered on his face.

Deep in dreams, raised arms chanted, "Heil Tony! Heil Tony!"

He never saw the little girl staring at him. He didn't even twitch. He was far too absorbed in being worshipped.

Chapter Forty-Four

Joplin
Day Seven

"DUSTY, WAKE UP. Please, Dusty, can you hear me?" A small voice filtered around the broken images in his sleep.

"Mmmm?" He tried to turn over but couldn't. His shoulder had fallen asleep. A tongue licked furiously at his face.

"Scooter, stop it!" a voice whispered harshly. "Dusty, please wake up." A small hand beat his chest.

The confusion fell away like a flimsy blanket, and he acclimated to the world around him.

I've overslept? Shit...

"No, you haven't, Dusty, but it's that man. He's at the back of camp asleep. He's, um thinkin' about a woman he hurt and people in funny pants with boots. They're stickin' their hands up in the air shouting his name. You gotta come, Dusty," Jessie pleaded, trying to make sense of the images in Tony's mind. "I could hear him in my sleep. I thought I was dreamin', but then it woke me up. He's still there now, but I've got to stop thinkin' about him."

Dusty stared bleary-eyed at Jessie, trying to figure out what she wanted, what she'd just said. Then he bolted upright.

Tony – at the back of camp? *He knows.*

"Yes, he does, now c'mon, Dusty, you don't have thoughts he can hear, so he won't know you're coming if you're careful. You're the answer, Dusty. My dreams said so. *Come on!*" Jessie's panic spurred him to get moving. Scooter turned circles in his excitement.

"My thoughts – I'm fuzzy, everyone says so. Why didn't I think of that?" Dusty looked at her, but he knew why. "Because we have you."

"No. My dreams go two ways, Dusty, and one of them is so bad, I can't even think about it. He...he...no. Just get your shoes on." She tugged at him, pulled his jacket off the duffel bag, and tried to put it on him while he tied his shoes.

"Jess, you're brilliant. Remind me to give you a raise." He stuffed his arm in one sleeve, then finished tying his shoes.

She giggled but then her face sobered. "Please hurry."

Melanie opened the partition and stared at the two of them with her blonde hair shooting off in ways Jessie didn't know hair could do.

"What's going on?" Her eyes were sleepy, yet bright with panic. She listened patiently as Jessie filled her in.

"I'm going, Mel," Dusty told her. He squeezed her hand and on impulse kissed her lightly on the lips.

Jessie grinned. She knew Dusty and Melanie were meant to be together, but right now, their window of opportunity narrowed. The snakes slithered in her head and cockroaches scampered, the feeling Tony's thoughts gave her, and that meant he was about to wake up. Or in a dream like before.

"Mel, get John and Jake. Take Jessie so she can explain. But they need to stay back, because he'll sense them coming. Jess is right. I have the best chance to catch him." Dusty grabbed his Smith and Wesson and shoved it in the front pocket of his jeans. The bulge made him feel safe.

"Wait. I don't like this, Dusty. You can't go alone; that's stupid. Who else doesn't do the mental stuff? Wait a minute. Sanford – he knows how to turn it off. Remember what you said about him? *He has a serious gift*. Let's get him to go with you. Please." Melanie held Dusty's arm.

Jessie had already slipped out the canvas bedroom and gone in search of Sanford Grimes. Scooter scampered from fire to fire sniffing at snack remains littering campsites. He scored a big piece of bread crust drowned in melted cheese.

"C'mon, Scooter, stay close." Jessie ordered. Two minutes later, she found Sanford Grimes awake and dressing. His gift was far superior to everyone else's. Except hers.

* * *

WITHIN TEN MINUTES, Sanford and Dusty stole carefully behind canvas homes one at a time. They listened to roof-raising snores. Someone in a pop-top camper mumbled in his sleep. They slipped from tent to tent for cover. Dusty squatted and ducked behind the next and then peeked around to see if anyone had seen them. He felt like a cop in a bad movie.

I'm not good at this, and my knees hurt like a bitch.

Jessie hurried to John and Melanie as they gathered the others to explain the change in plans. Watches were an hour from spurring them into action.

"The son of a bitch sensed us, I'm telling you." John shook his head, and angry red patches bloomed on his cheeks.

"You might be right, but thanks to Jessie, we're making our move now. Austin, did you give them the rope and that bicycle chain?"

"Yeah, but he only has your gun, and didn't you say it only had two bullets left?" Austin stared at John, the tension in his voice tangible.

"Yeah, but I think he knows that. Melanie, does he have any other weapons?"

"I...I don't know." Melanie's voice quivered. "He might have his knife. He usually keeps it strapped to his ankle, but he doesn't sleep with it on. Jessie, did he put it on? Did you see?"

"No, I didn't see. I just needed him to hurry. And you guys need to stop thinking bad thoughts. Tony hears them. You'll make him suspicious." Jessie's brow furrowed, and she blinked.

He knows they're coming.

"How did you know Tony was here, Jess?" John knew little about her abilities.

"He's the bad man. I...I feel him."

Melanie shivered and pulled the little girl to her. She had a flash of memory of Tattoo Boy and Wanda.

If only Sanford weren't so old.

"His old is different, Melanie." Jessie let herself be hugged but stiffened.

"Who?" Valerie, like Dusty, didn't get much in the way of thought-speech. But Billy, Jake, and Jessie were having a conversation all on their own. Austin cocked his head like he was trying, and Bryan shook his, tired of the headaches.

"Sanford – Melanie's worried 'cause he's old. But he's not, not like regular old."

"Whaddaya mean, Jess?" Melanie turned and held Jessie at arm's length.

"He rode a motorcycle all the way here from Chicago." Jessie talked almost like she was in a dream.

"You're kidding!" Melanie's hopes flickered. If they were doing this to make her feel better, it was working.

"No. And he's special, Melanie. I don't know where he came from – he's not from Chicago – he was just there to see about the people. But something about him is, well, I don't know how to say it. I can't picture him as a kid or in a house like I can everyone else. He's just…just *this Sanford* and nowhere else." Jessie squeezed her eyes shut. "My head hurts."

"You mean you can see us other places?" Jake came over to Jessie and squatted in front of her.

"You held Becky in your arms in the middle of your living room. You broke things you want to go back and find some day. And…and Melanie and Dusty were attacked by a painted man. And Bryan loved my momma, but she didn't love me enough to leave her job. And Tristan's boyfriend jumped off a bridge Thursday night because he understood what was coming. She saw him do it. I…I see all of it sometimes. Then most times, it's like a dream." Jessie's eyes glazed, and Melanie pulled her close again, trying to hug away the awful images she must see all the time.

"My God, she must be exhausted." Jake stroked her hair. "She saw me with Becky. That was Friday, while I was in South Carolina. Did she know we would come here?" He looked around at the others.

"Yes, I write it all in my Diary or my notepad. At first, I just wrote letters, like to my daddy. Then I started recording people's names in the spiral notebook, what they looked like in my head, where they were coming from. Most of you fit the picture. Except Candi, she didn't, and Griffin." Jessie's trance-like state was hypnotic to the others.

The crack of gunshots broke the connection and echoed throughout the camp.

"Oh, God," Melanie screamed, then darted forward. But John caught her.

"NO! Stop. Give it a minute or two. Our chaotic thinking won't help. Give them a chance." Jake held up both hands to block anyone's rogue intentions.

Melanie looked over and saw that Jessie had wet herself. Matthew came staggering over, wanting to know what that sound was.

Tristan hugged him, while Bryan picked up Jessie. No one talked, no one moved, no one breathed for ten agonizing minutes.

* * *

JUST BEFORE REACHING Tina Dobbins' tent, Dusty saw a shadow outlined behind it. The silhouette was walking away from him, but Dusty couldn't be sure it was Tony. When he saw a khaki tie laying on a jacket next to a chair, he knew the good general was on the prowl.

Does he know we're searching for him? Or is he on the hunt for another victim?

Neither could be good. Dusty looked behind him, and his breath caught in his throat. Sanford was gone.

Dammit. Where'd you go, grandpa?

He paused, inspected the area behind him, but didn't see the old man or Tony.

I'm on my own. All that planning. If Andrews gets away, we're fucked. He'll blast us to Timbuktu. Our hard work, it'll all be over in a flash of light. At least it'll be painless.

"Don't give up, Dusty. You're behind him, and he doesn't know you're there."

Dusty stopped cold. He whipped around but didn't see anyone. Was that Sanford's voice? He dropped into a low crouch and took a deep breath. Was that right? Tony really didn't know he was there?

Continuing to follow the shadow, he stopped when the footsteps did. Before he could lose his nerve, he scampered to the side of the next tent and took a deep breath. He gripped the pistol in his right hand until his joints ached, his left bracing the pistol butt.

Just as he turned the corner, Dusty stared right into the barrel of a semi-automatic pistol. Tony's grin was the most sinister thing he had ever seen. Flashes of memory came to him. Tattoo Boy and Wanda brandishing their gun, the dangling belt buckle. The blood when the kid shot his own lover.

"Hey, wiseass, who's gonna help you now? You've done your good deed, found all these people a home – isn't that what you tell 'em on the radio? *You keep us connected.* People like you make me want to puke." Tony slapped at a fly buzzing by his ear. *When did those return?*

"What do you want here, General? We know Karla's missing. What did you do with her?" *Play the role, don't show you know he's Andrews. Maybe you can snow him.*

"She was a pretty fine piece of ass. Said she was gonna go for coffee or somethin'. I don't know. I'm not a stay-and-cuddle kind of fella. When I left her, she was tokin' on a Marlboro Light. Is that what this is about? That little girl tell you she saw me? Shit, she didn't even understand what she saw." Tony's gun hand lowered a millimeter. "She can't be but what? Seven? Eight?"

"Eight. She came back saying she and Matthew saw you pullin' Mrs. Davidson by the arm into the dark. She said you were mean to Karla. Is that true? If not, everything's cool. But pointin' a gun at me tells me maybe it's not. What is it, sir?" Dusty managed a fake smile.

God, don't I hate callin' you sir, you pompous prick.

Tony raised the gun and pointed it straight at Dusty's head. Dusty hesitated, confused at what the old man was doing.

"Shoot him, Dusty, shoot the bastard now. This is your window. He knows."

The voice – didn't Tony hear it?

"He's going to shoot you now, Dusty. It's time. Watch his finger. I can hear him. Shoot him. NOW!"

Just as Dusty gripped his pistol tighter, Tony squeezed the trigger.

A menacing click took a moment for both men to register. Dusty lunged at Tony. He grabbed Tony's hands, yanked the older man to the ground as seven shots fired rapidly into the night. Six hit the tree beside them, and one slammed deep into the ground. Dusty jerked Andrews over, pushing his face into the dirt. He sat on Tony's butt, straddling him and shoving his head harder into the ground. He rammed the muzzle into the back of Tony's neck, seething with anger.

"You stupid motherfucker. You were gonna kill me. I don't like people who try to kill me. The last one is rotting in a building in Dallas listening to my radio station. And he didn't even like my music."

The words spewed from Dusty's mouth as spittle sprayed Tony's back. Adrenaline possessed Dusty like an animal gone rabid. Just as he clicked the handcuffs tightly around Tony's wrists, Sanford appeared behind them.

"Where've you been, old man?" Dusty's sweaty, wild-eyed expression struck a chord with Sanford. The old man smiled.

"I was with you, Dusty. The whole time. Ask him why he was confused by his gun not firing. He just loaded it." Sanford smiled again, his silver hair catching the firelight. A calm washed over Dusty as if he swam in it. His adrenaline slowed, and he saw an ocean with a small boat drifting lazily in the summer sun. People on the beach sunbathed, held hands, and carried babies. There was no glass scattered everywhere, no carnage, no metal heaps of junked cars – no bodies.

"The future is yours now." But as Dusty stared at Sanford, the man's lips never moved.

You were in my head, old man.

Sanford Grimes turned and simply walked over to a chair and sat. Dusty watched him go and then heard the chaos of others running toward them, realizing screams had followed the gunshots.

"Oh, my God, you caught him, Dusty!" Melanie threw her arms around Dusty, and he kissed her firmly on the lips. They stepped apart quickly and blushed as everyone yanked Tony to his feet.

"Oh, fuck. I'm in the middle of a goddamned soap opera." Tony spat, and Dusty popped the maniac right in the mouth.

Jake took Tony by the shoulder and pulled him away.

"You better kill me, cowboy," Tony hissed at Dusty, "because when I get loose, you will all die. I swear to God, you will die the slowest, cruelest death you could ever imagine. I have chemicals that will make your teeth rot out, your eyeballs bleed, and make Agent Orange look like bug spray. Mark my words. None of you can stop me. Tavares, Basinger and his beady-eyed VP, John's renegade in D.C., they all died because they thought they could. Look where it got them. I'll escape, I'm tellin' you. I will escape. I *always* escape."

"Not this time."

Andrews whirled around, and his face truly faltered seeing John Basinger standing five feet in front of him.

"John..."

"Welcome to my world, Tony. Yours is over. We've had enough death, enough violence. Think rehabilitation or don't think at all, because if I hear evil thoughts rumbling in that ugly head of yours, I will blow it off. I'm beyond scruples – ask Kyle. You killed my friend. Lock him up, boys, and chain him down." Big John grinned, but the smile never touched his eyes.

"Wait!" Tony bucked, thrashed about until Austin and Billy each got a leg, and Bryan and Jake held his torso. They flipped him over and dragged Tony to the cage to join the other animals.

* * *

"WHAT THE FUCK?" Nathan scrambled away as a bucking older man landed inches from his head. Hands came through the chain link, yanked Tony backward until his cuffs were next to the fence. Austin threaded the bike chain around the cuffs and snapped it.

"Fucker. You nearly blew me up. I hope you four have a real nice time." Austin backed away, while scores of people stood and stared. More walked up, whispering, asking what had happened. The camp was abuzz.

Austin's southern accent made Tony look up. The pure hatred that contorted Andrews' face confused the college boy. He could have no idea the repulsion the demented man felt toward him at that moment.

"Kids, meet Tony Andrews. And Jamie, if I were you, I'd steer clear. He thinks he's a real ladies' man," John added, grinning.

"Damn, that's gonna hurt after a while," Kyle said, staring at the restraints that tugged Tony's shoulders backward.

Jamie stared at him, her distaste evident in the curl of her lip.

"Who the hell is this?" Nathan's disgusted sneer made him look like he had a bellyache. "Tony Andrews? Why does that name sound familiar?"

"Your new buddy. Make him welcome. He's killed almost as many people as you all have. That's an exaggeration, of course, but you can certainly compare numbers."

Nathan turned and saw all the faces, the smirks, the judgmental gazes of people who despised him. He snarled at them, making a few jump.

"Pretty ironic, isn't it? These four sharing a chain-link cell?" Dusty put his arm around Melanie's shoulders. "Who's the yuck-yuck now?"

Tony jerked and made a low guttural sound in his throat. Images of Devontre Eilenstein holding his eleven-year-old face in a mud puddle while everyone laughed and chanted, "Phony Tony, phony Tony, phony Tony" rambled through his dementia. He yanked the fence as he thrust forward and growled.

Jamie yelped in surprise, and Kyle jumped up to get some distance from the crazy man.

Man, get me the fuck away from this freak. Nathan got off his cot and went to the other side with Jamie and Kyle.

"I'M NOT A FREAK, YOU FUCKING PRICK. AND STOP CALLING ME THAT NAME! I'M NOT A PHONY, YOU COCKSUCKING SONUVABITCH!"

Tony fell over exhausted. His brain reeled with the memories, past overlapping the present, sanity melting into madness. When he slipped into unconsciousness, Jamie, Kyle and Nathan got a glimpse of the man's brain-speech, and all three of them lunged to the fence and began screaming to get him out of there.

* * *

IT TOOK A while for the mass of people to disperse, to ignore the lunatic's rantings.

Dusty said it was their only twisted entertainment. But when Tony settled down, everyone wandered back to their campfires to replay the events, to share insights, anything other than going back to sleep too soon.

There were nightmares to be had, Griffin stated with a foreboding that scared Jessie.

"C'mon, it's almost daybreak. We've gotta get some sleep. Stop being so cryptic, Griffin." Jake smacked the man's arm and then said he was turning in.

"Where'd Sanford go?" Jessie asked Dusty. He walked her back to camp, with Bryan and Matthew on the other side of her.

"Um, he'll be around when we need him." Dusty smiled, but Jessie worried that Sanford was gone, and she wanted him to come back. She felt safer with him there.

When everyone said goodnight, she insisted that Bryan tickle her back and tell her a silly story.

"Uh, what kind of story?" Bryan brushed the brown hair from her face, then started tickling her back over her T-shirt.

"Something funny."

"Okay, well once upon a time, there was this little girl..."

"And a cool teenaged homie sidekick," Matthew interrupted.

Bryan and Jessie laughed.

"Okay, and an *immature* teenaged sidekick. And one day, all these people were going to see 'N Sync at the Edward Jones Dome."

"Huh-uh, *Nelly.* Man, get with the times. Justin Timberlake done left them white boys in the dust years ago." Matthew waved Bryan away.

Bryan had a hard time resuming his story without laughing, but finally managed. "Okay. God, Matthew, you crack me up."

"Yep, that's my job. Go on, man, This story's weak."

"Don't stop ticklin'," Jessie slurred, on the brink of sleep.

"Okay, well, this girl got tickets to see *Nelly* and even won backstage passes."

"Sweet!" Matthew interjected.

Jessie giggled, and Scooter's tail thumped in response.

Bryan continued the plotless tale, punctuated by Matthew's comments until Jessie fell asleep. Bryan would have to work on better stories...like her daddy's. But dumb was better than silence. She just didn't want to think about the bad man anymore.

"G'night, Jess. I'm right over there if you need me." Bryan kissed her forehead when her breathing evened and went to his side of the partition where his and Matthew's cots were. She mumbled something but within a few minutes, the tent fell silent.

Twenty minutes later, human howls pierced the early morning. Jessie buried her head under her blanket, and Scooter whimpered and crawled onto the cot with her, nearly squashing her. Matthew moaned for it to stop and did what most others did – plugged fingers in his ears.

The howls didn't die for nearly thirty minutes until Nathan Kirkpatrick finally punched Tony Andrews hard enough to knock him out.

In her sleep, Jessie high-fived Scooter.

Part Four
Hide & Seek

"An eye for an eye only ends up making the whole world blind."
– Mahatma Gandhi

Chapter Forty-Five

Joplin
Day Seven

"SO, HOW DID you do it? I mean, my company was deep into the research, but obviously we were years behind you three," Tony rasped. The growling had left his throat raw. "By the way, where is the fourth guy?" Tony darted his eyes around them so he could be sure no one was listening. The gawkers had dispersed to eat breakfast.

"He was dealt with. And your company was more than years behind. We did probably seven years of work in six months. We're brilliant, Tony, far more brilliant than any of the goons you had working for you. But that crazy act you got goin' – that's *good*." Nathan's pompous air remained undiminished.

"So, what do you think we could accomplish now? The four of us could take over, couldn't we? I've got the plant, the equipment, the kahunas. What do you three have?"

"The brains. We masterminded a plot that was far beyond what anyone could have ever dreamed. And it's only just beginning. Last night at midnight was another launch – targeted primarily for Europe and Asia, but it also hit fifteen smaller cities in the U.S. One of them in mid-Kansas, I believe. Wasn't it, Jamie?" Kyle's holier-than-thou tone didn't affect Tony. It mirrored how the CEO felt most of the time.

"I don't remember, Kyle. Jesus, we were setting up a hundred cities at a time by the sixth day, weren't we?"

"Yeah, the last noon launches were for fifty, mostly in Japan, Australia, and Russia. When we went to the midnight runs, those were a hundred. And they think it's over in eight days, but it cycles back again for two more launches. We have a one-hundred-city rerun on Friday. That'll be fun because we set that for all the big cities in the U.S. again, just to be thorough." Kyle popped his knuckles, watching Tony with each crack of the joints.

Tony now understood what John had told him about the three prisoners he had been holding in Chamber Number Nine. The cockiness belied their actions. To orchestrate mass destruction that killed their own loved ones didn't fit their demeanor. And that syrupy Texas drawl clawed at Tony's veneer.

"So what happened to your leg, hotshot?" Tony studied the arrogant, good-looking kid. Blond hair, blue-eyes – an Aryan dream child.

"Took one in the hip and in the knee. They dressed it, gave me antibiotics to prevent infection but with the damaged muscle, I'm doomed to a serious limp. I exercise it every day, but there's not enough room in here to do much." Kyle stood, as if motivated by the idea, and stretched. "I used to be a helluva football player. I could lay out for a pass..." Kyle's face clouded.

Tony tuned into the boy's frequency.

Manny sprinting downfield, a defender eating his dust, me on a cross route. That pass Perry Donner threw had been a beauty. Manny dove, and the cameras popped like lightning bugs. District champs and friends till the end. Didn't mind sharin' the glory with my best friend. Not then. Damn you, Julian. Oh, God, Manny, did you survive X-86?

"Yo, Kyle! Damn, where'd you go?" Nathan stared hard into the eyes of his partner.

"Huh? Oh, sorry." Kyle fell silent, aware of them watching him. Spiders scuttled through his thoughts, making him shiver.

Hmm, Kyle, you have remorse. What happened? What did Julian do?

Kyle jerked his head up and stared Tony straight in the eyes. "None of your goddamned business. Stay out of my head, you stupid fuck."

Jamie and Nathan stared, confused.

"What the hell're you talkin' about, Kyle? You losin' your marbles like him?" Nathan's forehead wrinkled.

"He can't do it?" Tony cocked his head, then turned back to Kyle.

"No, neither one of them can, I don't think. I didn't know anyone could until Basinger took us outside in Dallas. All these people were talkin' to me, and I thought I was losin' my mind. Fuckin' freaked me out. Then when I got here, I knew others could hear my thoughts, so I learned how to shield them. There are a few here I can't resist, but most I can. That little girl...she's on another level."

"You can hear what people are thinking? All this time sitting out here under this damn tree, and you knew what I was thinking?" Jamie's voice rose, attracting a few people's attention.

"Sorry. You don't transmit that strong, if it's any consolation. And...and I've been too busy shadowing my own to worry about you two bozos." Kyle looked down and then peeked up at Nathan, who still said nothing.

You asshole. You've heard all my deepest, darkest thoughts? I've got scary ones. Can you handle them? Nathan sneered, but the expression wavered.

"Yes, Nathan, I can. You don't scare me." Kyle turned back to Tony. "But you do. You're reckless."

"Well, you're the ones trying to destroy the planet. I'm just getting a little redemption, seeking a little revenge. Isn't that what you wanted?" Tony now directed his questions to Nathan, deciding him to be the more directed of the two men. And the lack of mental telepathy could be an asset. Tony had yet to determine Jamie's value in the grand scheme of things. His chauvinism ran deep.

"The implications are already worldwide. Should be at about eighty percent devastation by today, after last night's release." Nathan exuded pride. The totality of the project gave him a strange sense of accomplishment. "We've surpassed Timothy McVeigh, Ted Kaczynski, David Koresh, even Adolf Hitler. Who could dream they would be seen as small potatoes compared to Nathan Kirkpatrick? I'll be in every history book written – whole chapters devoted to the NAO. Our vision will be the wave of the future." Nathan's eyes gleamed.

"We, Nathan, *we*. You didn't do this alone," Jamie corrected.

"True," agreed Nathan. "But once they start the interrogations, you'll collapse – women just don't have the brass to finish. You've been a splendid partner, probably the smartest person I've ever met, and I've met quite a few. One man in Waco can give you a run for your money. And Kyle? Your conscience has always been a shortcoming. The little sister, and all that crap. Families must be expendable. It's the only way a plan like this can be executed flawlessly. Don't you agree, Tony?"

Jamie backed away from Nathan and retreated to her cot. She didn't look, she simply walked backward until her knees hit the metal frame forcing her to sit.

"See?" Nathan shook his head at Jamie and then turned back to Tony.

"Yes, I agree, Nathan. But you must develop a little style. It's good to know you have comrades – that makes sense. Fellow militants. And you had planned to go there to hide out, but John caught you. Do they know about Waco?" Tony no longer attempted to mask his admiration.

Nathan basked in it. "No, I don't think so. And John didn't catch us. Hell, he wasn't even around until the next morning. Fucking Jack

Barnes, the prick, had to go and get nosey. Caught us celebrating in the staff lounge and got suspicious."

"Actually, Nathan, you pulled out your gun and blew everything. If you could have controlled your fucking temper, we probably wouldn't be here in this cage getting sunburned and listening to that God-awful light rock shit." Kyle's face burned with anger.

Tony made a note of it – a civil dispute could be helpful later.

"Fuck you, Kyle, you self-righteous sonuvabitch. Sometimes extreme measures must be taken."

"Yeah, extreme measures put us in a freakin' cage," Jamie countered. "I'm cold, I'm tired...I can't sleep on this God-forsaken cot and I want a hamburger. And quite frankly, I don't give a rat's ass what they know anymore. They can't stop it anyway."

"Well, I think we can get out of here if we work hard enough and cover each other," Tony claimed.

"How?" Nathan looked skeptical but was always open to suggestions for escape. *I'm beginning to like you, Tony. Sorry I clubbed you last night.*

"I'm going to lean forward slowly. Look under me and see what I've managed already." Tony scooted forward an inch or so and then leaned to the right as if he were about to fart.

"Shit," Kyle muttered.

"All right!" Nathan exclaimed. "But they only give us plastic silverware. How'd you do that? Why'd they uncuff you anyway."

Jamie stared – What good'll escape do now? But then a faint hope of Charlie hiding in Waco brought a smile to her face.

"I threw my shoulder out of socket." Tony snickered, as all three caught a brief glimpse of a six-inch hole he somehow managed to dig in the early morning. He sat back before anyone walking around might see.

"This," he motioned, and lifted his pant leg to reveal Dusty's hunting knife. "I'm gonna make them regret leaving me uncuffed. They're so fucking gullible."

"How did you dig that, old man?"

"Hey, Nathan, old age is an illusion. Don't ever forget that. I pulled it out of his ankle holster when we were struggling and slid it in my sock. Cut me pretty good." He tugged his sock down, revealing a deep slit that should have had stitches. Jamie felt an empathetic cringe in her stomach.

Voices behind them caused Tony to release his pant leg, scoot back a little to make sure the hole was covered, and pretend like he was scratching fleas in his arm pits.

He barked at the two people whispering something, making them both jump. They scurried away when Tony began to growl again.

"Man, you're nuts," Nathan grinned. "That's great cover."

Chapter Forty-Six

Joplin
Day Seven

"HEY, DUSTY, HOW'S the campaignin' coming?" Melanie stood on the floor of the Hall, marveling at people's posters.

Dusty had gone all out – he placed posters on everyone's windshield, taped a flyer on each tent in their campsite, and was working on a large banner to hang over the voters' table. Valerie had also shown him how to design a poster and then scan it onto magnetic sheets. Dusty planned to slap one on every car.

Melanie read the banner and laughed out loud. Bryan came over to see what tickled her and burst into giggles. Candi braced herself on Melanie, laughing so hard she could barely breathe.

"I'm so glad someone else can offer a little comic relief. That was a big job, and I've been flying solo for so long," she proclaimed in her throaty voice.

That sent Melanie into fits again.

Tristan stepped back to inspect what was so funny. "Oh, my God. Austin, Jake, you gotta come see this." When four or five others circled around a blushing Dusty, she read the banner aloud.

"If you believe he's for us, vote for Mr. Morris," she read, pronouncing the *for us* so that it rhymed with his last name. "And he kept you connected too, so give credit where credit is due. There ain't nothin' crusty about Dusty!"

Jake leaned against a table, laughing so hard he fell against John who'd just walked into the auditorium. Everyone was bent over, snorting and cackling.

"What's so funny?" John read the banner and covered his mouth to keep from joining them. Jessie, Matthew, and Melissa came to see what the hoopla was all about.

"Crusty? Honestly, Dusty – that's too cheesy for pizza," Candi added, tickling Melanie's funny bone again.

"It was supposed to say rusty, not crusty," he corrected. "Besides, if it's that funny, then you'll remember it, right? Isn't that the point? Huh? Fine, I'll change it to 'He's our trusty Dusty'. Happy now?" Dusty raised his eyebrows. "Geez, you people need a life. At least if you're gonna stand here and poke fun, take some of these and put them on cars. I'm not going to waste them. And who'll help me hang my banner? I know I won't ask Melanie. I think she may've wet her drawers."

Jake and John grabbed an end, both grinning so big Dusty wanted to belt them. His comment had made Melanie giggle again, and he had the urge to ask her if he was right.

She bit her bottom lip to stifle further giggles, so she could try to answer. Her reddening face made it clear to Dusty that this proved to be a difficult task.

The three men stood on chairs to tape the strings on the rails that circled the entire auditorium, separating the second level seats from the floor. They jumped down and inspected the banner, bigger than all the other signs, that hung over Dusty's table.

The Hall's floor was outlined with small tables delegated to different "politicians" – each on the outer edge, the out-of-bounds area if it had been a basketball game. None of the others had a banner, cheesy or not.

"There, miss smarty pants. You just see. I bet I win, and it'll be because of my banner." Dusty gave Melanie a raspberry, then pinched her bottom as he walked away. Candi smiled and Jessie clamped her hand over her mouth in an *Ah, I'm tellin'* expression.

"C'mon, Matthew, we've gotta hit the high road. Melissa, are you up for a long bike ride?" Jessie's three-year edge on Melissa factored into approximately twenty years. Even Matthew understood he might be pretending to be the big brother, but he did what he was told.

"Sure," the curly-haired girl chirped. She looked more than a little like the youngest of the Brady Bunch daughters.

"Where you goin', Melissa?" Melanie watched the trio head for the door.

"We're going house shoppin', wanna come? I know we can't pick them out 'til Friday, but we're gonna get a jump. At least look at the ones in the area." Jessie's big blue eyes gazed innocently at Melanie.

No one has ever said no to you, have they?

"Once, but he thought better of it when I whined – my daddy, I mean. He was the best." Jessie's smile wavered, but she flashed teeth to overcompensate.

"I bet he was. And he would be so proud of you, young lady. You three go have fun. I'm gonna stay here. But be careful, okay? Watch out for her. And stop to rest when you need to."

"She's in good hands, Melanie," Jessie said, following Matthew and Melissa toward the lobby.

"Hey, Mel, you hear about the fax from Harrisburg?" Dusty jogged over to her and put his arm around her like it was the most normal gesture in the world. Butterflies fluttered in Melanie's stomach, and she turned too fast and bonked him on the chin with her head.

"Oh, shit, sorry." Melanie massaged her head.

"God, I know when to keep my hands off," Dusty said, rubbing his chin. But he was grinning.

"Not anymore." She pulled his arm and put it back around her. He leaned in close and kissed her gently on the lips.

"They got our message that we had caught Tony. Quite a few people in Harrisburg were mighty relieved. Seems like General Parker practiced his act in Lancaster before bringing it here. And they're following our lead with house cleaning and the barter system. So is the community in Portland, Oregon. But they've stagnated at a hundred fifty-three people. Harrisburg has almost three hundred. I told them we're holding steady near five hundred. I'll keep spending mornings on the air just in case there are more, but I'm losin' hope." A cloud of sadness passed across his face but was gone in a flash.

"Yep, and I've faxed both settlements our newest paper, giving them the lowdown on Tony. I want to paint a proper picture of him," Valerie explained, having walked up behind them. "The decline of a powerful man, induced by insanity and X-86. Tomorrow's will be the best piece. I want people to know everything about him. It will be an important part of our new history, don't you think?"

Dusty did, so he had motivated her to interview John, to get the details on Tony's life as a CEO and then after. John shared everything he thought pertinent with Valerie. He described Kenny's death as best he knew it and relayed what Tony had told him about Brad Tavares.

But he told Valerie her best source would be the devil himself. She hadn't gotten the nerve to do that yet. She would wait for the added information from Friday's inquiry.

By dinnertime, Valerie had written the article that would capture everyone on Thursday, the one-week "anniversary" of the X-86 release. That would be a day for everyone to remember those they had left behind, the strong who survived to lead into a new age, and the mistakes they planned to never repeat.

* * *

THROUGH THE COURSE of the day, the new and improved foursome took shifts watching for onlookers while the others continued digging. By nightfall, the hole began to curve up under the fence. The cover of dark allowed them to scrape and scoop the dirt, lining it on their cots, under their covers.

If only John Basinger had remembered to bring the Sony voice recorder as he'd intended, Thursday would have held its place in history as the seventh day and not DE Day – Day of Escape.

Chapter Forty-Seven

Joplin
One Week Anniversary – The Seventh Day

Dear Diary,

Today everything fell apart. Before I got up, it was already the worst ever. It was supposed to be a good day but instead Dusty was screaming - his face so red I thought he was going to pop. Then Scooter would'nt stop barking, and when me and Matthew got up to see what was going on all I could see was Melanie crying and Jake yelling at people. John could'nt even talk he looked so mad. And they used bad words, Diary. Real bad words. I won't even write them here.

When I finally got Melanie to tell me, she said the bad man had escaped - he dug a hole! That scares me so much, Diary. He has hurt so many people. I think he's worse than those three because he hurts people right when he's looking at them. Not from a computer. John said at least they had found the Silver Bullet, whatever the heck that is. But everyone was mad, Diary, real mad. Only one of the other prisoners got loose. Nathan. He's with the bad man now. Kyle and Jamie tried to leave, but they got caught. Thad sat on one of them.

Jake kept yelling that if everyone would have listened to him and put them in the local jail, this never would have happened.

Valerie said they should have kept a gard posted there at all times too. She got mad, saying they had gotten "lacks." I dont know that word, but I think she meant stupid. Then Dusty yelled for them to shut up, something about being a Monday morning ~~corterback~~ quarterback (I want to spell words right, but that one was crazy!). I don't know what that means, but I could tell he was tired of people complaining about things they couldn't change now.

Everybodys real mad and I was so happy cuz we found the perfect house in Arbor Hills yesterday. It had four bedrooms, one for me, Matthew, Bryan, and Tristan. If she wants to live with us - she's been spending lots of time with Bryan and us. It has a pool, but its not real big. It has a diving board but no slide. I told Matthew that was OK I could live without my cool slide from home. The basement was real neat. It had an air hockey table, a pinball machine, and even a big-screen TV. Matthew liked that a bunch. He even scouted for another house in the nayborhood for Storey.

Matthew and I helped Melissa find a real neat place just four houses away from us. That would be the bomb if they lived by us. It was just as pretty as ours.

I think I'll stay in the rest of today. This whole thing started last Thursday so we were going to have a bonfire for the people who died, but now everyone is hunting for Tony.

I hate him, Diary. He makes me real mad. Things were going real good until he did all this. I think he just wants ~~attenchion~~ attention. I hope they catch him, and, Diary? Daddy wouldn't like me to say it, but I hope they're real mean to him. (I hope they hurt him.)

Valerie is mad because of her great story on Tony. Now she said she better be ready to write a something or other. Some kind of follow-up to the first one. I hope they catch him and nobody gets hurt. When Bryan went too, that scared me real bad. I already lost my daddy, I dont think I could stand it if Bryan got hurt too. He really is like my Uncle. Him and Dusty and Jake all three. But I still miss my daddy so much - I think about him everyday.

Well, I'm going to play Matthew in a game of checkers I guess. Hes bummed too. It dose'nt sound so fun, but I'll try. Since its daytime, I won't say goodnight to daddy and momma. I'll write again tonight.

Love,
Jessie

* * *

"HE WILL KILL us, Dusty. Mark my words. If we don't find him, we're dead. And Nathan – shit, I can't even comprehend what he's capable of now. With some tweaking, I'm sure he can modify X-86 and kill the rest of us. God! How the hell did this happen?" Jake slammed his fist into the front dash. Dusty had the Mustang opened up, doing close to eighty on Joplin's main drag.

"Check with John in the air." Dusty motioned to the walkie-talkie in Jake's hand. "And then Griffin."

"Hey, John, see anything from up there?"

"Negative. Jack's covering the town by grids. Let us know if you have any tips." John's voice clicked off, but Dusty suspected Dr. Basinger had a great deal to say that he wouldn't. Not until they caught Tony.

"Griffin, what's your 10-20? Any sign of them?" Jake trembled as he let go of the transmit button. The bright red blotches on his cheeks let Dusty know just how angry he was. "A fucking hole. How the hell did they do that, and us not notice?"

The only poetic justice, Dusty knew, was the fact that Jamie and Kyle lay cuffed to their cots, out cold from the heavy dose of codeine Thad and Billy had forced down them. If only they had thought to do that to all of them sooner.

"Uh, we're on Main Street and no sign of him," Austin replied, his voice breaking up.

"Okay, thanks, Austin. Tell Griffin when he reaches the college to go right and circle back. Hey, Chuck? Any sightings?" Jake released the call button and waited.

The airwaves hummed, silent – an eerie dread clenched Dusty's stomach. "Oh, God."

"Chuck?" Jake repeated and waited.

Dusty slammed on the brakes, sending the Mustang into a full tail-spin. Jake braced himself with the dashboard, and Dusty steered into the spin until he came to a halt and slammed onto the curb outside a shopping center.

"Damn. Sorry." Dusty peeled out and headed in the opposite direction flying straight toward Checkpoint Charlie's tollbooth.

"Attention, cars one through ten. We have no response from Chuck. I repeat, we have no response from Chuck." Jake pulled his map out of the floorboard and pointed to the star that marked Chuck's location. "If Tony broke through it, he's got I-44 in his sights. Check the other roadblock on Main Street, Austin."

Dusty stiffened his arms, feeling like Speed Racer on a mission for God. He tried to imagine what would have happened if Melissa hadn't needed to go to the bathroom at seven thirty. Two women had heard the little girl screaming, scrambled out of their tents, and shrieked even louder when they saw Kyle halfway through with his jeans snagged by a belt loop. He freed the loop, but he had frozen and stared at them in panic. If he hadn't, he probably would have made it. Instead, he flinched and then caught his shirt on the fence, slowing him by ten or twelve seconds. That had been just enough time for one of the ladies to grab a piece of firewood and clobber him over the head. Thad had raced to their rescue less than a minute later to hogtie the prisoner. In the melee, no one could find the keys, so they scrounged a pair of cuffs and fastened him to the fence.

"What the hell?" Dusty was the first to come running followed by two St. Louis men and Billy. Thad, proud of his restraints, said he would just sit there – literally – on Kyle if necessary, until they found keys to the cage.

Jamie stared at them like a deer caught in headlights. She crouched on all fours, ready to escape. When the ladies had screamed, Jamie laid her head down on her forearms and screamed that feminism sucked.

If chivalry hadn't been dead, she would have been the first one through, she admitted later. But Tony finished the hole while she and the others covered him. It seemed fair to let him flee first.

Their Corning Ware breakfast bowls made incredible digging tools. When Melanie brought their cereal, all four of them glanced at each other in excitement. Plastic spoons wouldn't work, and that had been the panel's worry, hadn't it? But the bowls. The blanket covering the hole hadn't drawn Melanie's attention, though Kyle panicked that it might.

Jamie was worried about all the dirt spread evenly on and under the cots. If anyone inspected closely or lingered too long, they would see it. That spurred them on to finish before breakfast.

"Check the teams on foot. And Scooter, maybe he's sniffing them out." Dusty was desperate now.

* * *

"DUSTY! THE LEXUS!"

Dusty squinted and floored the accelerator. Up ahead, the tollbooth was leveled, splintered wood with the Lexus plowed over it and stuck. The car's wheels hovered in mid-air, with the chassis wedged onto a pile of debris.

Jake started ranting into the walkie-talkie that they had a visual on Tony's car, rammed head long into the checkpoint station. "Spread out and come in from all angles in case they're on foot. I repeat, *they're on foot!* We'll let you know more when we get there."

In less than a minute, Dusty skidded to a stop, and both men bolted from the car. They clawed through rubble until they saw a man's hand. Jake threw aside a broken piece of plywood and moaned. Chuck Keeler's mangled body was crushed under the front left tire of the Lexus LSI.

"Ah, God." Jake stooped down to feel Chuck's neck, nearly severed from his shoulders. "No pulse."

"Thank God. Look," Dusty pointed. Jake saw that the burly man's legs were gone, as well as half his right arm. "Dammit."

Dusty turned a circle, looking at hotels, stores, restaurants, and gas stations. "They're here somewhere." He felt the hood of Tony's car, still warm and ticking.

* * *

"SHHHHHH. I HEAR something." Nathan held his breath. "Stop panting. They'll hear you." He flicked a rotten banana peel off his knee. "Ugh."

Tony situated himself in the two feet of garbage. The dumpster wasn't full because Thursday had been trash day on Joplin's business strip. He slipped his undershirt over his mouth and nose to block the smell. He concentrated, trying to get inside Nathan's head. But static, like a waning radio station, made his brain ache. He would have to trust the kid and vice versa, but the CEO didn't like flying blind. He'd gotten used to playing God, in as many ways as possible.

A revving engine passed slowly by the dumpster they were crouched in. They were two blocks over on Main Street where both felt their chances of cover improved tremendously. Tony couldn't see the mangled mess of the tollbooth anymore, or that stupid Neanderthal standing in his path.

The big man jumped out of Tony's way at the last minute, but Tony had shown him. He turned and plowed the bearded thug right into the checkpoint station. Nathan screamed at him for totaling the car and their chances. But Tony had gotten out of worse jams.

"We're sitting ducks here," Nathan complained. He peeked out over the dumpster's lip, pushing away the week-old garbage. "We could've been halfway to Waco by now, you idiot."

"Kid, you better shut the fuck up, or I'm gonna shoot you." Tony sat at the bottom of the garbage bin, unaffected by the smell and liking the solid steel walls of protection. He waved the pistol at the kid.

"You know where our compound is? You know the combination to the vacuum chamber? If so, knock yourself out." Nathan ducked back down, squatting but refusing to sit in the two feet of rank trash.

"You better not be yankin' my chain," Tony threatened. He was frustrated by the prospect of a six- or seven-hour drive, depending on how clear the highway was, but knew he had to be patient.

He'd resisted driving all the way to Waco, demanding they check out the Silver Bullet first. But there was no time, and he knew it. Now, as they hid in a giant metal trash can beside a bookstore, a loud rumbling engine pulled into the parking lot less than fifty feet away.

Griffin Stevenson slowed the newly acquired Dodge Dakota as he and Austin surveyed the area. "I wish I hadn't given Billy and Tristan my new Dooley. This baby's too small."

"We're not playing demolition derby, Griff, c'mon. They're on foot. Just keep your eyes peeled." Austin rolled down the window and leaned so far out it, he sat on the edge.

Tony imagined John right outside the dumpster, waiting to cut the old man's throat. *Doin' Kenny pissed ya off, didn't it?*

A fleeting memory of two boys holding a butter knife to his neck made Tony sink deeper into the filth. The boys wanted his lunch money, but Tony didn't have any. He got free lunch, but he had been too proud to admit it. His hatred of poverty and subservience grew stronger with each cruel deed his classmates subjected him to.

"Hey, Griff, you hear that?" Austin cocked his head.

...pissed ya off, didn't it?

"Yeah," Griffin whispered. "Is it him?"

"I don't know. Go that way," Austin said, pointing toward the side street by the dumpster.

Nathan and Tony didn't move a millimeter.

John, you're an asshole. You had such potential. It'll be a shame to kill you, but this small fucked-up town needs a makeover.

Tony had to focus for a moment to remember where his laptop was. *The Silver Bullet.* That would be a problem. He would have to get his other one in D.C. The hurdles continued to rise in his path, and it pissed him off that he had to perform for these menial people.

"We've got somethin'," Austin whispered into the walkie-talkie. *The Silver Bullet* rambled through his head.

"We're comin'!" someone shouted before Austin could turn it down.

"This is stupid. I don't like bein' trapped here. Listen," Nathan hissed.

Voices came from every direction.

"We've gotta make a move. I'm slippin' out. Can you see anything?" Tony asked, peeking over the edge. His heart raced. He could make out people in the parking lot, heading toward the stores. His skin itched from anticipation and maggots somewhere in the rotting garbage below. His mom once left remnants of a head of lettuce out on the counter for days until squirming maggots swarmed the decaying leaves. The idea that they slid over his ankles brought a gorge into his throat.

"Looks like they're checkin' out stores – I'm goin'," Nathan asserted, and flipped over the edge of the dumpster. He landed on his feet and dropped into a crouch. He scrambled to the side, blocked from the street's view.

Tony followed and hunkered down behind him. Nathan backpedaled toward the corner of the building. They made their way behind the store and a bank next to it.

"Look!" Nathan pointed to an Expedition parked at the drive-thru. All the windows were open as if inviting them to join it in a playful romp through town.

"Don't mind if I do," Nathan answered.

Tony was checking out a Ford SUV parked next to the building but without luck.

Nathan eased the door of the Ford open, then slouched in the front seat, out of sight. He felt keys dangling from the ignition and leaned around to see an SMSU Bears key ring. "God bless you."

Tony saw the score and scampered to the Expedition's passenger side. Nathan started the engine as quietly as he could. He fought the urge to shush the motor. A whoop-whoop from overhead sent him into a panic.

Jack Simpson piloted the chopper while John and Haden scanned the area from the air, searching for moving vehicles or the fugitives on foot. Radios buzzed as Dusty and Jake conferred with the chopper and nine other cars in the hunt. Pairs of investigators had taken to foot, armed with walkie-talkies and pistols or shotguns. The order was clear: *shoot to kill.*

Tony and Nathan ducked below the dashboard in their newly acquired and fully loaded Ford Expedition, waiting for the helicopter to pass.

"Do we make a run for it or wait?" Nathan whispered. The engine idled.

"Shit if I know, Nathan. I don't think we can stand to wait, do you? They're gonna hear the truck as soon as they come outta that shop. Let's ease around the back of the building, over there," Tony said and pointed to the left, behind the bank and farther away from the dumpster. "I won't be taken alive again, I can tell you that much." He patted the knife, now wrapped in a sock sitting next to him on the seat.

"Okay, I'm gonna press the gas with my hand to stay outta sight. You peek over the dash and guide me. I'll creep, so when they come out I can just stop. Maybe they won't be able to tell we're moving. This may be painful, but I want the fuck out of Dodge."

Nathan shifted into drive on Tony's cue and eased his way around the back of the bank.

Why does every word you say have a fucking extra syllable? The Texas drawl was about to drive Tony to drink. *I wa-unt the fuck out of Do-uhdge. God.*

"All we gotta do is get around to the other side, get back on Main Street, and we're right at I-44. Forty-four south should be a quick right." Tony's nerves jumped every time Nathan tapped the brakes, and he forced himself to resist the urge to stab the kid repeatedly just to lighten his own stress. "Go easy, kid, they'll see your tail lights."

The Expedition rolled around the bank, and both grew brave enough to sit up in their seats. Tony, on point, saw the beagle jump in front of them, causing Nathan to slam on his brakes too late to tell him to just hit it. The stray raced in front of the building. When Tony watched it go, he saw two men sprint toward them, shouting into walkie-talkies.

"Shit, GO! Here they come! GO!"

The shout scared Nathan's foot into action. He rammed the pedal to the floorboard. The Expedition fishtailed as it skidded onto Main Street and zigzagged around the few stray cars along the side of the street. The clean-up commission had removed most but hadn't finished. That was on the agenda for Friday.

"Where are they?" Nathan yelled above the roaring engine.

Tony's heart pounded so hard in his chest, his ears throbbed with the beat. "Uh, I can't see them, but they had walkie-talkies, so I'm sure they're radioing someone."

Just as the words passed his lips, Tony screamed for Nathan to stop.

A helicopter dropped and hovered inches off the ground directly in front of them. Nathan slammed on the brakes. The Expedition's tires squealed as the SUV skidded and turned sideways. Nathan floored the gas, heading to the right onto a small side street.

"Are you there?" John screamed into the walkie-talkie.

Griffin slammed on the brakes of the Dakota to block the SUV's path at a stop sign. Bryan wheeled a Chevy 4X4 behind the Dodge, and Billy whipped the Dooley in front of it. The metal barricade, perpendicular to Nathan's path, gave him nowhere to go.

The Expedition didn't have time or room to stop. Austin flew out the passenger door, and Griffin scrambled frantically across the seat of the truck to get out, but before he could, the Ford plowed into him at better than fifty miles per hour. Tristan and Billy bailed from the Dooley just in time, and Bryan dove out of the 4X4.

Crunching metal, shattering glass, and Griffin's screams brought one team running from the next street. Austin scampered frantically from the Dakota's sideways thrust. He rolled, panicked by the path of the swerving Ford. Onlookers couldn't tell if he was going to make it or not.

The SUV's entire front end looked like a crash test demo. Seconds passed as Bryan and Billy neared the truck – each taking slow, careful steps with pistols drawn and hammering hearts.

"Come out with your hands up, motherfuckers!" Billy shouted. Tristan held a metal pipe in her hands, following Billy and Bryan.

"Griffin! Can you hear me? Austin, where are you?" Bryan yelled, as four other men raced to the accident.

"GET BACK!" Billy screamed.

Nathan revved the Expedition, burning rubber as it was thrown into reverse. It stopped, and barreled head first into the mangled mess, backed up, and slammed into the roadblock again. The Dakota skidded sideways another ten feet, giving Nathan room to maneuver. He reversed again and veered around the mangled Dodge, barely missing Austin.

Nathan wiped the blood from a cut on his forehead and sped down the new street, shoving the shattered airbag between his legs. He had no clue which direction he was headed. Tony's airbag supported the older man's lolling head but was deflating. On impact, Nathan had been pinned against his seat but groped for Tony's knife and slashed his airbag to bits, gagging on the metallic air that whooshed out of it.

"Tony? Hey! Tony! Wake up, man!" Nathan floored it, not caring now whether he made it or not, but he agreed with the CEO – he wasn't returning to the pen. Fingers of smoke streamed from the Expedition's engine.

"Tony?" Nathan reached over as the air bag flattened and pulled Tony sideways to lie across the seat next to him.

Andrews was unconscious, and Nathan didn't have time to worry about him. If he slammed into the floorboard, oh well. Tony knew the plan – escape, no matter what. With the reflexes of a cat, Nathan took a hard left onto another street just as the helicopter lowered to block him. But this time, no Dakota blocked his way. He raced back onto the main drag hollering that he was one bad motherfucker.

The SUV wobbled precariously on two wheels during the sharp turn, then settled back onto all four. Tony moaned beside him, and Nathan shouted jubilantly. He was back on Rangeline and saw the sign for I-44. *Which way did the old man say? South, you idiot, South!*

"I'M THE MAN!" Nathan pumped his fists with the adrenaline surging through his body.

"Shut up," mumbled a shaken Tony Andrews.

"I'm the man! C'mon, chopper, show me whatcha' got!" Nathan accelerated this time and headed straight for John.

"PULL UP, JACK! PULL UP! HE'S COMIN RIGHT FOR US!" John screamed, leaning back in his seat as if it would help.

Haden closed his eyes. Jack yanked the control stick back as hard as he could. The Expedition's luggage rack scraped the chopper's landing bar, sending it into a dangerous wobble. Jack righted the helicopter and made a sharp turn to follow them. John let out his breath, signaling that Haden could look.

"We're in pursuit!" John yelled into his walkie-talkie, hoping to be heard over the whipping blades. The Ford Expedition sped down Rangeline, taking the exit ramp so fast it veered on two wheels for a split second.

"We see him, too!" Dusty shouted, caught between wanting to check on the accident victims and knowing they had to catch the fleeing vehicle. "Hey! Melanie! Is the roadblock set-up? We're gonna need ya!" He roared onto the south I-44 exit ramp, his heart hammering.

He wanted to kiss Jimmy Starnes and Ben Neuheisel for thinking of jacking rigs across south I-44 when John had brought the guilty trio to their camp. Ben claimed if "the mutts ever managed to get away, it would be their getaway route – all Texans return to Texas."

Now as many as twenty members of the camp had headed straight to the road block to monitor and secure it.

"We're here, Dusty. Ben and Jimmy weren't able to get any more eighteen-wheelers over here – they were either flipped over or jackknifed so bad they couldn't maneuver them. But we've added trucks, and Valerie just dropped a spike strip she found at the police station. So we're ready." Melanie didn't sound convincing to any of them – prepared maybe, but not eager.

"Okay, everyone, they're south on 44 and we're lettin' them think they're gettin' away!"

"Great," John muttered, still a little shaken from his brush with death. "Jake, tell Dusty to be careful. Nathan's ruthless. He was willing to ram a chopper."

"You're kidding!" Jake turned to Dusty, who was gripping the Mustang's steering wheel tight enough to bend it.

"Huh-uh. I wouldn't kid...Hey! We've got him now. Jack, hang back. Okay, Dusty, I see your Mustang, and someone's in the Dooley comin' behind you. It's mangled as hell. Roadblock, they're bearing down on you."

"We're ready, John!" Melanie called out, Valerie shouting something inaudible in the background. "Hey, guys, Valerie says to keep 'em on the pavement for the spike strip."

"We'll try," Dusty answered, followed by John's laughter in the chopper overhead.

"We're armed and ready!" Ben barked. Twenty rifles simultaneously took aim for the horizon where they knew the SUV would appear any moment.

John signaled Jack Simpson to circle back, while Haden peered through binoculars for the Ford Expedition. John knew that, crashed front-end or not, Tony Andrews meant to escape.

And John Basinger meant to stop him.

Chapter Forty-Eight

Joplin
I-44 South

"SHOOT TO KILL, Melanie! Tell them I want that son of a bitch dead!" John laid down his walkie-talkie and grabbed his own binoculars.

"John?" a voice crackled over the airwaves. "Jake, you or Dusty hear me?"

"Go, Austin, what is it?" Jake released the talk button, while Dusty floored the accelerator. He felt a strange dread.

"Griffin's dead, Jake. That sonuvabitch killed him." Austin clicked off, but not before they heard the boy sniffle and let out a moan.

"Dammit." Jake closed his eyes, remembering his Sean Connery buddy, days on the road, and teasing the older man for his sexist comments. One of his first friends in the days after Becky. "I want to rip this asshole limb from limb."

"You'll have to wait your turn," John snipped. *That punk racist killed Victoria and my babies.* But Tony scared him worse.

"There they are!" Haden shouted, making John drop his radio.

"GO, JACK, GO!" John ordered.

The helicopter's nose drooped to the ground and zipped forward, making it hard for the men to stay in their seats.

Below them, a battered Ford SUV sped down I-44 thinking it was scot-free.

"Shit!" Nathan rammed his fist against the roof of the cab. "Won't these fuckers just go away and die?"

Tony saw the tractor trailers barricading the highway, with smaller trucks flanking them on the side.

"Hold on, Tony! No airbags to save us now!" The rugged SUV's speedometer trembled at 95 mph. A light stream of smoke swirled through the gaping edges of the hood.

Nathan braced his arms against the steering wheel, ready to maneuver. "Hold tight, old man, we're gonna test the all-terrain ability of this motherfucker!" Nathan's shouts were barely audible over the whipping wind and the voices screaming in Tony's head. The windshield was void of glass from the impact with the Dakota, and the passenger side window had splintered into an incredible design. Tony studied it wondering how such beauty could be formed during such a frantic disaster.

I could be on the beach sippin' a Dewar's. I chose this shit.

Tony's head jerked savagely as the Expedition suddenly dipped into the deep ditch to the right of the highway. They slammed hard against the embankment. The Ford stalled momentarily, but Nathan flipped the ignition hard, and they barely slowed. They plowed through the grassy field parallel to I-44. The bouncing caused Tony to slam his head into the roof. Stars erupted as Nathan whooped with excitement that Tony couldn't quite muster.

The Expedition stalled again with its shortened front end and belched dark gray smoke from the engine. Nathan coughed as the burning smell filled the cab. Lights flickered on the dashboard, but then the SUV resurrected, like a phoenix from the ashes.

Barreling through the bumpy field as far from the ambush as he could, Nathan saw men rushing for cars. He curved even farther into the field even though the terrain worsened the more he deviated from the highway.

As the SUV came parallel with the roadblock, even with twenty feet between them and the highway, Ben Neuheisel signaled for everyone to open fire.

"OH, SHIT!" Nathan hollered, as bullets riddled the Expedition. One hit Nathan immediately in the calf and a second into the bicep of his left arm. "AHHHHHHH. I'M HIT!" he screamed in pain as another whistled past his face. Tony dove into the floorboard, cramming himself as far out of the line of fire as possible.

Nathan zoomed around the rigs and thumped ruthlessly through the ditch and yanked the SUV back onto I-44.

"YEEHAW! We got you, you crazy motherfuckers!" Nathan howled, despite the pain. He thrust his right fist into the air victoriously. His left hung limp at his side, and Tony grimaced to see Nathan guiding the speeding truck with his right knee. The smell of blood made Tony's head swim, his stomach roll. The burning engine only added to the bouquet.

"Are we home free?" Tony asked, pulling himself out of the floor space and peered all around them. In the side mirror, he saw cars in pursuit but half a mile back.

"Think this thing is gonna hold up?" Tony watched smoke stream out of the front, burning his throat and eyes.

Before Nathan could answer, a dull thud hit the roof of the Expedition. Both men looked up and a dawning panic surged through them. Tony's face lacked any expression, and then his brow furrowed.

You sonuvabitch.

A second later, an explosion ripped through the SUV, flipping it on its side and sending it into a twenty-yard skid sparking along the pavement.

The Expedition slid off the highway down the embankment and another twenty feet through field grass and rock. The chopper came to rest ten feet away, and John raced over to the demolished SUV. It looked like a battered stunt vehicle in a Hollywood film.

John came to an abrupt halt as Tony Andrews slid out through the glassless windshield. *I'm the real Phoenix, not this stupid piece of shit.*

"Freeze!" John shouted. But Tony continued to slide down what remained of the front hood, ripping his shirt and scraping a deep gash into his left forearm. He dropped to the ground, his legs collapsing. On his knees, he looked up at his old friend and broke into a shit-eating grin.

"I still don't know how the hell you got away. I *killed* you, you motherfucker. I killed you. Bombed your ass. You should be dead," Tony rasped. Smoke, airbag dust, and all the screaming made it difficult for him to speak. He chuckled, a gruff sound that evolved into sputters of choking laughter.

For nearly four minutes, John waited.

"Something got your funny bone, Tony?" John's gun stared Tony straight in the eye. But Andrews continued to bait the big man with the menacing smile. John took a step forward, less than ten feet separating them.

"You can't do it, Fat Man. You don't have the balls. Now me, I'd have leveled my ass before I even sat up. You're too humane, John, too fucking moral. Makes me sick. 'Course we've been friends damn near forty-years. Haven't we?" Tony's smile faltered as John Basinger cocked the revolver and took aim, right at Andrews' head.

Visions of Victoria dying without him flitted through John's mind. The business trip to Detroit kept him away from his wife and his ten-year-old twins on their dying night.

Did they cry for their Daddy? Did Victoria hate me for not being there? I'm sorry, Tori, I'm so sorry.

"Well, Jesus, John, don't grovel over your dead fucking wife. *I* didn't kill her. *They* did. Now come help me up." Tony reached out, as if he really thought John was going to do it.

John's blank stare confused Tony. And then Basinger smiled back at him for the first time.

Andrews blinked.

You're not a murderer, John, you gotta let me live...my day in court and all that American bullshit. Me, on the other hand, I'd...

"Wrong. I'm not the man you used to toy with. When I pull this trigger, I'm going to plant one in your gut, then your chest, then your neck. I'll finish with one between the eyes, but you probably won't feel that one. Maybe not even the two before." John's emotionless expression wiped the smile from Tony's face.

A split second before the first bullet ripped through Andrews' abdomen, he begged, *No, John, no...*

Tony's body hitched and jumped with each impact before crumpling to the ground. The first two shots were true to their mark, but his convulsing body sent the rest into his jaw, an ear, and one over his head.

John dropped the gun.

Nathan crawled through his glassless side window that now faced the sky and held his hands high in the air.

"Don't shoot! I'm not armed!" Nathan stared at ten rifles aimed at him as men took slow steps forward. Seconds passed – someone called out and asked if they could shoot. Then a smile crossed Nathan's face. *You won't fuckin' shoot me, even if I want you to. Damn, I wish I had a gun.*

No one answered. Cars slammed to a halt nearby, and Jake and Dusty came running, never taking their eyes off the emerging prisoner. Haden stood frozen outside the helicopter, staring at his boss and wanting to clap him on the back.

"No!" Jake screamed, as he raced around the demolished SUV and stood panting between the marksmen and Nathan. He motioned for them to lower their weapons.

Nathan twisted, watching guns drop in response to Jake's order. He pulled himself out and dropped to the ground, screaming in pain from his wounds. When his left leg hit, it crumpled and he grabbed it, bawling like a baby. Dark patches of blood covered him – from the gunshots to cuts all over his arms and face. When Jake shouted for him to lie face down, Nathan did, then put his good hand behind his head.

I don't wanna go back. Jesus, why didn't you shoot me?

Good question, Jake wanted to answer. The firing squad had their orders. They shouldn't have hesitated.

But then Jake understood. It had been easy to fire into a moving car but not at the face of a human being. It was what separated the survivors from the three who orchestrated this whole mess.

"Thank God," Melanie shouted, as chatter erupted and people jumped from the arriving cars.

"Nathan, you are one lucky sonuvabitch. They had their orders." Dusty shook his head. Then he grabbed Melanie and held her.

"Lucky, my ass. I wanted to die. For my mission and my friends in Waco." Nathan grimaced as Ben, Valerie, and Candi lifted him to his feet.

"My leg. Ah, Jesus, it hurts." Blood oozed from the wounds, and he staggered, unable to bear weight on it. His left hand hung limp at his side.

Ben yanked the injured arm over his own shoulder to half-carry the man, who howled in pain and then fainted. Candi, strong enough to drape his other arm over her shoulder, helped carry him to a truck.

"Waco. Makes sense," Jake said.

"Yeah. But I ain't in no hurry. You?" Bryan turned to Jake.

"Not one bit."

"I gotta get back for Jessie. She's gonna be worried sick." Bryan hesitated, stared at the mangled SUV, then climbed the embankment to the blacktop. Jake followed him.

"I'm sure she knows, Bryan. Something tells me she already knows."

Bryan grinned, nodded, and joined scores of other people cramming into vehicles to head back to camp. Let someone else worry about Nathan.

They had houses to claim.

Chapter Forty-Nine

Joplin
The Eighth Day

DEAR DIARY,

Everybody is sad today. We buried Griffin, Karla, and Pam Brinkman, the lady Tony shot. Then they all talked about the ~~in~~, ~~inkwery~~ the thing tonight (I dont have the energy to get my dictionary). Everybody got to question the bad people and I guess from what Melanie said there's gonna be a bunch more cities hit again. The three bad people were as helpful as they could be, even the one on crutches, but there's just no way to stop it they said. Made lots of people real mad.

It lasted a real long time too Diary. I just left a little while ago. I did'nt think people were ever going to stop asking them questions. They kept going way too long. Dusty said he thought the three of them could do more about the X-86, but they just wont. I dont know, Diary, but I'm glad theyll be in the jail now. Its nice with that big ugly cage gone. I told Melanie I didn't really understand all that scary stuff, and she said that what it really means is we cant save a bunch of other people who might have survived the first time. Now everybody in the whole wide world is going through what we have. Most everybody in other countries will die, she said, just like in America. That makes me real sad.

Everybody has been quiet all day. Jake, John, and Billy are going to some city in Texas tomorrow where theres a bunch of people. Jamie told them where the hideout was and that she wanted to know if her brother was there. Nathan said many of them will die if they open the door but John said they could maybe talk to them and let them know what is going on. Just knowing others are out there waiting, and that the world is'nt so bad after all might help. But everybody here is wondering if they're good or bad people. Jamie and Kyle said most were family and friends. Nathan said there might be some not-so-nice friends of his. John smiled real big and said he would take care of that. I think maybe he meant beating them up or something, Diary. I hope he didn't mean worse. My dreams are all better now, and I don't think there's going to be any more killing. I hope.

The best news, Diary, is the bad man is dead. He made me mad because he killed Griffin and I liked Griffin a lot. Dusty says that Tonys with the Devil now, and that makes me feel lots better. I cried when they brought Griffin back, and so did Matthew, even though he won't admit it. Austin is hurt pretty bad, but Melanie said a few broken bones won't hold that kid back. Storey, Matthews regular sidekick now, is helping Candi take care of him. (I think she likes Austin, Diary, Storey said so.) Matthew and Storey let me tag along today when they went bike riding and you know what, Diary? Storey is from Chicago, and his dad, Mitchell Roberts, was an actor - a real actor! Anyway I wouldn't tell Matthew this, but I think Storey is WAAAAY cute.

Cindy, a real nice older lady, says all the bad stuff is over except people dying of the X-86. Not that that's good, but no more bad people will blow us up. She said no one else here would die until God decided to take them. She's real smart, Diary, almost as smart as Sanford, who is back now. He was gone yesterday, but hes going to stay now. Jake said they both have powers as strong as mine, but I think it's silly. I don't have powers - I have dreams. Anyway, Jake and Dusty think that'll wear off as the X-86 leaves the air. But I like the thought-talk - sometimes I play jokes on Matthew cause he can't do it. And, Diary, Storey can!

Thad, the big man with mussels who swings me from his arm, he agreed with Billy that even when the X-86 wears off, many people have learned how to do something with their brains that lots could already. Its called ESP, and the X-86 just made us better at it. I hope so! I practice it sometimes so I won't forget. Dusty can't do it, Diary, and it makes him SO mad. But Jake says that will make him the best mayor.

I hope he wins. And I hope him and Melanie adopt Melissa. She's a sweet kid, and then she would be my neighbor. Me and Bryan start moving into our new house on Monday. The whole town is having a give-away at the big Sam's Club. All of us can exchange furniture and get other things like clothes and school supplies.

Can you believe we get to go to school, Diary? Tristan doesn't want us to get bored and she was a teacher, so she's going to hold classes at Memorial Middle School. Isnt that cool, Diary? We won't be in a grade anymore, but all of us will be in classes together. And at a middle school! We're going to start after Labor Day, she said, so she can get the school all cleaned up and have computers ready for us (maybe she'll let us play computer games!). She and Austin are going to teach us, which is cool and all us kids are real excited. I think theres twenty-seven of us, Tristan said.

And the best news, Diary, is that Bryan is going to let Matthew come live with us. Isnt that great? And Tristan too, he said, as long as its okay with me. That sounded so neat, and I told him so. She's the best, and I would be living with my own teacher! How neat is that! He was real happy, I could tell.

A whole family, Diary. Daddy wouldn't ever give me a brother or a sister, but now I have one. And a dog! Scooter is the best. (Even though he chases Candyi's cat Rudy. Rudy's not too smart, Diary. He keeps coming back and making Scooter chase him!) I think Daddy would like Matthew and Scooter a lot. He wouldn't care that Matthew's a different color. It's funny, but no one seems to care about that kinda stuff anymore.

I hope Daddy isnt jealous. No matter how much I like Bryan or Jake or Dusty, I still love my daddy best. I wrote a poem for him, Diary. It's on a scrap of paper, but I'm going to add it after this. Bryan's going to take good care of me and I think that wood make Daddy happy. In a way, its like getting to be close to Momma, because Bryan talks about her more now. He tells me how much she loved me and missed me. He said she was a workaholic and he explained how that made her mess up with me.

But its okay. I just wish I could tell them about all this. About all the stuff I've done, and that Im okay. I hope they know.

Sometimes I hear his laugh in my head, Diary, and it makes me cry and smile all at the same time. Strange huh? Bryan said its okay with him if I call him Uncle Bryan. He knows I already have a daddy. Sometimes that big lump in my throat won't let me swallow when I think about Daddy.

Well I am tired and sad now, Diary. You have got only three more blank pages, and then its time for me to get a new one. Melanies going to help me pick one out. Billy and Valerie are both working at the Office Max. They write all the news, and Billy's already started a book about everything that has happened. Several other people help them run the paper.

Candy got Ben, Jimmy, and Thad to help her get Sam's Club opened so people can get the things they need, so we can rashon it, Candy says. We don't use the new money yet, but they said it won't be long before the new plan starts. I better get a Diary before then. But you'll still be my first Diary, and that'll make you extra special. Jake will be the chief of police and Bryan will be a deputy - I don't want them arresting me for stealing a Diary!

Goodnight, Daddy, I love you. Goodnight, Momma. I miss you both.

Love,
Jessie

A Poem By Jessica Bayker

I love my daddy best of all
Even though he's not here with me now.
But I think he would be proud of how strong I've been,
He's the one who showed me how.
So when I move into a house with my new family,
It won't be a competition or a test.
No matter how much I like them,
I will always love my daddy best.

Epilogue

Sixty Years Later

THE LINE TURNED the corner, so it was hard for Justin to see the box office.

"Man, are they selling tickets yet?" Fourteen-year-old Justin Roberts craned his neck, wondering if he was ever going to get tall like his dad.

"Your grandma really in this picture, Justin?" Landon didn't look at his friend to wait for the answer, because he was bobbing up and down trying to see the front of the line.

"It's her book, moron. When they asked her to write the screenplay, she laughed and said if she did, she wanted a small part in it. She plays some woman whose friend gets killed by Tony Andrews while they're at the camp in Joplin. I could just kick myself for not going to the private screening because of friggin' soccer camp." Justin's blond hair hung in his eyes, and he swept it back, hoping everyone in the crowd knew who he was.

People in front of the teenagers stirred and looked back at them. A few whispered and stared.

"Are you really Jessica Bayker Roberts grandson?" A lady looked at Justin, and he guessed her to be a thousand years old. Wrinkles and sagging skin made her look almost alien.

"Uh, yes, ma'am. She's the bomb, too. This movie is based on all her diary entries from those eight days. She tells stories about it all the time now, but Grandpa Storey says it took her a long time to want to talk about it. He said writing the book took her twenty-five years!" Justin swelled with pride as others gawked at him.

"I've heard a lot of stories about her and that dog, Scooter. That's one of my favorite parts of the movie, I think. The scene where Scooter comes waltzing into the kitchen with Matthew and Jessie. And then she adopts him and loves him with all her heart. They say that dog lived to be twenty-nine." The woman's misty eyes dropped, and she stroked the flap of skin dangling from her neck.

"You saw the movie already?" Justin couldn't believe it was only the second day of release, and somebody was standing in line to see it again. He wanted to correct her that Scooter only lived to be twenty-one, but he was too in awe of her second trip to his grandma's movie.

"Yeah. I saw it last night when it opened. Everyone's been waiting for this since, well, really since it all happened. Several of the survivors wrote about it, but nothing like this. She captures it just exactly how it happened. I wasn't part of the central force, but God knows I lived through it. I came to Joplin when my group in Kansas couldn't make a go of it. I owe my life to your grandma and her friends." The old lady paused, and Justin saw a tear stream down her cheek. *Could be old age. Grandma gets watery eyes a lot too.*

"Billy Ferguson published several short stories about it," she recalled, as if talking to herself.

The lady standing beside her nodded, like she remembered that. "Valerie Barnett-Kinsey, I'm sure you've heard of her or even know her, won her Pulitzer for Journalism for all her work in chronicling the years after the X-86 Apocalypse." The lady fell silent for a moment, and Landon looked at Justin and shrugged.

"Yes, ma'am. Valerie and Austin both come see Grandma all the time. They're *real* old. Like in their seventies. But lots of her friends are old. They celebrate lots of anniversaries and stuff together. And they've had to go to quite a few funerals in the last few years. They make Grandma real sad." Justin shuffled his feet. "Ma'am, did you ever hear about Charlie Mantel? He's one of my favorites because he started out bad. Grandma says she didn't put much in the movie about him because of all the controversy. She wouldn't talk about it much; I could tell it made her pretty mad. So I never knew what all the controversy was, do you?"

The line began to inch slowly, and the buzz of anticipation hummed around them. Voices bled over one another, but Justin wanted to hear what the lady knew. Another survivor's rendition of what had happened to the famed man made him antsy. It was a mission of his to discover the truth about the dawning of a new time, years he'd heard so much about. And about such a central player whose time was cut short. What he learned in school didn't compare with the real stories. His history teachers didn't know the half of it.

"Well, Charlie was a hero, son. No matter his faults in the early years, that doggone Movement. His sister spent a lot of her time in prison working with him to help make a difference. She never apologized for what she and the others did, and that made a whole heap of people mad at them. But Charlie. Huh. That boy became front and center with Dusty Morris and Jake Thomas. Those three really are like the original founding fathers. Washington. Jefferson. Adams. There were lots of other important people, but those three were like gods. When Charlie got murdered, that caught people way off guard. Scared 'em real bad, actually. We didn't have many of those and still don't. That's one of the greatest qualities Dusty and Jake instilled in the survivors. But poor Charlie."

"Who do you think killed him? My daddy says Tony Andrews himself came back from the dead and did it," Justin purred with his wicked horror-movie voice.

Landon hit him hard on the arm. *Stop it, Justin. You're creepin' me out, man, please?*

Justin smiled and nodded at Landon. His best friend hated when he talked evil like that, said it reminded him of the new horror series patterned after Andrews. The serial killer couldn't die, and at the end of every movie said something really scary in a shaky, ominous voice that Justin could imitate to a tee.

"Sorry, man."

The lady smiled. "I thought you could do it. I can sense it usually."

Few possessed the power still. It dissipated gradually from generation to generation, but some seemed to hone it better than others. She was never fortunate enough to do it very well, though the youngsters' thought-speech was loud and clear. Most of the survivors who had the ability passed it on to their children. Rumors flew that Billy's children and grandkids never even had to talk at the kitchen table. Or so the legend spread.

"Well, boys, I'd say that one of the NAO thugs who had been in the cellar with him for those thirty-three days probably did it, but many don't agree with me. Even though Brendon Highsmith went on to denounce the NAO – you probably don't remember them and that's a good thing. Anyway, a few of the others Nathan Kirkpatrick invited to Waco still believed in his cause. Four or five of 'em were watched like hawks for years. Jake's FIA investigated them forever, probably still wishes he could, bless his heart. Retiring had to be hard for him. Crime was epidemic before the meltdown, but that man. Well, I'd say he's one of the greatest things since sliced bread." The awe on her face was hidden from Justin as the line moved forward.

Those exiting the noon showing streamed by them, talking ninety miles a minute.

"...can you believe we really used to have people in the world like him?"

"...God, the acting was incredible, but it's so sad when that old man dies in that truck.."

"...I hated that asshole. I think he's worse than the three themselves, don't you?"

"...that little girl was somethin' else. And the kid who went on to be President...wow. What a pair they must've been in real life, riding bikes all the way home from the Arch. Dang."

The conversations continued past them, and Justin itched to get his ticket.

"Hey, Justin," Landon whispered behind him.

"Yeah?"

"Your mom and grandma are still real tight with Jake, aren't they? I mean, like they practically live at your house, don't they?" Landon peeked back to make sure folks could hear him. *I'm royalty by association.*

Justin grinned and nodded. Uncle Jake, as he referred to all the friends his nana called by that title, was older than God, but cool as shit. His stories and then his incredible life following the bad years were the stuff of legends.

Landon had marveled at his friend's connections to the New America's fabled beginnings. When he first sat down to dinner and recognized faces from TV, he couldn't talk for fear he might choke on his food. Justin had beamed at his friend's astonishment.

Famous dinner guests were part of Justin's heritage, and important to him. His grandma once told him to cherish the things he held dearest, because they might be the ones he would want to hold onto the longest but probably lose the soonest. He knew she was speaking of her dad, his great grandfather, who had died in the meltdown. She said many died from the chemical, but the emotional meltdown took its share of victims, too.

"I'm glad I didn't have to live through it, Nana. Would you do it again if you had to?"

She hadn't responded for the longest time to the question he asked that night. He feared she had fallen asleep as they sat on the couch in his living room.

"Well, Justin, I'd have to say yes, because look where the world is now in comparison to what it was like before. Now, the population's still weak, but we're getting there. But world hunger is over. There are no homeless people. Violence is pretty much controlled by the prison program we've got in place. Heck, we don't even really have poor people because of the Human Rights Amendment. My friends and I had an opportunity most people will never have – to change the world. To erase the negatives and replace them with a thousand positives. I certainly missed my daddy for a lot of years, and still do." She paused and wiped a tear from each eye. "But to see the road we traveled and where it's taken us? Naw, I can't say I'd give that up for anything. I'm a sixty-eight-year old woman who still feels eight when I talk about those times."

Justin pulled his card from his pocket, ready to get his ticket and the biggest tub of popcorn he could carry.

"Hey, let's get some Hot Tamales, too. You wanna share some with me?" Landon pulled at Justin's shirt, trying to keep up as the line moved fast now. Once the window opened, it only took seconds for them to swipe their cards.

Does a dog hike his leg? Heck, yeah!

"Well, boys, enjoy the movie," the wrinkled lady said. She reached out and shook Justin's hand like he was the most important kid on the planet.

"Thank you, ma'am. I will. I hope it's as good the second time for you." Justin smiled as she pulled open the door and disappeared inside.

"You shoulda asked her name," Landon said, swiping his card and following his friend inside.

"Yeah, I should've."

The two boys traipsed to the concessions, placed their orders, and turned around to inspect all the posters. One huge banner showed the title and a little girl standing in Forest Park with a dog at her side and the Arch in the distance. Another displayed a maniacal-looking man pressing a gun against a black man's head, the White House in the background. But Justin saw the coolest one: a building with thirteen people and a dog sitting in front of a walled ramp. His grandma sat leaning against Uncle Bryan's legs, Aunt Tristan holding his arm, Dusty and Melanie beside them, with Austin, Valerie, John, Jake, Candi, and Griffin behind them. Matthew and Storey lay in front on their bellies with chins resting on their hands.

It was a *real* picture – not the actors. It made him anxious to get to his seat.

I've seen the real photograph. As they got their tub of popcorn, drinks, and candy, they saw the last poster as they stood outside the theater – a huge chain-link cage with three people cowering inside and a Mafia-type digging to get out.

It made Justin shiver. He'd seen photo albums with all their pictures, several of the cage, and too many of Andrews. He didn't like looking at them, but Grandma told him it was important to see them.

"Aunt Valerie's photographs chronicle our survival, our ability to overcome these people, even convert them. Sort of. When she won that Pulitzer, I'd never seen her so happy."

"But then they gave the whole Joplin community the Nobel Peace Prize – a group recognition for all they had done," he reminded, because he always thought his nana should've gotten her own plaque. But the group one was fine with his grandma, and she had it on the wall in her den. "We couldn't recognize the few when the rest provided the backbone," the script read.

"C'mon, let's sit up front!" Landon tugged Justin's arm, nearly making him spill the popcorn. It smelled so good, he reached his tongue out and nabbed a kernel.

He pushed the seat down with his butt, careful not to drop anything. He shoved the bucket between his knees and put his soda in the hole to his right. Landon plopped into the seat to his left and started chattering.

Justin's head swam. He could never have imagined sitting in a dark theater waiting to see his grandma's movie – and what a sensation it had already created. Before the lights dimmed, he looked around at the packed theater. Random empty seats remained on the side and a few in the first row, but not many.

In the months that followed the opening, moviegoers sat through the already renowned classic time after time. Justin loved the talk shows his grandma appeared on, the rave she incited.

The movie played at the theater for thirteen months. Justin saw it five times.

Again, his grandma had stirred the hearts of thousands. When *8 Days* hit the bookshelves, Justin hadn't been old enough to understand the impact – nor the anticipation that preceded it.

Former President Francis, his own grandma's adoptive brother, publicized openly for several years that she was writing the account, that she had waited thirty years for the wounds to heal so she could start sifting through her journals. People waited as though she were Mother Mary herself.

In a lot of ways, she was.

Her story inspired them all to continue to be better people. And in the end, the once precocious little girl who had warmed her daddy's heart as she bellowed the words to "Maybelline" would motivate the world to continue what she had started. The Victrola had become a mythological icon to the family, and every person knew the words to Chuck Berry's classic by heart.

Justin basked in her presence and idolized the woman who had helped save the world. His dream was to someday be as important as she had been. And then he realized that what she tried to tell him was true – *all of us are that important to someone.*

Prequel to 8 Days – 2005 Release

The Movement

"CRAP." BEV TUGGED at the suitcase's zipper. She had crammed it as full as she could and sitting on it wasn't helping. When she got it most of the way closed, she heaved it into the Chevy's trunk.

Their most important – and lightest – belongings lay on the curb in front of a house she had helped paint. They had even replaced the windows last summer. She had intended to wallpaper the kitchen in July, frowning now at the finality of never getting the chance.

James speed-walked to the end of the driveway and plopped paper sacks on the ground behind his wife. She turned and stared at the bags straddling the sidewalk's cracks.

...step on a crack and break your mama's back...

She thought her daughters would take off their training wheels and skin their knees in a few years on this same chipped concrete. A lump of emotion lodged in her throat.

"Don't, Bev, we can't second-guess ourselves. We don't have time. Just throw it in. Don't worry about the damn suitcases." James draped the clothes still clinging to their wire hangers across the sacks.

"Don't yell at me, James. And if that's what you want, quit dropping everything on the damn curb. Put it in the car!" Bev's voice hitched. The clog inched closer to freedom, so tight now she could barely swallow. If she started to cry now, she would never stop.

"Mommy! The girls are cryin' again!" Charlie stood on the porch with his primer in his hands. He complained to his dad that some classmate would stake claim to his pencils and all the other cool things in his desk, but James insisted the rest had to stay. Charlie resituated his Astros' ball cap and kicked at an acorn that had fallen on the porch. He grinned when it cleared the bright yellow forsythia bush.

"C'mon, Charlie, let's go inside. I'll get the girls. Be a man and help Dad with the other bags – think you can do that?" James squeezed his first grade son's bicep and oohed over it while steering him into the house. He gave a quick look up and down the street, sharing his wife's paranoia. Bev recognized the over-the-shoulder glances, the feeling of being surveilled and controlled.

She brushed a few strays of auburn-flecked chestnut hair from her face and took her husband's advice. She arranged the bags in the back seat of the Chevrolet sedan. She knew there would be little room for the kids, but she could put Charlie in the front and the babies on her lap.

"Mom! Here's my stuff. Don't forget my stuff." Charlie came tearing out the door with a small suitcase and a satchel of toys. He ran a circle around his mother. "Can I take these? And my Hot Wheels?"

"Yes, baby, you can take these and your Hot Wheels." Bev reached down and hugged Charlie fiercely, but he squirmed from her tight grip. His silky hair smelled of Johnson's shampoo. A sob swelled inside her, but she swallowed it.

"I'll go get my cars. Where are we goin', Mom?" Charlie looked up at her, squinting into the bright June sun, but she could still catch a hint of the green eyes that she knew would someday woo the hearts of women everywhere. She hoped.

"You'll see...it's a surprise! Hurry up and get your things. Then climb in front, okay?" A sliver of fear shot down her spine, leaving her chilled and uncertain. She glanced up and down the street, knowing her neighbors were peeking around curtains or through small, upstairs windows, wondering what the Mantels thought they were accomplishing by running.

Bev knew the neighbors sympathized, but none would openly cheer them on. Bev prayed they didn't hope to win favor with the Panel by placing a warning phone call.

The slamming door startled her, and before she knew it, James was beside her shoving a few more things into their car. Panic screwed his face into an unfamiliar expression. He had sat Jamie and Jennifer on the lawn in their polka dotted jumpers, fingers in mouths and wonder in their eyes – too young to understand and young enough to forget.

A siren in the distance made the butterflies in Bev's stomach flutter – and a few minutes of panicked packing had the car jammed to the gills and the sidewalk empty. James situated Charlie in the front, helped Bev get the girls settled on her lap and raced around to the driver's side. Bev rolled down her window and tried to memorize their house – their first home together.

Birds chirped, dogs barked, and children on the next street over laughed as if it were any other day.

"Road trip!" James threw the Impala into gear and drove down Mason Drive like they were going for a Sunday picnic.

"Go the other way, James. The back way." Bev tightened the lap belt around herself and the twins. She scooted close enough to Charles that she could throw an arm in front of him if she needed to.

He obeyed the speed limit – he didn't need any unnecessary attention. He finagled around construction on Front Street then turned left on Main, eager to beat pavement to the highway and leave Kleberg County in the rearview mirror.

"Shit. There's Don at the A & P – duck!" James turned and waved, as if he didn't have a care in the world. He came to a stop at the intersection and prayed he could keep Don Bailey from seeing his family crammed into the front seat – that would be a dead giveaway.

Don waved and furrowed his brow.

"He's probably wonderin' what the hell we're doin'. All this junk piled in our backseat," James whispered through the fake smile he had plastered on his face.

"Hey, James! Where're you goin'? The Salvation Army?" Don laughed, but James just waved him off like his buddy was a joker. Bev groaned as she lay across her children, and James drove on trying to act nonchalant.

"Don's gonna be suspicious." James sped up and hit the city limits four minutes later without saying another word. When he glanced in the rearview and Bev dared to turn and look, they both took a deep breath and let it out slowly.

Bev sat back and cradled her sleeping babies and thanked her lucky stars Charlie hadn't started fidgeting yet. But she wouldn't feel better until they got to the highway. Or Corpus Christi. A little distancc would ease the sinking dread clutching her bladder.

But chewing away the gray ribbon of Highway 77 didn't provide any relief. Because less than twenty miles outside of Kleberg County, home of the Javelinas of Texas A & M-Kingsville, a police cruiser flashed its blue and red lights.

James thought he could outrun them, but maybe it was nothing. Fingers of panic clutched his stomach because he knew better – he hadn't been speeding.

* * *

"HOWDY, FOLKS. NICE afternoon, ain't it?" The officer chewed his toothpick like a piece of cud, then swished it to thc other side of his mouth.

James and Bev said nothing.

Charlie shoved his mom's arm off his shoulder, the Hot Wheels box losing its appeal with the real deal beside him. The babies slept soundly in Bev's lap.

"Well, I got Thomas Witherington back here wants to have a word with ya, Mr. Mantel. I'm sure you understand." Officer Toothpick tipped his hat as if he were inviting him for a cup of coffee.

"Uh, well, we're goin' on vacation, and, um, we're on a strict time-frame to get to Florida by tomorrow. Got reservations in Birmingham tonight. Hopin' we can make it that far." James' hand trembled but he braced it on the steering wheel. Once the lie felt sure on his lips, he ran with it.

"Well, Mr. Witherington still needs a word. You know the drill." Officer Toothpick chewed and smiled, a knowing smile. Tanned skin, white teeth, and crystal blue eyes – the face of the messenger, one Bev would never forget. She shivered as James grimaced, opened the door and said he would be right back.

"You better," she whispered. She stroked Jamie's cheek and Jennifer scratched at her own. Their long dark hair framed thin faces so identical, only the mole on Jennifer's left eyebrow allowed Bev to tell them apart.

She glanced in the side mirror and watched her husband disappear into the back seat of the police cruiser. Dread settled around the ham sandwich she had eaten for lunch.

* * *

"JAMES, HOW LONG has it been?" Tommy Witherington stuck out his hand as James slid into the roomy back seat. It wavered before the man realized James Mantel had no intention of shaking it.

"A long time. What's the meaning of this, Tommy? I can't take my family on vacation?"

"Ah, no, James, it's nothin' like that. But you know how it is. People talk. Saw Don at the A & P, got a call from a neighbor, and quite frankly – it alarmed me. Bein' as you're a new daddy. How old are the twins now, damn near one, aren't they?" Tommy cocked his head with genuine interest.

"Nine months." James paused, not sure how to play his cards. "Tommy, I'm just goin' on vacation and money's tight. Brought a few things to sell to the Goodwill. You know how it is...three kids can really put a cramp in the pocket book. They've got a real nice one in Corpus – a Goodwill, I mean – and we were going to do some selling or trading there before heading on to Birmingham. Kids have never seen the beach. We should be in Florida by Thursday. Plan to stay about five days. If that's all right with the almighty Panel." James scoffed, spitting the last out like a swig of sour milk. His distaste of the domineering Panel couldn't be avoided.

"Okay, James. Okay." Tommy weighed the words before gesturing toward the door, the signal that Mr. Mantel was free to go. "But consequences are dire, you got me? You know how The Movement feels about abandoners. *It just can't be.*"

"Good grief, Tommy, I'm going on vacation. You people are paranoid. And I know it can't be – I was on the panel. I grew up in Kingsville, remember?" James gripped the handle and pushed the knob to let himself out. He turned and studied Tommy Witherington's expression. "You really think I would leave like this? I'm not stupid, ya know. If I were leaving, I'd do it in the middle of the night, not in the broad daylight."

James Mantel got out of the car, steadying his trembling hands, and gave a sarcastic two-finger salute to his old neighborhood baseball buddy. When they were ten, James had gotten Little Tommy down and rubbed dirt in his face to shut him up. Tommy always talked too much, egged people on.

Things weren't so different now that Tommy was First Lieutenant to the Grand Dragon.

The window glided down on the patrol car and a voice warned again that *it just can't be*.

James got back in the Chevrolet and put a hand up for Bev to give him a second. Fear and worry cloyed at his insides like rotten hamburger on a hot summer day. He turned the key in the ignition, put the Impala in gear and eased back onto Highway 77 no longer with escape in mind but survival.

But The Movement's mantra repeated menacingly in the back of his mind. *It just can't be. It just can't be. It just can't be.*

He prayed they weren't right, because a hint of a threat he'd received a year earlier replayed in his mind – *three children are more than enough for any man.*

About the Author

Barri L. Bumgarner freelances for *School & Community*, *Something Better*, *CoMo* and *Family* magazines. She received Writer's Digest 72nd Annual Writing Competition honors in 2004. Her short fiction has appeared in *Rock Springs Review* and *Well-Versed*. Her young adult novel, *Dregs*, is being adapted for the stage and is set for an April 2005 release. Ms. Bumgarner divides her time between teaching and writing. She lives in Columbia, Missouri, and is at work on her fifth novel.

Photo by Tam Adams